# THE WOLF OF DALRIADA

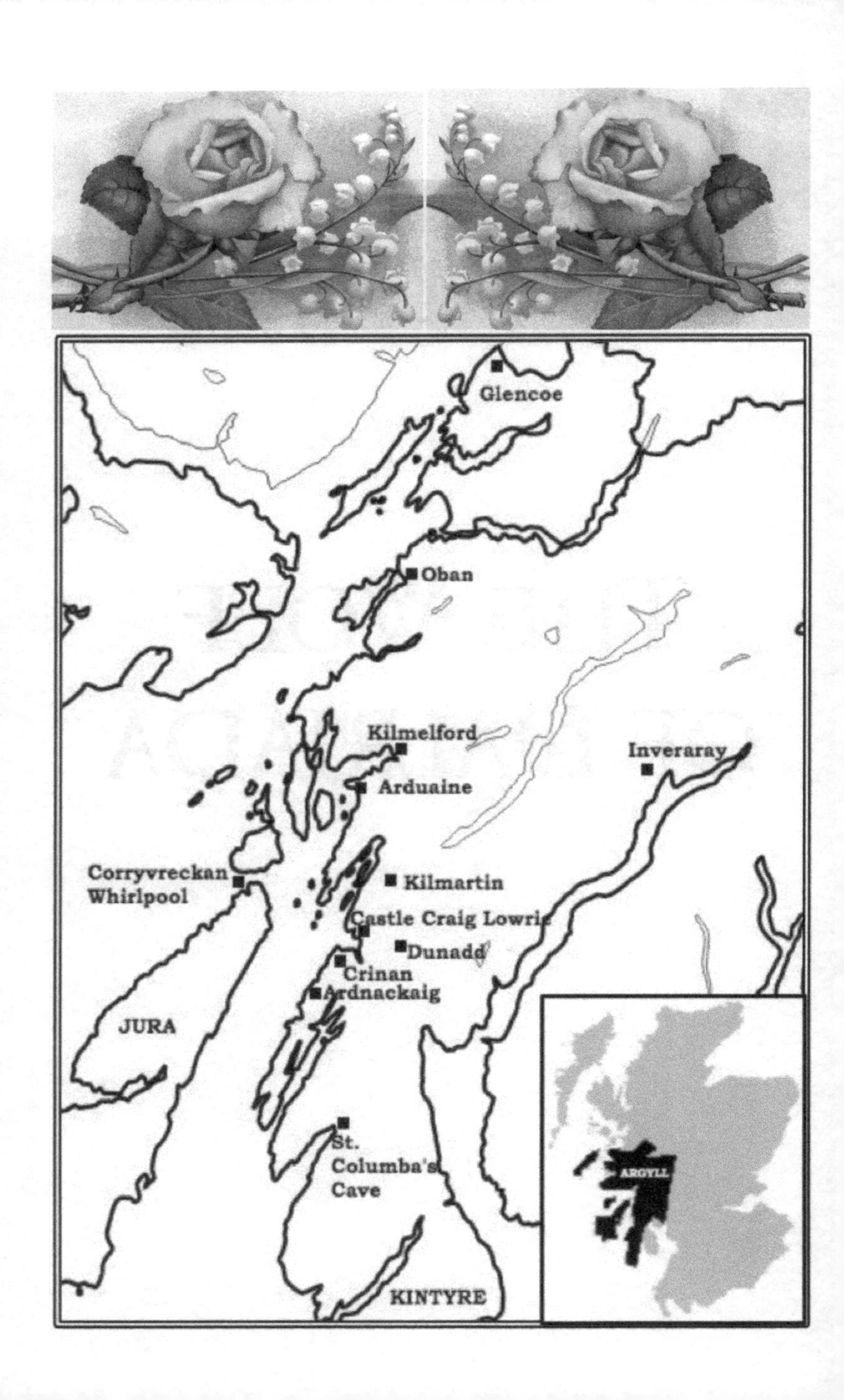
Glencoe
Oban
Kilmelford
Inveraray
Arduaine
Corryvreckan
Whirlpool
Kilmartin
Castle Craig Lowrie
Dunadd
Crinan
Ardnackaig
JURA
St.
Columba's
Cave
KINTYRE
ARGYLL

Matador
9 Priory Business Park,
Wistow Road, Kibworth Beauchamp,
Leicestershire. LE8 0RX
Tel: 0116 279 2299
Email: books@troubador.co.uk
Web: www.troubador.co.uk/matador
Twitter: @matadorbooks

ISBN 978 1785899 904

British Library Cataloguing in Publication Data.
A catalogue record for this book is available from the British Library.

Printed and bound by CPI Group (UK) Ltd, Croydon, CR0 4YY
Typeset in 9/12 Bookman Old Style by Lonely Furrow Company Publishing, Wirral, UK.

Matador is an imprint of Troubador Publishing Ltd

Elizabeth Gates

# The Wolf of Dalriada

For MB

# Prologue
## Versailles, 1783

THE SUNLIGHT on the leaves reminded me of Burgundy. I lay in the grass looking up and beyond, into the sky, so far, far into the sky. And I longed – so much – to see *Maman's* face. But *Maman* did not come.

Instead I heard a voice, not French, but soft. 'Who is the beautiful little one?' the voice said. *'Mignonne!'*

This was followed by laughter – gentle and kind. Like *Maman.*

I sat up then and saw the lovely lady whom I had often seen in the palace of Versailles. From far away, across the Hall of Mirrors, she had always seemed so unreachable, so encrusted with hard jewels, so untouchable, gliding across the floor, in layers of hooped skirts, weighted with rich heavy brocade.

But now, she was, close to me, dressed in what Papa would call 'soft muslin' – with a delicately transparent sash and a straw bonnet trimmed with entrancing feathers. She carried a single rose. And, here in the glade, her hair was not powdered and grey like an old woman. It was a natural, burnished red. This woman was so different from the woman I had seen at court. So much younger. So much more like *Maman.* Someone I could perhaps love.

I stood. I saw the need to do so in the faces of the women surrounding her. They were her creatures. Every time she spoke, their long white necks twisted outwards – like cranes – to hear what she said. Every time she laughed, they laughed too. I was waiting for them all to leave me alone in the glade but they did not. She did not.

'Little one,' she said, kneeling to speak to me. I heard a gasp from her ladies. 'Little one, will you take a message for me to the King? I'm sure you can run more quickly than any of us! It is a very special message that I ask you take. It is a secret.'

I was proud to be asked. I was proud as she fingered the dark blowing curls of my hair, proud as her hand traced the curve of my cheek. At the word 'secret', she touched my lips.

'My Lady!' said one of her women. I could hear outrage roughening the edge of her voice.

'Yes, you are right,' she said, laughing. 'It is bold of me on first acquaintance to ask such a favour. But, I am bold. I shall take this chance. And you will see. *Mignonne* will not let me down. Come into my humble home, *mignonne.* I shall write a note and then you will take it to my King for me.'

She laughed again. I did not know why. I was only nine years old, after all. But I followed her out of the glade and into the little village. Although this looked as if it had been there forever, men had only recently started to build it. It was a garden of play. First the lady and I admired the cows, Blanchette and Brunette, scratching at their polls, which they liked. Then, we stroked the soft and brightly-coloured wallflowers. And, at last, we came to an enchanting cottage – larger than any cottage I had ever seen. Still laughing, the lady led me inside, and then even further, into a grand room where she seated herself at a pretty little desk, to write her note.

When she had finished a few short lines, she rolled up the delicate parchment and placed it in a leather cylinder. This had a charming crest tooled upon it – which I later learned was her own. And, then, she glanced at me like a conspirator. 'So, *mignonne,*' she said, 'What do you think of my *Salon de Compagnie?* I see you looking around. Like a little bird – alert, perhaps a little afraid, no? But brave – even so. Tell me, what do you think?'

'I think some of its furnishings very pretty, madame.' I was used to giving my opinions on this sort of thing. Papa relied on me. I spoke up clearly.

'Only some? Tell me – what does not please you?'

'The curtains, *madame.*'

'And what do you not like about the curtains?'

'Too much red, *madame.*'

'Too much?'

'Too much.'

'Hmmm. I shall change them, then, perhaps. But what do you like?'

'I love those – the blues, the greens, the warm ivories, the browns, pale as caramel.'

'And what do you like best of all?'

I looked round and then I saw, almost out of sight in a corner, a collection of dolls. These were dressed in the most beautiful silks and satins. They looked like the ladies of the court. One was particularly lovely, its face soft and welcoming above its rich clothes and real jewels. Without a word, I touched it and – as I do – I lost myself in the feel of the fabric.

'Do you like her dress, *mignonne?* I made it myself. Yes, I did. Am I foolish to be so proud of that?'

'Oh, no *madame.* Not foolish at all. I should love to have a doll to make dresses for. And such dresses. You have so cleverly worked them. I love the hidden seams...'

I could have continued but the lady's companions were beginning to hiss – like geese. I had been too free with my opinions, perhaps, I thought. But the lady laughed, pleased. 'Well, I see you like my dolls. And my taste. Apart from the red. Which I don't much care for, myself, now you have drawn it to my attention. Tell me, *mignonne,* what is your name?'

'I am Adelaide de Fontenoy, *madame!*'

'You are proud of your name.'

'I am. It was my mother's name.'

'And where is she?'

'She is dead, *madame.*' At that moment, I thought I should cry but was glad I did not. The lady came across the pretty sunlit room and hugged me then. Her companions began to cluck in alarm but she ignored them, 'Well, Adelaide de Fontenoy, will you do me a service?'

By now, I was her creature. I would do anything for her. I nodded, unable to speak, and waited.

'Take this to the King. I am inviting His Majesty to a performance of a play. Just him. No-one else. At my own theatre. In *Le Petit Trianon* Palace. It will be so romantic. Just him. And me. So take care that no-one else – up there – reads this note. I suspect you know how to slide invisibly through the crowds in the Hall of Mirrors. You have done so, often, I think. Am I right?'

I nodded again, taking the leather cylinder carefully and respectfully in both hands, with a pretty curtsey – as Maman had taught me.

'And you shall have a doll like mine but larger – to help you make your own dresses – for yourself. A *mannequine*. Now,' said Marie Antoinette, for it was she. 'Now run!'

* * *

Within the half hour, I had run to Palace. Wearing a court dress, I thought to be hampered but, because I was a child, the one I wore was cut above the ankles, and I could run in it, very fast. Even so, as I crept through the vast Hall – miasmic with stale urine and ordure – worse than a farmyard – it was difficult to see where the lady's King might be. I needed sharp eyes and quicker wits.

I ignored Papa who broke off his conversation with the big English lawyer, Sir William Robinson. But, even then in 1783, when I was only a child, the look of that man, Robinson, made me shudder – a foreshadowing perhaps of how much I would come to loathe him. Papa was inviting me to his side – flapping his hands – but I pushed away into the crowd. Easily done. On most days, there could be as many as ten thousand hopeful courtiers, diplomats, tourists and beggars standing around in the Hall of Mirrors and along the corridors of Versailles. Difficult to catch anyone who does not want to be caught.

I crept on and on and then I glimpsed my sister, Gabrielle, in the distance. She was carrying some bolts of silk. Though only twelve years old, she was disappearing through some ornate doors into an ante-room, following a grand lady who clearly wanted a fitting, there and then. Gabrielle, my lovely elder sister, would always oblige a client. Papa used to call her his *petite femme des affaires* and her commercial sense was her real contribution to our business. Papa made hats. I sewed – quickly, neatly, beautifully – pulling everything, colours and fabrics, together in the most lovely confections. But I had no head for business. Not surprising. I was, after all, only a child. And, although she could also sew well, Gabrielle liked to maintain the order book and count the coin. So we were all happy.

Gabrielle waved to me. I waved back but did not go to her. I had something very important to do and Marie Antoinette, herself, had promised me one of her beautiful dolls as a reward. And I wanted that doll.

I pushed on, drawn into the maelstrom of the crowd but, at its heart, I took time to look about me. And, when the fat, shy King was left alone for a second, I fulfilled my commission. His noble companions were all squabbling among themselves. They were grotesques, all of them. Pomaded wigs, painted mouths, patches on pockmarks, faces and bodies gross and liverish or scrawny with disease – these courtiers looked like pigs fed the wrong food. I crept through them easily – they were so quarrelsome they did not notice me. I pressed the crested cylinder into the shy King's hand. He glanced at the crest and smiled and then I turned and slid away again. I was beneath the notice of the crush.

It was then that I saw him.

Much taller than me, and a few years older, the boy was part of – but not belonging to – an entourage of diplomats there for the signing. Too young. Too sad. English, I thought at first. But then I noticed he was not wearing breeches. He was wearing what seemed to me then a strange sort of costume. I liked the black velvet jacket, with lace frothing at the neck and the silver buttons. But the kilt as it is called – it looked warm, too warm perhaps for France.

Some French courtiers nearby were discussing him – rudely – and staring – rudely. I guessed he did not speak French but, I could see, he recognised how impolite they were. He stood with his arms folded across his chest, tapping his lip with his thumb. I could see menace in this but they seemed quite unaware.

They – men and women – spoke of how handsome he was – *'Le Petit Prince'.* Their sniggers and cackles made me suddenly feel very unwell. I was about to run from the Hall of Mirrors into the Park. I wanted to feel the fresh air on my face. But, as if I was captured in a bubble of time, something about him held me there. I heard one woman – perhaps kinder than the rest – say, 'Leave him. He is too young and innocent – or too old – for such games. Besides, he has just lost his mother – and his father. He will not be in the mood for love.'

Laughter – cruel – met this. The boy did not know what had been said but I could see his loneliness was complete. On impulse, I pushed through the crowd and took his hand. I tried to say something but, over the hullabaloo in the Hall of Mirrors, he could not understand. He leaned down to hear me repeat it. I did but still he did not understand. So, I kissed him, my lips brushing his cheek – as downy as any young boy's but dry, so dry. Any tears he may have shed in his past must have been short-lived but I could feel waves of hurt coming off him. Sorrow flowed from his azure eyes and overwhelmed me. He had lost his mother and I remembered *Maman.* And he and I, we shared a secret now.

I put my finger to my lips. But I could hear Gabrielle's voice, calling to me. 'Adele, Adele, come quickly. We must work. We have a gown to make. Quickly, I need you.'

So I crept away from the young boy but not before I heard his name, echoing behind me, in the coarse whispers of the Hall of Mirrors.

The beautiful boy's name was Malcolm Craig Lowrie.

# Chapter 1

## Dalriada, Argyll, Scotland

## 1st January 1793 (Ten years later)

GAELIC CALLS spin a web through the mist in arcs of soft sound. Fear unsteadies the unseen flocks on the scrub heather hillside as men and dogs weave a trap around them in the darkling night. Once the flocks are penned, then the lanterns are turned towards the south. The watchers wait in silence.

Meanwhile, down below, at Crinan Loch-side, a horse's muffled hooves slither on the cobbled apron before the Castle Craig Lowrie gate. The slope is steep and wet with winter but the horse keeps moving forward. Then, at the forest's secret edge, the muffles are removed, swiftly, deftly. The rider – dressed in groom's clothes and wrapped in a stolen plaid – climbs into the saddle. Which way? They take the track north from Dalriada towards Oban.

* * *

Watching from castle battlements, eyes – azure, intelligent – pick out the moon-cast shadows as the rider moves away in dusky night. 'Safer out there than here, at present,' Malcolm Craig Lowrie thinks. 'I will know where to find her – when I need.'

He pauses for the tiniest shard of a split moment. He wonders how it would feel to love and be so loved – as that young girl is. Then he turns back to his task in hand. A laird with five hundred armed men at his call, he is waiting – as always – for yet another attack.

The Laird of Craig Lowrie knows he irks King George III of England – who fears any challenger in the north. The King believes all Highlanders to be *Jacobins* and he shudders in his palaces at the thought of the revolutionary French. The Craig Lowrie also more than irks the Campbell clan chief, the Duke of Argyll. One of the Duke's many present interests and intentions is to recover the tongues of land – the rich pastures and verdant forests of *his* Dalriada. He wants returned the land that the Craig Lowries have taken in their relentless surge onto the mainland out of the Isle of Jura. So, as Malcolm Craig Lowrie knows, the next attack will come, as always, from the east and from the south.

But first there is the truce for the burying of the dead. Malcolm Craig Lowrie looks down onto the dead Campbells, lying on the foreshore of the lochside, the night-dark sea fretting them where they have been placed by Craig Lowrie men. Their kin will take them within the hour. The dead English soldiers lying alongside may be removed too – although of that he is not so certain. He shrugs. Those who are not taken will float out upon the tide to feed the fishes. He has in decency ordered a minister to say a few words of committal over them. He can do no more.

But his own kin, treacherously slain – they have been taken by their fathers, brothers and sons, in honour, to their graves. These, dug deep and piled high with stones against the foxes, cluster to Castle Craig Lowrie walls and the clansmen, like their forefathers, lie facing the east in hope of the resurrection. They sleep in the Field of Cairns, resting safely, between the castle and the sea. And, caught in a silver web of duty, Malcolm Craig Lowrie watches over them where they lie.

He also waits for the next attack, whenever that may come. Perhaps with the Wolf Moon tonight. Or with the Storm Moon in February. But, of one thing he is certain, he will not be waiting long.

* * *

Meanwhile, out in the forest beyond Chambered Cairn, now uncertain, the rider checks and turns. In low-lying mist, she bypasses the village of Kilmartin and then meets a major fork in the woods. One track, well-worn and heading due north, leads to Oban. She fears it. There will be other riders, soldiers perhaps, on that track. The second track is less travelled. *Fewer people,* she thinks. So, keeping the moon – the Wolf Moon and the largest of the year – to her left, the girl takes the second trail which leads towards the northeast. As she rides, from time to time, she scans the moonlight behind her but spectral clouds rising out of the mist on the trails tell her nothing. These spirals could be clansmen or soldiers tracking her. Or they could simply be deer breaking from the woods, crossing the bare land to find more shelter. Anything. Standing tall in the stirrups, she also listens for hooves. But the ancient woods here – oak, birch, hazel – clatter with the hunter and the hunted, animals hoping to feed, smaller animals hoping to live. She hears nothing beyond their call and screech.

The young girl is afraid. She came here, to Dalriada for a wedding and witnessed a murder. But she presses on, urging her mount forward, her lips whispering close to his alert ears.

Dawn comes and the bracken turns red in the new light. She slides up beyond the tree line into the desert hills, looking for swathes of grass for her horse – the huge Friesian, descended from the warhorses of her Northumbrian home. He needs his feed. She finds tender shoots searching for an early Spring, alongside a clear burn, bubbling out of the snow-melt-sodden earth. These are numerous and succulent and, while her horse grazes, she rests. And, as he sleeps, nestling like a giant grouse in the scrub, she sleeps, huddled to his warm flank, ignoring the penetrating cold in the bright sun. She dreams, slipping back to Castle Craig Lowrie.

In her dream, she sees *steel like ripping teeth biting into the heart of Castle Craig Lowrie. The priest shrieking and running – but was this before or after she was fully declared wed? The dream is unclear. She watches again as the hand of her bridegroom – James Craig Lowrie – is torn from hers. Men down on the rushes – writhing, wounded...The hiss of doused sconces. Acrid smoke spiralling into dark air...The heart-broken cry of 'Treachery!' And Malcolm Craig Lowrie – standing astride a fallen man, the man's head forced back with white throat exposed. Malcolm Craig Lowrie – his eyes glittering and the dirk in his hand flashing through artery and vein and windpipe of the fallen man below. And blood – the gush of it, the bubble of it, the smell of it.*

Startled, she awakes. For a moment she cannot remember where she is. Hills stack away to the north, rampart beyond blue rampart. And, below her lie the shining waters of Loch Awe. But, an English girl far from home, she does not know the names of either. Then, shivering in the winter-burnished heather and muffling the stolen Craig Lowrie plaid around her, she becomes aware of the smell of gunpowder in the air. Across the frost-rimed woods below, she sees drifts of smoke rising from the clachans. She knows nothing of the Clearances but, since the events at Castle Craig Lowrie, she knows despair in a human voice when she hears it. That sound now shrills in the glens and rackets from hill to snow-brushed hill, as women keen for loss.

Weary beyond hope, the young girl wraps the rough plaid more tightly around her and falls asleep in the heather. She dreams again. And, then, again, she wakes with shock. Two children and an old man stand over her. She springs to her feet at the sight of them and of a youngish woman, leading a work-worn garron to this place above the tree line. The old horse is struggling with the incline and with the palette it drags behind. There is silence, broken only by the voice of the woman softly repeating the garron's name – 'Kelpie! Kelpie, Kelpie!' The horse stumbles and tries again, pushing on up the slope with its heavy burden. On the palette is a battered tin box, heavy with what is left of their lives.

With the sunlight of winter dusk, low and blood-red, to the west of them, all the Highlanders, even the children, have sunken eyes and cheeks grooved as oak bark. Brought up as an earl's daughter – with plentiful food on the board and a soft bed to sleep in – these faces shock her. Confused, she asks, 'Is this the right road for Oban?'

'Depends, laddie.'

The old man settles himself on a boulder. He takes out a clay pipe. He hesitates for a moment, searching for the English words for what he wants to say.

'Depends which way you want to come to Oban by.'

'The shortest.'

The old man turns his head to the west – a slight movement.

She shakes her head. 'I came that way.'

He continues, 'We are headed that way. But perhaps you would not be wanting to go in step with our Auld Kelpie – on your fine horse.'

He says nothing more for a moment and then, 'Well if you have reasons for not taking that road, you must take another.'

He offers her a smoke. Her groom's clothes disguise her well, she thinks, and refuses politely, adding, 'Is there another? How do I come to Oban now?'

'You must cross the loch or travel east around it. If you go east, you can rest at Kilchurn. The old castle, in ruins, at the head of the

Loch. No-one comes there now. We killed all that lived there and broke the stones. As we were bid. As you'll see. No-one comes there now.'

The old man thinks for a while. Then, with a deep breath, he finds the words. 'We are loyal to our lairds. They bid us fight. And so we do. That is our way. It is our honour. It is our obligation.'

The young girl in groom's clothes voices the thought the old man cannot bring himself to air. 'But it has not served you well. The soldiers...'

This speech is not welcome. There is a silence. In the old man's breathing, she hears an echo of despair again. But then he shakes himself and explains the way she must now take.

'Beyond Kilchurn, you go on then towards Ben Cruachan – the Peak of the Coracle. But, no matter who comes, you must stay on the track – all the way through the Pass of Brander. Do not be tempted by the hills. On foot, Ben Cruachan itself alone would take you nine hours. There'd be no riding up there. Keep to the Pass, with the Falls of Cruachan to your right, to the east, and the way to Oban to the west, it could take you one, maybe two, days.'

The young girl in groom's clothes looks at Ben Cruachan across the water. For her, it is now a signpost for Oban, and for safety. But, before she comes to the town, she knows there will be a long trail beset by dangers. She falters.

'Is there another way?'

'No.'

'Only this?'

'Aye. If you will not now go due west with us, you must keep to the northeast trails and then – beyond Taynuilt – cut due west again. Walk with the waters of Loch Etive. That will bring you to Oban town – and whatever it is you seek.'

The woman with the baggage has heard how the young rider seeks to go from this place of no comfort. The long hard ride ahead moves her to pity and now she says, 'Have you eaten?'

'Not much.'

'It is hard, travelling on these hills.' She unfurls what she has in the baggage laid across the saddle of the old garron. 'Here, laddie, some flatbread for you. You eat it – little by little. Not too much. Not all at once.'

A piece of the barley bannock – rough and blackened – stops the ache in the belly of the girl in groom's clothes. As she nibbles its corner, the bairns gaze at her, trying to return her smile. Their wizened faces are streaked with a grime of tears. They are children but their lives are now joyless.

'Then,' the young girl says, 'here – take this.'

From her saddlebag, she pulls out a large green stone, its edges shining in the sunset. The bairns reach out to play with it, grasping at a memory of games. For them, it could be a toy. She offers it to the woman who looks at the old man. The old man dismisses it with a wave of his twisted hand.

'Will you not take this for them to play with – with my thanks?'

'Your thanks? For what?'

'For bannock and the path to Oban.'

For a moment the old man is silent. Then he bows his head – a slight movement, again, but seen by the girl in groom's clothes. Then she tosses the green stone into the air. As the dying sunlight flashes on its clean-cut sides, the bairns run to catch it. They laugh. The old man and his daughter smile. They have not thought to smile again so soon after the soldiers came.

'And...' The girl in groom's clothes is supplicant but respectful. 'And, I would beg your silence.'

'They'll not be hearing of you from us.'

This is all the old man says but it is enough. Then he and his family make their way west, taking the shorter route to Oban.

Now, the girl in groom's clothes wraps up the remains of the bannock in her bedroll and straps the bag containing emeralds to her saddle once more. Then she takes milk from an early suckling ewe, wild on the hills, squeezing the teat rhythmically as the milk fills a wooden cup she has brought with her for the purpose. Food and drink restore her but, when she has finished, she bites her lip and leans into her horse's neck. Sated with bright grasses, the horse waits, breathing softly, as she tells her sadness. But there is no answer – nothing but silence in the dusk. The winter sun has now set and horse and rider must take an eastern route through the night.

# Chapter 2

## Sir William Robinson's Private Journal Entry, Robinson Park, Arduaine, near Oban – 6th January 1793

*WHEN LADY Emma Bamburgh walked through my Oban office door today, my first instinct was to throw her out. Among other things, she smelled of horse sweat. She was covered in grime, had short spiky, matted hair and was wearing breeches. The curve of her cheek made her seem vulnerable. Attractive. But, she looked like a boy and I thought – because of my curious discomfort – I was on the turn. Things like that do happen to middle-aged gentlemen like myself – though not often. I found her upsettingly exciting. I also found myself offering her a chair – although I did not bother to dust it. And, she then launched* in media res *– a tale of the usual mayhem associated with the Craig Lowries. I made verbatim notes, of course. And, when she reached The Tale of The Murder, she looked at me with those challenging green eyes of hers and – though it was hard for her to say the words – say them she did. She stated – quite clearly: 'I believe Malcolm Craig Lowrie has killed his cousin, my betrothed, James Craig Lowrie.'*

*I could well believe it. I judge Malcolm Craig Lowrie more than capable of internecine murder.*

*A pretty tale then followed of how she escaped and rode north, alone, from Dalriada towards Oban. But, beyond Kilmartin, it seems, she missed her way. The pretty tale became incoherent. She was rambling, I suppose with nerves, but it was a picture that seemed to ring true in the detail – she rode, it seems, nearer to fifty miles than the forty-mile track direct from Dalriada to Oban. If she'd taken that, she would have passed not far from the Park gates. And it was hard riding – five winter nights of it. Thank God the snow we had before Christmas was gone. She was lucky. No snow at the moment but it will come. Even Highlanders would think twice about a ride like that. Silly girl.*

*But, what she said next has left me anxious. I refer again to my note. She said: 'All the time, I felt I was being watched. But when I looked around, I could see no-one.'*

*A mystery, then. Was this simply a young girl's excessive sensibility? Or was it something more serious? Would it be a Kingsman or a Campbell? If so, they would surely have taken her. As she said, and I've recorded: 'I am in no doubt that I would be a trophy worth their while.'*

*This option – handing her over to the Campbells – could of course be worth my while too. It would build my credit with them. A not insubstantial part of my income already depends on the business of helping London-based drawing-room clan chiefs – such as those of the Campbell septs – to the title of the clan lands. And facilitating the Clearances. And negotiating with New World traders on the clan chiefs' behalf. I would not want to jeopardise this happy arrangement with the clan chiefs by being found to support an enemy's cause. Country farmers' wills and distillers' probate would be as nothing alongside the loss of that revenue.*

Robinson stood and went to the window. His Park lay before him. Its manicured lawns and carefully-raked gravel drives reflected – and had reflected for at least eight years – his ordered life. It was a matter for pride but also a comfort to him.

Robinson still shuddered at the thought of the clamouring creditors – and worse – who had occasioned his hasty departure from London in the early '80s. Giving Prinny's potential mistress the clap had been unfortunate. And there was the business of his mother. And her jewellery. So, in 1783, he had attached himself and his legal expertise to the party of British diplomats negotiating the Peace of Paris and the withdrawal from the British Empire of the American Colonies. Hoping at best for anonymity, he had scurried off to the Continent in their wake. But then what had he found? With joy, he had found there such temptation – banknotes, gold, silver, works of art. And Adelaide. The beautiful nine-year-old child...

He dragged his finger along the window sill. Dust rimed on it. He would have to have a word with Adelaide. No, not Adelaide. The house steward.

Still, in spite of a little neglect – to be expected when a house was ten years' old – Robinson Hall was the finest house he'd ever seen, the best money could buy and situate well away from the smell of fish, and the prying eyes of burgeoning Oban. He was satisfied. 'No intrigues, no violence. Just a comfortable life! I have absolutely no wish – at my age – to re-locate. I might have to remove to Fort William or worse, and start again. I'm not so young as I was. And, of course, there is "Lady Robinson". Mysterious, dark, lovely Adelaide, my little French canary.'

He tried to picture the woman known as 'Lady Robinson' in the north of Scotland. Caithness, say. Windswept, untidy, without all her silks and brocades. He sniffed. The inexorable process – the building, the selection of the furnishings, the waiting, the unpacking, the mess, the upheaval – would weary him. He had already laid out thousands and thousands of guineas on 'Lady Robinson's Versailles whims'. And the silence he had bought – ten years of it! Move somewhere else and he would have to buy it all again. Otherwise, there would be more of his linen washed in public. And more danger that his creditors and persecutors would find him – even after all this time. He struck the windowsill. It would be intolerable.

He returned to his desk and contemplated his journal. Its leather binding and vellum pages were pleasant to the touch but then he remembered that, in spite of all he had invested in Lady Robinson, this was his only true confidante. This was where he could clear his mind, explore possible solutions to his problems, examine his innermost thoughts. He took up his pen again.

*'Setting all this aside,'* he wrote, *'if not a Kingsman or a Campbell – was whoever was watching the girl – trailing her perhaps to my office – a Craig Lowrie man? This is a truly dreadful thought. The Craig Lowries – all hard, hard men. And now on her trail? And straight to my door?*

*'I am of course no fool. I could be bought by someone, on some side, in all this business. I am for hire, after all. I could, I suppose, for the sake of my own safety, switch sides – if Craig Lowrie has need of an English-trained lawyer. He's certainly rich enough to afford my fees. But no, he doesn't much bother with the Law at all, from what I gather. That would not work. Worse, he seems actively to dislike the profession. There are tales. The heads of several of my legal brethren have been found along – or are thought to be floating out beyond – the Mull of Kintyre. With Malcolm Craig Lowrie's name attached to the stories. And I don't want to join them!'*

He sat back and poured himself a neat glass of port. At the end of her tale, he recalled, the young girl had reached into her saddle-bag and drawn out two leather packages. The first held a strange object of twisted silver – it was the bent but complete setting for a necklace, without stones. Then she had reached for the second package. Emeralds had showered from the leather – some huge, some tiny, all glorious. She had clipped the stones onto the silver setting. Some of the claws had broken away, but enough held. And, at last, Robinson had recognised it. This was the Bamburgh necklace – Robinson had seen it on Edwin Bamburgh's wedding day, when the Dowager Bamburgh had graced Edwin's new bride's neck with it. And this was now this slip of a girl's dowry. *Was this proof that she was a Bamburgh daughter?*

Robinson scratched harder and more quickly with his quill. Before he needed to replenish the ink, he needed to get his thoughts down. *'Eleanor Bamburgh was then indeed beautiful and I was then indeed enslaved. And now, here, in my offices, it appeared, was sitting her fifteen-year-old daughter! How strange life can be!'*

But, one emerald, large to judge from the setting, had been missing. When challenged, the girl had lied. She said she'd bought some winter fodder on the road near Eredine Forest for herself and her horse, Berry. *Unlikely,* sniffed Robinson.

The old lawyer chuckled and sat back in his chair to consider this. 'Curious name for such a powerful piece of horseflesh,' he thought, 'now eating huge amounts of hay in my stables, no doubt. "Berry"? Short for "Barbary" apparently? Now "Barbary" – a much more suitable name. An excellent pedigree, I understand, with some racing blood. Good over the jumps and also on the flat. And unsurpassed stamina, I gather.'

The digression had entertained but it was time to return to the matter in hand. Robinson sighed and wrote in capitals. 'ACTION POINT FOR ME: RETRIEVE THIS STONE. IF THIS STORY IS TRUE, AN EMERALD IS A) FAR TOO VALUABLE FOR WHATEVER SERVICE WAS RENDERED AND B) IT WOULD BE A USEFUL MARKER FOR ANYONE LOOKING FOR HER.'

A slight frisson overcame the crusty old lawyer. How had so beautiful and appealing a young girl – cast adrift in the world without a protector – managed? *Where had she slept, for example?* To his surprise, she had told him, 'with Berry'.

Most women would draw the line at sleeping with a horse, he

thought. He began to write again, scratching words out onto the vellum as quickly as his thoughts came to him. *'But my horse-savvy friend Bamburgh – he could have sired such a woman. I am persuaded. She is indeed who she purports to be. In general, I would say I'm uncomfortable with being forced to behave well. But, I confess it, I find I'm being drawn in. Something other than venality is coming into play. And it may be the worse for me.'*

Robinson paused again. Fear was making his brow damp. He stood up and moved to the window. The moon – what these heathens called a Wolf Moon – had leeched colour from the hills and turned the Sound of Jura milk-pale. And somewhere out there but closely – so closely – involved with all this was the one man, above all, whom Robinson would not like to cross.

'Wedding-day widowhood?' he thought. 'Malcolm Craig Lowrie will soon be clamouring after her. Witnesses – even this far north of Carlisle – are not the ideal loose cannon. So what to do?'

He returned to his journal, thinking through the quill.

*'I've weighed up the options,'* he wrote. *'Handing her back to Craig Lowrie, I've considered and dismissed – she's Edwin's daughter, after all. But, for the time being, concealment up at Robinson Park does seem possible. She could masquerade as my niece, perhaps – come north away from sickness in Carlisle, for the air. Adelaide could take her in hand – as she does everything.'*

He paused, shocked at his own change of heart and policy. He tapped the desk as he re-read what he had written. Then he made a note. *'I've always kept Adelaide absolutely without intimates. What if she made friends with this young girl?'*

He rubbed his temples, his wits dulled by the situation's layered complexities. His whole frame tensed. He took up his quill again and wrote, *'Of course, in all this, there is the threat of Malcolm Craig Lowrie. I suspect I could make an enemy of him. Not ideal. Even if he does not know where the Lady Emma is, yet he will know she is being helped. And he will regard anyone who helps her as a danger to himself. In this case, that person and I will be one and the same. And this will be very dangerous. So what to do?'*

He stood and paced. It helped. When he sat down again, he was calmer. He wrote confidently, 'ACTION POINT: A WORD WITH THE PROCURATOR FISCAL. A WRIT OF OUTLAWRY MUST BE ARRANGED SO EVERYONE BECOMES CRAIG LOWRIE'S ENEMY.'

Robinson chuckled – congratulating himself on arranging the appointment of young MacDougall as Procurator Fiscal. The Lodge had proved valuable again and again since he had helped found it two years before. 'Freemasonry has its uses,' he thought, smiling.

Then reverting to his journal he worked through his new solution to the Craig Lowrie menace. Quickly, he wrote, *'He could be killed on sight as an enemy of the King. And the reward? That would be collected – perhaps in this case not necessarily by the hand that does the killing. And the forfeiture of land to the King? That would involve legal intervention. Which is where I could help. Neat. Very neat. Safety and profit. Perfect.* Caput lupinem gerat. *Let Craig Lowrie bear the wolf's head!'*

Then, whistling quietly, he crossed the Library, locked his journal in a secret compartment in the wainscot and rang for his house steward. It was time to have his bedchamber prepared, his bed warmed and a glass of the finest contraband French brandy set by his bedside.

Robinson had a plan.

# Chapter 3

## Oban and Robinson Park, Arduaine, Argyll – 7th January 1793

'YOU'D BETTER come up to the Park with me,' Sir William had said, the evening before, and something edging his voice had set Emma off like a colt – she had startled and flared – but then he had chuckled and said in a tone that was intended to re-assure, 'Lady Robinson is waiting for you.'

Barbary was to be tied to the carriage and Emma was to ride within, with Sir William. But Emma refused. 'I couldn't tie Berry to a carriage. He could not bear it. He would fight and hurt himself.'

'Oh? Really? Is he not trained to do as he's told?'

They were standing at the southern dock-edge in Oban, outside the lawyer's offices. The sun was setting and they had two hours' ride before them at least. The groom was holding the horses still and gentle and Barbary was eyeing the team. As Robinson was speaking about him, the whites of the horse's eyes flashed but, under Emma's hand, he did not move. 'I shall ride him to the Park,' she replied. 'I shall follow the carriage.'

Sir William sighed but acceded and then the lawyer heaved his bulk into the carriage, wrapping himself in a travel rug and a muffler. At the tap of his cane, the groom moved the equipage forward and Emma, now mounted, followed. Between her knees, she could feel Barbary curious but biddable. She laughed. 'Just one more journey, tonight, and then you can rest,' she whispered.

Then they set off, away from the dock, across the river bridge and up the track out of the town. The coming night was black but the darkness was underlit by the dying sun and the Wolf Moon was rising quietly. At least the journey would be dry overhead, although recent snowmelt had left the track wet under hoof. And, at last, after twenty miles in the murky wake of the carriage, rider and horse reached Robinson Hall.

Though weary almost to nausea, after six days on the road, Emma thought to go into the stableyard to settle Barbary. But Sir William said, 'Rest and you'll be sent for.' And Robinson's Chief Groom eased the reins from her hands.

Emma was led to her new quarters. She immediately dismissed the maid, collapsing onto the bed as she did. But, in due course, morning came, the sun breaking into her rooms from the east, and she awoke, still dressed in groom's clothes. Hunger twisted her stomach and she looked towards the door, hoping the maid would return with a hot chocolate, as would have happened at home in Northumberland. But no-one came.

As the sun rose higher, so did her hunger, and still, no-one came. She had been forgotten. At last she crept down to the stables to find Barbary and share some of his breakfast oats. 'No honey!' she thought, but nudged him out of the way.

Still there was no sign of the Master or the Lady of the House. Only a few grooms going about their business. Emma tacked Barbary. She could wait no longer. She needed air and movement. The grief of days was threatening to burst her heart.

Robinson Park lay in the dawn and horse and rider galloped around the bay, up the woodland rides, onto the hills. They jumped paddock hedges. They scrambled over the rough terrain. But, Emma realised, she felt no better. The memory of Jamie's hand as it slipped from hers had harried her all the way on the trail north. It had made her lose her way. It had made her forget to eat. It had almost forced her into the way of soldiers. And it harried her now.

But, at last she paused. It was time for Barbary to rest and crop grasses. And, as Barbary grazed, she sipped some water from a young burn, springing just below the ridge forming the eastern boundary of the Park. Then she lay down on her stomach in the grass. The gnawing at her insides, she found, seemed less this way.

It was about noon and, looking down from her vantage point on the ridge, she could see how truly grand Robinson Hall was. It was laid out, in the lea of a small wooded mound, protecting the house from the prevailing westerlies and almost at the top of the sunny south-facing slope beneath her. Low hills ran from Arduaine all the way down the coast of the Sound of Jura as far as the outcrop where, she realised, Castle Craig Lowrie stood. These hills concealed Robinson Hall from the direct track to Oban north of Kilmartin and she now realised how grave her error had been in taking the route along Loch Awe. The bleak Craig Lowrie stronghold must be no more than two to three hours ride from here.

She shuddered and studied the Hall again. She glimpsed the long drive hidden by rich ancient broadleaves as it led up to the east-facing main entrance of the hall and she could see where the carriage having unburdened itself of Robinson would usually sweep off round the north end of the Hall to the stable block and the kitchens. But on the southwestern side she could also now see an extension, isolated and solitary and largely concealed from visitors. However, thought Emma, this wing seemed cherished. The rose beds lying in a parterre with a southerly aspect were tended by a number of gardeners – she counted five – toiling in the winter sun. Men were also busy repairing guttering, broken in recent snow storms. Nothing would be left undone which maintenance required – unlike the rest of the Hall, which seemed to need some paint. The render had begun to flake. This was puzzling.

There was something else. The windows of this wing shone, as bright as if they were mirrors. Emma looked more closely. That in fact was what they were. Huge mirrors, capturing the sun, reflecting silent hills and a pewter sea. Emma – a young girl brought up in a castle – was intrigued. This was exotic, unlike anything she'd ever seen. But, she also realised, all this must be to the taste of the *chatelaine* of Robinson Park, the mysterious and invisible Lady Robinson.

'But why has she not shown herself?' Emma said aloud. Barbary raised his head at the sound of her voice and she stood up. The horse had mud spatters from today overlaying the mud spatters of the previous evening. No-one had tended him and Emma felt ashamed.

'Come, Berry,' she said. 'It is time I made you comfortable.' She swung up into the saddle, glad of her groom's clothes, and set off along the ridgeway and down its woodland rides at a gentler pace.

At last, she cut across the driveway and now knew she could follow it up to the rear of the Hall. But, as she passed the eastern facade, she had again the strong sensation she was being watched from one – she did not know which – of the huge black windows of the main section of the Hall. Glancing up, she thought she glimpsed a pale figure but she could not be sure. 'A trick of the light on glass,' she thought. Then, she shivered and urged Barbary into a spanking trot in the direction of the stable block.

As she dealt with Barbary in his loose box, a footman arrived to say a bath had been poured for her. Emma finished her tasks with Barbary and, leaving him comfortable for the night, she then followed the silent footman to her room where she found a servant's clothes laid out – a clean, plain robe, several sizes too large but passable, a petticoat and a shift. She bathed and dressed, quickly and – as was her custom – without a maid's help. A supper of broth and bread, fruit and cheese, and the most delicate of tiny pastries – sweet and delicious – had been brought and she ate quickly and with relish. Then the footman returned and told her she would be 'attending Lady Robinson'.

'That sounds grand,' thought Emma. 'But I don't think she can be grander than I. Her husband is only a knight, after all. Very wealthy and powerful, no doubt, but only a knight.'

As she walked along behind the silent footman, Emma compared what she saw to her home, the castle at Bamburgh. Some of the features of Robinson Hall struck her as distinctly odd. She was looking for traces of her host and hostess and she could find none.

Designed by one of the finest architects in the country, Robert Adam, Robinson Hall was only ten years old 'and the furnishings...! At home everything we have is shabby, used by generations of us and, here, almost every thing is new. New drapes, new rugs...'

But these, Emma noted, were few in number. As she walked, bare floorboards and plain furniture featured throughout. Not a flower graced the surfaces. Portraits of the long dead – dark in oil – lowered over her and dank air had settled like a pall of neglect on the rooms she passed. 'This house,' she thought, 'is quite as austere as I would imagine a Quaker's house to be – as if Sir William was a bachelor! And there is no spoor of Lady Robinson in all this.'

Emma's thoughts now went back to the rose parterre and the warmth and care lavished on that and she shivered at the mystery.

Ahead of her, the footman walked without a word until, at last, they came to a linkway. Here the servant's candle sputtered. A cold draught broached the new building at this point. Emma gulped but then her eyes opened wide. At home in Bamburgh, small, diamond window-panes kept out the wind, nothing more. In Castle Craig Lowrie, windows were no more than slits for arrows to pass through. Yet, through these arcaded windows with their immense panes of glass held in place by the thinnest of wooden frames, by day she would be able see all the way to the Dalriada hills, perhaps even as far as Castle Craig Lowrie. But her delight faltered. The glass against the darkness made her shiver. Menace surrounded her. This mute footman was leading her she knew not where and she knew not whether Lady Robinson was friend or foe.

Then she was across the linkway, and she found another world. Candles – shimmering in mirrors – blazed and the lushness of light dazzled Emma. And suddenly, in a cosy pretty sitting room, she found seated by the fire was the most beautiful woman she had ever seen. This woman was so lovely, Emma gasped.

Lady Robinson glanced up at Emma as she walked in. But she was occupied with embroidering roses on to silk – apple-green, delicate, pure and another moment passed before she paused.

'Should I not be wearing black?' Emma said.

It was already a difficult conversation. Lady Robinson had not risen and curtsied. She was clearly expecting Emma and Emma was expecting courtesies which she now knew would never come. 'This woman, not much older than me, is neither Scottish nor English. And she is not as middle-class and pedestrian as her title makes her sound.'

'Evidently not,' Lady Robinson said. 'No black,' she repeated. Her voice, lilting and soft, confirmed Emma's suspicions. Lady Robinson was foreign.

'But if I'm a widow, I should be wearing black, shouldn't I?' Emma asked.

'"No black." Robinson said. "No black!"'

Lady Robinson bit through the thread. 'Are you a widow?' she asked.

At this point, Emma realised she did not know herself and said so. But Lady Robinson showed neither shock nor surprise. She tidied up her embroidery and looked at her visitor with the frankness of an equal. Emma tutted. 'How are we to proceed?' she thought. 'She knows who I am. She should at least be polite.'

But Lady Robinson explained nothing more. Like a professional seamstress, she said, 'Strip to your shift.'

Emma stripped. Then Lady Robinson measured her shoulders

and back, chest, waist, hips, the length from nape to floor and noted everything down. Without ceremony or apology, she pushed and she pulled. Emma bore it, her teeth clenched. It was close, intimate. She could even smell the perfume with which Lady Robinson dressed her hair, wreathing a delicate web around the two young women.

'What is that scent?' asked Emma.

'*Muguet des Bois*. You call it, "Lily of the Valley". The *muguet* sprang from Eve's tears when she was banished from the Garden. In the language of flowers, the *muguet* signifies a return to happiness. I keep some by me. A return to happiness, that is what I hope for.'

Emma shivered in her shift.

'Now, sit by the fire,' Lady Robinson smiled and, grateful, Emma made herself comfortable. Cake and tea had been laid out for her. She nibbled and sipped but, after supper and tea, she no longer feared hunger. And she wanted to watch Lady Robinson practice her magical craft.

First Lady Robinson pulled the life-size *mannequine* across from the corner into the centre of the room. Emma was intrigued by the crude effigy with its rouged cheeks and pouffed hair and more was to come. The doll's body was adjustable and Lady Robinson, consulting her notes about Emma's measurements, tweaked it into what must have been 'Emma'. Emma almost clapped her hands. Then, without a pause, Lady Robinson took up some shears and, on a huge old brown worktable, cut out numerous shapes in some fresh plain linen. Each cut into the cheap rough cloth, Emma noted, was made without the benefit of marker or tacking and entirely without falter. Then Lady Robinson's needle and thread flashed through the weave – over and over again – until a bodice started to take moulded shape. Emma was enchanted by the speed and the skill.

At the same time, under Lady Robinson's instruction, two silent sewing maids worked in the distant shadows of the room on a petticoat template. When they did exchange a word it was in Scots and, Emma realised, whatever she said to her hostess, they would not understand. Emboldened, she asked, 'Is this how I am to be dressed from now on? I will look like a serving wench in that cloth.'

'On Sir William's instruction,' came the reply, 'I am to make you two day gowns and two dinner gowns. And some nightgowns. He says you are to look like the Ladies of Oban, but, I am sure, you will look better, better by far. They are all, I am told by him, twisted with the weather. Farmers and fish-wives or bourgeoises, he says. You are to blend. But, you, you are a beauty.'

Emma recalled her father's view. She had often heard him say, not without affection, 'Gawky, red-haired little thing!' But she had never been called a beauty. She was not sure what to think of that.

Then, holding up the rough gown, its seams to the outside, Lady Robinson said, 'Here. Try this on.'

As her arms slid through the makeshift sleeves and her head emerged, Emma began to see what pleasure could be taken in any gown created by Lady Robinson. The young woman possessed prodigious talent for fashion. Hardly surprising, thought Emma, realising Lady Robinson was French.

At this point, Lady Robinson seated herself at her sewing table and began to firm up the pinned seams with more of her strong, even tacking stitches. But, in the gleam of the firelight, with her eyes down, her fingers constantly moving, nimble and quick, she suddenly asked, 'Your story?'

At first, Emma was taken aback. But, encouraged, she told the tale. Lady Robinson said nothing, keeping her eyes lowered. She continued to stitch – hundreds of neat stitches, chain after chain – but, then, she asked, 'You, you travelled alone? Without a maid?'

Emma flared. 'Who would have been my maid in that awful place? Jennet Awe? That Craig Lowrie woman who dragged me away from the fighting – away from Jamie? She would never have been any protection for me. She was never MY maid. Oh, I know she cut my hair so I could escape and I think it was she who drew back the bolts on the postern gate. Yes, that was brave, I suppose.'

Emma had admitted this with uncharacteristic ill grace. She fidgetted on her chair and blushed at it but Lady Robinson was saying nothing in reply. Instead – so slightly Emma almost missed it – the French woman shrugged. But the misery of days was welling up now and Emma could not stem it.

'People should think about what I have lost. Why worry about maids and what was seemly? What I have lost is so much more!'

'True,' said Lady Robinson.

Emma stood and paced. She said, 'I'm fifteen years old and I've lost the man I've always thought I would marry. Everything my Lady Mother promised me would happen – that's just not happening now. And I don't know what will. Is that not cause for grief? Is that not cause for sympathy – even from people who hardly know me?'

Lady Robinson's huge eyes had been shining in the light but, now, became smoky with something like grief and Emma was sorry for her outburst. She had not thought to ask the questions that crackled around the head of Lady Robinson. What horror keeps this young woman living in such isolation? Nineteen years old, married to that dusty old man and childless? 'These Robinsons,' Emma thought, 'are not close. There is something mysterious here, it makes me cold inside to think about it. Something dark. Something I would not want to know, perhaps.'

Lady Robinson – surrounded by soft light, resting on soft furnishings, amid soft colours – clearly lived separately from Sir William Robinson. And, to Emma, brought up in a tumble-down soldier's home, where everyone lived cheek-by-jowl, this was the strangest arrangement of all at Robinson Park.

Now, however, though feverish with confusion, Emma smiled and Lady Robinson smiled back.

'Yes,' thought Emma, 'I really think – in another time and place – we could laugh together. We could have been friends, perhaps.'

Emma prattled on. Lowering her voice to prevent the maids hearing her, she confided, 'If my father had willed it, I could have been affianced to some old man – for no better reason than to bring money into the family coffers! Father is bartering, horse-trading, all the time, with anything and anyone at his disposal. I was so pleased – and relieved – when my "match" turned out to be Jamie. I remembered Jamie from when we were children. Playing on the beach at Bamburgh, admiring the puffins, throwing pebbles at the waves, racing our ponies. He was my friend then. And I thought he would be my friend now and forever. It is so unfair. And, knowing my father, even now I may be married off to some old man.'

Now, Lady Robinson spoke again. 'You mean, a man like Robinson.'

As she said this, she ripped her finger on a pin. A drop of blood bloomed, hovered and fell onto the linen bodice. Then it wicked outwards from its heart centre. No amount of washing would ever remove it now. Emma bit her lip, picking up a piece of linen rag to bind her companion's finger, and pressed the wound hard.

But, Lady Robinson removed the rag and, with a smile, revived the conversation. 'Jamie? Tell me more of this Jamie?'

In Lady Robinson's beautiful rooms, in a safe, warm halo of firelight, the shock of Jamie's death overwhelmed Emma again. She had chattered on about maids – and marriages to fat, old men – as if Jamie had never really existed. But he had.

'Everyone loved Jamie,' she said. 'His smile could lighten a room, I know it. I've seen it. We all laughed when Jamie played the fool. He was so funny, so wild in his plans. Loving to play the Laird. Jamie clowned and swore he was going to take over Argyll. He was going to trounce the Duke and make him run back to London. How we laughed.'

But there was another question in the firelight.

'And this man, Malcolm Craig Lowrie?' Lady Robinson asked, her eyes cast down to her task. 'What of him?'

Emma said, 'I know little of him. No-one does.'

But she was suddenly on the edge of her chair. Malcolm Craig Lowrie was raw power and menace – which she tried to explain. 'They call him "The Wolf of Dalriada" and that suits him well, I think. The last wolf in Scotland has been killed, I believe, but I could not say its spirit does not still walk. Not when I look into Malcolm Craig Lowrie's face. When I look into his eyes, I think I see the wolf returning.'

Lady Robinson had stopped sewing and was listening intently.

Emma continued, 'Where Jamie delights, Malcolm Craig Lowrie is silent and mirthless. But, I believe, Malcolm Craig Lowrie – if he wished – could very well "trounce the Duke", could very well "take over Argyll".'

'But, he, it seems, is loved too. No-one ever questions him. Everyone does exactly as he wishes. Even clanswomen – like that great, thick Jennet Awe. Her rough voice seemed to soften when she spoke of him. And Jamie, too. Jamie loved him.'

Emma suddenly wrapped her arms round her body – trying to prevent a sob. She blurted out, 'If Malcolm Craig Lowrie has killed his cousin, my Jamie, who loved him, he is more than bad. He is evil. And who is now left who can punish him? And I am afraid, so afraid, he will come after me. And what shall I do then?'

Suddenly she wanted to cry and never stop. She longed for her mother to be there to comfort her but, seeing the Scots sewing maids staring at her, Emma smeared away the tears from her lashes and returned to her chair. Lady Robinson did not move and had no comfort for her. But she let her sewing fall and then she took Emma's hand, saying quietly, 'What men think, it is all a mystery to us. Who they are. Good? Evil? How they hold their hearts. How they hold our hearts. All, a mystery. We understand it only in patchwork. Only in rags.'

Both young women were now lost in unhappiness but, pressing Lady Robinson's gentle fingers, Emma thought, 'Yes, now we are friends.'

Suddenly, Lady Robinson seemed to make a decision. She stood and drew out from a linen press multicoloured bolts of muslin, silk, velvet, brocade. 'Look, Emma,' she said, 'these have come – secretly – all the way from Paris. Touch them! Feel them! Are they not magical?'

Running her hands over the fabric, Emma was beguiled. She almost forgot Jamie and Malcolm Craig Lowrie.

# Chapter 4

## Robinson Park, Arduaine, Argyll
## 8th January 1793

IT IS MORNING. Sir William Robinson is reading the private journal of Lady Emma Bamburgh, while the Lady Emma rides out. He congratulates himself. He suspected she might write a journal – most girls do – and his search of her quarters would have been feverish, had this been necessary. But the journal came to his hand quite easily and his suspicions were rewarded.

Now he is comfortable in his library, with Oporto wine to hand and a footstool for his gouty leg. He is alone – apart from his spaniels – and has settled down to enjoy a young girl's thoughts. He has always believed the acquisition of information – bought, stolen or whispered – is what keeps him safe but he also takes unbridled delight in the wonder of young girls on the cusp of womanhood. He supposes he will enjoy this.

He flicks open the journal and the first words he reads are, '*I know that fat old man's my father's friend! And I know he's promised to help me. And I know I shouldn't think of him this way! But there's still something about him I don't like. Something, I fear.*'

Robinson chuckles at this and sips his port, shifting slightly in his chair. The spaniels at his side awake – alerted by his growing excitement.

'You'd like me even less if you knew I was reading your every word,' he says and chuckles again. This time, the spaniels return to sleep.

He leafs further back to a mention of Adelaide. He discovers her despair at her powerlessness – and Emma's – in the face of male ambition and desire and this amuses him. To his delighted surprise, Adelaide understands she is governed. But she is also aware that this 'management' is achieved by the tricks of a travelling conjuror, tiny scraps of information released when he, Robinson, chooses. This is how it works.

'Quite', says Robinson, chuckling again. He is finally learning how Adelaide thinks and may find out more useful things from this young girl's journal than from any other source so far.

But, he wonders, why did Adelaide not tell the Lady Emma that when she comes of age, he and she will marry? Then she will become 'Lady Robinson' in every sense, not merely using his title for the benefit of servants. Surely that would make him more 'acceptable', more honourable, in the Lady Emma's eyes. Robinson shifts in his chair, kneading his painful stomach. He is no longer comfortable but feels compelled to read on. Emma's script is childish but – for a horsewoman and an aristocrat – she is prolific and he is grateful for all the information she is supplying.

Then he reads:

*'But, what happened next was horrible!'*

Robinson is brought to abrupt concentration. The girlish hand continues, describing with unequivocal horror, what passed between himself and Lady Robinson the evening before when he paid the sewing room a visit. Seeing the events set out – with no opportunity to explain himself – cuts him to the quick. He had told Lady Robinson Emma's story and explained that she wanted to buy passage to Revolutionary France. But he now reads: *Had Sir William used mention of France to hurt Lady Robinson? Was he waiting for a sign of Lady Robinson's weakness so he could turn the knife? The sewing room was filled with Sir William's sense of triumph. It smelled bad – like the old flesh they give hounds. A game seemed afoot there and only one of we three players seemed to know what the rules were. And I was reminded of what Lady Robinson had said: 'They do not tell us everything.'*

*Until it suits, it seems. I wondered what was going to happen next.*

*Then, as I watched, it began. He stepped across the room again – heavily and deliberately. A predator, yes. But also, strangely, he moved around these private rooms as if of right...because, I suppose, this house belongs to him. Because, I suppose, this wonderful woman belongs to him.*

*But, as she stood, primping the template on the* mannequine, *Lady Robinson's back was rigid. He would receive no welcome there, I thought. And I was glad. His fleshy lips, his hands so rough and fingers so thick and so coarse. I had to fight down a groan of revulsion at the thought of him touching her...*

*However, more was to come. A curl had escaped from her upswept hair. It lay there – perfect black – on the gleaming skin at the nape of her white neck. And, as I watched, he noticed it too and his fat and sweating hand was reaching out to touch it. Slowly, so slowly. I could scarcely breathe.*

*And then, I heard it. Cold. Venomous. Lady Robinson hissed. And then she spun on her heel. Candlelight flashed on steel. The blades of her sewing shears were at his throat.*

'Non!' *she said.*

*That was all she said. 'No!' But, in that one word, I could hear so clearly her loathing for this man. I could feel the ugliness of the story there. And I gasped. And for the first time, it seemed, the two of them remembered I was there.*

*Then Sir William straightened up and half-bowed – stiffly — from the waist.*

*'Adelaide,' he said. 'My Lady!' (This to me.) And he left, his spaniels at his heels, claws clicking across the flags of the linkway as he returned to the main house.*

*I could not speak. Lady Robinson lent against the table for a moment, holding her forehead with her delicate fingers, breathing deeply. And then she simply turned back to her task, to continue making the template that would form the basis for my new wardrobe.*

*I am now crying too much to continue this, tonight.*

Snapping shut the journal, Sir William heaves himself from his chair. What he has read has unnerved him. He feels ridiculous and vulnerable. This is not how he likes to see himself. He started reading the journal in the hope of learning a little more about events at Castle Craig Lowrie and perhaps pleasuring himself with a young girl's pubescent thoughts. But this has not happened.

Once more, he goes up the servants' stairs to the Lady Emma's guest rooms, replacing the journal with care under her pillow. The smell of spaniel will linger in the room but he does not think of this. His mind is swirling the new information of how much his 'wife' loathes him around and around, as he walks out into the Park. He climbs to the belvedere looking out over the coast to the west. Above all, he can hear the roaring maelstrom of the Corryvreckan, miles and miles away across the sea. He shivers at the menace it sends on the rising winds.

'The situation here,' he says to himself, 'is becoming intolerable.'

* * *

Fresh from her ride, Emma breaks in upon the rooms set aside for her. She has been told they are her private quarters and will be treated as such and with the respect due to the daughter of an earl.

But then, with her senses enlivened by winter, she catches some trace scent on the air. She recognises a blend of spaniel odour and of Oporto wine on a man's breath. She goes to her bed and raises the pillow. Her journal is lying there – almost as she left it. But not quite. The book is turned upside down. She gasps. She knows full well what has happened. She takes the journal to the hearth and, tearing out the pages, one by one, she burns them all. She weeps. It is her life she is burning and she knows she will never write a journal again. She also knows that 'respect due to the daughter of an earl' means nothing in this household. Everything depends on the whim of the Lord and Master of the House. And she is now as much a prisoner here as the beautiful Lady Robinson.

* * *

## Robinson's most private Journal, written later that night and then held under lock and key in his bed-chamber

*I don't understand what's going on. Adelaide?*

*When I brought her here, I had such hopes. At least, I hoped she would love me. That was the first thing. It was me, after all, who took her from that foolish court and that foolish father in particular. And have I not been proved right to have done so? The whole country – France – is up in arms. Revolutionaires everywhere, baying for heads on stakes. How would she have survived in that? My little canary.*

*She looked so full of promise on the boat across, I remember. With the curve of the cheek and the lip, rounded and shining in the candlelight. So very kissable. But, she was so afraid. So very small and so very afraid. Every time I drew near, she was like a trapped creature. Dangerous.*

*I did think she would grow out of all that. But no, I know the blade is still there, hidden in the sheets. Her bed would be a dangerous place for me. Perhaps even for any man. I don't know.*

*But there is something else. Something I would sooner confess to no-one. Something I can scarcely bring myself to write down. I am not far from meeting my Maker. When the pain in my gut first came to me, I felt it was a warning from the Almighty. Before I could even touch her, I was warned away! And now, the pain comes – worse and worse, more and more, night and day. And I am terrified that, when I stand before Him – which will surely happen soon – I will have nothing to offer Him in the balance, nothing to put against my sinful life. Nothing but my pure, pure Adelaide. Will He not acknowledge on my deathbed how I have protected her? Will He not be merciful because of that? Will He not take account of how I have cared for her, fulfilled her every wish and whim. I have given her everything, everything she has asked for – except, it is true, except for freedom. But, even so, will He not remember how I have borne her resistance without complaint – and without retribution. With forebearance. With restraint. Surely Adelaide will be my atonement. Surely Adelaide will be my redemption. Surely Adelaide will shine for me like the star she is. And my Maker, surely He will give me credit for that. And I will be saved. Saved from His eternal damnation. He is so close now – I can almost feel His breath upon me. He is the pain that tears at my gut.*

*But, if she is to be my redemption, why – when I see her – can I not escape the deadly sin of lust? Surely that is the cruellest joke on His part – that I am forced to endure the temptation daily. To be aware of the drift of the scent of her in the air. To have had to watch candlelight flickering over her budding breasts at table. To feel that I would like to push her up against the wall and take her – as I do the sluts, slatterns and whores of the town and of the kitchens. Yet, in spite of all this temptation – so powerful I can scarcely breathe – I don't act on it. So she will be my redemption. Surely. If God is just...*

*Yes, I think it has been a mistake to bring the Lady Emma Bamburgh here.*

# Chapter 5

## Letter to Pettigrew, Robinson & Pettigrew, Solrs, Carlisle

### Dated 9th January 1793

*PETTIGREW, my dear fellow!*

*Here is my assessment of a situation currently besetting us.*

*The Lady Emma Bamburgh is apparently the virgin widow of the young fire-brand James Craig Lowrie of Dalriada, whom, she believes murdered on their wedding day at Castle Craig Lowrie – near Crinan in the south of this region – by his cousin and clan chieftain, Malcolm Craig Lowrie.*

*I can well believe this. As you know, I do listen to servants' gossip and they are always forthcoming with admiring tales of Craig Lowrie witch-spawn devilry. Personally, I'd outlaw Black Malcolm, as they call him, as soon as look at him. And, in fact, this is what I've decided to arrange. More of that, soon.*

*But, the Lady Emma fears for her life. She had to escape. For all she – and the rest of us – knows, Malcolm Craig Lowrie may have his own designs upon her, her title and her dowry. So, yes – contrary to all my instincts for self-preservation – I have her here. But the question remains – if she is indeed wed and/or widowed – what exactly is to be done with the Lady Emma Craig Lowrie? Well, at present, she thinks to buy a passage to France – a nonsensical option in my view. She thinks all the trouble over there will blow over, which I sincerely doubt, and she has friends. It will all be well, she says.*

*But, if going to France is indeed the plan, you'd better send young Pettigrew north. She'll need an escort. I can't go. As you know, even if the old order is changing, even if I could bear the sea voyage, I sus-*

*pect I would not be generally welcome in Paris. I shall give the matter further thought but in the meantime, young Pettigrew's presence is required.*

*I'll be in touch again when I know more. Same precautions. Same secrecy.*

*Ever your humble and obedient servant,*

***Robinson***

# Chapter 6

## Oban, Argyll, Scotland
## 11th January 1793

WHEN SUDDEN WIND lifts the sail, the rigging shifts and a mariner, Jean le Pecque, feels the harsh lash on his back. He is surprised and his bare foot, damp in the Scottish air, slips on the ropes. He falls. Then his scream comes abruptly to silence and, on the deck, his crew-mates flow over his sprawled form like ants over food.

* * *

On the quayside, these events are observed by Lady Robinson. She sinks back onto the silk cushions of her carriage. She is shivering. She would not care to die like Jean Le Pecque – 'knowing you are falling to your death for those long, long seconds before the end.'

She whispers to her chaplain, Father John Stewart Macdonald, 'Make sure it's him. Then, if it please you, find the letters again. If it please you, bring them here.'

She is urgent. Her chaplain glances at her in enquiry. Then, he slides into the crowd – becoming, as she watches, one of them. He has, she thinks, a talent for invisibility when it suits. Now, the stark sounds of Oban – the shouts and the clatters and the groaning ropes – din in her ears. The smells – old fish, horse dung, human sweat – make her want to retch, while all she needs is to observe her chaplain. Everyone and everything seems intent on preventing this.

But she sees the chaplain has reached the French brig, *Espoir.* He is about to climb the gangplank but he is forced to pause. Some sailors are manhandling the dead mariner down it. The chaplain signals and the bearers halt. He raises the coarse blanket – which serves as a shroud – to look at the mangled corpse. Then he drops the stained cloth, covering his own face for a moment with his gloved hand. The smell of the broken body – its skin no more now than a bag to hold blood and bone and damaged organs – cuts easily through fish market smells. Lady Robinson imagines she detects it on the air.

The sailors do not question the chaplain. They wait in deference as he slides his hand over the seaman's rags. In and out. He is searching the corpse as if he had authority to do so. He has not. It is a manoeuvre hidden in plain sight. It works. Then he crosses himself.

After a few words with the crewmen, the chaplain walks up the gangplank. And, now, as she waits, Lady Robinson is gripping the carriage side so hard it hurts her fingers. But, amid preparations for sailing that evening – cargo stowage, sail re-reefing and trimming – she sees no-one stop the chaplain. Then he disappears below. He will now be searching the man's hammock and the brig's rough-hewn ribs close by it. He will question passing sailors. There is nothing he will not do to find the letters and the leather cylinder that carries them – crested as it is with the insignia of the court of Marie Antoinette.

Slow moments slide past.

But, as the Lady waits, there is a sideshow.

The French seamen struggle with their misshapen burden on a creaking lych cart, their hobnail boots slipping on the quayside cobbles and the metalled wheels grinding with the turns demanded. But, where the sailor's head should be, the shroud falls flat and the sight shocks the crowd. Fishermen stand silent. Even Highlanders – gaggled on the dockside, waiting for their forced passage to foreign parts – have pulled off their bonnets in respect. Their women cover their hair. There remains, thinks the Lady watching in the carriage, a certain dignity in this bleak cortege.

This does not last.

A young woman bursts through the crowd. At first, she tears at the corpse's shroud where the head should be but then she re-coils, hand to mouth. Then she claws more deeply into the dead sailor's clothing, finally pulling free a hand. She seems to be looking for something to recognise. She seems to recognise a ring.

Then the woman screams – a long, slow animal cry. This harrows the watching crowd. Some turn their heads away. For a moment, Lady

Robinson thinks perhaps she should send Jean Le Pecque's woman some money. But, she remembers, she does not yet know for sure whether the dead sailor and Jean Le Pecque are the same. Then she sees Father MacDonald walking towards her, through the awed and whispering crowd. His face is as still as a tomb.

Once more at the carriage door, the chaplain says, 'It was him. No letters. They must have been taken.'

'Already? *Certes,* he won't yet be cold.'

'These are poor people. Letters mean money.'

'Is there an accusation in this?' she thinks. She says, 'Those letters, they won't do anyone much good but us.'

'Perhaps. But if whoever has them takes them to an officer. To one who can read...He will pay perhaps.'

On the bow of the *Espoir,* the figurehead hovers over and then slaps down on the chilled waters of the Oban docks. It is the coarse representation of a young woman – skin, unnatural white, slashed by scarlet lips and framed by crude, curling yellow hair. Her bosom blooms from her dress. She offers her sailors hope.

'But hope of what?' Lady Robinson wonders. 'Love, a better life, a safe voyage, home? So,' she thinks, 'so...'

She bites her lip, reluctant to recall her own voyage to Scotland all those years ago, on that same brig.

Father MacDonald is now commissioned to track down the lost letters before the crest of the court of Marie Antoinette is recognised. These are dangerous times, even so far north, especially so far north. But the Lady and her chaplain have done all they can here for the moment. The chaplain will make his enquiries later, when the working folk on the quay are more ready to talk – perhaps in the evening – though they will know little for certain, thinks Lady Robinson.

'And will say less,' adds the priest.

According to usual schedules, the *Espoir* would soon have been underway. In the normal course of things, the ebb would be set, and able to bear the brig out into the Firth of Lorne at nine o' clock, seven hours from now. But the death of Jean Le Pecque has delayed the usual sailing. The brig will not now leave until the morrow – despite what its owners would prefer. Lady Robinson considers this. It gives more time, twenty-four hours at least, for the chaplain to find the letters. This is some comfort.

In all these concerns, Jean Le Pecque is forgotten by everyone except his woman.

'Where next?' the chaplain asks.

'The Fish Market, of course.'

Since she was twelve, Adelaide de Fontenoy – also known as Lady Robinson – has had the running of Robinson Park. As a child at the court of Marie Antoinette, under the tutelage of her mother and at the side of her sister, she learned how to do this and – from choosing daily menus to counting linen to supervising maids and arranging flowers – she does it well. 'It is almost pleasant,' she often says to herself, 'to run a great household.'

Her *chatelaine* duties also allow her to go to market in the Port of Oban. No British woman of her apparent rank would make these visits but, as a French woman, she is expected to be nice about the choice of ingredients for the Robinson Park kitchens. However, she has to take care. Would Robinson accept her concern for the freshness of fish as reason enough for tiring his horses? This is improbable, so she makes the four-hour return journey to town – at least once every six weeks – in secret. She rides dark-cloaked, hooded and veiled, accompanied by only her chaplain and the Chief Groom, in a carriage draped with black linen to hide its insignia.

Even so, in this, she knows, she is bold. If Sir William Robinson – the Oban magistrate who at this moment is inspecting the body of Jean Le Pecque – were to know she came to town like this, he would be angry. She shudders at the thought of the consequences. More rigorous incarceration? An offer of violence? Perhaps even the rupture of the sole and final link with her sister, Gabrielle.

But now, with the loss of those letters handed into Jean Le Pecque's keeping not much more than an hour before, things have taken a turn for the even worse. Almost unable to breathe, Lady Robinson works her fingers into the folds of her gown. But the light film of silk fails this time to soothe her.

'The Fish Market, yes, the Fish Market,' she repeats. They must maintain a credible pattern of activity. If discovered in town, they must avoid arousing Sir William's suspicions. He believes her, she thinks, to have broken totally with France; to be totally within his power. He must not know the truth.

Receiving her instructions, Father Macdonald turns to command the Chief Groom to urge the patient horses and the carriage forward, to the side entrance of the Market Hall. There, as they have done many times before, the Lady will wait with her list as he directs and the groom completes her errands.

But, then, the chaplain pauses. Lady Robinson has laid a hand on his sleeve. It is not appropriate. She does not notice the slight quiver this has triggered. She does not notice how the lines of his long, drawn face soften for a second and how, almost imperceptibly, his lips part as if to speak.

'Who is that?' she asks, looking past him into the crowd.

Not many yards from her carriage, someone else has been observing events. A tall but graceful man stands apart from the clustering fisherfolk. He is sleek and glossy as a raven. His greatcoat flows snugly over the line of his muscled shoulders. The coat is perfect. From generous collar to polished boot, it is perfect.

'French tailoring,' Lady Robinson thinks, 'it is impossible not to take pleasure in the couture talent of her fellow countrymen.' And the coat's owner? 'Perhaps an *aristo* officer from the *Espoir,*' she first surmises. But there is more. She sees that this man has the sea-washed skin of the north. He is not French. He is a Scot. She studies the man in black more closely. In the pale sunshine of the afternoon, his dark hair gleams where it falls in a spiralling tail down his back – longer hair than is fashionable in this north-western Scottish seaport. 'This is a man without fear or favour,' she thinks, 'a man who calls no man "Master!"'

Then, he turns. His eyes scan the crowds. He is hunting. But who or what is his quarry? When his eyes come to rest on hers, she sees they are blue as the turquoise seas of the Isles. She cannot help herself. She gazes at him and her lips part in the softest of smiles. He gazes back openly but he does not smile. With a gasp, Lady Robinson lets the door blind fall. There is something about this man, about the thought that he will come again into her life at some point soon, that takes her breath away. But she is sure – absolutely sure – that he will.

She steadies herself – counting slowly – and John Stewart Macdonald quizzes a passer-by.

'Who is the Laird?' John Stewart Macdonald asks.

'Malcolm Craig Lowrie,' comes the reply.

In the carriage, Adelaide, Lady Robinson, hears fear crackle in the passer-by's voice. But, when she looks again, Malcolm Craig Lowrie is gone.

# Chapter 7

## Late afternoon at The Three Fishes Inn, Oban, Argyll, Scotland 12th January 1793

THE FIRE CRACKLED and spat. Malcolm Craig Lowrie shifted in his chair and wondered whether, after all, it would be better for everyone just to burn the letters. After reading them, he knew, they were trouble, particularly for the women they were intended to pass between.

And there had been that troubling incident with the little French woman, Marie Le Pecque, who brought them. She had tumbled in through the door, gabbling in French. 'Did she know I would understand?' he now wondered.

Loyal Rab MacDonald, his tacksman and house steward, had struggled to keep her out but she would not be denied.

*'M'sieur,* I beg you, hear me!'

Craig Lowrie signalled to Rab MacDonald, The woman was to be allowed to speak to the Laird but she was prevented from approaching too near by the huge mahogany desk between them. Craig Lowrie would then watch for the untruth in what she was to say. There was none, he was pleased to note. As it turned out, she was widow to the sailor who had fallen to his death on the *Espoir* the day before. More than that, he could see, she was angry.

'My husband, he was courier. Courier between these two women. I don't know who they are. But I loathe them. I detest them. How could these women – whom I have never met and never harmed – have such power over me? They have left me alone, without friends, in this cold, damp country of yours. I have no money. I must find work. And they have made me a beggar. Help me! Help me, *m'sieur!'*

'Why me, *madame?'* Touched by the beautiful face, the eyes luminous with tears in the firelight, Craig Lowrie could not help but be curious about her.

'Because you can, *m'sieur.* I see you on the Docks and I think, "Yes, that man there, he can help me." Something about the eyes...otherwise...I do not know. I do not know how I will live. Now my Jean is dead. And it is all the fault of these, these women...'

She spat in the fire.

'I do not know the women,' was his soft reply.

At this point, she plunged into her shawl and drew out a worn leather cylinder, its stitching strained, its edges and seams scuffed. She opened it and pulled out parchment, scattering it without care over the polished wood of his desk. She picked up a few sheets at random and handed them to Craig Lowrie. A glance told him they were in no particular order and he realised she could not read. The letter contents were safe, then.

'These letters, my Jean, he carried them for these women. For money, it is true. But the money, it is not enough! Not enough to lose my husband.'

She bit her lip and waved the papers towards him with more insistence. 'And I want justice,' she added, snatching the papers back to her breast.

Craig Lowrie simply said, 'Justice? Very grand. Money? More likely?'

'I have none. I have neither. And money, it changes how you see things, *m'sieur.* You – you can afford morality, I expect. I would have hoped to be able to live that way too. To live with honour – as a good man's wife. And, as I would hope now, as a respectable Christian widow. But, without money, I cannot. I simply cannot.'

'You say so.'

'I do.'

'Show me the letters.'

'Pay me.'

'You are bold.'

'I am desperate.'

'True, *madame.'* And Craig Lowrie signalled again to Rab MacDonald, this time to find the necessary recompense. The woman thanked him, with some flattery about his goodness. This amused him. His usual reputation, its flames fanned by his agents, was quite the reverse. Men called him The Wolf, he heard. But now he sent her away with hope. Rab MacDonald would find her some respectable work, he said. She was then bundled out, counting her gold. She seemed content.

Craig Lowrie was satisfied. His intention had been in part charitable. But, of course, although he did not yet know what, he also knew there was some profit to be had in all of this. The trick lay in identifying the senders and intended recipients. And, so far, he had no clue.

He looked at the pet name at the beginning of the letters. It was a family name, he was sure: light, inconsequential and anonymous to all but those in the know. The same was true of the signatures – simply 'A'. The women were sisters, separated by quantities of sea. The letters were intended to travel between Oban and Paris.

'And the answers must come back the same route,' he thought, picturing the trafficking of mail in these dark, uncertain times – letters would pass to and fro but with the utmost difficulty from the unknown Parisian *citoyenne* to farmer to sailor to whom? The concealed identities did not surprise him. This would be the first precaution.

'Like raiders on the hillsides, melting into the dawn,' he thought 'nameless, faceless, unknowable, silent.'

And so – with no great expectations – Malcolm Craig Lowrie settled down to re-read his 'purchase'.

* * *

***2nd January 1793***

*My dear, dear Gabi!*

*Did I tell you I've refurbished my rooms? Now, you could not tell them apart from* Le Petit Trianon, *I'm certain. I've adopted precisely the Queen's rustic style – though, principally, it is true, I have done so to escape the harshness of the Scottish style. I'm only young, after all! So, here, in my rooms – based precisely on what you have told me about the Queen's Versailles Apartments – I have created something, something light and fresh. These rooms, they have become a symbol of 'home' for me. And I do so hope, so very much, to come home one day.*

*But let me explain how I have used your information. You would be delighted. I have adapted the motifs you sent me. The rose and the lily of the valley – these are my favourite flowers, absolutely. Thank you, thank you, dear Gabi! Of course, neither does so well out-*

*side this far north so I've covered the walls and panelling with rosebud and lily designs. And on the silk curtains – apple-green! – I have designed pockets so, when roses or muguets are in season in the garden outside my windows – a much shorter time here than in France, I can tell you – I have the scent of fresh flowers filling the room. And, in the winter, I have the musk of dried roses filling the room with fragrance. Just like hers, just like the Queen Marie Antoinette's. Thank you for telling me about everything in such detail!*

*And I have been able to choose some wonderful ceramic bowls for these pots-pourris. Sadly, the craftsmen around here are not able to execute frescoes but they can make a fair hand of crafting flowers in wood or plaster or even, when encouraged, papier-mâché. But there are some good potters here. You should see the results! Even She would be proud.*

*No crystal blowers, though. Some over at Edinburgh but that is too, too far away. (Everything is, apparently, much too dangerous, south of here). So no crystal – as yet. Nor have I adopted the robin's egg blue of the* Trianon *– it can look harsh in the northern light. But, with candles, I have been able to warm up the panelling. And, for paint, I have chosen creams and ivory whites and the colour of mocha. And I love being here – in these rooms. This place is a sanctuary and no-one comes here without my express invitation.*

*But, there is something else I must explain to you. In my rooms, my dear sister, I have adopted the Queen's taste for mirrors. There are mirrors everywhere. You may think it, but I have not done this from vanity. I have done this so I do not forget who I am. Is that strange? I need my reflection around me so I do not forget.*

*And, each morning, when I rise, although I feel alone, and lonely, I choose what I am to wear so carefully! Where I am to warm my cheekbones with rouge! How I am to set my hair! Some English women, I hear, wear a morning cap to save themselves the trouble. But I, I sit before the mirrors and every day I re-create 'my self'...*

* * *

The content of this letter was private, sisterly stuff, about fashion and decorating rooms. And about what – with the revolutionaries hammering at her gates – Marie Antoinette favoured. This irritated Malcolm Craig Lowrie. 'The people want bread,' he said to himself. 'And the woman uses flour to sculpt her hair.'

But it was clear too that, although these sisters were not high-born, they had had the ear of Marie Antoinette. They had hung on to the French court's coat tails – with some success. And, it was even clearer, one of them was now here in Scotland. Near Oban.

He read the second letter in the bundle – with much more attention.

* * *

***January 9th***

*Dearest G!*

*I must tell you. Extraordinary things are happening. Let me tell you everything!*

*Yesterday, it was a bad day. I was bored to sobs. Even my morning toilette could not cheer me. Then – strangely enough – it was R who rescued me from this low mood. Over the breakfast table, he suddenly stopped reading about racing (!!!) in his newspapers and spoke. He told me a young girl was come to stay. I was to make her some new clothes and keep her identity a secret. I of course promised to oblige. How could I not keep 'secrets'? I, who never see anyone!*

*But R said nothing more. After his kippers – pickled and smoked herrings, you would loathe them – he went to write letters. I prefer to spend our time apart, anyway, and I'm so glad when I do not see him again until the evening. As is usual.*

*But, throughout the day, the young girl he mentioned, I could see her from my windows and my terraces. I watched her without her seeing me. And, all day, she rode her horse, throughout the parkland, backwards and forwards. Like a caged animal. You know, I find this obsession with constant need for movement slightly ridiculous – and so very British. But, even so, I was moved by her. I realised she was driven. Driven by something that had all the appearance of fear and grief. And I became more and more curious.'*

Craig Lowrie sat up and began to scan the pages, searching for information – as much as he could glean – from the script. The writer continued.

*'I watched her return to the stable yard. She rode in with an enormous clatter. Her horse – Berry, its name – is huge. Strong. Powerful. A man's horse, I would say, although I am scarcely the person to judge, as you know. But, she waved away the groom and then she groomed her horse herself – long, sweeping strokes – loving strokes, I remember thinking – and, as I watched her, I saw her wipe some tears away with her sleeve. She looked like a little girl, then, and my heart went out to her.*

*Then, it was I who organised a bath and a supper, and a gown-fitting for her. So, suddenly, my dear sister, it appears I am to be seamstress to an English earl's daughter. Yes, absolutely. This is what I have found out. More real, you may agree, than our father's career in royal millinery!!!*

*And I'm so happy you sent those bolts of silk two ships ago. (Silk has now been banned with you!!! How dreadful that must be!) I used some for the curtains, as you know. But lots remained and the liquid quality of that green silk, it matches this young girl's eyes – but perfectly. Such loveliness is breath-taking. And it will be a joy to make gowns for such a figure. She is immature, and tall, like most of the northern English (which she is). But perfect, flawless. And as you know, my greatest talent, it is my sewing.*

*But, I lose my way – the silks you sent, the velvets, the brocades – the touch of them, the shades, tones and hues, the perfumes...I cannot put this less strongly...this young girl is entranced, as entranced as you and I. And I, I am really hopeful my life now changes. First, my new rooms. And now this! Perhaps a friend!*

*As to the fitting, it flowed along beautifully. Why would it not, with such raw materials? We started with a linen sack but a mouthful of pins soon shaped the seams in and out, tuck by tuck – she is so slender. And then we settled, I to my tacking and she to a chair by the fire. The maids were there, as usual, dealing with petticoats and under-shifts but they only understand Gaelic so we were quite safe to talk. So I turned to my own work. And she, to her story!'*

There was a break in the letter at this point. Craig Lowrie sifted the pages and found the addendum. He noted a shift in the hand-writing. The script seemed to show sudden high emotion in the writer. His interest quickened.

*'And this is such a story. You will never have heard the like, I think. The girl had escaped from some cruel captivity in the Highlands. There had been a wedding day and a murder and soldiers and chaos and evil and terror!'*

Craig Lowrie was now stock-straight. This was all sounding familiar. The writer pushed on with the story. *'But, when she was telling the tale, the Lady E quite lost the look of a lost child – so appealing, so darling in its way. Her eyes and her mouth – they became dead, no expression, frightening. When I saw this, I shuddered. Oh so much, Gabi!'*

On another piece of paper, Craig Lowrie found, *'But, while E was telling me about her journey north, I thought, there is more, so much more she is not telling me. The story veered off. The story now, it was as nothing. But I am a good listener and I know when to stay quiet and when to press. I know how to wait, too. Ten years of long practice, in thrall to R, have given me that skill. I was prepared to wait. I continued to sew, to give her time and freedom to recover. But her story absolutely burst from her now.*

*'She had wed her childhood sweetheart only to see him murdered before her eyes on their wedding day. And by his cousin. That's how she came to be in Oban. Oh, for a moment, she had thought to come to France, when she saw a French brig at the quayside. But the captain wouldn't take her horse! Some ships will, I know, but not that one. And she wouldn't leave it. I know – strange – so British – as I say. Then she saw R's nameplate – the name was familiar to her, from her father, the Earl. When she saw the nameplate on his office door, she rang for attention.*

*'The facts are jumbled. I don't know what's true. I don't know what is not. But this man, MCL, it seems, he is powerful, here, in the Highlands. His reputation as evil is widespread. But what a coincidence! Could he be the same person as the "Petit Prince"? All these Scottish people, they all seem to have the same or similar names, so probably it is not the Scottish boy from so many years ago. But then to have exactly the same name! And I, I cannot remember quite where I could have met a Scottish brigand? Or how? Apart from Burgundy and Versailles, I have only ever known this house in Scotland. And Oban, I suppose, on market days. But then, I dare not talk to anyone but the Father. Such a mystery!'*

'Indeed!' thought Craig Lowrie. Had he and the 'A' of the letters met before then? He could not re-call it. He thought back over the years – particularly those spent in France. Many women, it was true. But the 'A' of the letters, he could not single her out. He started to read again, eager for more clues.

*'And for what reason would he kill a young cousin?' you may ask. I certainly did. But the Lady E's response, it saddened me. She said: 'Does a man like that need a reason? Land, power, title? And then she added – oh, it is so sad, my dear sister – she added, 'Everyone, it seems, can make a profit out of me.'*

*'She was out of her chair now. Pacing. It was the same hunger for movement, I'd seen in her earlier, riding all day. I thought of animals*

*again – animals in grief. Then she sat by the fire, spent. She is only fifteen after all.'*

Craig Lowrie by now knew the identity of at least one of the people in the letter. He turned over page after unsorted page and then he found a page, bled in part by tears.

*'He walked right in to my rooms. We became aware of this only when the sewing maids stood to disappear but these are my staff and I signalled to them to sit down and carry on with their work. But to just walk in. Without invitation, leave or courtesy. With his spaniels wet from the field, pushing their way forward to the fire. He kicked the dogs aside and then, settled and comfortable, rocking from side to side, warming his great hams before the flames and he took it upon himself to tell me the young girl's story. The stench of wet spaniel was making my eyes water but I said nothing, Gabi, nothing. I accepted this intrusion – I have to. My fire is lit at his expense. I must accept these things. And, I would not give him the satisfaction of a protest. Without a word, I slipped the Lady E a house robe and then placed the linen template on the mannequine. As he boomed on, I behaved as if I ignored him, primping and picking at the template gown. When he had finished the tale, I asked simply why the Lady E had come to us for help. His response was a mixture of the laconic – he's a lawyer, after all – and the melodramatic – also a lawyer's skill.*

*'Because of the relationship of kith and kin,' R said and mentioned his old friend her father and then her mother. But, while he was speaking of the Lady Mother, his eyes were watching me.*

*All the while, he was swelling up like a sweating toad. Then he drew out his snuff. (My rooms have reeked of that – and of wet dog – for hours!) But, I did ask, 'If she had the money for France, why not go?'*

*Even more loudly and almost beside himself with triumph, the fat old fool riposted, 'Because – my little French canary – she needs my help. As her father's friend. Because, my dear, things are in chaos over there. Because, my dear,* La Belle France *is in revolution.'*

*I did not miss the reproach. He knows I would sooner be with you – however changed France may be – than here with him. But, at that, I shrugged and started to pin up the linen template again.*

*'I can't fully describe to you what happened next. But, I can tell you, right there. In front of that young girl. He tried to touch me again.*

*'I cannot bear it, dear, dear sister. For ten years now, I have tried to keep him at bay. Ever since that first time – on the ship coming*

*here from France. Do you remember that? I was only nine!*

*'Since then, I have slept always with my shears at my side – just in case – a blade for him and a blade for me. He has not forced me – yet. Which, I suppose, is a mystery in itself. But, oh, he seems always to be trying to come closer. Suddenly, without warning, I will find a hand on my skin. Feel his breath on my shoulder. Smell the stench of it. And I can't bear it.'*

Craig Lowrie was absorbed now by the tale and he hastily picked up another page. It read:

*'The Lady E is the virgin widow, he jokes. But, if so, me, what am I? A virgin mistress? Oh, I am sure he lets his colleagues think I am his "ward and not yet out", that he is my guardian and that we are to be "married" when I am of age. He will swagger up and down the town, meeting people and greeting them, passing the time of day and I am sure he will answer all enquiries regarding me with some credible reason – my not being "out", for example – as to why he never takes me to town or introduces me to local worthies. When he dines out, he dines alone. He never allows me to meet anyone. I should not be surprised, dear sister, if I have a reputation for extreme frailty among the townsfolk of Oban.*

*'But, I am sure he believes it gives him huge glory to have a young French "wife-to-be" at home, especially one who was brought up in the court of Marie Antoinette. But, I'll wager, he would never admit I was only a trainee milliner! And what is worse, the daughter of the milliner who was only ever ONCE in favour with the Austrian Queen...*

*'Unless of course he has never told anyone anything about me at all!!!!*

*'That I suppose might be possible. He brought me here for some very special reasons of his own – as we know. Disgusting, foul reasons. He, even he, may not want to have that discussed. I may yet be a secret.'*

# Chapter 8

## At The Three Fishes Inn 12th January 1793

'THIS "EVIL COUSIN" – what a reputation I have!' Malcolm Craig Lowrie smiled, rolled the letters up again and fed them back into their leather cylinder. 'But', he thought, 'this R also seems to have an Achilles' heel.'

Rab MacDonald was waiting across the room. A thick-set man from the Isles, more used to cattle than people, he said little but thought much. On the surface of things, he was preparing food for Craig Lowrie's supper, a simple dish of oatcakes and mackerel. He did so with care, his attention seemingly on the task, his eyes lowered, his hands busy. But he was listening, even so, and when he paused, the Laird found his house steward looking at him in expectation.

Craig Lowrie went to the fire, folded his arms and tapped his lip in thought. 'But who are these people?' he said to Rab. 'And where is this happening? This is surely the Lady Emma but where is she and with whom? There is no clue to that. This letter is written with some craft...It offers no directions. No landscape information. Nothing to identify a residence sufficiently grand to house the daughter of an earl. And no indication as to the name of the host.'

Rab poured a glass of claret and took it to his Laird. Craig Lowrie took it, cupping the crystal bowl in his hands to warm the wine. He sipped thoughtfully and continued, 'This "grand house" must be somewhere, somewhere sufficiently close to Oban.'

The Lady Emma was no doubt safe there for the moment. But

he needed to know where 'there' was. He would set his agents onto this and soon. The horse's name – Berry – would surely help. Yet enquiries about the Lady Emma had so far yielded nothing and Highlanders, he knew, could keep secrets for hundreds of years, even unto death. It was a matter of Highland honour and of obligation. It was his creed too. He understood it.

'But,' Craig Lowrie reminded himself, 'Highlanders also love a story and stories have always come to them. The ten-year-old mystery of a French girl-child in the thrall of an old man – now that is a good story. It would buy food and shelter – such a story. Someone must have heard it. But, even so, someone powerful up in the hills was keeping that story secret, along with the whereabouts of Emma Bamburgh. Perhaps Emma's "protector" was using the code of clan loyalties for his, or her, own purposes. And did that make him, or her, Scottish? Or devious?

'However', Craig Lowrie reasoned, 'down here in the port of Oban, people are torn away from their clan loyalties and starvation can be a rigorous paymaster. Silence may be alive in the hills but here, among the desperate, perhaps it could be broken. And perhaps,' thought Craig Lowrie, 'as with Marie Le Pecque, a little gold could now ease the breaking.'

He strode to the window and gazed out for a moment. Expanding Oban would become more powerful. Even now, travelling far into the north, even English tourists came to see the Oban sights. One such was the new distillery. Whisky, now out of the illicit stills in the hills, would make Oban famous and fashionable and respectable and even *bourgeois*. And, as Oban lay even further north than his own footprint on Argyll – by a good thirty miles – he could not help but be intrigued by the changes wrought, changes which had flanked Dalriada and Crinan Moss and passed him by.

He returned to the papers, scattered over the desk, and began to sort most of them away into the drawers except for the leather cylinder that he placed carefully where it was not generally visible. Although it was partly concealed by ledgers, Craig Lowrie knew it was trap bait. But, as yet, he did not know what animal would come for it.

Then, he was filled with renewed impatience.

There were undercurrents swirling through Argyll and, recalling his years spent with his uncle Argyll in the French court, Craig Lowrie recognised their precise source and felt their keen menace.

To ensure survival of his clan against Argyll, he knew, he would have to move with infinite care through the treacherous shallows of the new Scotland. Oban and Argyll were just a starting point.

Rab laid a place for his Laird on the desk and offered to serve the mackerel but Craig Lowrie could eat with little enthusiasm and waved it aside for now.

'Oban dances to the new tunes,' he was thinking, 'while the old songs stay in the Hills and the Isles. And we of the Hills and the Isles – we are like the *daoine sith.* The guardians of the Portals. We are used to the old, harsh order. We know its rules. We can live and die with those. But what if we are forced out of the hills? Then, if we want to "endure", we must learn the new tunes to dance to.'

Oban would teach Craig Lowrie what they were.

# Chapter 9

## At The Three Fishes Inn 12th January 1793

MALCOLM CRAIG LOWRIE had earlier that month decided to keep some rooms in Oban and the anonymity of *The Three Fishes Inn* had appealed to him. Neither landlord nor customer would ever ask for a name or give it to anyone else. There would, of course, be those in the quayside crowds who knew the Craig Lowrie but they would remain silent – an echo of old clan loyalties. And, in that trust, he could enjoy the simplicity of the room furnishings and the plainness of the food. In the dark, rough-beamed rooms set aside for him, the mahogany desk where his papers lay was a very handsome piece of furniture. By contrast, in the bed chamber off the receiving room, his bed was a single truckle bed, dark and solid, and took up very little space.

'Yes, this will be a comfortable den', he thought. He was pleased with it. In the south there were a host of riding servants and war bands under their own commanders who would hold Castle Craig Lowrie and his lands in good order for him. Just five hours' ride away – and another world. And, here, at *The Three Fishes,* he had easier access to those Oban undercurrents and the gossip that would help him understand the new Scotland. He needed both.

Now, a sea wind caught at the inn, threatening to shatter the smeared glass of the casement window as it tugged it loose. Disturbed by the sudden noise of bustling Oban, Craig Lowrie abandoned the desk and moved across the room to secure it. But then, he paused, watching the quayside crowds argue over fish and whisky. And, as he did so, he saw him again – the priest from the Quay, the companion of the Dark Lady. Craig Lowrie watched as, where the flood tide splashed over the stones of the dock next to the Market Hall and across the water from *The Three Fishes,* there moved the wraith-like figure of the priest. He had to admire the way the priest passed in and out of the shadows, at times no more than a blur, at times blended to invisibility, with only a flash of lamplight picking him out before he was gone. By the look of him, he was asking questions as he moved along. And sailors and fishermen alike were wiping their greasy hands on their clothes and bowing their heads to receive the priest's blessing. One after another, the quayside workers pointed to *The Three Fishes Inn.* And, Craig Lowrie realised he was himself the priest's quarry.

In the same second, he also knew, that his 'anonymity' on the dockside was already compromised. He had assumed loyalties to his name that perhaps had been forgotten, no longer existed in this battered, transit port. He had made a mistake, perhaps, assuming Oban still had a Highland fishing village way of thinking. And, if so, he would be angry for it. But, this state of affairs had good and bad to it. If the fisherfolk could be bought by a priest's blessing, he reasoned, they might sell their information to Craig Lowrie agents. The price had only to be right, had only to better what was already on offer. What had the Le Pecque woman said? 'You can afford morality.' She and the rest of the poor could not.

'So,' Craig Lowrie muttered to himself, 'are you coming to find me? Or is it the letters? And who are you, anyway, my friend?'

This priest was certainly someone's agent.

'But, if this man has a defining feature,' thought Craig Lowrie, 'it is pride. He has a back like a ship's cannon ramrod. And he's no-one's lackey.'

Craig Lowrie tapped his lip in thought, 'So, some other power is at work. Love? Duty? And who pulls the strings? Does the Dark Lady of the Quay pull your strings, priest? And, are she and the "French sister" one and the same? And, has the hunt for the Lady Emma suddenly become easier?'

Craig Lowrie caught his breath at the thought of the Dark Lady. He had seen her for only a moment but, in the hours since Jean Le Pecque's death, he had thought again and again of her face, shimmering in the darkness of the carriage. And he knew the Lady Emma was only part of the story as to why he was still here in Oban – not away, hunting on hill ground, where he felt secure in the knowledge of where the trails led.

He returned to the desk by the fire to wait. He did not have to wait long. Within minutes, Rab MacDonald opened the door and the priest walked in.

For a moment, the priest paused in the centre of the room, while, in his hands, his black priest's hat – the only outward sign of his office – revolved slowly. His fingers moved with attention, not fear, around the broad brim. His eyes slid from side to side, still checking. Then the room's plain furnishings seemed to help. He was perhaps reassured by an absence of show.

'You're the Craig Lowrie?' enquired the priest.

Craig Lowrie did not rise from his chair at the fireside desk but nodded agreement. He was a man who appreciated straight dealing. He appreciated the priest's next question. 'The letters, you have them?'

'I do.'

'How much do you want for them?'

'How much do you want them?'

A sum was named. Craig Lowrie hissed softly through clenched teeth. 'You want them greatly then.'

'Not me.' The priest hesitated and then asked, 'Will you sell them?'

'Now, why would a man like you want to buy letters, written between sisters, containing nothing but trivial details of fashion and romantic notions?'

'You've read them?'

'But, of course.'

'In French'

'Aye.'

Both of them?'

Both men knew what the second contained – nothing to do with fashion and romantic notions.

'Aye.'

'You're a man of many talents, Malcolm Craig Lowrie.'

'Because I speak French?'

Craig Lowrie stood up and then threw another log on the fire. He was watching the priest as he did so and saw the old man covertly scan the desk. Craig Lowrie saw him pause. What was he looking for? His eyes had stopped moving when he saw the leather cylinder peeping out from behind some ledgers.

'They're there.' Craig Lowrie was aware the other man's hand had moved to what could have been a *sghian dubh* in his black coat sleeve. He smiled. 'Will you be trying to kill me for them? Or are you going to give me the money you offered?'

'I would not be killing you to save the money.'

'But you would be killing me to save your mistress?' Craig Lowrie straightened from the fire and turned to face the other man. "The Dark Lady?" On the Quay? One of the sisters? And "the fat old fool" of the letters? Her guardian?'

The priest's face iced over.

Craig Lowrie continued: 'And you'd be prepared to kill me because I've read the letters – because I know she's French and would rather be in Paris even now – because she's of the court and she's in danger – because I know she's unhappy. And because she's had a visitor. Yes, I can see that would make you want to kill me. If I were to scan the situation wrongly...or tell the wrong people...killing might be a reasonable choice. Or you could buy my silence.'

'How do I know you'll keep your word?'

'I haven't given you my word yet about any of this. You also do not know whether or no I had the French sailor killed for the letters. Or whether some other party brought them to me – who had read them first. Your decision to kill or not is, if I may say so, a delicate one. Would I be of more use to you dead? In which case you may take the letters – without paying – but not survive your first encounter with my man at the door. Or would I be of more use to you alive? And an ally? Aye, delicate and difficult.'

For a moment, each man regarded the other. But Craig Lowrie was amused. There would now be either a fight or a pact. A pact would be better. He liked the old man's way of dealing and wouldn't want his blood on his hands. He turned his back on him to show how little he feared him and pulled the leather cylinder from the pile. From it, he extracted the voluminous sheaf of papers, made a show of examining the crest, then walked round the desk and dropped them on the polished wood. The priest counted out coin alongside them. This was a challenge, Craig Lowrie knew, but he glanced at the stack of coin and shrugged.

Money was always useful. It would pay for something. But Craig Lowrie's silence – now that would put this man – and whoever sent him – in Craig Lowrie's debt. Craig Lowrie knew he could then, if necessary, kill either – perhaps both – when he deemed fit. But at the moment, both were alive and both owed him something for silence. Silken threads bound both to him. And he could tweak the thread from time to time, to let them know he was there – until such time as it would be more useful to yank it. He was satisfied. He'd called the priest's bluff and won.

The priest withdrew the *sghian dubh* from his sleeve and placed it in his bootleg. He picked up the leather cylinder and tucked it into the sleeve where the knife had been. He turned to go.

But – at a slight signal from the Craig Lowrie – Rab Macdonald had moved from the shadows.'Will you no take a drink, before you go?' he asked the priest.

Expecting little and still amused, Craig Lowrie watched as Rab offered one of the two waiting crystal goblets. The wine – its colour unfurling in the light and its savour drifting upwards through the room like the scent of flowers – was French and of highest quality.

'No!'

Craig Lowrie shrugged again – noting that there had been no offer of a blessing. Then Rab MacDonald – with the instinct of servants – opened the door for the priest to leave.

Craig Lowrie raised an eyebrow, thinking the while 'And I now have the fine idea that the beautiful Dark Lady of the Quay will soon know more of me.'

He glanced at Rab MacDonald who nodded and then both men clattered down the stairs, to trail the priest through the quayside crowd.

# Chapter 10

## On the Oban Quayside 12th January 1793

OUTSIDE, THERE WAS no sign of John Stewart Macdonald. As Craig Lowrie had thought, the priest had a talent for disappearing. So Rab set off down the quay and towards the town to find those fishermen who at the end of the working day might be willing, for an ale, to tell a tale or two about the Dark Lady and the priest. An Isles man, Rab could claim kinship with most of them – which at times like this could be useful. They might speak to him, whereas they would not speak to those who could not claim their kinship.

Craig Lowrie turned to walk in the other direction. It was a short route from *The Three Fishes Inn* to the end of the quay but there may yet be someone who could give him information about where the priest came from and who, apart from God, he served. In any case, the walk would clear his head, muzzy from the events of the day.

But when he paused to light a pipe, he noticed an old man and a young woman, two bairns clinging to her skirts. While the bairns tossed a toy between them, the old man and the young woman were dragging a box to the quayside. The toy caught Craig Lowrie's attention. It was not a ball. It was not an old piece of sea-glass, weathered by the Corryvreckan maelstrom. This was something bright, shining in the harbour flares. He drew closer. 'That,' he thought, 'is an emerald. I wonder. Have I seen that before? On the Lady Emma's neck?'

He moved closer to the small family. At last, he thought, he could hope for progress but he would have to make enquiry with some delicacy. Was Emma dead? Had the emerald been stolen? Or was there some other story here?

'Now stay here and wait, faither. I'll be back as soon as I've spoken to the factor.'

With that, the young woman pocketed the emerald and towed the bairns into the crowd and out of sight. The old man began to pull at the box. It did not move. Craig Lowrie stepped in. The box was light. 'Where would you be wanting it, faither?'

'Just there, laddie, just there.' The old man's eyes squinted up at the newcomer in the twilight gloom on the dock and Craig Lowrie guessed he would see only the vague outline of a young man, dressed as a Highlander, offering help. The offer of help had been respectfully made. It was accepted.

Craig Lowrie put the battered box where the old man's crooked finger pointed. Then the old man sat down, hunching himself around his thumbstick, gazing out to the tip of the Isle of Kerrera across the bay. He seemed disinclined to talk and his pale eyes were, the young man noted, wet. Craig Lowrie drew out another clay pipe from his *plaid-neuk.*

'Will you smoke with me, faither?'

The pipe was taken, space offered on the box. Craig Lowrie sat but some minutes passed before another word was spoken. The silence was eloquent and dense. Craig Lowrie waited, unsurprised when the old man said at last, 'You're a Laird, maister.'

Craig Lowrie caught the bat squeak of bitterness. He did not respond to that but asked 'You and your young – you travel alone?'

'Have to. My son, he's in Africa. Fighting for the Laird. And for the King. I'll not see him again. I did not know it at the time, but I've said my last goodbye to him.'

Craig Lowrie said nothing but drew on his own pipe. The old man – encouraged by the silence – continued, 'His wife, his bairns, and me, we have all been told to go.'

Then the old man turned his eyes from Kerrera. If he wanted to ask his Laird why this was happening to him, his Laird was not there. But the young Laird, sitting next to him, would stand as proxy.

'The men came to our home. Soldiers and muskets. Sheriffsmen with batons. Doing the Laird's bidding, they said. I find that hard. I cannot believe that. They dragged everything out of the blackhouses that would burn – we hid what we could in this box – and the valley was blue with smoke. Some of the cattle were taken off to new pastures but some were driven away onto the moorland – the old beasts, weak – once strong and useful. But old now, and weak. Some canna see. Or move easily. They'll die soon, out there on the moorland, in the snows. I wish I was with them.'

Craig Lowrie let the tale come at its own pace. The old man resumed.

'I went and asked the minister why this was happening? I was told if we did not obey the King, the Kirk and the Laird, we were evil and destined for Hell. I could not believe that. So we waited in the burning scrub for word from the Laird. But only the factor came. He said the land was to be cleared for the sheep. He said passage to the Americas had been arranged for us, "for our own good." He said a ship was waiting at Oban to take us to Liverpool and we should hurry. We have come on foot as fast as we could. But it has taken us some days. I am too old. And the bairns are too young to move fast. We had our old garron, Kelpie, with us but he could pull only the box. He could no longer bear weight on his back, so I walked. He gave us everything he had. And now the Oban town-rats will have him. We may have missed that ship. If so, I've no doubt there will be others.

'But we are still hoping for a word of kindness from the Laird. None has come, yet. Too sad himself, perhaps. And now we're bound away from our land. When the time comes, I'll not lie with my forefathers. And, if he comes back, my son will not see his children play where he played. Even if he comes home, he will most likely never see them again. And I know I will not see him. I will not say to his face, "God be with you, Johnny." That perhaps is the hardest of it.'

The old man looked at Craig Lowrie, who still said nothing. There was nothing to be said. Emboldened by grief, the old man asked, 'Will you be treating your kin this way, Laird?'

'No – I hope to God, no.'

The old man breathed a death rattle of a sound. 'Thank'ee, Laird. Thank'ee.'

'What is your name? May I have it?'

'The same as my Laird's.'

'May I have it?'

'Campbell. John Campbell.'

'Well, John Campbell – I wish you "Godspeed!"'
'Aye, to Him. It cannot be long now.'
John Campbell turned his eyes back to Kerrera, his eyes full. Then he turned again. 'Your name, Laird?'
'Malcolm Craig Lowrie.'
'God bless you, Malcolm Craig Lowrie!' The old man stood and they gave each other their sword hands. Craig Lowrie felt the bones through the old man's skin. There were no muscles left to pad them but the grip was steadfast. Then John Campbell sat down again and spoke not another word.
Craig Lowrie placed his tobacco pouch on the box beside the old man and then left him, looking out to the hostile sea that would most likely be his grave. He knew after this night John Campbell would not look on Scotland again.
As he turned away, Craig Lowrie recalled there had been no word of 'an emerald' in the old man's story. 'The jewel has no value for him,' he thought. But he now knew he was on the Lady Emma's trail, and closer than before. He also knew listening to his tale was the greatest gift he could have given John Campbell in his darkest sorrow. And, though heart-sick, Craig Lowrie would have to rest content with that.
But, as he turned away, he caught sight of John Stewart Macdonald in the shadows on the Quayside. 'That was well done!' said the priest. Craig Lowrie shrugged.
'These are godless times, priest.'
'None knows it more than I.'
'Aye, I suppose you would.'
Craig Lowrie slid into the darkness of the ramshackle buildings alongside the waiting priest. 'I should have thought you'd be away by now.' He paused. Why did it give him pain to mention her? 'To the Dark Lady of the Quay. With the letters.'
'Nothing so easy.' And Craig Lowrie heard the fear in the old priest's voice, although the man's outward appearance was as stiff and upright as when Craig Lowrie had first seen him. The young man stood for a moment in silence, thinking *This is a night for tales.*
Then he invited the priest to say more. 'What then?' he asked.
The white-faced priest looked at him hard, as if weighing the value of his interest and that was difficult to gauge. 'I think I may need some help where I'm going. Pray God I'll find it.'
'I'll pray God you do, too. France, is it, then? With the letters?"

'With the letters.'

There was much that Craig Lowrie wished to know about from whom and from where the letters came. But he recognised that some bargaining was now in place again. The old priest was as discreet as the confessional. He would not be bought with coin and fear did not make him prattle. Craig Lowrie decided on a different tack.

'So. So,' he said, turning his gaze to the docks. The *Espoir* still rode at mooring there. With a nod in the direction of the French brig, he said, 'Your passage to France on the evening tide?'

John Stewart Macdonald winced. Craig Lowrie had hit the nerve. Craig Lowrie pressed the advantage. 'I have routes to Paris, myself. Not used for a while. But there are still those who when they hear my name would help you.'

'A brigand's name. Would they be brigands then?'

Craig Lowrie inclined his head – slightly – and then lost patience. 'You seem to have little choice, if I may say so. You are about to embark on a journey that men half your age would avoid if possible. To a country where Christian law has been suspended. If I were you, I would take what offers of friendship I could find.'

'Friendship? Is that what this is?'

'It is.' Craig Lowrie leant against the wall, watching the old man absorb this. The conflict within the old man was palpable. The priest was desperate, so desperate, to take the letters to France but fear and age were making their presence felt. His body was failing him. He was daunted and he disliked this truth. And now a brigand offered him 'protection'. Hope. But, with Craig Lowrie's help, he could do what he had promised, his dearest wish. Craig Lowrie read this and waited.

The priest was a plain-dealing man. He said, 'And what could I bring to this "friendship"?'

Whatever it was, it would not be betrayal of the Dark Lady of the Quay. Craig Lowrie understood that. However, some compromise was inevitable.

'Information.' Craig Lowrie's response was frank and curt.

'Information?'

'Information. About France and what is happening there.'

'Now why would a man like you need to know what is happening in France?'

Craig Lowrie smiled. 'Because I do,' he said.

John Stewart Macdonald could scry nothing from Craig Lowrie's face.

Then he said, 'And how – on my travels – will I find this protection?'

Craig Lowrie accepted this as agreement. 'Scots – MacDonalds of the Isles – will meet you whenever you need to be met. Show them this.'

A leather pouch was hanging from Craig Lowrie's kilt belt, alongside dirk and sheath, and pistol. The priest sniffed. With weaponry like this to hand, he knew Craig Lowrie could have killed him. But he had not and now, Craig Lowrie reached into the leather pouch. The priest leant forward. There, suddenly, in Craig Lowrie's hand, shone a ring – an emerald cabuchon, its slender shank, gold, its setting plain. As the priest studied it, the quayside flares lit the green depths of the stone. It was like looking into the sea. A beautiful thing. 'Jacobite?' he whispered, fear drying his throat.

'Was,' said Craig Lowrie and turned it over. The flare above them now picked out a mailed fist, holding a cross, engraved on the reverse. The words in Latin, 'By land, by sea' were visible. As were the initials, MCL and the date, 1783.

'The date?' croaked the priest.

'The year I became a Laird,' said Craig Lowrie, simply. Impatient now, he indicated it was the time to take the ring. It was time for the priest to accept what that brought with it. The priest eased the ring onto his finger and saw the MacDonald crest shining through the stone. 'You're a MacDonald then,' the old man said. 'A kinsman.'

Craig Lowrie said nothing but offered his hand. The old man shook it. 'I will bring you information about France,' he said.

'It is enough,' said Craig Lowrie. He said no more and made his way back to his rooms at *The Three Fishes* to wait for Rab MacDonald's return.

Within the hour, Rab MacDonald returned.

'I lost him!' he said, dipping his eyes.

'No matter,' said Craig Lowrie. He was by the window, watching the *Espoir* set sail. 'I expected no less.'

Rab MacDonald made his report. He had approached several of the fishermen and sailors now lounging on the dock. 'There's no knowledge of where he comes from. And the carriage he rides with has never insignia to identify it. They see it only when a French ship comes in...They don't know what the connection is. Someone pays for silence on the quay.'

'I wonder who? The priest's name? Is it known?'

'That, they could tell me. His clan is known in these parts and scattered in the glens. He could be one of many.'

'His name?' Craig Lowrie double-checked from habit rather than need.

'He is Father John Stewart Macdonald – a kinsman – though I stay in the Isles and do not know him, myself.'

It was now Craig Lowrie's turn to be silent. He had caught sight of Father John Stewart Macdonald, standing on the foredeck of the *Espoir,* as she slipped out of port on the evening ebb-tide. The priest's chin jutted into the storm-laden air but his back was no longer straight. In the crumpling form of Father John Stewart Macdonald, Craig Lowrie could now see John Campbell, the despair of old men swept onward by powers too cruel to listen. However proud and powerful these old men had been once, they were proud and powerful no more. It was a savage lesson in change, he recognised, one of the first of many that Oban would teach him.

From the casement, he saw some newly-arrived bands of clansmen, jostling on the docks. Some would be standing with their Lairds' tacksmen, believing they could all yet travel to new lives with honour. Other families would have been sold to the New World by their London-based Lairds and would be travelling without the covenant of a Laird's care. The end result was the same. All were the victims of the Highland Clearances. They were waiting for passage, while sheep – profitable, rich-wool-bearing Cheviots – grazed on the reed roofs of their ruined blackhouses, infested their homes.

'Yes, everything is changing,' thought Craig Lowrie and turned away from the casement with a shudder before settling down to read the papers on his desk. Saying nothing more, Rab MacDonald again brought him the plain oatcakes and mackerel, which this time were accepted.

# Chapter 11

## Sir William Robinson's Private Journal Entry 27th January 1793

PETTIGREW'S SILENT. Dismayed, I suppose. Quite naturally so. A writ of outlawry against Craig Lowrie is no longer possible in Scotland. Brieves, as they call them, of this sort are now obsolete. But there must be some way – some legal trick or fiction – that will protect me in this. Who do I know in Edinburgh?

And Edwin Bamburgh's reply came today, in the saddle-bag of a rather greasy but necessary spy. And I'm not very happy. Edwin's letter says:

*'Too dangerous at present for her to travel home. Stay with you perhaps. I shall well reward you...'*

This seemed promising.

Then, *'But – if the ceremony took place – according to the marriage contract I had drawn up, she is now heiress to half of Dalriada. Get it back for her. Hire an army if necessary. English mercenaries should fit the bill. Try Carlisle. I'd send you my troops but they're otherwise engaged on His Grace's business. But I'm sure you'll make shift. Yes, hire an army if necessary. Your old friend, B.etc...'*

Bless my periwig, I say.

# Chapter 12

## The Hillside of Ardnackaig
## 7th February 1793

THE RAM BREAKS from the pen.

'Wasting his energies,' mutters Tam Sween. The Early Spring Tup is underway but this delay is using daylight. The clansmen have brought the ewes down from the crags to the good grass on the cliff top but they cannot stay many days. The winter fodder needs to recover. 'And', says Tam, 'I should nae ha done that.'

The young dog lies dead in the pen, broken as the stones around it. Inexperience left it vulnerable to a ram in his prime. 'But, the dog'd never been promising,' Tam Sween re-calls. 'It'd always been wilful, intent on hunting sheep.' And, in the tradition of the hills, the old shepherd had decided, time in a pen with the ram would cure its predatory instincts.

'So it has,' Tam says to himself. But the cure has carried with it extreme penalty. The ram has made short work of the pup. To bring the remaining dogs to him, the old man whistles softly through his teeth. They slither to his side, Bess as ever in the vanguard, panting in her desire to please. But suddenly Tam stiffens.

Malcolm Craig Lowrie has appeared at his side – his face, grim. 'The cliff's too close. Put a dog over there, one that knows what to do!' This is all Craig Lowrie says. It is enough.

The shepherd obeys, calling to the dogs in the old tongue, the Gaelic, softly, so as not to alarm the ram. It is Bess – brave and loyal – who pricks her ears and ripples over the grass to the cliff edge. 'Doing the Laird's bidding,' Tam Sween thinks, his mouth so dry that the commands – whistle and call – scarcely sound. Picked out by a setting sun against the shadowed sea, the dog now stands at the very edge of the headland. The ram lowers its head and begins to run and the shepherd prays the ram will turn. It does not. But it is canny enough to stop when it has butted the dog into the darkness. Bess falls over the north-facing cliff without a sound. The shepherd's jaw sets but he says nothing.

Craig Lowrie's eyes narrow. Without a word, he takes off his riding coat and hands it to the shepherd. Then he walks off, across the ragged land, without breaking step. His kilt swirls in the flow of menace in his stride.

Wary, the ram moves away from the edge and, with malevolent eye, watches the man, moving across its field of vision. Recognising a force of nature, stark and powerful in the gloaming, the animal shifts further up the slope.

Craig Lowrie does not falter. Sure of foot, he reaches the place where the dog went over. Without pause, he follows the cliff edge up and then cuts across the headland. He is moving around the ram but he has caught its attention and it swings to face him.

'The Laird's taking the path Bess would have taken,' Tam thinks. Blaming Craig Lowrie for the loss of Bess, Tam Sween has no reason now to like the man but the tension between Craig Lowrie and the ram meshes him in. The sun is low in the sky, large and blood red over the Sound of Jura to the west. Craig Lowrie is now in dark silhouette against it and the ram is faltering but transfixed. Tam Sween licks his dry lips.

With hardly a movement, Craig Lowrie signals to his men and, silently, ready with dirk and targe, eyes on Craig Lowrie and the ram, the clansmen form a tinchel between the points of cliff edge and pen. The danger is vivid.

Big as a stirk and heavier, the ram could easily take out a man. But even so, the plan, the shepherds recognise, is not to harm it. Rams have their uses. Men, on the other hand, as each one standing on the hillside believes, are forfeit to the good of the clan.

Craig Lowrie takes out his own dirk from the leather pouch slung to his chest – twenty inches of metal polished to mirror brightness. Holding it above his head, he catches the sun – dying now but still bright and clear on the tilted steel. He shines the sun's light directly into the ram's eye.

At first, the ram lowers its gaze. Then it raises its eye to the man it recognises as its predator. But, wherever and whenever the ram tries to face down Craig Lowrie, light pierces its eye, sharp into the nerves behind. It hurts. Grumbling, the ram backs down the hill, taking a run now and then as if to break the line of men. But the drumming on the targes turn it back. And still the light and the 'devil' bearing it comes on. Tam Sween blinks but once back in the pen, the light finally falls away and the ram quietly crops the luscious grass. Men run to make good the walls but not before Craig Lowrie picks up the body of the young dead dog and tosses it into the heather scrub of the headland.

'For the foxes,' he says, to no-one in particular.

Then he adds, 'We'll eat the ram. It's feart of a dirk and sunlight. Its lambs will be weak on the hills. I'll to Lochgilphead tomorrow and fetch another.'

Tam Sween, for the first time, looks Craig Lowrie in the eye. 'So it's all been for nothing, then?' he says, thinking of Bess.

'Aye.'

The old man says nothing more, bows his head and clasps his hands before him for the Laird's brogue. Craig Lowrie sweeps up onto his horse. But, before turning away, he pauses. He leans forward and touches the old man's shoulder.

'You've lost old Bess, today, Tam Sween. My dog's in whelp. Ask in the yard for two of the pups – the best.'

Tam says nothing but his eyes glimmer in the sunlight. Then the woods between Ardnackaig and Crinan fold round Craig Lowrie, as he rides back to the Craig Lowrie stronghold.

The men Craig Lowrie leaves behind know what to do. The tup is over till a new ram can be found. Craig Lowrie has detailed clansmen to take the raddled ewes back up onto the hills towards Cnoc Reamhar to overnight pens high on the ridges. And, with drumming and whistles, the men are moving the edgy animals up the drovers' trails towards the open pastures on the tops. Only a few of the Craig Lowrie shepherds – including Tam Sween – stay behind to make the rest of the flock secure in the tupping meadows on the headland.

But silence comes at last. Now, with a moment to grieve, Tam's hand moves down to where Bess would have raised her head and licked him. Her absence clutches at his heart. 'A new pup,' he thinks, 'for an old man.'

And this is the moment when the raiders choose to attack. The warning Tam Sween hears first is the light scrape of unsheathed metal on stone. Then, all round the flanks of the tupping meadows, he sees men rise up from the ground. These men of the shadows are silent as wraiths but then a cry breaks from them like the roar of a river in sudden spate. The line spreads to sweep the field but two in the vanguard of the Highlanders' charge are heading for Tam. It is a matter of seconds, but, old as he is, Tam Sween is ready with his dirk when they reach him. As they close in, in a single movement, he slashes both throats, exposed in the war cry. In shock, the two raiders stand for a moment before crumpling together to the earth. But the sight of their collapse enrages their kin and they swirl to take Tam Sween to the ground. It is a clean kill.

The other Craig Lowrie shepherds are not so lucky. The raiders' numbers force submission. The shepherds are disarmed of their dirks and bound and they wait to see what will happen now. But, certain they will not be disturbed, the raiders are lazy in their looting of the shepherds' camp. There is not much booty here – these are poor people – but the raiders take what they can. There is much laughter. And then they dispatch the shepherds and move out, taking the few remaining Craig Lowrie ewes with them.

Only one man is left standing to tell the tale. Deliberately released, Rab MacDonald slips and tumbles down towards the Craig Lowrie stronghold – on the trail of the Laird himself. His story will be an old one. He has seen how, in their last minutes, his kinsmen have known shame. He has watched as his kinsmen, defenceless, were thrown from the cliff. He has heard, as they fell to the rocks, his kinsmen's prayers that their Laird will avenge them.

# Chapter 13

## The Kitchen at Castle Craig Lowrie 7th February 1793

'THE LAIRD.' The whisper hissed round the shadows of the kitchen and, of the Craig Lowrie serving women, only Jennet Awe remained in the light. She was listening as the groom took the Laird's horse in the castle court and Craig Lowrie ran down the scullery steps towards her. He was taking them two at a time, as he'd done since he could walk. Jennet Awe smiled.

'You'll be needing broth,' she said, reaching for a ladle. This was her domain. She had no intention of bowing her head and disappearing from the Laird's sight. She was not like the other women. She had some power in this household.

Craig Lowrie nodded and slid onto a bench – while the women in the dark recesses watched him in silence. Shapeless, bruised and scalded, they would wait till the Laird had eaten and left and they could resume their work. But he scarcely glanced at them, Jennet noted, nor at her. Thinking of other things, he was tapping the table.

'Here it is!' said Jennet Awe. He stopped tapping. She had heeled him but he had, as she recognised, not meant to imply impatience.

The bowl of broth – thick with chicken, carrot and barley – steamed in front of him and, with his dirk, he hacked off the corner of a fresh barley bannock. He dipped it deep and watched the bread moisten in the brew.

Jennet Awe said nothing. Before his arrival, she'd been about to make more oatcakes and now she continued her daily duties. She began to work the oatmeal and bacon fat and water in a huge bowl but she was watching him as she did so. Then she sat down across the bleached table from him. The oatmeal bubbled in the bowl.

'Something bad?' she asked.

'On the cliff. Tam Sween's Bess. Tam'll be in to ask for a whelp.'

There was a pause.

'I see,' said Jennet Awe. But she thought better of asking another question and stood up to go back to her baking. He meanwhile finished the broth, sighed and glanced up at her and she looked directly into his eyes. White bread dough, English-style, prepared and proven earlier, now slapped down – again and again – on the scrubbed table. 'I've looked out for him all his life,' thought Jennet Awe, 'I am still.'

But, before she could speak, shouts from the yard broke in upon the quiet kitchen. Suddenly a man was framed in the doorway and, even with the light behind him, the mud and blood spattering tunic and kilt was stark to see. It was Rab MacDonald.

'Come, come quick. See what they have done!' Rab MacDonald was yelping.

'No, you tell me! Now!'

But, exhausted by fight, flight and grief, Rab MacDonald had no words for his Laird. 'It's better you see.'

And Craig Lowrie was gone – with Rab MacDonald not long behind him.

Jennet Awe sprinkled the table with dry oatmeal. 'It'll be raiders, again,' she said. 'Mark me well.'

The serving women moved from the shadows. 'Had we better not go to find out?' asked one, bolder than the rest.

'We'll know – in good time – when we need. When the Laird comes home.' Jennet Awe was rolling out the soft dough into huge circles. She impressed each into eighths with a knife and then, with infinite care, she leant over the rounds to glaze them.

'But...'

'Nae "buts", lassie. Since he was bairn, the Laird has known better than you or I what we need to know.' Jennet Awe bit her lip. Then, briskly, she swept the oatmeal rounds into the oven and onto the griddle. It was time for the oatcakes to bake but Jennet could hear, somewhere in the castle, women – wives, mothers, daughters – already keening for loss.

* * *

Although garron horses are bred for the work, scrambling up towards Ardnackaig for a second time that day had been hard for Craig Lowrie's mount. She had been ridden hard up the tracks both times and the way down to Castle Craig Lowrie was never easy. Now, turned loose on the rich grasses of the tupping meadows, the pony was tempted to graze and rest. But she couldn't settle to feeding. Something on the wind – a scent, a sound – made her flanks shiver. And she stood alert, as Rab MacDonald explained to his silent Laird, 'Not long after you left, they came. The raddled ewes were back up on their way towards Cnoc – their flocksmen with them. The rest – less than half – were being penned down here for the night. The shepherds were making camp. Unarmed but for dirks. They, they were too few...'

Craig Lowrie looked around. His kinsmen lay dead on the rocks below and the scrub above, with Tam Sween among them. But, though hacked to death by rough and angry hands, Tam's face was calm, almost content. 'He and Bess were not long apart,' Craig Lowrie said, understanding.

He paused at the sight of each fallen man and marked well his passing. He said each name for the last time. But, among the slaughtered clansmen also lay the hulk of the ram. Castrated, it had slowly bled to death – an intended insult. Craig Lowrie knew it for message of hatred.

'Come this way!' said Rab MacDonald. 'There's more.'

*Could there be?* Craig Lowrie walked behind his steward towards the Snow Moon, rising in the east, at the southern neck of the headland by the Dun. An unmistakeable sound took his breath from him. Before he saw the gibbets, he heard the creak of rope on wood – as two small bodies turned this way and that in a lazy breeze off the sea. He recognised the two distorted faces. He'd set these young boys – not old enough to help with the tup – in the south as watchmen. These were children, the children of his kinsmen.

'Who did this?' he asked. 'Who did this?'

'The war-cry was "Cruachan!"' replied Rab MacDonald.

'Cruachan!' Craig Lowrie repeated. There was no doubt then. It had been Campbells. He looked around. The disembowelling of the two young boys had splashed blood onto the stones of the ancient Hill beneath. The stones would carry their fear, and his clan's grief, always now. The land was sullied with it. He bit his lip, a slight movement but hard. He licked the small line of blood away, the tip of his tongue carrying the bitter promise.

‘Caterans’ he spat, using the old word. The old feud that never died now rode again. It needed the old language. But then he paused.

*Had these murders arisen from the savage impulses of wild men eking out harsh life on brutal hills? Or had murder arisen from something cold, something almost entirely grown within the darkness of a human mind, somewhere off the hills – in a civilised drawing room, perhaps?*

He shuddered. In that moment, there on the moonlit crags, he could not be sure. He could not think. There was a will, raging in him, to hunt down the men who had done this and it threatened his ability to follow the trail. He had to regain control.

His men watched in silence as Craig Lowrie climbed the joints of the gibbet. Quietly he cut down the children, one after the other, and carried each to earth. This was their final human embrace. He said nothing. Tears lined the watching eyes, and mouths were grim lines of pain but the watchers also knew to say nothing. There were no words for this.

He laid the small corpses on the ground and, kneeling, closed their eyes. ‘So young, they’ll have needed no shriving,’ he said, by way of comfort to the clansmen.

He pushed the heels of his hands into his eye sockets and then stood up, turning to Rab MacDonald.

‘Call the men from the hillside. Save what meat from the ram you can. And carry our little kinsmen home. The raiders, they’ll not be back tonight. But they’ll pay. The Campbells will pay for this. I’ll to Inveraray now. To visit my kinsman, Argyll.’

# Chapter 14

## Inveraray Castle
## 8th February 1793

ARGYLL POURED THE compost into a new pot and, slowly, teased out the delicate orchid tendrils with his practised fingers. He wanted to ensure they were the best position for the plant to draw in air and moisture. When he at last spoke, an edge of impatience had begun to glitter in his quiet voice. 'Spit it out, boy.'

Outside, the Scottish winter howled its worst, making the glass roof jump and crackle but the still air in the Duke of Argyll's new planthouse was humid. The air was fit only for plants and, it seemed, to the Duke, not much else. Craig Lowrie, he could see, would have sooner been in the weather outside. The boy had ridden for almost three hours but did not seem to have noticed the wildness of the terrain or the bitterness of the weather. And, it was not the atmosphere that was driving the young man to pace the hothouse as if trapped.

Still waiting, Argyll watched the rain run off Craig Lowrie's hair, and down his neck, and the whisper of a memory of Craig Lowrie's mother came to him, a soft echo of her face in the line of her son's cheekbones and in his lustrous eyes. Argyll resisted the temptation to send a servant for dry clothes. He indicated Craig Lowrie should sit. Craig Lowrie did so and then stood again.

'These young boys,' said Craig Lowrie at last, 'they were your kin too. And the others. They were all your kinsmen.'

Argyll dipped his head in deliberately slight acknowledgement. He turned his attention to a small larch, beside the newly-potted orchid.

He picked up some shears and snipped off a twig and tiny cone in silence. Then he said, 'Are you asking me to start a blood feud?'

Craig Lowrie sighed at the Duke's seeming slowness.

'That's started already,' he snapped. The Duke bent attentively over the larch, assessing it, as with an artist's eye. He tutted. 'The balance is wrong,' he said and put away the shears. He then turned to face the younger man but still he would not engage. He smiled.

Some could have mistaken this as innocence. Craig Lowrie did not and his sense of being played by a skilled sportsman did not help his temper. But, even so, with supreme effort, he stopped pacing, looked the Duke in the eye and laid down his terms.

'No, I want the names of those who did this. And I want the killing stopped.' He paused and then added. 'At its source.'

The Duke let the additional remark pass. He waved his hand, dismissing the demand. 'You ask much, boy.'

'Not much for a kinsman.'

'And if the perpetrators are also kinsmen?'

Craig Lowrie now knew this was the truth of it. 'Your decision,' he challenged.

Without answer, Argyll moved out of the hot house, walking along shadowy corridors and into the blazing light of a castle withdrawing room. Craig Lowrie had no choice but to follow him.

Waving a footman away, the Duke poured himself some brandywine. Then, after a studied pause, he gestured to Craig Lowrie that he should take some too. Craig Lowrie shook his head and waited. Time spent as a boy with the Duke of Argyll had schooled him well in patience. He remained standing in the centre of the drawing room – a focus of the tension between the men. The Duke was obliged – finally – to engage.

'Well, I'll do it.' The Duke said these words as if this were a fresh decision and not one that he had already known he would take. 'But I want some things in return.'

Craig Lowrie was now vigilant. Was it coming now? Would he discover the reason for the atrocity on the hillside at Ardnackaig? And, further back, what lay behind the treacherous attack on the Craig Lowrie stronghold on Emma's wedding day? *A message. A message in blood. From Blood to Blood.* Such discovery seemed unlikely...He almost admired the *sang froid* of Argyll who was still maintaining a political appearance of ignorance.

Then, as if following a trail on a different line of country, the

Duke continued: 'You know, I never know which tartan you'll wear, my boy. I always wonder, when the Craig Lowrie turns out – will you be a Campbell? Or a MacDonald? Or some other clan? I'm never sure. It adds such piquancy to our meetings.'

Craig Lowrie said nothing.

The Duke broke cover, 'So I want you, as my tacksman, to wear the Black Watch.'

Even Craig Lowrie had to gasp at the affront to his honour and the honour of his clan. 'You want the Craig Lowries as part of your Highland army? As your sept?'

The Duke smiled. 'I do. This is part of my price to name the murderers – when I find them, of course. Clansmen may have the right to ask their clan chief to police their petty squabbles but, in my case, they don't usually have the satisfaction. If I intervene on your behalf, I shall expect from you and yours demonstrations of profound clan loyalty. That would be only just and fair.'

Both men knew that this was a fiction. Campbell Justice meant that as Chief Justice of the region, Argyll could pack his juries with Campbell men. But, here in the withdrawing room of Inveraray, the charade of disinterest and lack of involvement continued and the Duke said, 'If *you* want me to hand over alleged murderers, I am prepared to make an exception. I shall involve myself. But I'll want to know where you stand.'

'And you would want me to stand where you can see me.'

'Precisely so.' The Duke looked at Craig Lowrie and changed his approach yet again. 'You would be something of a feather in the cap for my Highland rabble. The Wolf of Dalriada.'

'There are those who would say I'd blend in quite easily. A cattle rustler policing cattle rustlers.'

'I think we know who they are.' The Duke slumped into his chair. Scottish winters made him ache. He longed for the warmth and welcome of the London court. But his mind flashed with alertness, as he waited, smiling, for Craig Lowrie's response. He added, 'And we know what we know.'

Craig Lowrie shifted with unease. Honeyed words from this man made hairs on his neck prickle. 'You said "some things"?'

'Emma Bamburgh.'

Craig Lowrie said nothing. Argyll probed again.

'Emma Craig Lowrie?'

Craig Lowrie still did not respond.

'The marriage – did it go ahead, then? Pity. Pity. I had my own plans for the young bride. But still, the situation is not entirely lost.'

Argyll was turning over the possibilities in his mind. Whether widowed or single, Emma Bamburgh was still a bargaining counter. One of his acolytes could certainly oblige, even to the point of marriage, if the Duke willed it. And he did. He wanted Northumberland stitched to his current cause, with a twine of steel. He looked again sharply at Craig Lowrie, waiting before him. 'I believe her husband was killed,' he added. 'Some say, by you.'

'I killed a traitor – the man who left open the postern gate for the King's men and the Campbells.'

'Was that James?'

Craig Lowrie did not reply.

Although by no means sure, the Duke took this as a shamed admission of guilt. For the likes of Craig Lowrie, he knew, it was not so much admitting to murder but admitting one's kin was treacherous that was a matter for shame. He left the young man uneasy for a moment and then, continued, now impatient, 'No matter, I want the virgin widow – or whatever she is – here.'

'Why should I have her?'

'Mebbe you do. Mebbe you don't. But you could. And you probably will.'

The Duke and Craig Lowrie looked at each other. The Duke had played his hand – a calculated risk. *But then not so risky,* thought Craig Lowrie. He had been placed as ward with his uncle and clan chief Argyll after the death of his mother and father. There were therefore historic ties, loyalties and obligations between them. Argyll was relying on this.

Argyll scented the pause and reminded Craig Lowrie sharply of what he owed. 'I gave you your first whore,' he said. 'French. Very skilled.'

'Ah, yes!' said Craig Lowrie. 'Amelie. She was very kind. To a young boy of fourteen.'

Argyll clearly expected clan loyalty. But, even so, Craig Lowrie knew, this clan loyalty would run only one way. If the Duke willed it, Craig Lowrie knew, he would not survive the hour.

*Argyll wakes every morning to a new game,* he thought.

But today's game, it seemed, was part of a game that had already lasted several months. If the Duke needed Emma, as it seemed, the game could only be that the Dukedoms of Argyll and the Northumberland become brokers for power within the Union of the Kingdoms of Great Britain. The Union was still reeling from the bloody nose the Jacobites had given it in 1745, fifty years earlier. But it had and would – comfortably and ultimately – survive that. And Argyll would relish a future role in a United Kingdom. But, before that could happen, Emma Bamburgh would have to serve as the bridge. *A neat plan,* thought Craig Lowrie, *if ambitious:* turn Emma into a friend of the Argyll cause; influence – with subtlety – her father, Edwin Earl Bamburgh; and then influence – with subtlety – the mindset of the gouty Duke of Northumberland – the Percy who only reluctantly went to the London court nowadays and was thus immune to the blandishments there of the present Duke of Argyll. And this was the crux of it. Argyll needed Emma. And to reach her, he needed Craig Lowrie on his side.

But here was a sticking point. Craig Lowrie did not want to serve as the Duke of Argyll's tacksman. He did not want to receive favour from the kinsman he trusted least. And he would never choose to lay his people open to dangers already stalking the Highlands. In Craig Lowrie's heart, the memory of John Campbell raised itself. Unlike other Argyllmen before him, Craig Lowrie would never sacrifice his clansmen to greed. He would die first.

But the Duke was not finished in his demands. He stood up and began to circle Craig Lowrie. His closeness filled the Hall.

'One thing more,' he said.

An animal instinct for survival screamed through Craig Lowrie. But even he was completely unprepared for what came next. 'I'm tired of all these games we play, Malcolm. I want you to change your name.'

The Duke went back his chair and slid down with relief upon the cushioned seat as Craig Lowrie spat out, 'To what?'

'Campbell.' The Duke smiled and refilled his own glass but this time, with water. 'Campbell, of course.'

# Chapter 15

## 14th February 1793

### In the greasy saddle bag of Robinson's Agent, leaving Sir William Robinson's Office, Oban

*DEAR BAMBURGH,*

*Brought your Emma to town today. It was time. If she is indeed the relict of Jamie Craig Lowrie she needs to make a will. My view, anyway. So here we came, her dressed in normal clothing for once.*

*(I know she is your daughter, but really! This obsession with fresh air and exercise!) She was wearing some sort of day gown and jacket that Adelaide, Lady Robinson, has made up. (She does very well very quickly, I must say). And Lady Emma looked quite a picture. Quite delightful. And her face is as lovely as her mother's was at fifteen. I expect you remember our rivalry for the lovely Eleanor at that stage. You've been a lucky man, Bamburgh, I cannot deny it.*

*I digress. The Will. There is – it turns out – a problem. Lady Emma could not swear, by anything that's holy, that she saw JCL killed. She believes she did. But she never saw the body. And there seems to have been a funeral. But, she says, only the men attended. They are so primitive, these Craig Lowries. One step up from cave-dwellers, I should say. Anyway, what is the long and the short of it? No sight of a body. That does not mean there is not one. Only that we have no proof that JCL is dead and therefore no proof that she is the relict and due to inherit the estate. I know you wanted me to hire an army etc etc but, until I know JCL is dead, there is simply no point.*

*On another matter, please send disbursements as requested in documents attached to this letter.*

*(You will see a bill there from my Scottish colleague, a Mr MacKay. I had asked him in to the office to bear witness to Emma's Will – because we're on Scottish territory. But, as Emma would not swear, there was nothing he could do. So, I'm afraid, his fee is all for nothing. I thought he might waive it – but no!)*

*This also holds up another issue. I was counting on Emma's witness statement to prove* in absentio *Craig Lowrie's ill intent towards the King and his supporters – this time, the Campbells. A circuitous route, involving the implication that JCL was working for the Campbells and therefore a Kingsman. And I had every intention of having MCL outlawed under the Treason Outlawries (Scotland) Act 1748. But the murder of his cousin cannot be proved without Emma's testimony. And she will not comply. I explained matters to her – to a certain extent – and she was drawn by the thought of punishing MCL but, when it came to it, she could not, so she would not, swear. She seems to think the Almighty would not be pleased if she swore without absolute conviction. Really. I cannot do anything with her. Perhaps when you come to fetch her, you can. When will that be, incidentally?*
*Yours ever*
*Wm Robinson,*
*Attorney at Law.*

* * *

***14th inst***

*Pettigrew!*
*This business – of EB and JCL and MCL – grows more peculiar and costly by the day. No money yet from B. No evidence that Lady E is widowed. Or was even married. Strangers watching everyone's movements in town. Not sure whether they're King's men – in which case, fine – or CL men or some other faction entirely – in which case not so fine. There are also rumours of blood-letting in the hills. Beyond Crinan. But who is doing what to whom, I have not an idea. I am too old for this kind of excitement. And am feeling almost too unwell – my gut, y'know – to take an interest. Send young Pettigrew post-haste. I need a hand with this.*
*Yours ever*
*WR.*
*PS. B wants me to hire an army. On mature reflection, I think I will. For my own safety. Now, there must be sufficient rabble in Carlisle for you to send me up a few English mercenaries along with your son! And I've a second consignment of blood-stock passing through*

*Carlisle soon. They could all travel together – a jolly excursion for them all. I would be obliged if you would attend to all this post-haste.*

* * *

***February 15th 1793***
***Entry in Robinson's most private journal, kept under lock and key at Robinson Park, Arduaine, nr Oban***

*Major frustration of my plans here. Without Lady E's witness statement, I have no evidence of malfaisance and murder of a Kingsman by MCL. It may be that he murdered his cousin – bad enough and possibly sufficient – or it may be that he murdered someone working for Argyll. If the latter, I would hope – with his Grace's help – to outlaw MCL with ease. I could then add a Bill of Attainder into the mix. I am sure that – on behalf of His Majesty – His Grace, Argyll, would then have the 'management' of the extensive CL lands. I think I would also push for a Corruption of the Blood clause – a nice touch – safeguarding the Duke's rights in perpetuity – just in case there are any other claimants – illegitimate or otherwise – around the place. MCL could quite possibly have spawned some progeny somewhere. Some weird Scottish form of* ius primae nocti, *I suppose. Best to be sure they couldn't inherit.*

*And, the upshot of all this is that His Grace's gratitude would be mine, and mine alone.*

*Of course, His Grace does not know me yet. I am just some English lawyer who has been helping his factor over title to the clan lands for some years now. But he will know me! And soon. I shall seek an appointment with His Grace and see what can be done about MCL via that route. All properly formal and with appropriate respect.*

*If my life, property and safety were not involved, what fun this would all be! What entertainment I could have!*

# Chapter 16

## Robinson Park, Arduaine, near Oban 15th February 1793

AS SHE WATCHED Robinson help the newly-gowned Lady Emma down from the carriage and the groomsman take the whole equipage out of sight behind the stable block, Adelaide's hand slid up the heavy brocade drapes of her apartment – soothed as ever by their silken touch.

As was her custom, she had risen late, breakfasted lightly, dressed with care and was preparing to shut out the day. And, although the northern light was at the height of its power on this early Spring day, behind her, the servant was already lighting candles.

Adelaide shivered and drew a cashmere shawl around her. One by one, she continued to place roses in the pockets stitched into the brocade curtains. This was her concession to a summer long gone – the placing of roses, captured and dried in their moment of perfection, into the tableau she daily created in her rooms.

When at last the day was shuttered out, the servant gone and she was alone, she turned to regard her image in the mirrors plating every available area of wall, each casting back reflections in stacked row upon row, to infinity. Adelaide did not like what she saw.

The gown, it was true, was well enough – white muslin with silver and red embroidery, nipped in at the tiny waist by light stays. She also liked the *mouchoir anglaise,* frothing with lace, which clung to her fingers, and the glorious *fichu menteur* that settled modestly over the swell of her breasts and gently circled her body.

But her head of dark luxuriant hair, piled extravagantly above the crown of her head, seemed to contrast uncomfortably with the diminutive delicacy of her features. Only her huge black eyes could match it.

And her face...?

The Lady Emma's radiant complexion had shown her what a nonsense rouge could be. But, Adelaide now feared her own skin had begun naturally to take on the hue of the flour and water paste that Marie Antoinette so favoured. Was she, Adelaide, at nineteen, already too old to be considered a beauty?

She turned this way and that, appraising the mirror images. But she feared it was true. Each feature of her appearance had its perfections but together they worked to instill in her a fear of mortality. Her smoke-dark eyes were now no more than huge pools of sadness – lightless, leaving her nothing but despair.

'And why is that?' she wondered.

Nothing in her life had given her joy since the day when her father had called her to that sordid card-room at Versailles. Around them, stale smoke had mingled with the aroma of wine sediment drying in the crystal goblets. Half-eaten meat and cakes and stained clothing lay abandoned. And the child, Adele, had shuddered with nausea.

But then had come a hope of escape from the life she so hated. 'You are to go to Scotland, my child,' her father said. He spoke without looking at her. He was by custom a man proud of his skills – milliner to Marie Antoinette, he always announced on his business cards – but she could not see that pride here in the broken man, slouched before her. Fear suddenly fretted her.

Even so, she chattered breezily on.

'And when shall we return? Is Gabrielle packing for us now? Could I take my blue gown – the one you made me for Christmas?' she asked.

'No. You are going alone. Well, not quite alone.'

And then it was revealed. This father – professing to love her – had staked her in a game of cards and lost. And the victor – Sir William Robinson – now claimed his prize. Soon after she heard this, her father stood and left her. He did not look at her. His last words to her were *'A Dieu!'* And then there had been the parting from Gabrielle...

* * *

The sea voyage north had been *un cauchemar,* she recalled. In all her short life, she had never felt so ill. But, this was not entirely without advantage. While she was lying in her bunk – the stays of the ship swirling around her – Robinson respected her privacy.

However, a few days into the voyage, off the coasts of Ireland and Wales, feeling slightly better, she struggled up onto the deck. And, there, within minutes of breathing the clear air, and watching sea birds fly alongside the ship, she began to feel better. She began to dream of freedom – freedom from the lascivious court that she so hated – and she still had a child's brave thirst for adventure.

But then she heard a snigger. Two of the crew, held in the rigging like wingless birds, were grinning at her. She felt their eyes travel over her body, encased as it was in its now shabby court gown. She heard the words *'petite maitresse'*. She knew they meant her. She heard the words *'le vielliard'*. She knew from these words she now belonged to Robinson. Then, as she turned to run from the deck, she found Robinson standing behind her, watching her. He had clearly heard the sailors and derived some satisfaction from it. Adele ran down to her bunk and vomited again. Robinson was close behind her. She whipped out her sewing shears – holding them before her like a crucifix. Hesitating, he smiled and then backed away, seemingly reluctant to engage with either the shears or the soiled bed.

'Time enough, little one,' he grinned and disappeared.

Adele vomited again and, even now, ten years on, whenever the old man – gross and losing his teeth – came near her, that same feeling of nausea returned.

So Robinson had yet to claim his prize. But, how long, she wondered, how long could she resist him and how long would he display his puzzling forebearance? She had always been grateful to the serving maids and the dockside whores who had submitted to him in her place. But, as he aged, she knew, increasingly few would bed him willingly or even for payment. In the not too distant future, she felt he would, inevitably, turn his attention to her. And how long then would his strange forebearance last?

In Adelaide's *Petit Trianon* – as she was pleased to call her own quarters at Robinson Park – the mirrors glimmered with her image. They were telling her what she perceived to be the truth. She was, like Robinson, growing old. And she knew full well, somewhere beyond these interminable hills, and this dull, grey sea, Life was being lived – but without her. As if she had never existed. That was a truth. Sooner rather than later she would have to accept it.

So now she took her place at her desk, took out a pack of cards and laid out the columns for Patience. When she was ready to play, she lifted the first card from the waiting pack. It was the Queen of Hearts. There was nowhere for it to go.

# Chapter 17

## Robinson Park, Arduaine, near Oban 15th February 1793

THEN, THE DOOR burst open, the candles guttered and there, framed by the daylight, stood the Lady Emma in her riding clothes.

'Adele, come, ride with me. It is such a beautiful day.'

Startled, Adele shook her head. 'I cannot ride,' she said.

'Why not?'

'I have never learned.'

'Never learned? How can that be?'

'When I came here,' Adele explained, 'I was too young for any of the riding horses.' She turned away, to busy herself with her sewing projects – to avoid the challenge in Emma's frank green eyes. Robinson had not liked to admit that, Adele remembered. *Too young for the horses, too young to be his wife.* And so had grown the legal fiction of his 'ward'. A thin veneer of respectability. He had encouraged the servants to use her future title – 'Lady Robinson' – to bolster it. It had succeeded. For him, for them – but not for her.

Emma was not deflected. 'But how can you have lived here, trapped indoors, with such country around you? It's unnatural.'

'At first, my chaplain, Father Macdonald,' persisted Adele. 'He took me out, riding pillion. Every day, we went out. At that point, it is true, I almost came to love the hills. And sometimes, in the woods, when the sun shone, I thought again of the places where I grew up. No, not of Versailles. Of Burgundy. Of Yonne. I remembered my mother, in the woods, the sunlight on her hair. No, not Versailles or

Paris. In Paris, it was mostly just my father and – and, after *Maman* had gone, it seemed always to rain.'

Her hands plucked at the silks on the *mannequine*. Emma drew in her breath as if about to speak but Adele cut across her. She did not want to speak of Burgundy.

'When I grew too tall – or too old for it to be seemly – those excursions, they stopped. I was obliged to take the carriage. And that meant Oban. Nowhere else. Just Oban. And very rarely. Always chaperoned by the Father. Sometimes, in secret, when Robinson was away and, when a French brig was in dock. To hand over, or collect, the letters, *tu sais*. The letters for Gabrielle. But always, just Oban.'

But didn't you ever want to ride out again – on your own – freely?'

'Of course but...'

'But what?'

'I knew I would not be allowed. I felt that. I felt I would have had to beg. And that would give Robinson something, some advantage. I do not ever want to give him such a thread to hold me by.'

Emma pressed further. 'But would you not come with me?'

Adele paused. The impulse for freedom still burned in her, the freedom of the woods in Yonne, and she longed to run towards it. So, defying the rules locking her into her fetid isolation, she said at last, 'I am not afraid. I will come. But, how is this to be arranged?'

* * *

With some assiduity, it seemed.

For several days, Adele's duties as *chatelaine* of Robinson Park were neglected. Left to her own devices and without Adele's talented direction, the housekeeper drew up her own daily menus of Highland fare, involving, to Robinson's discomfort, rather too many oats. Also – without rebuke to the maids – dust settled over the main house like a shroud. And, in *Le Petit Trianon,* Adele stitched – swiftly, obsessively, without thought of food or sleep. The *mannequine* now took pride of place at the centre of Adele's salon.

Marie Antoinette herself had given this sewing doll to the beautiful girl-child who had so beguiled her and there had been such excitement when it arrived at the de Fontenoy lodgings in the Rue Maitre Albert, all those years before. But soon after, it had become a parting gift, a legacy.

True, to appease the child appalled at the prospect of leaving

France, Robinson had arranged with some difficulty for the *mannequine* to be transported to Oban. But, she had come to realise, his kindness had been selfish in object and not to be trusted.

Thereafter, during the long years of her incarceration, Adele had used the *mannequine* to create sumptuous gowns, equal to any at the French court of the 1770s. These, in rich cavalcade, had dazzled Robinson at dinner after dinner and kept the young wearer, as she believed, unapproachable, untouchable – like Marie Antoinette in the French court.

But, now, using Paris fashion plates, Adele intended to create for herself a wardrobe of riding clothes and, inspired by Marie Antoinette, these would include a *redingote.* Military in style, complete with smuggled and expensive enamel buttons, this was a deliberate departure from her usual feminine gowns.

As she sewed, she recalled long epistolary discussions with Gabrielle over what social critics had written in the heady days of the 1770s. One had written 'The Parisian in general is inevitably abstemious, eating very badly out of poverty so he can pay the tailor and the bonnet seller.'

*But,* Adele and Gabrielle had agreed, *this missed the trick. Clothes were more than frippery.* Marie Antoinette's *redingote* had helped the Queen demonstrate her strength. Adele hoped for the same. And, when she tried on the finished *redingote,* Adele felt a flood of power. Thus encouraged, the young woman sent to Oban for several more pairs of leather riding boots.

Meanwhile, on her visits to the stable block to tend to Berry, Emma was studying the other horses. She hoped to find a suitable mount for a novice rider but that was proving a harder task than she ever imagined it would be. The plan to teach Adele to ride seemed ready to founder in its infancy. But Emma persisted.

* * *

One brisk March afternoon, a few weeks later, the young women were taking a turn about the Rose Parterre Terrace before dinner. Adele wanted to see for herself the ravages of winter and think how the gardeners could best repair them. As she explained to Emma, soft with the promise of rain, the wind mostly came from the south west and, as the parterres were laid out to the south east of Adele's apartments, the roses – traditional, formal, French – were protected from the salt air. Even so, sometimes, cold winds blew down from the hills and Adele grieved that the struggling roses had no shelter from them. She was considering the possibility of a new wall to catch the sun. 'And I shall ask that the grooms bring up the ordure from the stables too. It will help.'

At the mention of the stables, Emma broached again the subject of finding a horse. They had paused by a fountain, to let the clear waters trickle over their hands.

'There is Tavish,' said Emma. 'Robinson's mount. He is a big, heavy, good-natured Clydesdale. We would need to take up the stirrups. But he would be gentle. Like sitting on a table,' she suggested. 'Good for a beginner.'

Adele at once rejected Tavish. 'No more favours than absolutely necessary from Robinson,' she said, searching for a kerchief to dry her and Emma's hands. 'I do not wish to be more obliged than I need.'

Emma then watched as Adele twisted off a dead head from a rose. 'Why not?' she asked.

'The whole of my life – everything from my breakfast to my nightcap – it is in the gift of Robinson,' Adele said. 'I know, it is just the way of things for women like me – cast adrift, dependent on a 'protector'. I am a practical woman and I have long since resolved to make the best of this arrangement. But I also know, perhaps this 'generosity' is pre-payment. Perhaps some day there will be some service I will have to render. This cannot be changed. And, when that time comes, I will have little or no choice but to submit. I hate that thought. And I hate myself. But, until then, to preserve a tiny bit of dignity, for myself, I do not ask for anything. I may say I want something. But I do not ask.'

She removed another dead rose head – careless with anger. A thorn found her hand and drew blood. With a small cry, she put her lips to the wound. Then, as Emma bound her hand with the kerchief, Adele added, 'And, often I think, were I at home in the French court, it would be no different. There would, equally, be someone who would pay for me. This is inescapable. For women like me with no fortune. And I could say nothing about it. *Tant pis.* But I will not ask Robinson. For anything. I cannot.'

Emma was shocked for a moment into silence. Then she countered, 'But – your *couture,* as you call it. Such talent! Could you not survive without a – a protector?'

'I would not know where to start. My sister Gabrielle, it is true, she has a *sens des affaires*. But I do not. My life here, it has been so bizarre. I am not well-equipped.'

Emma agreed. Adele's was a *bizarre* life. It seemed so to her too. She examined her own. 'At home, in Northumberland, no-one spends money unless they have to,' she said. 'And, it seems, my father only ever opens the coffers to pay for soldiers for the Duke. Or, I suppose, to pay for visits for himself and Mama to the English Court. Or horses, I suppose. What he most fears is the loss of land and power and what he likes most is horse-racing – and that makes him spend money. But he does so, very reluctantly, for any other cause. And he would never just give me what I asked for. Like your riding boots – I have never had such boots. Such soft leather. You will be able to feel the horse's flank through them! And the horse will be able to feel you! Wonderful.'

As they started to walk along a gravel path, Adele occasionally tugged at a wild plant, which had self-seeded in the wrong place while Emma continued to chatter.

'On the other hand, there are advantages to Father's disinterest. I can always go where I want and say what I think. Sometimes too much so, perhaps. My Lady Mother always says I must learn to rule my tongue and be ruled by my husband.'

And she – is that what she does?' asked Adele. She was always intrigued by Emma's tales of British family life. In her heart she wondered whether she could ever have had such a life.

'Hmmm, I'm not sure. Between you and me, I think my Lady Mother is also forthright in her way. That is possible for us, English women, living in the north. We can breathe. At home, we can at least breathe. We do not live by so many rules as Mother and Father do at court. As you seem to, here. And as for the French court – from what I have heard – the number of rules there! I should feel quite stifled. I should die, I think. How can people live like that?'

At this, Adele laughed, surprised by her own laughter. So rare was this, it sounded almost to have come from someone else. Then, she hugged the young girl. 'But no Tavish!' she added, wagging her finger at Emma, who giggled. 'No Tavish. No more obligation than necessary to Robinson,' Adele repeated.

*But,* thought Emma, *what other choice of horse exists?*

The other horses, she could see, had not been well treated by the lawyer's servants. Ridden with urgency on the Master's orders, hard in the mouth, they were difficult, edgy and headstrong. There was not, it seemed, a calm mount in the yard – except for Berry.

At the thought of sharing Berry, Emma shied. She understood every flicker of Berry's muscles, every snuffle he emitted, every thought he could be said to have. She did not want to share that closeness. But Emma also knew that here, even though trapped in an isolated house in wild country, she had unexpectedly found a friend. And, in Emma's view, friends shared.

Later, after dinner, seated by the fire in Adele's salon, Emma was restlessly shuffling Adele's fashion plates. These portrayed not her style of thing at all and it was some relief when Adele asked how they were to proceed with the riding project. Emma put down the fashion plates and resolutely straightened her spine.

'We start by making friends,' she said. 'I will lend you Berry tomorrow.'

Adele, however, glanced across at her. There was a grace note of feeling, hanging on the air between them. She was silent for a moment and then she said: 'Emma, you teach me how to ride Berry. When I know what I need to know, I promise I will ask Robinson for a mount – that will be hard but I will do it – and we will then go riding; you on Berry and me on my new horse.'

Emma smiled. 'What friends we are!' she said and gave Adele a hug.

Adele laughed again. Since Emma had arrived, Adele had begun to feel that to be close was not always to be threatened. For the first time in ten years, she felt, to be touched was not to be burned.

* * *

One of Robinson's grand schemes had always been to create a racecourse on the lower pastures of the Park. The old lawyer took pride in the idea, thinking to introduce what he considered the civilised sport of racing to the Highlands. To further these plans, through a Glasgow bloodstock merchant, he had bought some young thoroughbreds and these he would add to the Robinson herd. Bred for racing, they would bring grace and speed into the line but they sadly lacked endurance. He felt they needed Highland toughness, the equine toughness that could keep going all day no matter what the weather spat out – up and down the glens, across moorland, burdened with full-grown stags, doing the master's bidding. His Highland stock was infused with a touch of Arab and a touch of Percheron and this, he knew, was what the garrons would give these delicate creatures from the south. He also hoped to breed winners to match Bamburgh's over the two miles of the Doncaster St Leger.

'Stamina, courage – and with something in hand for the finish', he repeated to his grooms, as if reciting the recipe for an elixir.

But now he needed to settle the new stock in with his carriage horses, his riding mounts, the draft horses and the Highland ponies, cobs and garrons of his ghillies and keepers. This would steady their temperament and – after the comforts of the lowlands – accustom them to Scottish Highland weather. So, when the first batch of the new horses arrived, he had the whole herd turned out into the lochside paddocks to enjoy the spring grasses 'and to make friends.'

At first, against the homespun roughness of the natives, the quality breeding of the newcomers gleamed. But, a few days later, as Adele and Emma walked towards them, they found the temper of the herd in the new paddocks had become calm, content and unified. Even so, as Emma well knew, any threatening move, however slight, and the newcomers would be away, testing the boundaries for an escape.

'I wonder?' she said.

*'Quoi?'*

'Could we try...?'

*'Mais, oui!* What do you want me to do?'

'Enter the paddock. And then stand quite still.'

Adele nodded, moved forward and then stood – alone – almost in silhouette against brightness of the hills. Emma watched her. Adele seemed so small and everything around her seemed so huge. But, even so, something about Adele held the gaze. Was it the tilt of her head? The line of her shoulders? Emma couldn't identify what it was. She could only recognise Adele's quiet magic. And, even though the horses continued to crop, Emma knew they were watching the young French woman, too.

Adele knew how to wait. Resting her eyes on the horizon, she quietened her breath, standing still as stone. And, for the first time in a long time, she allowed herself to become aware of the hills around her, dimpled green, against an achingly blue sky. She could hear skylarks above the sea meadows. She closed her eyes. Time was suspended. She was free at last. She could almost weep for the joy of it.

Watchful still, the herd caressed grass with their soft mouths. Then, one of the new horses – a black mare – stopped cropping and raised a head, ears alert, gaze steady.

'Finely bred but kind,' thought Emma.

Then, without urgency, the mare left the herd. With no little courage, it seemed, the horse closed the gap between her and the young French woman. Once close, she breathed gently into Adele's neck. Adele opened her eyes but did not move. She spoke, in the low, musical tones she remembered her mother using in Burgundy. She was reliving a memory long obscured by horror and the mare listened to the tale. Curiosity overcame fear as she nibbled at Adele's sleeve. Adele laughed quietly and, then, turned slowly to stroke the velvet of the animal's neck. She ran her fingers through the rich, full mane. She allowed the horse to lip the back of her hands. Then, prompted by some instinct, she walked away from the horse back towards Emma, who was resting on the paddock fence. She asked 'What do I do now?'

'You make friends,' said Emma. 'It will be easy. She has chosen you. Stop now, turn again and look.'

Adele did so and then caught her breath. The mare was following her, coming close. The animal lowered her head. It was a deep and trusting bow. Adele bowed her head, too. She kissed the horse's mane, passing her hands kindly over the animal's neck and shoulders. The mare quivered with pleasure and, murmuring softly, Adele wove a skein of trust between them.

'I shall call you "Sirene",' she whispered, drowning in the darkness of the black mare's eyes.

# Chapter 18

## Robinson Park, Arduaine, near Oban 1st May 1793

AS THE BAROUCHE passed through the gates of Robinson Park, Silas Pettigrew scented money. His tongue quivered at the thought and he was obliged to dab the corner of his mouth with the lace kerchief trailing from his velvet cuff. On arrival at the main entrance, when he was shown into the Library to await his host and left alone, he took the opportunity to confirm his suspicions.

He picked up a candlestick. He liked its sculptural style, the chasing was exquisite and the silver was excellent quality – marked in 1768 in Paris by Robert-Joseph Auguste, the French King's silversmith. It was a thing of rare quality and beauty – with a talent for survival. Pettigrew knew most of the silver of the French court was constantly under threat of being melted down to make coin to fill the royal coffers. He sucked his teeth, full of admiration for the achievements of Robinson, who had clearly smuggled this and the other silver pieces now gracing his library out from under the noses of an increasingly watchful France. Pettigrew sighed and lovingly polished his finger marks away with the greasy palm of his hand. Another job for lazy maids, he thought, replacing the candlestick.

Now he turned his attention to other items in the room. The chairs were Chippendale. A long journey for these, too, he said to himself, easing his languid form into one, better to admire the rugs scattered on the wooden floors – French from Aubusson. Everything around him spoke of taste and coin. He had the growing conviction it should belong to him.

He reflected on his situation. The law practice in Carlisle was now too small for both him and his father and, short of the old man dying, there seemed no way of advancement. But Silas Pettigrew was a man who could plot for the long haul. He had heard of his father's partner, Sir William Robinson, up in the north, in Argyll country. The aristocracy of that region, the Campbells, were friendly to the Duke of Cumberland whom he one day hoped to have as a client. Once Cumberland was a client, the Campbells would also be friendly to Pettigrew, would be able introduce him to sources of wealth just aching to be spent as the town of Oban grew up around the new distillery. Growth seemed inevitable. And, Pettigrew believed, a gilded Oban would simply yearn for English lawyers like himself to help its denizens make sense of the Union and interpret English law for them.

Nothing escaped the sponge-like Pettigrew. He now considered the dust left by the maids on the bookshelves in this room. There was money here certainly. But also neglect. He wondered. *Was there an advantage for him in this?*

Lawyers were a closed-rank brotherhood and, however little they may discuss matters outside the ranks, in-rank gossip had rippled with the lovely Adelaide de Fontenoy, French, young, beautiful, familiar with the court at Versailles. And lost in Scotland. But more important, even than this – so his father had said – she was not yet officially married to Sir William Robinson although she at times seemed to use his title. *His ward then,* thought Pettigrew. *Robinson's intended? An heiress, perhaps? Not interested in the smaller details of house-keeping, certainly.* The dust from the bookshelves had stained his fingers. *Not interested in Robinson, then. No desire to please. Perhaps ripe for the plucking.* His tongue moistened his thin lips. He would find out.

'Good afternoon, young Pettigrew!' Sir William burst into the room. 'My dear young fellow, I'm so sorry I wasn't here to meet you. Down at the stud, don't you know? Minor problem. Too many horses, now, with this second batch. Stabling issues – nothing serious. I'm delighted you consented to travel with my armed guard – and the livestock. Much the safest way north at the moment, I can tell you. And I'm grateful to you, my boy. Very grateful indeed. For all I know, those English rapscallions might not have bothered to come north without your being there, needing an escort, and so on...'

Pettigrew shuddered at the memory. Noise, dust, smell – he had thought the journey would never end. It was only that, as his father had advised, keeping an eye on the English mercenaries and the bloodstock would please Robinson. At present, this was a crucial part of his strategem.

His host continued – affability in person. 'Will you take some refreshment after your journey? Then we can talk. Your bags are already in your room. I hope you'll be comfortable there.'

Pettigrew clicked his teeth – a small dismissive noise, the significance not lost upon his companion. Pettigrew would worry about creature comforts later. For the present, Pettigrew was afire to learn what he needed to know about his mission. Why he'd been sent by his aged father to this far outpost of English civilisation? And what profit could he turn from it? He indicated, however, that he would take some wine, admiring the jewel-like richness lent to the claret by the superior quality of a fine Irish decanter and goblets. He was not disappointed. The quality of the wine matched the quality of everything else. Pettigrew felt he had found a place on earth where he could be comfortable, indeed. The plotting for the long haul began.

Sir William Robinson's tale of Emma Bamburgh did not disappoint either. From his father, Pettigrew had received the briefest of briefings, based solely on Robinson's letters. But this young woman was the key to it all, he was sure. Gently balancing the goblet of wine in the palm of his hand – as if weighing it – he asked the older man: 'The issue then is whether she is truly married and truly widowed?'

'Indeed. There are of course no witnesses. Craig Lowrie's men are silent.'

'And have you asked him?'

'You don't just 'ask' Craig Lowrie something. Finding him is the first trick. He's everywhere at once. He's involved in everything, everywhere, from Oban south to Lochgilphead and the farthest point of the Mull. Not to mention the Isles. And there are rumours – all the time – of murders, of rustlings, of blood feuds. Now he's rumoured to be part of a Campbells' land grab. Now he's ducking the Kingsmen and trouncing them into the Loch Awe. And the next thing you hear is he's taking rooms opposite my office, dressed for all the world like a gentleman. No, you don't just ask Craig Lowrie whether he's killed his cousin or not. It won't do. It won't do at all.'

Pettigrew sipped his wine.

Robinson continued: 'We've Emma Bamburgh here disguised as your young sister, Dilly Pettigrew. A hot coal under the roof, I can tell you. My people are, I believe, as silent as Craig Lowrie's to an outsider. I pay them handsomely for their silence. And they never leave the park. Well, only very, very few of them, the ones I trust to guard their tongues or lose them. But you never know. Gossip is gossip, after all.'

'Seems to me,' said Pettigrew, 'seems to me you have to flush out the fox. If you can't go to this brigand because of landscape difficulties and blood feuds and so on, bring him here. Dresses as a gentleman, you say. Courtly manners, then. Nothing easier. An invitation. To a rich lawyer's new home – what could be more attractive to a brigand?'

Robinson blinked.

Pettigrew was good at this. Straight to the nub of the matter, he went. 'We need to test Emma Bamburgh's disguise as Dilly Pettigrew. If that fails, we need quite another strategy. But I doubt the Laird'll recognise her. I doubt he bothered overmuch with the arranged wife of his cousin. In the normal way of things, I doubt Dilly Pettigrew will need to appear other than as Dilly Pettigrew.

'But we need to know whether he does and how he treats her. If she is heiress to some of his lands, he'll want her where he can see her. If he truly killed her husband, he'll have some plan for her himself. Maybe even want to marry her. We need to know what's in his mind. As I say, I suggest you invite him here. "Dilly Pettigrew" can earn her keep. She can bewitch him. She can find out what he's up to.'

'But, she's a child.'

Robinson had now stopped primping the wine table and slumped into a chair. Pettigrew sipped his wine again, watching as Robinson turned over in his mind the many possibilities.

'She couldn't do it,' Robinson said at last. 'She's too much the English innocent – apart from some romantic notions about Jamie Craig Lowrie she held before she arrived for her wedding day. I don't believe she knows what to do with a man. Horses, yes. But, a man like Craig Lowrie, she'd be tongue-tied, surely, never mind wheedle his innermost thoughts out of him. She's no coquette. She's too straight. Demme, she won't even sign a witness document against the blasted Craig Lowrie – whom she fears and detests – because she cannot be sure she saw him kill his cousin.'

Pettigrew shook his head with impatience. 'Such nicety,' he muttered. Then he added, 'Adelaide, then?'

'Lady Robinson?' Across the room, Robinson had stiffened perceptibly.

Pettigrew noted a sensitive edge. 'Oh, I think we can both acknowledge she is not your wife. And not Lady Robinson by any stretch of the imagination. I'm sure you have taught her well – over the years.'

Robinson, as Pettigrew recognised, was trapped. The extent to which he was trapped Pettigrew couldn't know. But Pettigrew recognised a trapped creature when he saw one. For the first time, since he had left Carlisle for this God-forsaken country, Pettigrew indulged the possibility of enjoying himself. He stood up. 'I'd like a bath, if I may. The road was dusty. Before I meet the ladies, you understand...'

Robinson found himself ringing for the maid to pour Pettigrew a bath.

# Chapter 19

## Robinson Park, Arduaine, near Oban
## 1st May 1793

AS PETTIGREW LUXURIATED in the copper bath, easing the travel dust into oblivion, a plan presented itself in its fullest form and Pettigrew was delighted with it. He liked plans to have a simple but powerful outline and this was one of his finest to date. But he wouldn't tell Robinson too much just now. Robinson was a canny old bird, by reputation and in fact. The Library silver and furnishings – which had come out of the French court little by little over a long period – were proof of that. Oh yes, Robinson was canny. Pettigrew wanted to be sure of him. And couldn't yet.

But, as he had thought, there was money to be made out of all this. And he knew where it would rest – finally. It would rest, he swore, with him. As he saw it, Emma was rich. And, by all accounts, beautiful. And, by all the available accounts to date, widowed. Emma's father was powerful. And canny. Had he not organised an unlikely and hugely desirable inheritance for Emma, while appearing to arrange her dowry? The value of the legendary Bamburgh jewels paled to insignificance alongside the lush and productive Craig Lowrie lands. And these were a prize worth politicking for. And Pettigrew was the man to do it.

But Pettigrew still needed to know what Craig Lowrie's weaknesses were. And he needed to know what the Duke of Argyll thought about English Law and whether he would need another English lawyer, in addition to Robinson. There was so much to know, so much to do. And he, 'Pettigrew, Silas', was the man for the challenge. He laughed out loud – surprising himself and the manservant he had been assigned. He was, he now knew, going to enjoy this.

Pettigrew's simple plan was that, with enough 'evidence' – whether true or false – Craig Lowrie would be hanged for the murder of his cousin, Jamie. His lands would be inevitably forfeit to the Crown. (Finding out what Pettigrew could do about that would have to wait). But, at a decent interval after the execution, Pettigrew saw himself marrying the murder victim's grieving widow who, thanks to the foresight of her father, just happened already to be in possession of a sizeable chunk of rich Craig Lowrie pasture land. With wealth like that behind him, he – Pettigrew – would then be in a position to buy and sell Robinson's practice up at Oban and entice the Scottish lairds and farmers into costly court cases under English law. At the thought of this, any earlier plans he may have had regarding Robinson's ward/mistress and her dubious inheritance were shelved. This was, he was sure, the way forward. Marriage with Emma Bamburgh. And, with two dukes on its books, the firm – to be renamed as *Pettigrew and Robinson,* or perhaps, even just *Pettigrew Attorneys at Law* – would put its stamp all over Cumberland, Ayrshire and Argyll. Not to mention Edinburgh and London. Steady work with the new middle classes, spectacular work with the aristocracy. The neatness of this plan took his breath away.

But as he took his place in the dining room – dressed in black silk, his wig elegantly and freshly pomaded to eternity, snuff box at the ready – his newly dreamt up plans vanished. Adelaide de Fontenoy came in to take her place at the head of her table and, in doing so, wiped his mind clean of any ambition save that of possessing her. Emma Bamburgh at her side was beautiful, it was true, but young and, because of that, insignificant alongside the incomparable Adelaide. And, for a moment, Pettigrew was stunned.

Then his brain swung into fresh computations incorporating the sublime Adelaide in his future plans for fame and fortune. There was no doubt about it. She managed an excellent table. This would be crucial for the society hostess he intended she should be. He observed *la service à la française* at Robinson Park had all the vital elements for elegance. The Chelsea and Indian porcelain felt like egg-shell to his connoisseur fingers. He admired the jewelled colours of the paintings on tureens and the sauceboats. He marvelled at the centrepiece of dolphins carved in sugar, aware that Adelaide with courage and aplomb had ordered the employment of a French pastry chef and sugar artist in her Highland kitchens. And he was just about to deploy his own pewter knife, fork and spoon – whisking out his kerchief to polish them – when he noted the delicate silver cutlery lying close to his place setting. He shuddered with relief that he had not embarrassed himself and with presence of mind, used his kerchief to dab his wet lips instead.

Stretching across crisp linen, dish upon dish waited for him. The house steward, on Lady Robinson's command, had displayed each to advantage and Pettigrew's principle regret was that he could not reach all of them. Laid out in meticulous order, the dishes of the first course were marshalled – all cooling as Pettigrew shifted in his seat in anticipation.

Scanning the table and savouring the bouquet from the soup tureen as he did so, Pettigrew began to make his choices between the dishes laid out before him that he could reach. But, when he heard Robinson's dry cough, he was brought sharply back to attention. He realised that it was time for the Grace and that he had been waited for. He leapt to his feet, clasped his hands in piety and closed his eyes as Robinson began on the long paen of praise and thanks to the Almighty. He intoned: '*Nos miseri et egentes homines pro cibo quem ad alimoniam corporis sanctificatum nobis es largítus, ut eo utamur grati tibi, Deus omnipotens, Pater caelestis, gratias reverenter agimus, simul obsecrantes ut cibum angelorum, verum panem caelestem, verbum Dei aeternum, Dominum nostrum Iesum Christum nobis impertiaris, ut illo mens nostra pascatur et per carnem et sanguinem eius foveamur, alamur et corróboremur.*'

Not unconvinced that Robinson would say it twice on purpose to discomfort him, Pettigrew kept pace silently with an English version: 'We wretched and needy men reverently give thee thanks, Almighty God, Heavenly Father, for the food which thou hast sanctified and bestowed for the sustenance of the body, so that we may use it thankfully; at the same time we beseech thee that thou wouldst impart to us the food of angels, the true bread of heaven, the eternal word of God, Jesus Christ our Lord, so that our mind may feed on him and that through his flesh and blood we may be nourished, sustained and strengthened.'

But, while thus occupied, he could not resist the opportunity to study further – while their attention rested on higher things – the Lady Emma and Adelaide de Fontenoy. True, the Lady Emma was a beauty in bud. She was tall and gleaming and fresh but so very young, the bloom of childhood still coated her cheek. Adelaide de Fontenoy, however, he thought, would break your heart for lack of a smile.

'Forget' he thought 'all this nonsense of "Lady Robinson".' Watching her lips move in prayer, Pettigrew lost his place in the Grace. But, at this point, Robinson's intonation seemed to imply the winding up of the seemingly interminable liturgy of thanks and Pettigrew turned his attention from Adelaide to his host. To Pettigrew's shock, he found Robinson's eyes were upon him. And the old lawyer's expression was not pleasant.

But, then, at last, the company could take their seats. There were only four to dinner that night, with eight servants including the house steward and butler to attend them. And proceedings began with Robinson serving the soup. Initial conversation was limited and pedestrian, covering topics such as the inclement weather and the unpleasantness of travel through brigand country. This was of course a code for Craig Lowrie land but Pettigrew was glad of the anodyne treatment of the topic. It allowed him to give his full attention to the oysters brought up in his honour from the beds in the bay. He could enjoy the neeps – cooked to perfection with cream and sugar – served alongside beans and greens – asparagus and artichokes – and accompanying slices of roasted rib of beef, fresher than any meat he had ever tasted. And he would never forget the salad with a dressing, French to its core oils and wine vinegars. *Pure sunshine,* he thought.

In a flurry of linen, the diners waited while the first courses were cleared. And then arrived dessert – rout drop cakes and ratafia cakes and Portugal cakes – sliding onto the polished surface of the magnificent mahogany table without pause or mishap. In spite of a slight excess of dust in the Library, Robinson's household was in general truly manned by impeccable servants, thought Pettigrew. Then, French cheeses and a spectacular range of fresh and dried fruit – pears, apples, walnuts, almonds and raisins – tumbled forth, leaving Pettigrew almost beside himself. And wine settled in the goblets, gleaming through the darkening night.

When replete, Pettigrew felt equal, finally, to some conversation. He caressed his mouth with the napkin and began. 'The whole dinner has been quite delightful. Such a range of food, so delicately balanced. You are, my lady, a hostess of some note in the region, I should think.'

Adelaide who had no more than picked at her food was now selecting a little fruit and some nuts from dishes close by. She looked up at his compliment and demurred. 'Not at all, Mr Pettigrew. I am not well-known at all in the region.'

'Oh, but, Sir William! Is this not a great deprivation for your neighbours? Not to be able to see how to do things well and as elegantly as things are done in the French court. French dining is the highest standard throughout Europe. And you, you have the means to enlighten your close associates and their wives. Think what praise and honour this would bring our firm.'

Sir William paused about to reply but Pettigrew was relentless. 'You should, oh, you must allow your neighbours to visit and see for themselves your beautiful china, your exquisite cutlery, your wonderful furniture...and sample the delights of Lady Robinson's excellent table. Do you not think a party a good notion, Lady Emma? All the great and the good of the region here in one splendid glittering occasion?'

Adele had had enough of the discomfort created by Pettigrew's extravagant conversation. She thought she could hear a batsqueak of some other agenda. He was not sincere, of that she was convinced. But she could not yet identify what he hoped for. She ended the conversation, standing to lead the Lady Emma to the drawing room for tea. The gentlemen had no option but to stand as the ladies left but they then settled to a further glass of port.

* * *

**Robinson's Journal – sealed under key at Robinson Park, Arduaine**

*I have the measure of Pettigrew. He is ambitious, venal and greedy. And clever. And he thinks I am not – which is all to the good for the present. I wonder what his downfall will be. I suspect his desire to have His Grace as a client will come into it. But I don't think he appreciates that here in Argyll, what His Grace wants, His Grace takes – land, women, power. Simple as that. And I suspect that ease of acquisition must be the same elsewhere in the Kingdom. Pettigrew will be swotted like the nasty little fly he is if he tries to recruit the Duke for his own purposes and crosses him. It will end in tears. I could put money on that.*

*For now, though, I'll let him borrow all the books he needs from my library to turn himself into a plantsman – like the Duke. He's ruining his eyes, even as I write, trying to learn about orchids. I must say, I admire his dedication to his scheme. So much research. In an area of science so clearly alien to him.*

*And, socially, Pettigrew thrusts, feints and parries all to the tune of his own deadly air. Pettigrew is every inch his father's son. But could yet be useful for me.*

*However, I remain displeased. My main concern at present is that Pettigrew's fancy footwork does not cut across my own plans for the recruitment of the Duke in the matter of the outlawing of Craig Lowrie. The success of that venture is paramount. Even enhanced revenue comes a pale second. My life could depend on this alliance. And whippersnappers will only muddy the stream. Here lies danger.*

*Setting that aside, of course, first of all, I need him to find out what happened to James Craig Lowrie. When I sent for him, I thought SP would send out spies, or something along those lines. I thought the role of covert spymaster would suit him. And keep my hands clean – here in western Argyll.*

*But no, now we are to have a ball. Here at Robinson Park. And invite MCL. The Wolf to my fold, my private residence. The results had better be worth the expense. And the danger. And the breaking of my carefully-cultivated cover. The loss of a secret maintained for a decade. I'm not comfortable with that. Not at all.*

*There is some logic to it, though. Whatever Pettigrew says, I guess he is thinking that MCL will recognise EB – she was to marry his cousin after all – and he will attempt a kidnap. A bloody end for a kidnapper, perhaps. But with compensation, blood money, inheritance – EB will indeed be a prize. And, with MCL well and truly out of the equation. Neat, very neat. But, then what for EB? We'll wait and see. I suspect Pettigrew will come into the picture somehow, but how?*

*However, I don't like the way Pettigrew stares at Adelaide. Adelaide. More beautiful by the day. Less pale. Less sad. But still unreachable. By me. Why can I not forget what Emma wrote in her journal? Adelaide loathes me. That is truly intolerable. And unjust.*

# Chapter 20

## Robinson Park, Arduaine, near Oban 2nd May 1793

ADELE HAD NEVER thought before how much grooming could endear her to a horse. But when she saw how the mare, Sirene, shivered with pleasure as the brush swept her back and flanks, she found she loved to give the horse such delight. As Emma suggested, Adele had taken over these stable duties each morning before her now daily ride. The Chief Groom was at first surprised to see the Lady of the House, working in the stables. But the Lady of the House was even more surprised. She had never before seen the early light of day. Neither at the French court nor during the life she had created for herself at Robinson Park had she indulged in the drinking of breakfast chocolate before noon. But, since Sirene's arrival, she had turned into a lark – dressed and ready to groom the horse, learning all about curry combs and horse blankets – and she had come to savour the freshness edging the air. Could she, she wondered, become a country girl? Unbidden, the turquoise eyes of Malcolm Craig Lowrie rose before her. She tutted and slapped some straw from the velvet of her gown.

The day after the addition of Pettigrew to the household, both young women were more anxious than ever to meet in the stables. By mutual and tacit consent, they knew they would groom the horses and take to the gallops before reining in to a walk up through the forest ride to the hills. And, though the Park boundaries were now regularly patrolled by English mercenaries and a groomsman would be riding not far away, they would at last be able to talk without being overheard.

Once there – with the morning air rising to meet them from the summer sea and the Inner Hebrides visible through the purest sunlight – Emma turned to Adele and said: 'What do you think of Mr Pettigrew?'

'Hard for me to judge. I don't understand your English ways.'

'Don't be coy with me, Adele. What did you think? Truly, I value your opinion.'

'I found it odd.'

'What?'

'That Mr Pettigrew should suggest a ball. A ball, it could be so light. So exciting. It could be such fun. But it didn't seem so – well, coming from him, the idea of a ball...And, and, I don't care much for his way with oysters.'

The girls laughed but Adele was watching Emma.

'What troubles you?'

'As he flattered me – which I did not seek or enjoy – he watched you all the time. Like a snake, he was watching you. I don't know what he was thinking. I just had a sense of menace. I can't explain why. But yes, menace, that was it.

'Watching me? I didn't notice. I was certainly avoiding watching him eat. He's one of those men who snuffle while they eat – *dégoûtant!* Menace? Well...Perhaps I should steel myself. Perhaps...'

'Don't tease me, Adele. I'm afraid for you. And for me. It made me think of Jamie.'

'Don't you always?'

'Yes. Always.' The girl's reply had an automatic quality Adele did not like. The English way, perhaps. But then, Emma swung round on Berry to look straight into Adele's face. 'But last evening, I thought of him in a particular way. Even though I hadn't seen him for seven years, when we rode here to Argyll, I believed I was marrying Jamie for love. I truly believed that.

'Oh, my father had negotiated with Jamie's father – as though we were bloodstock, Adele. Estates, dowries, jewels – even an inheritance clause. But I didn't listen. I didn't feel that was important. As I rode across the country, all I could think of was the fact that I was going to marry someone I had sworn to love when I was eight years old. It was like a fairy-tale. The importance of inheritances – you can't imagine how little thought I gave them. But, it seems, these lawyers – Sir William and Mr Pettigrew – think inheritance is more important than I thought...'

She turned back to the heather track over the hills and faced the sea wind. But Adele heard her, clearly, as Emma asked: 'And, if I did truly love Jamie, as I thought I did, what chance have I of ever marrying for love again? Is it all to be negotiation? Is true love now at an end?'

There was a silence following this and then, Adele whispered, 'For some, it has never come and never will!'

Suddenly urging Sirene forward to Berry's side, Adele then said, 'Has Robinson something to do with this fear? Has he, Emma?'

'I don't know. I just had a feeling. No more than that. Last night. And I wondered why am I still here? Why has my father not come to fetch me? And what really happened to Jamie?'

Adele had no answer to these questions but leaned over to touch her friend's arm. Emma smiled through tears and then spurred Berry towards home, reckless of speed or terrain. Adele followed. And the groom, caught by surprise, trailed behind.

* * *

**Robinson's Journal, still tightly under lock and key in the Library of Robinson Park, Arduaine, near Oban**
**5th May 1793**

*Adelaide seems very fond of the Lady Emma. They huddle together – no other word for it. Always chattering. Always laughing. I have watched them from the windows of the Hall. I can just see the Rose Parterre from my chamber – and I see them deep in conversation, their heads together, their hair mingling. And I hear their laughter across the lawns. And I see them hugging and kissing each other. And there is no place for me in all of this.*

*I was right to fear that company – any company – would make it almost impossible for Adelaide to turn to me, as I had hoped. This is precisely why I have kept her so hidden, over the years. Any human contact – apart from her confessor, who is surely not human, anyway – could be distraction. I wanted her to come to me in affection and of her own accord. I did not want this diluted. I wanted to keep her pure – for the Almighty – yes! But if she was to give herself to anyone, I wanted it to be me.*

*And, now, the little wasted bird seems ready to sing. But, it seems, no matter how much I ache, I'll never hear that song. Thank God for the Oban whores and the serving wenches. A man could go mad, waiting for that little French canary to sing.*

*Yes, it was a mistake to bring Emma here.*

*And now they – Adelaide and Emma – want to have a ball, here at Robinson Park. A ball! To introduce Dilly Pettigrew to the world – well, Oban, anyway. And no doubt demonstrate Adelaide's considerable* chatelaine *skills. But what else could they be about? Although I remember the suggestion was Pettigrew's – for a ball – on one of these daily rides they take, the girls have brewed up this idea into a full-scale Assembly, including most of Oban. With candles. And refreshments. And musicians. It's ridiculous.*

*And where did all this riding suddenly come from? I could hardly say 'No!' when asked by the Lady Emma to let Adelaide ride out on the black mare. My brood mare to be! Of all the new intake! I didn't even know Adelaide could ride. She's spent so long hiding from the light in her apartments, how could she even begin to learn? It's all very puzzling. More than that. My lawyer's nose can smell a rat. But at the moment I can do nothing. Masterly inactivity, my principal used to say. That's what's needed. Masterly inactivity. And a watchful eye. There is a game afoot. I'll wager Adelaide's life on that.*

# Chapter 21

## Arduaine, near Oban, Argyll
## 10th May 1793

THE YEAR WAS wearing on. The nights were growing shorter, the days warmer, Spring had merged into Summer and still – apart from endless boundary patrols – there was no real action for the English mercenaries cooped up in the isolation of Robinson Park. They became slothful and quarrelsome and endured the time with gambling – especially as their officers had from the beginning made it quite clear that any steadings close to the Park were hostile to strangers and off limits.

But, against these orders and bored in camp, one mercenary decided he would take a chance. Though he did not know what he would find – 'a woman perhaps?' he thought – with several hours to go before darkness, he decided he would take himself to a nearby clachan. Whatever he found, he thought, it would have to be more interesting than yet more card games. So hidden from the view of the Hall, he now slid into the clear cold waters of the bay. Under the cover of the rocky outcrops flanking the brown shore, he waded around the headland. Then he pulled himself out of the salt waters and, with his shirt and breeches drying in the sun, he ran east along the sea-loch side. He was glad not to have gone later. Even in May, Scottish nights were cold and, in the gunmetal grey seas, he thought he should have caught his death. But now, he could feel Summer surging through him and he began to hope for better.

Then, the English mercenary found a blackhouse serving as a hostelry on the Oban track. His spirits rose even further especially as, when he appeared in the doorway, one of a band of tinkers, taking their ease from plying their trade between Oban and Glasgow, offered him a glass of rough whisky. But, as he adjusted his eyesight from bright sunlight to the gloom of the blackhouse, he noted the tinkers' faces were suffused with agressive greed and the mercenary decided he would not be mentioning Robinson Hall. All his instincts were warning him of mortal risk for anyone who might be held to ransom by these passing low-lifes. Instead, he drained the dirty glass, made a joke and settled down companionably alongside them to enjoy the banter and fend off their curiosity.

At last, tiring of his reticence, the tinkers – now loud with drink – turned their attention elsewhere. They lost caution and began to gossip. And, having escaped the turgid atmosphere of the camp, the mercenary congratulated himself. He had done well, he thought, to duck out from under the watchful eye of his officers and he now cheerfully mopped up everything said, like a bannock in stew. Somehow, he knew, someone somewhere would pay for what he was learning.

However, trouble was brewing as the drunken tinkers prattled. They began to challenge their fellow travellers. First they tried to engage three silent Highlanders, clustering round a table away from the light. However, the Highlanders continued to eat the coarse broth before them with no apparent interest in what tinkers had to say.

Then the tinkers noticed one man holding himself apart from the rest. Seated with his back to the only window, this man's face was hidden in the green gloom of the blackhouse as he cleaned an old claypipe. He was dressed, as the tinkers observed, quite unlike the saffron-bloused and plaid-draped Highlanders on the opposite side of the room. Though kilted like them, he wore a different tartan and his stock and shirt were made of pure white linen. Warm cloth dyed in the subtle shades of a broadleaf forest in summer constituted his jacket. He was a gentleman and, the tinkers thought, alone.

'Will you look at that kilt pin?' said one of their number, deceived by drink into believing he was whispering. 'Now that's worth money. It's a rich man, it is, wearing that and, look, no pistol. No broadsword. Only a dirk to cut his bread with. But he could spare that pin fine.'

'I've seen that pin before. Of that, I'm certain,' the tinker leader said, grasping uneasily for an elusive memory. 'That's one of the finest kilt pins I've ever seen. I'd be sure to remember it. But where?'

'Has the man no other pins and buckles to his clothes? Rich men, I'm told, carry their wealth on them around here. Too afraid of thieves to leave it at home.'

'Afraid of thieves, you say? Aye, look, silver buttons. Good, solid silver – enough to pay for a handsome funeral.'

And, admiring the display of wealth, the tinkers stood up, the better to menace the man on the window settle. But their leader halted them, triumphant. 'I have seen that pin before. On the docks, at Oban. By *The Three Fishes Inn,* lads, that's where I saw it! And the fine gentleman we have before us.'

Suddenly wary, the English mercenary rose from the table. His neck hairs were bristling with caution. He made his excuses, slipping out into the yard to relieve himself, and, as he stood in a dank and stinking corner of the yard, he heard the tinkers inside the blackhouse becoming even more voluble. He shuddered in anticipation.

They had seen a way to wealth. They wanted the silver kilt pin, with its craftsmanship and its jewels, and the solid silver buttons – and any other items of value the silent man with the claypipe might have concealed about him. They went across to sit at his table, unaware that the Highlanders behind them had stopped eating and that the dark atmosphere in the blackhouse was now dangerous.

Then, one tinker, his garlic-laced breath wreathing round the silent man's face, spraying spittle from his broken-toothed mouth over the silent man's rich clothing spoke. 'Here, alone, without weapons – with so much silver about you. D'you always travel so weighted down? Well, this is very fine. Very fine. Mebbe the time has come to share your wealth around a little. Lighten the load. With us, mebbe. With us. Your friends.'

The tinkers had lurched to their feet again. And the mercenary – who now felt the better course was to stay in the yard – heard the tinkers' leader say, 'Bide now, you're him. The one they call "The Wolf". Lads, did you hear tha'! This man here, there's a king's ransom on his head. He's...'

The mercenary did not wait longer. He fled the yard as the tinkers pressed on to their doom. Gleeful, their leader was now exhorting his leering companions to attack while – uninvited – he used the silent man's name. At this point, Malcolm Craig Lowrie lit his pipe and raised his eyes. And, the last earthly thing the garrulous tinkers saw was a flash of azure.

Within the hour, their dismembered bodies had disappeared into the moorland peatbogs and their pots, pans and tinker tools been distributed around the hill crofts. No-one would ever come to look for them nor find them if they did. But, when his tacksmen returned to the blackhouse, Malcolm Craig Lowrie took his pipe from his mouth and asked, 'Where is the Englishman?'

'Not among those bodies,' Rab MacDonald replied.

Craig Lowrie thought for a moment and then said, 'No matter. When ye've eaten, find him – or his trail. He won't be gone far. Not on foot. Not round here.'

As the Highlanders settled gratefully to their food, the Laird retrieved his weaponry from under the settle. He slid his pistol into its loop on his kilt belt and his dirk into its sheath, took some bannock from the table and added, 'I'm to Oban now. When you can, bring news of him to me. I want to know what an Englishman's doing here so far north in Argyll.'

He put his hand on Rab MacDonald's shoulder and added, 'You know, I feel, Rabbie, that suddenly that we are closer to the Lady Emma than we've been in months. Wherever she may stay, and with whom, I'd wager that Englishman holds the key.'

And he was gone.

As Rab MacDonald was returning to his broth, an old woman appeared from the shadows. Too old to be afraid, she began to pick up stools and clear away the tinkers' pots. Rab went across to help her.

'Here, mother, I'll help you. We're sorry for your trouble. Where should I bring these?'

She said nothing but nodded to the scullery, eyeing him with suspicion as he carried the crockery through the dark and broken doorway. But, when he returned to the table, he possessed information as tenuous but sure as a blood smear on heather in the hunt for prey. He believed he knew where the Englishman had gone and, when he and his fellow Highlanders had eaten their fill, they would be able to check the trail and take the news to the Craig Lowrie before dawn. 'A good day's work,' he thought.

The old woman came in again with more broth for the Craig Lowrie tacksmen and smiled. 'I'd have told you earlier, kinsmen, if I'd known you needed to know,' she said.

* * *

Pettigrew had spent the afternoon considering the ball. His mind was particularly exercised by two invitations and, in Robinson's well-endowed library, he had toiled away composing the form of wording most likely to entice the Duke of Argyll and Malcolm Craig Lowrie to the evening's entertainment. When he had suggested inviting the Duke and the brigand, Robinson had seemed lack-lustre so he had decided to proceed without his host's knowledge. It seemed to Pettigrew essential that these two notables should come to Robinson Park, the better for him to acquaint himself with their 'hopes and fears'. He believed that there was no substitute for a close and detailed knowledge of one's opponent's strengths and weaknesses. And, when content with the fruits of his epistolary labours, Pettigrew decided he would, at five of the clock, permit himself a full indulgence in yet another delectable dinner at Adelaide's table. But, before that, the problem still lying ahead of him was that of delivery to his special guests and he decided on a stroll by the sea before dinner to consider this.

Robinson's servants had been curiously resistant to bribes and threats of any sort, he felt. This intransigence seemed ill-willed. He could not believe loyalty to Robinson was keeping them unbiddable but, it was clear, without Robinson's permission, they would not leave the Park. And he was not yet ready to reveal all his plans – particularly relating to Argyll – to Robinson and so enlist his help transparently. Though irked, Pettigrew would have to find another way.

While engaged in these musings, Pettigrew became aware of heavy breathing and splashing, as of a man running through tidal waters that were flowing against him. Then, staggering round the headland, came the wild-eyed English mercenary – fighting to breathe as though the hounds of Hell were after him. *Convenient,* thought Pettigrew. He always found fear useful in recruiting help and this man was ripe with terror.

At the sight of Pettigrew, the mercenary halted abruptly, unsure which way to run now. But, Pettigrew stood still, drizzling coin from hand to hand, until the mercenary mesmerised by the stream of silver was calm again. In spite of everything, the mercenary was still sharp enough to recognise Pettigrew as a potential market for his hard-won information and, in return for a single shilling, Pettigrew learned that, according to the tinkers, a man of extraordinary power had taken rooms at an Oban quayside inn, *The Three Fishes.* No, the mercenary had not heard his name, but, thought the feverish Pettigrew, *could this be the man he needed to find? Could this be the Craig Lowrie?*

And he determined to know the truth of this by morning.

Silas Pettigrew was no horseman and, while standing in the stable yard of Robinson Park in the cool of the Scottish summer evening, he explained to Robinson's Chief Groom that he usually travelled by coach. Even so, relentless, the Robinson groom had gone in search of a horse. When he returned, it was with a Highland pony – short and broad.

'Not a quality horse.' Pettigrew sniffed.

'Reliable. Keep going all day. Never throw you.'

*The man could have meant it kindly,* thought Pettigrew. But somehow he doubted it. The groom did not bother to say more and left Pettigrew and the animal to assess each other. From the baleful look in its eye, Pettigrew understood this Highland Pony was not best pleased to be out in the Scottish gloaming. Night rides, Pettigrew suspected, were something the younger horses usually did and this pony seemed to be of the opinion that a warm stable was more appropriate, on such a cool evening. But, Pettigrew had made up his mind and, with the aid of a mounting block, he whirled his languid form across the recalcitrant pony. Then, the animal began to amble along the long, winding and pitted track towards the burgeoning lights of Oban and, with the setting sun to light his task, Pettigrew settled down to write the name of the groom in his notebook. He had a growing list of people he would punish in due course – when his plans came to fruition. The groom's name – yet another Macdonald – was the most recent of them. And the two-hour ride gave him considerable scope for note-taking.

*This discomfort had better be worthwhile,* he thought peevishly, cursing the mercenary, *I'm missing dinner.*

But, once at *The Three Fishes Inn,* Pettigrew recovered his dignity. Sitting for a while in the bar, nursing a rather fine local whisky, he waited and watched. And, blood-hound that he was, with comparative ease and in due course, he found a way of achieving what he had come for.

A group of farmers and townsfolk – all men – were assembling. The conversation was a low hum but 'upstairs' came through, clarion-like, to Pettigrew's alert and waiting ears. It tied in precisely with the information he had bought from the English mercenary.

Satisfied, Pettigrew moved among the ragged assembly. He bought a round of drinks, became part of the group and trooped upstairs in its wake. And Pettigrew's hand knocked on the door to gain entry.

The men sidled in. Some, Pettigrew noted, now wore fear on their faces like a badge. But the young man standing at his ease by the hearth fire was unperturbed. Malcolm Craig Lowrie was studying each one of them with no sign of recognition but, before anyone spoke, Pettigrew was sure, the Laird had placed them all. They mumbled their unnecessary introductions. These uncouth countrymen whose leasehold lands marched alongside Craig Lowrie territory were forming the new middle-classes in Oban. Their power was in their growing numbers. And, thought Pettigrew, Craig Lowrie's way of handling them was impressive. Even as a war-lord and, by repute, a brigand, Craig Lowrie had a talent for political finesse. He was behaving, thought Pettigrew, in a civil – almost affable – manner towards them.

But, wondered Pettigrew, why were they here? Some suit of which he was as yet unaware? A lapsed lease? A disputed boundary? More work perhaps for Robinson and for him. But leases and boundary disputes were mere sprats to a mackerel shoal, considering the current potential revenues at stake for *Robinson and Pettigrew, Attorneys at Law*. Whatever the purpose for this assembly, it did not matter much to Pettigrew at the moment. His purpose in being there was quite different. He was there to assess Craig Lowrie. What he wanted to know was: 'Is this man capable of killing a cousin?' He rather feared he was.

Things were now moving on apace. A spokesman stepped forward and identified himself. *Oh no, yet another Macdonald,* thought Pettigrew, with a slight groan. Up here the world was thick with them. This Macdonald was another farmer, although this time from the north, and had a strong dialect and a stutter. Craig Lowrie waited for him to finish his greeting – in silence. The farmer then began to explain why he and the other visitors were keeping the Laird from his business while his companions continued to stare at the floor and, Pettigrew noted, Craig Lowrie continued to appraise each of the motley crew. As they shuffled and mumbled, his startling azure eyes scanned, checked and faced down each applicant. And, although Pettigrew had chosen to stand at the back of the rabble, in the shadows, he found himself disconcerted by Craig Lowrie's gaze. When his turn came, he covered his own awkwardness by busying himself with his snuff box – as he watched Craig Lowrie and as Craig Lowrie watched the others – and him.

At last, attuned to the brogue, Pettigrew came to understand what the farmer was talking about. To his surprise, Malcolm Craig Lowrie was being invited to join the board of the new distillery.

'Will you consider it, laird?'

Craig Lowrie paused. 'When I stand on the hills of my land, I can see forty-three illicit stills. I can find *usquebaugh* whenever I need it. Why would I be part of this? Why do you ask me?'

'It's the future, laird. Will you no be part of it?'

'What would it entail? I have never thought to be a distiller.'

It was explained that Malcolm Craig Lowrie would not be required to ladle the grain or bottle the product. Pettigrew smirked at the thought.

'I would hope I would not. But what do you hope for? To have someone you call a brigand on your board? Is this sensible? Or do you hope to tame me by this? Turn me into one of your middle-class citizens? Do you hope this will constrain me?'

The consequent silence seemed impenetrable and Pettigrew was aghast at Malcolm Craig Lowrie's ability to incise to the heart of the matter. The man's boldness in argument would serve him well in court, he thought.

'Will you consider it, laird?' repeated the farmer from the north. Craig Lowrie did not answer. Then, suddenly, he smiled.

'I will. I will join your middle-classes, gentlemen.'

These were not 'gentlemen' but they accepted the flattery as a token of friendship. The relief in the room was palpable. Malcolm Craig Lowrie was to be one of them. If that were so, he would not attack them. There would be no 'difficulties' in getting the whisky away to the south, to Glasgow. Profit was assured. Pettigrew, too, felt relieved. His plans did not involve the complication of the recently-improved post- and military roads being subject to lawless attack. Safe passage for all – but particularly for him – throughout the Western Highlands would suit him best.

The burghers looked around them. To celebrate this new partnership, an invitation to sit and drink some of the claret visible on the desk would have been re-assuring. It did not come. And the farmer from the north said at last, 'Well, we'll be leaving you then.'

'If you will.'

The door opened and one by one they reversed through it – except for Pettigrew. Standing apart and now clearly not one of them, he stepped forward and extended a hand to Craig Lowrie. For a moment his eyes searched out Craig Lowrie's direct gaze but could not hold it for long. This man did not have any real subtlety after all, thought Pettigrew, irritated. Craig Lowrie made civilised people uncomfortable.

Then Pettigrew's hand was being shaken. As his knuckles cracked with the strength of the other man's grip, Pettigrew was feeling suddenly unwell and he turned to leave. His mind span with disappointment and dismay – he had failed, he thought. But then, as he reached the door, he smiled. He heard Craig Lowrie say, 'At last!'

As Pettigrew's indolent form slithered away down the stairs and into the dark stable-yard, he was leaving Craig Lowrie holding a hand-written card. It was an invitation to a Midsummer Night Ball at Robinson Park, at Arduaine near Oban. And Malcolm Craig Lowrie would be sending his accepting note to Adelaide de Fontenoy, otherwise known as 'Lady Robinson'. As Pettigrew had hoped, Craig Lowrie had taken his bait. *At last, indeed,* thought Pettigrew.

Another matter was also resolved. The mercenary had proved himself – and his information – reliable and Pettigrew was possessed of sufficient coin to keep the man loyal. His difficulty in delivering a secret invitation to the Duke of Argyll was no more. The mercenary would now serve as Pettigrew's postman and his creature.

# Chapter 22

## Oban, Argyll
## 10th May 1793

A MIDSUMMER BALL has been announced that will allow the inquisitives of Oban their first viewing of the newly-discovered (by Oban, anyway) Palace in the Hills. Arduaine is two hours' carriage drive to the south of the town but even so, the gentlemen and ladies cannot believe they have not known about this reputedly wonderful house until the moment when the stylish handwritten invitations arrived on their breakfast tables. The stunned silence that greeted these tastefully-produced invitations did not last. It soon gave way to feverish speculation, led by the Doyenne of Oban Society, the new distillery manager's wife, Molly Ballachulish. And the salons of Oban had rarely had such bones to chew on. But Oban society took to it with gusto, particularly in the salon of No 1, The Crescent, North Shore, where Mrs Ballachulish lived.

'My dear, do you think the Lady of the House will have chosen to decorate Robinson Park in the manner of the French court?'

'I hear she is straight from there – last week, the rumours say. Newly come to Scotland. An *emigrée* perhaps, driven out by those dreadful Jacobins. Paris Aristocracy, perhaps?'

'Do you think so? Of course, French style is just what we need here in the north – a touch of civilisation. A touch of fashion. I long for it so. And we'll come to know how things are done in the French court. Edinburgh! London! Drabs in comparison.'

'But why do you think Sir William has decided now to invite us? After so many years of living as a recluse – and yet, it appears, a mere twenty miles from town.'

'Well, I have it on good authority, very good authority, that he has married this Adelaide de Fontenoy as a way of helping her escape.'

'No – really? Well, that is very handsome of him. Very handsome indeed. But she is only half his age I hear. If that!'

'Scandalous – if she is. Such a scandalous waste for our young men. We have so many handsome young fellows in town, who could look after a penniless aristocrat just as well as the venerable Sir William.'

'She may of course be very plain – it wouldn't matter then that he is so very old. She may also be very rich. As well as aristocratic. Yes, a wife like that would suit Sir William very well.'

'And there will be the other young lady too. Miss Dilly Pettigrew, here with her brother to escape the sickness in Carlisle.'

'Such a lot of very fine fashions we shall see. Paris! And Carlisle! Such a treat.'

'I can scarcely wait. Do you think Lady Robinson could advise me?'

'On what, my dear?'

'On the best way to wear my hair?'

'Well she may. But, though she may be French, she can't work miracles.'

'Well, she wouldn't even know where to start advising you on gowns. As a farmer's wife, so twisted with the damp and cold as you are, I regret to say it but nothing will look well.'

'And why did Lady Robinson send out her invitations as Adelaide de Fontenoy? Are they not married, mother? Do you not think that's perhaps another scandal?'

'Oh Fiona, how ignorant you are! It is the way of the French court. The ladies keep their own names and title.'

'Oh, Mrs Ballachulish – how very elegant. And exciting. And French.'

'Mother, what do you think Lady Robinson will serve as confections? I understand she has employed a French pastry cook.'

'Oh, Fiona, can you not think only of food?'

'Oh mother, how can you say such things when we are about to attend my first ball? How can I find a husband, if you put such things in my mind?'

# Chapter 23

## Oban, Argyll
## 10th May 1793

THE FRENCH BRIG, *Espoir,* eased towards the quay. The hour was early but the morning light bloomed, warming Father John Stewart Macdonald as he stood on the deck. Relief seeped through every line of his face – relief to be back in Scotland and relief to have accomplished his commission.

At the foot of the *Espoir's* gangplank, an empty carriage was waiting. This was noted but not commented upon by the dock workers who were silently manouevring bulky cargo past it. There were no insignia on the carriage doors and no other signs of its provenance. Even so, the priest signalled porters to place within it multiple if anonymous packages. He knew these contained bolts of damask, silk and brocade – smuggled right under the noses of the Parisian revolutionaries who had peevishly, he thought, banned silk not so long before. The packages were weighty and awkward to handle but the stevedores fitted them all in with skill. Then, negotiating with extreme care the many potholes along the unmetalled track through the hills, the laden carriage returned to Robinson Park.

The Robinson groom had also earlier sent the Chaplain's garron down to the Port. And, before he kept his appointment with Malcolm Craig Lowrie, the old priest intended to re-assure himself that Adelaide was well. The old man rode his sure-footed mount hard and fast and ahead of the carriage, as he had done so many times before.

And, as he rode, he recalled his first ride down this track. A decade before, impoverished and badly mounted, he had ridden from the north, cresting the hill with the morning. The craftsmen, he remembered, had just applied the final touches to the new buildings that had been raised in secrecy on the Arduaine promontary, screened by woodland and some distance from the main track between Inveraray and Oban. And, when he arrived, the builders were dismantling their camps, ready to go back to Glasgow, Edinburgh, Liverpool and London, from whence they had come. There, they would find more work and they would be allowed to spend their handsome remuneration – so excessive it bought not only their skill but also their silence. In his pocket, each craftsman carried a private note of commendation from Robinson that would open new doors for him. And, ever cautious, while he bought secrecy, Robinson had included checks and controls to conceal his whereabouts. Nothing had been left to chance in his strategy for laying false trails for the hounds.

'Whatever he's done, it's serious, Father', one man had told John Stewart Macdonald before he melted into the crowds of men moving out towards Oban and the waiting ships bound for the southern ports, their women trailing behind with luggage and children. The man's face, the priest noted, was white with fear at having said too much. However skilled these people were, they were superstitious and illiterate. They had supped, they believed, with the Devil – and without a long spoon.

Bewildering as all this was, the pall of silence had been absolute. Until Father Macdonald had ridden over the Oban road above Loch Melfort, he had not heard the breath of a whisper of what lay concealed in the hills. A palace, it seemed to him, a palace had been built and concealed in silence. He had, he remembered, shivered at the thought of the power of the money behind that silence. But, why such secrecy? He had wondered then and he wondered now and still the silence remained absolute.

Sir William Robinson had greeted him affably enough, explaining that – with his Lord Bishop's full permission – he, John Stewart Macdonald, was to act as chaplain for Robinson's young French Roman Catholic ward. With a huge retainer already paid into Church coffers, John Stewart Macdonald knew his services would also include 'total discretion' – in other words, silence. This requirement, Father Macdonald had felt, existed to ensure the safety of the 'palace's' owner and, in fact, while ringing for a servant to conduct the Chaplain to his new quarters, Sir William had confirmed its exigency. And smiled.

John Stewart Macdonald shuddered. As an inexperienced priest, he had gazed upon the face of evil and had seen it smile and remembered with shame his sense of his own complete inadequacy in the face of what he feared Robinson could do. He also recalled his first view of the child, his charge-to-be. Apart from her extreme beauty, the thing that had most clutched at his heart on that far off day was her extreme sadness. When he had come into her presence, at that moment so long ago, he knew at once that her protection and her salvation would be the two most important tasks he would ever undertake. And he had sworn to God that he would dedicate every skill, talent and strength he possessed to these holy ends.

'My friend, your Lord Bishop', the English lawyer repeated, presiding with apparent magnanimity over the meeting of chaplain and charge, 'has been most accommodating. I trust you will be too.'

'But may I ask you something, Sir William?'

'You may.'

'How does the young lady come to be here? She is but nine years old, you say. And, not from Scotland. And not of your faith.'

'You may ask.' Robinson turned away and picked up a paper knife from a Riesener *secretaire* settled between the windows of the room. He looked out over the Park and, absent-mindedly, drew the steel blade across the palm of his hand. He repeated his response. 'You may ask.' The tension in the room rose and, uncomfortable, the priest thought to re-phrase the question less bluntly.

Robinson however pre-empted him. 'Yes, you may ask. But I, I am not obliged to reply. As for my intentions. They are precisely that. Mine. And will remain known only to me until I choose otherwise. As for your presence here, let us say that was part of a bargain. A bargain on which I may at some point choose to renege. You, however, will no doubt make your own mind up over time.'

The shock in the room lapped around the sides. Then, suddenly Sir William changed approach, adding affably, 'Come now! I jest. We shall see how we all shall shift, shall we? Come, my dear!'

Still smiling, Sir William dropped the paper knife back onto the blotter, virgin on the *secretaire*. And the child moved to John Stewart Macdonald's side to take his hand. But, if Sir William was angry, there was no outward sign, as he said, 'Very well, my dear, for now. Take comfort, yes, take comfort from your Mother Church.'

Remembering how tightly the child had held his hand, the old priest now brushed his eyes and slid down from his garron. The waiting groom took the mud-spattered and weary horse away to the stable block and Father John Stewart Macdonald sought out the rooms of *Le Petit Trianon.*

And Robinson, catching sight of the priest as he himself sought out the kitchens – and more particularly the maids – asked himself, 'I wonder what news JSM has brought from France...'

* * *

'The King is dead.'

'Dead? How?'

'Executed.'

'And the Queen?'

'Taken.'

'And Gabrielle?'

Adele's hands tremble over the fabric she is working on. Servants no longer light candles during the day in her rooms and, today, she is in a garden room – attached to *Le Petit Trianon* – where morning sunlight suffuses unfiltered upon her. John Stewart Macdonald remains standing, moving his hat slowly through his fingers, as if to measure the brim helps him stay brave. He coughs. Adele lays aside her sewing, stands and brings the *mannequine* out of a corner to place it in the centre of the room. It is ablaze with sunlight. For the first time, JSM recognises the face. Though distorted, it is that of the Austrian Queen in happier days. Adele smooths brocade over the paniers.

'And Gabrielle?' she repeats.

'Alive. Your father, too.'

Adele hisses – softly but audibly.

'Gabrielle is making a living. For them both. She is making hats for women, for the *citoyennes,* flounced with red, white and blue ribbons. She's surviving. But she keeps your father out of sight. In case he boasts of –'

'Of the one hat he made for the Queen.'

'It would be enough.'

'Enough?'

'To execute them both.'

'What can we do?'

On Adele's face, he can see the question written but they both know the answer. John Stewart Macdonald is many things but he is not able to help her save Gabrielle. Time, the priest knows, has somewhat softened Adele's feelings towards her father. But, he knows, the sight of Sir William daily reminds her of her father Gabriel de Fontenoy's perfidy in handing her over to an old lecher. Because of his worldly vanity and folly, the milliner placed an innocent child in the power of a man she could never love and, although her father's mind may have long gone, this act of betrayal was and is culpable, thinks her chaplain. His profligacy has also cast Adele's pretty, charming sister, Gabrielle, in the role of drudge. Adele, her chaplain believes, will never be able to forgive the old man for that.

John Stewart Macdonald holds out a letter for her. The seal is familiar to them both.

'Thank you for your news, Father,' she remembers to say.

'I wish it could have been better, child.'

The priest leaves her to open Gabrielle's letter on her own.

* * *

*Adele, Chérie,*

*I am so pleased to be able to send you this note with the Father. Truly, he is the very best courier you could have found. Here, there is still some respect for the cloth so our letters and their bearer are safe. For the most part. For the moment. But there is still danger. We must be watchful – always. Remember our man and that accident. Sometimes I wonder. How could an experienced seaman, such as Jean Le Pecque, have such an accident – in dock? Don't you ever think that strange?*

*But shall the Father come again soon?*

*As if you could answer these questions!*

*Things are very bad here. We wait daily for news of the Queen's trial. Rumour is rife – you cannot trust anything you hear. But I won't say more of that now. The Father will tell you what you need to know. I will say only that the world is mad. We thought – our little family – that we were in evil times when you were sent so far away and all we could do was send letters and bolts of cloth and pattern plates. But you would not believe how the world has turned. And for the worse. What we used to do for fun, I now do for bread. But with no style required. No imagination. Just plain caps and endless, endless red, white and blue ribbons. I feel 'tricoloured' to death – well, not quite. Not yet.*

*Our father is low in spirit. Lower and lower each day. And he cries and rages and weeps for you. I can find no sense in what he says and sometimes, I feel, he doesn't even see me now. Yet, if we have a visitor, he seems to grow a little – grow towards what he used to be. Even so, I have taken to hiding him from our visitors – the neighbours, the tradesmen who call with the materials or food. I am afraid. If he once boasts of our former glory, we could be denounced. We live on the edge of the world. And the most vicious of all our enemies, Robespierre and his friends, gain more and more power by the second. So many of our former friends have suffered at the hands of these men. Name after name, I could tell you. And you would weep. Friends like Olympe de Gouges, perhaps? As children, we thought her kind, do you remember? And, do you remember how she filled us with all those lovely ideas of marrying for love. But, things change. Like you, she's been in the power of a man she could not love. And, yet, she always so wanted little women like us – and her – to be able to choose. Recently, standing on the hustings, she said, the Revolution has not freed us. In spite of all our hopes, we are no better placed now than we were before the blood-letting. As she says, women mount the block but still have no voice. She has argued women, as citizens, have the right to free speech. And women should be members of the political and public side of society. I don't really understand what all that would mean for us but these are amazing ideas, don't you think, in our times? And dangerous. Now!*

*But something she says I do understand very well. Women, she also says, manage property but we do not and cannot own it. And this is true. Look at me. I am in sole charge of our father's property but not a sou is mine. When he dies, I don't know what will happen... I shall have no home, and no protector. You are perhaps – after all – more lucky than I. Perhaps I shall be able to come to you. In Scotland. What do you think? That would be so wonderful. We could perhaps one day have our children together. Live together. Breathe the same pure air together. But I dare not write more.*

*Take care, my love, and send the Father to me again soon. It was such comfort to hear from him, my little sister – he who knows you so well, how you are, how you look, how you are loved. As you are here – even by our poor demented guilty father – and even more especially by me, your loving sister, Gabrielle.*

# Chapter 24

## The Three Fishes Inn, Oban
## 10th May 1793

THE NEWS THE OLD priest brought from France would have to belong to Malcolm Craig Lowrie before dawn. The priest was a man of his word – although he still wondered why a brigand like the Craig Lowrie would need news from Revolutionary France. Some further deep iniquity, he supposed.

But – a close-lipped Highlander by birth – Father Macdonald would not be telling Malcolm Craig Lowrie everything. Much of what he knew of the Robinson household would remain private and, he would not be mentioning the freshly-delivered letter from Gabrielle. This was not part of the deal. The deal was 'news from France' and there was enough of that to satisfy even the thirstiest curiosity.

But, having seen first hand what was happening in France, Father Macdonald knew Adele's sister, Gabrielle, would soon need to be brought out of there and, he felt, in the shadows of his heart, Adele would try to help her. He could anticipate everything unfold along the most horrendous course. As things stood, Adele would beg Robinson for assistance. And Robinson would demand payment – with whatever unimaginable horror that may entail. The reality of the situation was that, ailing and elderly, the old priest was now powerless to prevent this horror. But, much to his surprise, he found himself hoping there was just a chance Malcolm Craig Lowrie could. And this hope, though irrational, had persisted throughout his sea voyage and a day's riding.

But, there had been developments of which he was unaware.

Now, as he stabled his garron at the quayside inn where he was to keep his appointment with the Craig Lowrie, his attention was caught by a tall stranger following a disparate band of farmers and townsfolk out into the Oban night. The sight of the man set the hairs on John Stewart Macdonald's neck to standing. *Danger,* he thought. *For My Lady,* he thought. He did not know why he thought this, but he did. *That man means danger for Adele.*

* * *

The old priest has again ridden hard up from the Port and is about to retire for the night when he sees the light from Adele's rooms across the linkway. The oblongs of light falling out on the terraces are thin and flickering – candlelight, blocked by oaken doors and mirror glass. Unwelcoming. His knock on her door is tentative.

Once more, the old priest stands before Adele, flecked and travel-grimed. He is always particular in using the polite address. It shows his respect for her. 'You are well, My Lady?'

To his surprise, she kneels before him. 'Father, forgive me for I have sinned. Will you hear my confession?'

He raises her and leads her by her gentle hand to her *Prie Dieu,* listening for the rustle of her silk gown as she settles on her knees. He reaches into his travel bag for the artefacts of his office and prepares to offer her the comfort of Mother Church. When he is prepared, she begins without preamble. 'Hatred, I have spent ten years feeling nothing but hatred. And now, that sin has come to haunt me.'

He is shocked. He has never thought to hear the deadly sin of hatred so frankly confessed by one he knows to be so innocent. Her eyelashes, resting on the flawless face, are wet with tears.

At last, she pauses and raises her head. 'What shall I do to atone?'

It is the question of one who hopes atonement will save the suffering of another. It is a bargaining counter with God. It is sacrifice. He is wary. The priest seeks to comfort her but suddenly he is equally moved to be frank.

'Yours are the sins of omission, child. You have lived your life in a dark world. Yet you have not sought the light. And you have spent long years in not doing the good that was there for you to do. You have lived your life in the shadows of hatred but now there are calls to light that you can no longer deny. And you, only you can allow yourself to move towards it. The light is love, my child.'

'You mean, Gabrielle.'

'She is one who needs you, certainly.'

'What can I do?'

Adele raises her eyes to his. He falters. He is a kind man but, on this occasion, he must wait while she faces her devils alone. Only then, he is thinking, will she understand what must be done. He sees in her face that she understands that in this, for the first time in her life, she is truly alone. He bites his lips to silence, blesses her and leaves her to her thoughts.

The strangeness of what is happening is crackling around her – like summer lightning over the hills. But can she do anything? She paces. She picks up the letter from Gabrielle, from where it lies on the card table. As she does so, the movement scatters the cards beneath it. She was about to play Patience when the priest came to the door that morning, before his excursion to Oban. The cards were laid out, with precision, as if stitched onto the green baize. Now they lie as if cast to the four winds.

She re-reads the letter and then restores it to its leather cylinder, moving to hide it within the secret recess in the wall. She believes no-one knows of the existence of this recess – apart from the builder who made it and whom Father John Stewart Macdonald bribed to silence. And in it there lie ten years of letters from her sister. Now, as she knows from the letter, these may soon be all she has left of Gabrielle.

'*Tiens*. I have been so selfish,' she says out loud. 'And all this paper, this is not enough'

She can no longer just leave things to happen as they will. She has thought to do her duty by enduring. But now she looks at the image of herself, mirrored to infinity, on the walls of her rooms. And she knows something has changed. Her secret life in waiting is now over. She must act. But, for the moment, she cannot think how.

* * *

**Robinson's Journal, Arduaine, near Oban**

**Under lock and key**

*An extraordinary turn of events. Quite preposterous, of course. But quite extraordinary. Adelaide has asked me to help her. She wants me to go to France and rescue her sister and that fool of a father of hers. I cannot credit it. I said 'No!' of course. I'm too old for such jollies now. Even when I was young I didn't travel to France to go round rescuing people.*

*Still, she has asked me. Does this mean she has started to look kindly on me at last? Dare I hope for a softening in my direction? It must have cost her a lot to ask me. Surely, if she is moving towards me, if she offers herself to me, I will not have broken my pact with my Maker. She could still be my atonement – ten long years of waiting. She could still be my redemption. I can scarcely breathe at the thought of it. Could it be my little French canary will yet sing for me? Without my breaking my promise to the Almighty?*

*I'll not tell Pettigrew about this. Best kept between her and me. Who knows?*

**Robinson's journal, several days later. Still under lock and key**

*Adelaide is still fretting about France and what's going on there and Queen Marie Antoinette and Mademoiselle Gabrielle de Fontenoy and the whole army of them – but none of this helps me with what to do about the Lady Emma Bamburgh. Still no word from her father. And Pettigrew has turned into a loose canon. He was down at the Port some days ago, visiting Craig Lowrie. Oh, he thinks I do not know, of course. He thinks we are all fools up here. But, as he will find, there's precious little that I do not know about what goes on in this corner of western Argyll, around Oban. If I can browse Adelaide's letters from France, I can have Pettigrew tracked to the Port. What a fool the man is if he thinks otherwise.*

*But the Craig Lowrie lands are different. They are a closed book – even to me. I wonder how Pettigrew will worm his way in there. It'll take more than tagging on to a distillers' deputation to do that. Still Pettigrew's devious enough to pull it off. And he will report to me. At the moment, he believes he needs me. I think I shall keep it that way.*

*This is the sort of intrigue I have a taste for. Not performing outlandish and daring rescue attempts on Adelaide's behalf. Though, of course, she might reward me for those. No, France is far too uncertain for my taste anymore. I want a quiet life – not to go thundering round a foreign country on horseback, with peasants and pitchforks on every side. Whatever the prize.*

*What can Adelaide have been thinking to suggest it?*

# Chapter 25

## Robinson Park, Arduaine, near Oban 15th June 1793

AGAIN THE LADY EMMA is wearing the groom's clothes in which she rode from Dalriada to Oban. They have been laundered and mended and kept in her closet – just in case. But in case of what? She has not until now known.

She lies on the bed and waits for darkness.

As she accompanied Adele to Oban Fish Market that day, she saw the hooded man there again, on the docks. Had she been alone, he would have spoken to her, she is sure. But who is he? Is he perhaps her father's man? But, if so, why does he not just march up to the door and make himself known? Or is he from some other faction – Argyll's man perhaps? Or is he a Craig Lowrie man, reluctant to show his face in these places so hostile to the Clan, keeping her observed until the Craig Lowrie decides what to do about her? Will this man in the grey hood and cloak at some point make an attempt to kidnap her? Had he wanted, she is sure, he could already have offered violence. On her way into Oban from Robinson Park, perhaps? No, there are always armed riding servants around her and the carriage. Perhaps, when she has ridden out with Adele within the Park? A groom would be no deterrent to a determined assailant. It is true, the English mercenaries have regular patterns of patrol, but these could with some observation be avoided. But, no, in spite of opportunities to do so, the hooded man has not yet made any attempt to approach her.

Yet, nor has he concealed his existence. He has – with some bravado reminiscent of Jamie's style – been temptingly visible. She has caught glimpses of him, usually in town, watching her across the road or from the quay. And, presumably, he has chosen not to conceal himself. There has been something bold, something frank, about the way he simply stood there – forcing the passers-by to split and flow past like spate waters round a rock. As if defying the Almighty. And as if challenging the forces of evil, challenging Robinson. But if he is no-one's agent, thinks Emma, who is he?

And, when she and Adele drove back from town, there he was on the road to Arduaine. Still watching. And this place, Robinson Park, is meant to be so secret, she thinks. Was it by chance he knew she would be coming here? But, whoever he is, Emma has just seen the light of his fire by the gate of Robinson Park. She has not seen him so close to the Park before. But there he is, now, outside the Park gates. Is he watching her? Or is he watching over her? She cannot be sure.

*So many questions!*

She feels again the fear that ran with her as she travelled from Crinan to Oban. Fear running in the hills – she remembers fear taking her breath from her as she stood in the stirrups to turn and scan the empty lands. Fear that she is hunted. But she has decided. She is an earl's daughter. She will not be cowed. She will challenge him, whoever he is. Now. This very minute.

She slips down the servants' stairs. Without a candle, her dark clothes enfold her in the darkness of the stairwells. She is invisible as she penetrates the kitchens. For her, this is uncharted territory and she is pleased to find her way so easily. It is quite simple to reach the Park this way, so simple she would not have believed it. Suddenly she hears the smothered laughter of one of the slatterns who do the pots. She realises Robinson is finding his pleasures close to home tonight. But, repressing her revulsion at the thought of that great bulk quivering with lust and gratification, she slides a knife from the knife block and scarcely dares breathe as she eases the heavy oaken door open. For a moment, she considers Robinson's back, hefts the knife and wonders about the possibilities of delivering Adele from her imprisonment. But then Emma's purpose re-asserts itself. 'Another time,' she thinks.

The mercenaries' camp – built on the remains of the housebuilders' camps – is close to the house, with its cooking and other smells and the noises of sleeping men. But, above her, the Rose Moon is bright, sailing in the deep azure sky, and it is enough to see by as she skirts the alien encampment. She runs towards the gate but she runs on the grass, not on the gravel, and her footfalls are silent.

Although a light burns in the lodge cottage, all at the gate is quiet. But, as she approaches the Park boundary, she realises the iron gates are locked. For a moment, the lodge flare blinds her but then she turns away and feels her way along the perimeter rails, her fingers glancing over the weathered metal and bulky stone of the Robinson Park defences. She is led into darkness and away from the Lodge and from the house. But, as she moves along the boundary, she can smell and hear and – at last – see the fire.

She is not prepared for what she sees next.

The man in the hood is sitting with his back to her. He is intent on cooking a small animal on the fire, its flesh crisping in the heat. With a swift, careless movement, he slips the hood back from his head, the better to eat. But then he hears behind him the twig – brittle in the summer's heat – snap under her boot. He turns, dirk in hand.

'Jamie!' she calls out in amazement.

Months of unnecessary grief – and now, to her surprise, anger – swell the cry. The sense of loss that has become part of her fuels her outrage.

'Of course, who else?' he grins. 'You've caused me a devil of a chase, Em.'

'Me!'

'Yes, you. After you left the castle, I thought to catch up with you before you struck Oban. But no. The road was completely empty. Whatever did you do, girl?'

Still stunned, she is hardly coherent when she says, 'I mistook the trail. I came by Cruachan.'

She recounts the names etched on her memory by fear and loss. Crinan, Kilmartin, Loch Awe, Kilchurn, Cruachan, Taynuilt, Loch Etive, Oban. Such endurance, such pain, such needless grief, pushing her on and on and on. And now, here he is – eating!

'Good Lord!' He has the good manners to recognise her achievement but nothing will stop her now until she tears the truth out of him.

'And why haven't you come to the door? What is all this sculling about the woods – and the docks? Why did you not speak to me? Have you an idea how unhappy I've been?'

'Have you not heard? Your protector, your Sir William...'

'Not mine.'

'Well, him, anyway. He's seeking to outlaw my cousin. The Craig Lowries are – as that old buffoon lawyer would say – *persona non grata*. Hardly easy to call in for tea, now.'

'Oh I know about the outlawry – or the attempt. But it was based on your murder – the murder of a King's man, Sir William calls it. Is that not you? Are you not the man who let in the Campbells and the King's soldiery.'

'No. No. Not me.'

'Oh, Jamie! Why did everyone let me think you'd been murdered? That Jennet Awe...It was so unkind.'

'Safer, though, for you – not to know where I was. It appeared I'd upset Uncle Argyll in some way. So, easier for you not to know the truth, we thought. And neater to let you 'escape'. Uncle – well, his agents – would be busy with the castle and, even if he broke through, you'd be safer miles from Crinan. And then everyone thought I'd find you before Oban and be able to put your mind at rest, anyway. I did eventually catch sight of you – once – in Oban but you were always surrounded by Robinson and his men. You did look lovely though, Em.'

Emma brushed this aside. 'But who was the man, I saw...Who was the man who died, was killed...?'

'Oh, some Campbell man. Yes, a King's man. A traitor in our midst. Left the postern gate open. The Laird was angry! I've never seen Mal so angry. Like cold steel. All that killing...I think Uncle thought to bring us to our knees. But no, not the Craig Lowries!'

Finally recognising the need for some contrition, he lowered his voice, 'Anyway, the plan was to let Uncle think one of the Craig Lowrie cousins had died in the attack. Argyll does not like to be seen to be openly involved in these spats, says the Laird, and the possibility of my being murdered would keep him out of matters for a few months. But things are never that simple, are they? First, there was another attack – on the shepherds – over at Ardnackaig. And now, as it turns out, after all, Uncle Argyll wants you!'

'Me?'

'Yes, you. Don't ask me why! It's what Mal says. But we'd lost track of you. Until a sort of chance meeting near Arduaine. Things became much clearer after that.'

Their hands can only touch through the bars of the boundary –

so tall there is no way to climb over it. Emma thinks her heart will break after months of grief and its sudden easing but Jamie leans as close as he can towards her and takes her fingers to kiss them.

'I've missed you so much, Em. So much.' His voice cracks – a tiny, broken sound – and she forgives him the months of pain. And now they can at least talk, explaining everything that remains to be explained and more besides. Jamie also wants to know the precise layout of the Hall – interested particularly in Emma's description of the kitchen stairs. He also listens to her description of life at the Hall and the wonderful Adele. 'Oh, my love,' he says. 'You've both been prisoners. Did you not see that?'

Emma is considering again the truth of this when there comes the sound of English mercenaries, lumbering along the perimeter road on their patrol. With the toe of his boot, Jamie nudges stones over the fire's embers and, touching Emma's lips through the bars in farewell, he sighs and says 'Not a word. I will come again. And soon. Everything will be well. Everything. I promise.'

Emma watches him melt into the darkness, her heart tearing as he goes, but, as the patrol, disinterested, clatters past, she waits. For the mercenaries, walking the boundaries is now no more than duty and they no longer have a sense of excitement and peril. But, thinks Emma, now is not the time to disabuse them. Not yet. And, when the mercenaries have shambled off, she slides back through the bushes and runs across the lawns to the house.

As she does so, Robinson studies her from the windows of the Hall's Long Gallery. For now, he stores the information but he is intrigued, feeling sure that he has seen something significant. He hears Emma's chamber door slide shut and he chuckles with delight at the possession of knowledge – which, like all the other knowledge he possesses, he may at some point find useful.

# Chapter 26

## Robinson Park, Arduaine
## 21st June – Midsummer Night – 1793

AND NOW THE Midsummer Night Ball has finally arrived.

Although on the alert, the English mercenaries have been ordered out of sight, around the back of Robinson Hall, beyond the stable blocks but still within the Park. This is because Silas Pettigrew has suggested that their uncouth and unruly appearance might frighten the visitors. And, in truth, the visitors themselves – the great and the good of Oban and their wives – are left nervous enough by the seemingly endless journey up from the town. They are glad it is Midsummer Night and still light but the potholes on the track south are already seriously discouraging. As the *barouches coupés* slide and bump along, the ladies hope fervently that no brigands will force them to step down onto the road. Their new silken slippers would not tolerate the damp and the mud.

At the approach of the first carriage towards the lodge of Robinson Park, the gates are flung open and now, through eerie gloaming, the Robinson Park watchman hears ladies' chatter. The muffled sounds are dominated by the booming English tones of the Distillery Manager's Birmingham-born wife, Molly Ballachulish.

'Hush, now. Everyone, look. The Hall. Did you ever see the like? Oh, this is real style. Twenty-three glazed windows! And what a door! And this is just the Eastern Facade!'

'Oh, Molly, my dear! No, I never did see such elegance, I never did.'

'Mrs Ballachulish, don't you just wonder at the height of those steps? A stone staircase! Oh, this is what royalty would choose – I'm sure of it.'

Hearts are prepared to flutter.

Meanwhile, Sir William Robinson has found himself aligning dishes of almonds with the floral centrepiece on the buffet table. During the past week, Adelaide has been requesting the maids to divest the water meadows and the Park hedgerows of their flowers – poppies, thistles, marigolds, chamomile, wild roses and honeysuckle. And, against a backdrop of white heather, meadow sweet and wild carrot, these now sparkle in candlelit vignettes designed, absolutely, to charm his guests and fill the Hall with intricate skeins of colour and fragrance, redolent of the Highlands. Even Robinson is impressed – only distracted from his attentions to the floral displays by the polite cough of his house steward behind him.

'The first guests,' the man says.

Sir William is aware the steward is eyeing him with some caution. No doubt, in his experience, a host does not concern himself with table settings. And, in all honesty, Sir William finds it strange himself that he should. If ever entertaining Oban becomes an established part of his activities, he thinks, he certainly will not be found fiddling with the flowers – or anything else. But tonight he feels unusually nervous and he knows this anxiety began when, against his better judgement, he was persuaded to hold this event.

'The first guests are arriving, sir.'

Sir William spun round. 'Guests? This early? Good Lord, the ladies aren't down yet. Where's Mr Pettigrew? Who are they?'

'Townsfolk.'

From that single-word response, Sir William recognises how ill-conceived his servants feel a French-style Midsummer Ball to be – if held in the north of Scotland. *If the staff – who usually express no view at all – are doubtful, then, God help us all,* thinks Sir William. *And what does Young Pettigrew really hope to gain by it?*

In fact, the more he knows of Young Pettigrew, the more he feels the man is a loose cannon and more trouble than he is worth. But, now, at Sir William's signal, with a flurry of paper and a twang of catgut, the musicians burst into life – exploring a Highland version of Vivaldi's Winter Largo. Though not unpleasant, this is roughened by the grace notes of the bagpipes. It is also the wrong season.

*Bizarre,* thinks Sir William and goes to meet his guests.

There is some delay. The grounds seethe with *barouches coupés.*

The air quivers with fashionable ostrich feathers adorning the ladies' hair. Groomsmen shout and, as they are coaxed into spaces too small for them, horses noisily protest. The new *bourgeoisie* of Oban has arrived but cannot set down. The drive is blocked.

Alone on the steps, Sir William waits. In the absence of his co-hosts, Pettigrew and the Lady of the House – who, given her Gallic temperament, could easily decide not to attend at all – Sir William settles upon another unusual course of action. Protocol, as it is understood by all attending, must be breached.

'All very informal,' he says to each guest, when they finally extract themselves from the morass of the lawns. 'All very informal. Supper and dancing with friends. Please do go in. Please do go in.'

But the ballroom, he thinks, will be hard-pressed to hold so many 'friends'. It seems the whole town of Oban has turned out – at least, the whole of the new middle-classes. Client after client, he notes, is making the laborious journey up his stone steps, admiring porticos and pillars built with the fulsome revenues of his legal practice. They are admiring, he is amused to observe, what they have themselves paid for. But he continues to greet them with civility, and mostly by name.

* * *

Then Pettigrew appeared. Sir William allowed himself a flicker of the eyebrow. His own black silk evening dress, worn with pride a decade before at the French court and subsequently at the English court of St James' and at Holyrood Palace, now seemed shabby alongside the glorious Pettigrew. Pettigrew had chosen to appear as Louis XIV – the Sun King himself. He had interpreted 'French-style' as 'Fancy Dress'.

*The man has finally run mad!* thought Sir William.

But Pettigrew muttered, 'My, what a sight!' And, warming to his theme, he continued, addressing Sir William out of the side of his painted mouth, 'There are rich pickings here. These gowns, alone, will have cost the owners dearly. Pity they don't know how to wear them. But then,' he added with a sniff, 'any attempt at being fashionable would be doomed to failure in this part of the world.'

Returning his amazed eyes to his guests, Sir William did wonder whether Pettigrew had a point. The townswomen were waddling in waves up the steps towards the welcoming party. Many had chosen – out of some imagined deference to Adelaide de Fontenoy – to wear what they believed to be French court dress. However, stays failed to restrict waistlines. Too much rouge and blooming bosoms – gorged on new wealth – made ship's figureheads of their owners. And wide-hooped skirts swayed in a brisk sea breeze that threatened to blow them off course. *Oban Bay holding a fleet of foreign traders,* thought Robinson, vastly entertained and chuckling.

But, though the steps of Robinson Hall were now the setting for parody, for a venal lawyer, the sight was heart-warming. Such a client gathering of *Robinson & Pettigrew, Attorneys at Law* had never been seen before. The sheer numbers were impressive, the money represented almost impossible to calculate. And, under the spell of Adelaide de Fontenoy and embracing its destiny, Robinson Hall was ready to welcome them. *But,* thought the canny Robinson, recognising the hand of his junior partner in the arrangements, *Why has Pettigrew invited all these people?*

'I need to have a feel for local society.' Pettigrew commented as if he had heard.

'Why?' Robinson's eyebrows flickered again.

'These people need to protect their new money. They're not used to wealth. They'll need to put their new money in trusts. They'll need to make wills to prevent their money going to the undeserving. They'll need property transfers. They'll need me. They'll need us.'

*Young Pettigrew,* thought Robinson, *is building himself a gallows.*

At this point, the wife of the distillery manager broke from the fleet. The new distillery was the source of much of the new wealth now on display and Mrs Ballachulish carried the duties of social leadership. She was also trailing her unmarried daughter, Fiona, in her wake.

'Sir William, I do rather hope my Fiona can be a friend to the young Mademoiselle de Fontenoy and to your new visitor, Miss Pettigrew. At that age, girls do like to be able to gossip, you know, Sir William. And little goes on in this town that Fiona doesn't know about.'

'I like a little gossip, myself' replied Sir William, smiling. The young Fiona, pasty and smelling of indoors, would scarcely have access to his sources of news – the whores, spies and other low-life of the town – and would scarcely be up to challenging him. Even so, he politely offered mother and daughter refreshment.

Mrs Ballachulish, however, was not to be moved from her position at his side so easily. 'But where are the young ladies?' she continued, her fan fluttering even more than her eyelashes. 'We are all so anxious to see young ladies of such high fashion. Straight from the French Court, I hear. Tell me, does Mademoiselle de Fontenoy –'

'Lady Robinson,' corrected Robinson, adding inaudibly to himself 'Or very nearly.'

Mrs Ballachulish gleamed, like a spaniel on a quarry. 'Does the young Lady Robinson often hear from the Queen herself? From Her Highness. From Queen Marie Antoinette.'

*Mrs Ballachulish,* thought Robinson, *could not resist the siren-song of the name, 'Marie Antoinette'.* She clearly repeated the words as often as she could in her conversation. But, when Sir William looked into the woman's eager, up-turned face, he understood how immersed in ignorance Oban stood, regarding France and its Revolution. As indeed he himself would be without access to Adelaide's 'secret' letters.

*Should I enlighten this woman?* he wondered, as she wheezed with curiosity before him but he then abandoned the idea as far too time-consuming and probably not worth the candle.

He also wondered from her glazed expression whether she had understood the tidbit of information he had fed her, indicating how his ward would soon be his wife. This, he felt, was information necessary to his standing – to be delivered in the form of the tiniest piece of gossip in salons throughout the town. This snippet would render respectable the arrangements at Robinson Hall for the whole of his Oban clientele. And this was the woman, he felt, to do it. A day at the most, he was sure, was all it would take to spread the news of his impending nuptials and, looking at her panting bosom, he realised he need concern himself no more. She had the matter in hand. He could leave her now to make a start on the broadcasting of that very rumour.

Besides, he realised, a hush had fallen upon the thronging townsfolk. Adelaide de Fontenoy – a vision lit by sun, moon and starlight – had appeared at the end of the Hall and Oban was craning its neck to see. Unlike her guests, Adelaide had eschewed panier and pad. Instead, like Marie Antoinette in *Le Petit Trianon* at Versailles, she had adopted the *Chemiselareine* dress, its daring freedoms in tune with the grace of her movements. For those aware of such things, the only point of controlling structure was her high-waisted sash – made of silk as blue as the midsummer sky – which gathered in the folds of white muslin billowing about her. But the effect of swirl and cling was magical. Oban declared itself charmed and clamoured to meet her. And, now at her side, clamping his big hand firmly on her waist, Sir William laid claim. At last, at the entrance to the ballroom, he and 'his ward and wife-to-be' Adelaide de Fontenoy, were officially welcoming their guests and the party could begin.

It did not escape Robinson, however, that, with his usual arrogance, Pettigrew was already moving among the crowd – introducing himself. Some guests had met him before, on his clandestine forays into the town. But, Sir William could see, jaws were dropping as young Pettigrew clicked around the ante-rooms in his heeled shoes. With the addition of his wig, he was now a vision in gold brocade, standing almost a head taller than the rest of the guests.

*Ridiculous,* thought Sir William, eyeing Pettigrew. *The whole affair.* He now abandoned Adelaide de Fontenoy to the party, resentful of the stiff resistance he could feel seeping from her through his grip. *Like a reproach from the Almighty.* Weary of this game and out of sorts, he moved to the vantage point of the punch bowl as, in the blossoming chaos, more and more guests were arriving, the musicians played on and the house steward took over the duties of welcoming guests, complete with announcements.

*It is,* Robinson feared, *to be a long night.*

But, once at the refreshment table, he was just about to pour himself a soothing cup when he sensed a fluttering among the distaff side of Oban's new *bourgeosie. Alarm in the hen coop,* he thought. Some of the ladies were scurrying away with their daughters to the far side of the ballroom. Some – such as the courageous, and indefatigable Mrs Ballachulish – were pushing daughters against the tide towards the entrance. And daughters – such as Fiona Ballachulish – were rendered feverish at what they saw looking down the Hall steps and over the Park.

As the amber moon, clinging to the horizon, spilled liquid light over the eastern hills, there appeared a single rider riding a thoroughbred horse of rare quality. Nearing the Hall's sparkling granite facade, with a spray of gravel and an easy grace, the rider dismounted and then sprang up the stone staircase, two steps at a time. His shirt was of whitest linen, frothing at the neck with the finest Belgian lace; his sleek jacket was cut from luxurious blue velvet; his buttons had been worked in finest quality silver. His insignia were encrusted with sea-washed jewels. His long brown hair gleamed, loose in the midsummer starlight. And, when he flashed his azure eyes around the company gathered before him, the daughters of Oban to a girl swooned.

* * *

Malcolm Craig Lowrie, however, did not notice. Pausing at the head of the steps, he was beguiled by what he saw. The east-facing portico of Robinson Hall was dark but a central atrium ran all the way through the house, lit by midsummer sunlight from huge windows placed at the western end. Softened by exquisite tapestry and drapes, the Hall spoke welcome. But the fragrant wild Scottish flowers – gracing every surface – called up all that was most dear to Craig Lowrie and Craig Lowrie was enchanted.

Then, unbidden into his mind came the memory of the old man on the quay, of John Campbell. John Campbell, he remembered, had been forced to leave *his* heartland. The memory cut. At once, Craig Lowrie swung his hair from his eyes and moved forward to seek out his host, as good manners dictated.

But, as he pressed through the crowd, his mind was still alert. He had always been familiar with military architecture – such as the medieval keep at Castle Craig Lowrie – or demonstrations of aristocratic power such as the ducal arrangements at Inveraray. But now, as he moved through the anterooms towards the ballroom, he recognised a shift in the spirit of the times. New buildings, like those in Robinson Park, were now everywhere being designed by architects, such as Robert Adam, with solely domestic purpose, and this development in architecture was just one of many new and enlightened 'ideas' coming to the Highlands fanned by French thought. Intrigued, Craig Lowrie was particularly curious as to what these new ideas would mean for people like himself, the lairds of a hierarchical society in a wild country that did not easily submit to change. But, in this time of change, he also feared something important may be lost. He grappled with its identity.

The Duke of Argyll wanted to persuade him to be his tacksman but Craig Lowrie was wary. Once an honoured military leader, the tacksman was fast becoming a mere farm manager. And, in Argyll's case, this meant heinously rack-renting tenants or, worse, clearing the land of all human occupation. This did not seem to be an advance. *No, while my clan look to me, I'll be no man's tacksman,* Craig Lowrie thought, knowing he was now at war. *Ardnackaig!* The cry clutched at his heart.

But, here, on Midsummer Night at Robinson Park, he was looking forward to a few hours' holiday – particularly as now before him stood Adelaide de Fontenoy, the loveliest woman he had ever seen.

From behind her, the midsummer night's sun gilded her beneath the softness of her gown. A sweet-scented posy of lilies of the valley nestled in the warmth of her bosom. And, netting the miraculous sunlight, a silver braid tamed the drift of her hair, entwining its dark curls with fresh roses of purest white. Craig Lowrie already knew where he had seen her before. As well as this dream of a woman shimmering in light, she was also the Dark Lady of the Quayside. Hers was the beautiful face he had glimpsed in the darkness of her carriage. Hers was the unutterable sadness.

But there was more. He knew – with a deep awareness that rocked his world – that he had met her in France, ten years before. Then, fourteen-years-old and grieving, Malcolm Craig Lowrie had been enmeshed in the intrigues of his guardian, Argyll, and beset by French courtiers. But a silent and beautiful child had been watching him across the chaos of the French court. Then, with quiet wisdom beyond her years, she had taken his hand in hers and softly kissed his cheek – a simple kindness. He would have thanked her – heartfelt – for it. But, almost at once, the silent and beautiful child was gone, lost in the crowds, and he was left with only dreams. Oh, yes, Malcolm Craig Lowrie had been then – and was still – drawn on a silken thread to Adelaide de Fontenoy.

*'Madame'*, he said, approaching her. She offered him her hand. As he kissed it, gently, she sank into a curtsey and raised her beautiful eyes to his. In French, he enquired of her health, complimented her on her arrangements and wished her well for the evening. She responded to his questions in English. He asked her whether she missed France. She responded that she did but it had been some time since she was there and she believed it was all changed now.

'I believe so, *Madame'*, he said.

Politeness dictated he should now stop monopolising his hostess. He retired to the refreshment table. He accepted some water from a servant and continued to gaze at her – as, laughing, she whirled and sparkled through the ballroom. He thought of his mother. He thought of Jennet Awe offering him love and loyalty without condition. He had always accepted the love of both these women without question. He thought of the kindness of the French courtesan, Amelie. He thought of the women of the kitchen and the women on his tenanted farms. But now, suddenly he wanted to trace the curve of Adelaide de Fontenoy's perfect cheek with an ungloved hand and unpin the roses from her hair. He wanted to talk with this lovely woman till the sun rose. He wanted her to stay with him all his life. And, with shock, he realised, she was now and always his heartland.

He also recognised he was not alone in his admiration. All the good burghers of Oban, it seemed, were queuing up to offer her their sword-arms. Would he have to fight for the attention of this woman? Then, he noted – as his breath stopped sharply in his chest – she was glancing at him, as drawn to him as he to her. He wondered, *Is she remembering something of France too?* Yet there was something else in those glances. There was also distrust. He had to find out why. He set down his water glass and was preparing to cross the room once more, when Sir William appeared at his side.

'She is lovely, isn't she?'

With those few words, Sir William laid claim to Adelaide de Fontenoy and Craig Lowrie gasped.

Only a few weeks before, Rab MacDonald had found the trail of the English mercenary and followed broken, stained and torn vegetation through the woods to Robinson's hidden Palace. Then he had brought news to the Craig Lowrie at *The Three Fishes*. From Rab, Craig Lowrie had learned that the Lady Emma was a 'house guest' up at Arduaine. At the same time, he had learned that Robinson Hall's owner, lawyer and baronet Sir William Robinson, was to be married to a young French woman. And, on that very day, while delivering the invitation to this Midsummer Ball, Pettigrew had confirmed all this. But Craig Lowrie had not really made the connection until now. *How could that beautiful and silent child be married to this thing?* He was aware that alongside him, Robinson was perspiring profusely but all he said was, 'Aye, so. You are fortunate indeed. I am Malcolm Craig Lowrie. I am at your service, Sir William.'

'I believed you to be.' Robinson offered Craig Lowrie his hand and observed the young man from under his brows as he took it. Then, Robinson enquired about the arduous nature of the ride north and whether Craig Lowrie had come by carriage. He apologised for the *mêlée* on the drive and hoped the grooms had cleared the burghers' *barouches* to ease his path.

'They have indeed,' smiled Craig Lowrie. 'But – no matter, Sir William. I rode and only from the town tonight.'

'Ah, yes, your rooms. On the Quay.'

If Craig Lowrie was surprised, there was no sign. He merely responded, 'Precisely so.'

At this point, Pettigrew joined them. As he helped himself to yet more punch, his eyes were flashing round the crowded assembly, absorbing the sightings of commercial prey before him. But, when Robinson introduced Craig Lowrie, Pettigrew's weasel eyes flashed no more. Robinson thought to himself a lesser man than the Craig Lowrie would have quailed in the face of Pettigrew's sudden and undiluted interest.

'You came,' said Pettigrew.

'Did you think I would not?'

'You know each other?' Robinson asked with an appearance of surprise.

'Aye, Mr Pettigrew was kind enough some weeks ago to attend on me in my chambers down at *The Three Fishes.'*

'Now why would that be?' said Robinson, pouring a cup of punch for Craig Lowrie and one for himself. He was amused at the potential for entertainment Pettigrew's discomfort held. The fool hadn't yet realised that Robinson knew virtually everything, almost all of the time.

'Oh, never you mind that now,' said Pettigrew, apparently overwhelmed with excitement at the proximity of the Craig Lowrie. Robinson observed Pettigrew's mind racing with all the questions he wanted to put to Craig Lowrie about his lands. Craig Lowrie folded his arms across his chest, waiting, it seemed, for whatever would happen next. Pettigrew applied some snuff to his nostrils.

*And which question – in all politeness – will he ask first?* wondered Robinson.

Meanwhile, Adelaide de Fontenoy and Malcolm Craig Lowrie glanced at each other across the ballroom. And, hunting dog that he was, Sir William sensed it. Suddenly, he was not happy. *I must double the guard,* he thought.

# Chapter 27

## Robinson Park, Arduaine
## 21st June 1793

WHILE SIR WILLIAM was waiting for Pettigrew to finish the snuff-taking ritual which usually, he had come to recognise, heralded some move of devilry, Sir William was also thinking the musicians now needed to perform some music suitable for formal dancing. *A ball would not be a ball without dancing,* he thought. But, before he could do anything about that, Sir William found himself again accosted. His Gatekeeper stood before him. The man was stricken.

'Sir William,' he gibbered.

'What ever is the matter, man?'

'I couldn't stop them, Sir William. The grounds, they're breached. There're unauthorised armed men all over them.'

And, at that moment, the Duke of Argyll walked in. He stood at the entrance to the ballroom and allowed the company to register his presence. Even without a liveried entourage, from his demeanour, Sir William would have known him anywhere. But personally he would never have invited the Duke to anything as tawdry as this Midsummer Ball was turning out to be – due to the misguided interference of Pettigrew. This was not at all how he had planned his first audience with the Duke, when he had intended to broach the subject of Malcolm Craig Lowrie's outlawry.

*But who has invited his Grace?* Robinson wondered. Then the thought came to mind of Pettigrew's excitement, bubbling and spilling over, all evening. *The invitation must have come from Petti-*

*grew,* Robinson concluded, and, irritated, he was forced to cross the ballroom floor and, un-introduced, welcome Pettigrew's noble guest of honour.

Argyll accepted Robinson's welcome as his due and then moved forward into the room on a ducal progress. He addressed Robinson over his shoulder as he swept on. 'So, so. Quite, quite. And your lovely lady wife? Where is she? The incomparable Lady Robinson?'

'Soon to be, soon to be' Robinson began but then, Adelaide de Fontenoy appeared and curtsied deeply.

'Well my dear,' said the Duke, raising her up. 'Perhaps you'll introduce some of your guests to me. Are they tenants of mine? How amusing that will be! All of us together like this. How our Jacobin friends would enjoy that! And how beautiful you are – such hair, such eyes. I have only ever seen one other so beautiful.' For the moment, the Duke almost seemed prepared to abandon himself to reverie. Then he recovered, saying, 'Your reputation does you scant justice, my dear.'

Adelaide frowned. 'But I had thought my presence in Scotland – it was a secret. I cannot believe I have a reputation, your Grace.'

'The wrong word, perhaps. "Reputation". So given to denigration. Besides, I'm told, you are but recently here. For whatever reason that could be. However, whether in France or Scotland, there are few who would not be vanquished by your beauty.'

Armed as he was – broadsword to hip – this courtier style ill became the Duke. Robinson wondered where matters would go next. Craig Lowrie had at least had the manners to attend armed with no more than the *sgian dubh.* But, Robinson could see, His Grace was enjoying himself. His hand gripped Adelaide's arm like a mailed fist and together they cut a swathe to the refreshment table. The pain caused by his grip registered on Adelaide's face, something lost on neither Sir William nor Silas Pettigrew nor Malcolm Craig Lowrie.

'Ah, and my kinsman, Malcolm Craig Lowrie,' continued the Duke, pausing by the young man. He gazed pointedly at Craig Lowrie's kilt pin – the insignium of a MacDonald Laird of the Isles – and then decided to make light of it. 'Kilted as a MacDonald of the Isles today, I see. And your father a Campbell! Your mother had some strong power – even magical – to split your loyalties so profoundly.'

His smile did not reach his teeth and he added, 'You haven't responded to my proposal yet, I notice.'

'And news of the murderers?' countered the Craig Lowrie. Ardnackaig was never far from his thoughts. He still felt the weight of the young boys in his arms, the wetness of their blood.

The Duke held out his hand for Craig Lowrie to bend the knee before him. For a moment, no longer than a single breath, this seemed totally out of the question. And then, to Robinson's surprise, the young Laird seemed to think better of insult. Craig Lowrie bent his head almost imperceptibly over the Duke's ring – just this side of 'impolite'. The Duke hesitated, as if to say more but then moved on. Robinson was aghast. The significance of what had just happened – in this wild, uncivilised part of the Union – was clear. From Craig Lowrie, the Wolf of Dalriada, there had been the very slightest sign of deference – not enough for the Duke to be content but certainly given. *In return for...what?* wondered Robinson. His lawyer's nose scented dead rat – somewhere.

'And you? Who are you?' the Duke asked.

Pettigrew was beside himself with joy at Argyll's notice. He explained his position in the household and how it had been he who had sent the invitation to Argyll. Robinson – behind him – coughed but Pettigrew was unstoppable. *The man's impertinence was breathtaking,* Robinson thought. And Argyll, it appeared, thought so too. He held Pettigrew's gaze for a moment and then asked, 'Why are you dressed as the Sun King?'

Then the Duke seemed to tire of the conversation. He yawned and turned away, Adelaide still trapped by his arm. 'Dancing,' he said. 'Dancing that's what I came for.'

*Anything so patently untrue,* thought Robinson, *I've yet to hear.* Then, pleading dis-ease of the stomach and a preference for watching the young people dance – he retired to the punch bowl to watch proceedings. *More is afoot,* he felt, *than a desire to participate in an eightsome reel.* But the Duke seemed implacable. It was his pleasure to dance with the ladies, he said. The musicians and the piper shuffled through their music again. Vivaldi was abandoned. The conductor made a suggestion of formal court dance music, appropriate he felt to the occasion. It was declined. Discouraged, the conductor moved on to offer more traditional Scottish ceilidh music. The Duke accepted, his grip on Adelaide's arm never easing. The eights were established. The principals of the evening were obliged to stand up with the Duke. And the Duke settled into the dancing as if that was indeed his only purpose in being there.

From his vantage point of the punch bowl, Robinson could see the Duke's clear admiration of Adelaide. It was no more than he expected. As she moved, her lightness of foot was a delight, her dress clinging gracefully as she skipped and twirled. *Of course, of course.* Robinson had always recognised her beauty and now others could see it too. She was young; she was full of life. She was born for dancing and being admired. She bloomed in the candlelight of a ballroom – even in the false twilight of a Scottish midsummer night. Rescuing her from the French court, he thought again, was the best thing he had ever done. She was the loveliest thing he had ever known – truly a gift to God – at a time perhaps not too far in the future. And, he had to admit, watching Adelaide de Fontenoy create her own court among this disparate group of courtiers, he was jealous. Profoundly, dangerously jealous.

Now, he noticed, the dance had moved on. He lost sight of Adelaide in the *mêlée.* But he could still see how the Duke progressed. *The clever old devil,* thought Robinson. The Duke had quite without effort taken the hand of Miss Dilly Pettigrew.

Emma looked strangely older than her years tonight. Robinson considered it. Her appearance had trace notes of a secret, though Robinson could not at present guess what this could be. But against the provinciality of the company, she appeared no less than queenly. Dressed in green velvet, edged with silk, she was wearing the damaged necklace of the Bamburgh emeralds, which she had requested he remove from the safe-keeping of his quayside offices for this occasion. He could hardly have refused. *And her cropped auburn hair is trimmed intriguingly,* he thought, short at the back, curled at the front, a new style, named *à la victime.* Strange choice of words, thought Robinson, but something about this and her dress was not right. She seemed more to be dressed for the outdoors than a ball – *although of course, he knew little of fashion.* He decided to adopt his usual lawyers' policy. *When in doubt, do nought,* he thought. It had served him well in the past. And, for now, as the dance continued, it seemed *Miss Dilly Pettigrew* had no choice but to take the Duke's proffered hand.

'Ah, Miss Pettigrew, I believe,' the Duke smiled. 'You travelled North from Carlisle to stay here, I gather. Because of sickness, was it? Strange, I live closer to Carlisle than Oban is and I have not heard of plague in Carlisle. In fact, travellers come from there quite often to Inveraray – but with no tales of sickness at present.'

'It was a personal matter – sickness within the family.'

Ah, I see. And you have come to join your brother. How pleasant. How very pleasant!'

The conversation paused as the dance gave Emma to Pettigrew. As they danced, Emma watched Pettigrew for some moments, his tongue moistening his lips, his movements in the dance strangely disjointed as he turned his head this way and that to keep Adele in view. Then he seemed to realise that the hand he held was Emma's. The look he turned on her startled her. It was predatory. *But why her?* she thought, *He's clearly in love with Adele.*

Then the dance gave her back to the Duke.

'You don't speak with a Carlisle voice,' he continued, relentless. 'Northern English, yes, but not Carlisle.'

'I was sent away. To stay with relatives, Your Grace.' Emma was now uncomfortable. Her eyes lowered.

'And where would that have been?'

'Northumberland.'

'Ah!' said the Duke, more than satisfied with the discovery. 'I thought so.'

And the dance gave her back to Pettigrew.

'I tire', he said. 'Will you allow me to find you some punch?'

Emma could hardly continue to dance on her own so followed her 'brother' away from the floor. But instead of towards the buffet table, he led her into the shadows of the ballroom. She was alarmed. He had taken her wrist.

'Please, my lady, you must allow me a moment's private conversation. I admire you – tremendously –'

'Me?' Emma faltered. As she had seen the looks he gave Adele, she had no idea where this conversation could lead. But Pettigrew was not going to explain. Suddenly, he moved his grip from her wrist to her waist. And, incensed by his feelings for Adele, he lunged at Emma's neck with his protuberant lips. Emma's revulsion gave her a strength she did not know she had. She reached for the nearest weapon. This happened to be a plate and the noise of the contact it made with Pettigrew's head caused stillness and silence to ripple through the dancers closest to them. Pettigrew crumpled. He was now laid out like a king's corpse, his dreams of marriage to an earl's daughter as shattered as the plate.

# Chapter 28

## Robinson Park, Arduaine
## 21st June 1793

BEFORE HE CAME to this northern fastness, Argyll had been working on rumour. Emma of Bamburgh was 'loose' in the region – somewhere – he was sure of it. But where? Craig Lowrie, if he'd known anything at all, was silent about the whereabouts of his 'sister-in-law'. Nor had he challenged the rumour of his alleged part in Jamie Craig Lowrie's murder. Argyll found it hard to accept this reticence when more powerful men than Craig Lowrie would abase themselves to do his bidding. The young man seemed to foil him on every front. But, even when hard-pressed by a curious Argyll on these points, Craig Lowrie had remained tight-lipped and silent.

*Tiresome,* Argyll had been thinking. *The whole business.* From the moment over a mouthful of scrambled eggs at breakfast when he had thought of establishing a power brokerage between the kingdoms of Great Britain, he had wanted to lay his hands on the Lady Emma. She was his route to the hearts and minds of Northumberland. But where had she disappeared to? There were more false trails laid among these hills than a rabbit warren. No-one, it seemed, knew where anyone was, let alone an English girl with a fancy necklace, who should have stood out like the flames of a beacon against the heather. But no. Every clachan, every farm where she was reported to have been yielded nothing but the beginning of yet another trail. And most of these led Argyll back to the silent Craig Lowrie.

'Vexing,' he sighed. 'For a reputedly hard man, Craig Lowrie seems to call in outstanding loyalty from his tenants and stockmen. Or perhaps he disciplines them in ways that even I couldn't better.'

But then – when the situation seemed at its least hopeful – a strange invitation had arrived. By hand. At Argyll's door. About a ball, to be held at some place in the north of the region called Robinson Hall near Oban. Argyll would usually have not even heard about the invitation. His house steward would have seen to its less-than-polite rejection. But the man was bribed, perhaps? And the handwritten invitation had been placed on the board next to Argyll at breakfast. The Duke was intrigued. He had picked up the card. And – like Malcolm Craig Lowrie – had not been able to resist the bait that Pettigrew set.

The superficial purpose of the evening was to introduce a Miss Dilly Pettigrew from Carlisle and this had set the hairs standing on the back of Argyll's neck. Carlisle and Bamburgh were two places most significant in his current, ambitious strategising. But he did not want the usual pomp and circumstance to attend his movement round the region. This would set the doe running. So, in due course, he had bidden a good evening to her Grace, his wife, saying 'You don't need to attend this, my dear. I'll go alone. It'll be a tedious matter of keeping the *bourgeoisie* happy, I expect.'

He had then gathered his most trusted riding servants around him and headed north, convinced this 'soiree' would produce some news of Emma Bamburgh. But, if nothing else, he thought, even if the Lady Emma is nowhere to be seen, he would enjoy a dance. He also thought, *Why would a young Frenchwoman suddenly appear – without forewarning – as a Highland hostess? There is mystery here. But, at least the food will be good.*

However, the moment he saw Miss Dilly Pettigrew, he recognised her at once as the Lady Emma of Bamburgh. *How could she not be?* Tonight, there was a mock meekness about her but he sensed a degree of kindred aristocratic spirit. And she was wearing that famously vulgar emerald necklace – her dowry, he believed. She was the prize he hoped for. When he first saw her, he imagined that, at some quiet moment during the evening, he would deliver a subtle but pressing invitation and whisk Emma away to Inveraray. He would then be able to open discussions of her role in his expansionist plans and this would all be conducted in a civilised fashion with her as a 'house guest' until an alternative *modus operandi* presented itself.

But now, Argyll saw, the Northumberland girl had been exposed to the whole company by that buffoon lawyer, Pettigrew. *Pettigrew was supposed to be the girl's brother. What was he thinking of? Lunging at a young girl in the shadows. Of course, she flared.*

And, then, as a result, the Duke had been forced to set two of his retainers on her. Admittedly they had none too gently man-handled her from the anonymity of the alcove and the Duke found himself forced to address her as if she'd been caught taking the silver at Inveraray. And Oban had no doubt not missed a trick. *Yes, vexing,* he thought, preparing to take control.

'So, my dear, not Dilly Pettigrew then. I wonder. Would you be so kind as to introduce yourself now – in full, with no further deception? These games, they are not worthy of you. Lady Emma.'

'Perhaps, Sir, the niceties could have been better preserved if you had not told servants to lay hands on me in this way. I am a lady, an earl's daughter. You have no right to have your people touch me. If Jamie Craig Lowrie were here...'

Emma faltered, her voice losing courage.

The Duke's eyes narrowed. 'But he is not,' He spoke almost in a whisper. 'Or is he?' He looked around quickly but could see nothing amiss. He did not move but continued in the low voice that he knew every Oban ear was straining to hear.

'Perhaps he is not. But then this foolish little game you've been playing – it could be more sinister. I need to know what you meant by it. And, for a start, perhaps you could introduce yourself to these good people of Oban – with your full name.'

The Duke was insistent. He continued to address her from across the ballroom, his power creeping across the floor like a blood-stain. He knew what he was asking. The world was waiting for a public declaration of her widowhood or her wifehood.

Then, at the doorway leading to the kitchens, a man in a hooded cloak appeared.

'Jamie!' cried out Emma. And even the Duke of Argyll was wrong-footed.

# Chapter 29

## Robinson Park, Arduaine
## 21st June – Midsummer Night – 1793

ROBINSON'S MEN had not seen Jamie Craig Lowrie in their midst before it was too late. He had moved across the park and into the servants' hall while Argyll's men and Robinson's men – augmented for the occasion – argued the toss for the control of the grounds. Now here he was in the heart of the company. Emma heard the gasp of the Oban townsfolk and watched as the hooded cloak fell away from the tall apparition at the Duke of Argyll's side. Without a doubt, there stood Jamie Craig Lowrie. Emma felt an immobility descend on the crowd – dense and paralysing – even while the ballroom simmered with primitive hostilities and political responses. Jacobite or Kingsman? The thin veneer of the Oban *bourgeoisie* was being challenged. And the sight of Jamie Craig Lowrie – dressed in the once outlawed Highland tartan of a MacDonald, as his grandfather had been at Culloden, fifty years earlier – took Emma's breath away, along with everyone else's. Jamie Craig Lowrie was alive and well and a fine-looking young man. Everything Emma had ever dreamed of – growing up, picturing her marriage. And he was here, alive, with blood in his veins and light in his eyes and fire in his heart. And hers. He was hers – as he had said – no matter what and forever.

On the other hand, Robinson stood struck as if by lightening. He felt his plans for his future comfort, his life – even his salvation – splintered and sinking like lost vessels before the storm. His current strategem for the discomfiture of Malcolm Craig Lowrie – outlawry and the forfeit of land and title, perhaps even execution – had had as its main plank, the treasonous murder of Jamie Craig Lowrie. *But here – vexingly – stood the young firebrand. And far from murdered!*

In Jamie's hands were two broadswords. Now he tossed one high into the air. Emma watched it as it spun, glittering in the light of a thousand candles. And she saw it come down into the waiting hand of Jamie's cousin, Malcolm Craig Lowrie.

Until then, she had been so irritated by the jostling from Argyll's manservants she had not noticed Malcolm Craig Lowrie's swift and silent arrival at her side. And the first intimation she had that he was there was the sudden tensing of one of the men. As the servant's fingers gripped her, she could feel his lascivious over-familiarity replaced by fear. And then she heard the crack of bone and tooth as Craig Lowrie's fist found the man's jaw. She didn't wait to be asked. She turned to the other servant grappling with her on the other side. And her riding boot found the softness between his legs. Both of Argyll's men now fell away from her – crippled and speechless – and she was free.

'C'mon lassie, what's keeping you now?' Jamie grinned as she ran to him.

'You've taken time yourself, Jamie Craig Lowrie.'

'But you've bided, waiting for me.'

'Of course. I had no better offer.'

And the young lovers disappeared before the stillness in the ballroom could break.

Before he left, however, Malcolm Craig Lowrie turned to the transfixed Duke. 'Ardnackaig,' he said so that the whole of Oban could hear. 'I'm waiting. I want the murderer's head.'

Then he was gone.

Within seconds, the Duke was bellowing orders to his harassed men but the Oban assembly suddenly sparked into life and clustered to the doors and windows of the ballroom. Every man and woman fought to see what was going to happen and unintentionally prevented even the keenest and fittest of Campbell followers from making headway. Outside, without leadership, the Duke's company tangled with the townsfolk's grooms. Stockmen and shepherds as they were, the Argyll company made a good fist of it but both sides got broken pates and hurt pride for their pains. Robinson's imported army – the English mercenaries – might have made a better show, had they known precisely who they were supposed to attack but all the Scots seemed identical to them. And, once in the grounds away from Robinson Hall, Malcolm Craig Lowrie took control of the escape.

'Walk. Don't run. If we don't look as though we're in a hurry, this "army" will not be fashed by us.'

It was true. Argyll's riding servants had heard their liege lord's bellow and pushed up the steps to answer the call – sword drawn and pistol ready. But they met a down-flowing tide of the citizens of Oban, spurred on by the pressing thought it was time to seek the safety of their own beds. The charge of the Campbell clansmen – leaderless – was broken and routed by whalebone and petticoat. But, as the Duke himself would recognise, his men could hardly – in this new age of enlightenment – have perpetrated a slaughter of the *bourgeoisie.* As for the Duke, although used to having his own way, he was a political animal and he recognised a shift in the mood of the populace when he saw it. A massacre in pursuit of his own kinsmen and the young girl he hoped would be his 'house guest' would also, he felt, invite comment.

Meanwhile, Malcolm Craig Lowrie was saying, 'Uncle Argyll being there was an unpleasant surprise.'

Jamie side-stepped a wandering Campbell clansman, saying 'Certainly was. What did he want?'

Steering the Lady Emma through choppy seas of people moving inefficiently around the grounds, Malcolm suggested 'You? Me, perhaps? Or perhaps it was you, Emma? You, as bait for us, perhaps? Who knows?'

The Craig Lowries heard a shriek from the steps, as Molly Ballachulish sought to chivvy and make good her departure and a cluster of grooms attempted to back carriage horses into the shafts of the distillery *barouche,* the Ballachulish *equipage.*

'A punt then. Just to see what would happen. These aristocrats, they'd bet on anything,' continued Jamie as the Craig Lowrie cousins negotiated the rout.

'We did.' Malcolm smiled and shrugged. But there was no time to speculate. Within a few minutes, the cousins and Emma had walked through the camp towards the pre-arranged rendezvous where Jennet Awe and John Stewart Macdonald held their horses. It was time to go.

Once on her horse, Emma had time to admire the 'escape'. When Jamie Craig Lowrie had touched her face through the railings of the Park, she had known – with all her heart – that he would come for her. But, appearing at the ball had been a wonderful folly and bravado – so typical of Jamie. On such a public occasion. She didn't care that this was not sensible. It was a wild, wonderful gesture of romance – even if, for trouncing the Campbells yet again, Jamie's cousin, Malcolm, would soon have double a king's ransom on his head and Jamie might come in for a spot of outlawry too!

'Ride now, young lady' said Jennet Awe, bringing her to earth. 'And no ideas now – I'm here to watch your virtue. I'm your new Lady's Maid.' And, spinning to the south, the three of them gave their horses their heads.

Meanwhile, just outside the Robinson Park gates, Malcolm Craig Lowrie was still unmounted and motionless, gazing back at Robinson Hall. Then Father Macdonald laid a hand on his arm and said, 'You'd better go. Go on, down – beyond Craig Lowrie, to the Mull. I'll meet you all there. As soon as I can.'

'You?'

'I swear I'll perform the sacrament. I'll marry the young ones. As is fitting. As was intended. As was half-done.'

Only then did Craig Lowrie mount the horse tendered to him, 'I'll have to see the castle safe,' he said. It would now again be a target for Argyll. The country was about to close down. 'But Jamie can go on. He knows the land round there – what's ours – he can feed himself and Emma well. And Jennet Awe too. I'll remove Argyll's men from the Mull and away from Castle Craig Lowrie. I swear we'll have the wedding away from the threat of Campbells. They'll not be interrupting it again. I'll pin the Campbells down near Inveraray while everything's arranged and meet you all there, on the Mull. In due course. Don't fret. I'll find you.'

But, astride his horse, which was spinning ready for action, Craig Lowrie still gazed back to the Hall, now alive with light from moon, star and candle. The old priest tugged at his coat jacket.

'Make haste, Craig Lowrie. Argyll – or someone – won't be far behind you,' he said.

'I thank you for your help, John Stewart Macdonald'.

'I've had more words from you tonight, Malcolm Craig Lowrie, than in all our acquaintance. And I'm beginning to think well of you.'

Craig Lowrie paused, briefly reining in his horse. He studied the priest for the moment and said, curtly, 'I shouldn't.'

Then Craig Lowrie was away into the night and John Stewart Macdonald walked back to the Hall.

# Chapter 30

## Robinson Park, Arduaine, Oban
## 21st June 1793

ARGYLL WAS NOW READY to be off on the road to Inveraray. His 'adventure' had turned out far more disappointing than he had imagined it would. What should have been a pressing invitation to the Lady Emma to 'come and stay' had turned into an abduction – and not by him. And now he was forced to retire from the field.

No, he thought, better to go back to Inveraray and organise a sweep of the countryside around Castle Craig Lowrie. An example had to be made. Whatever the Craig Lowries thought, their lands were – and always had been – part of his fief. *But this was not a matter for the Oban bourgeoisie to concern themselves with.* He would now revert to the age-old way, the call of Blood. Nice concerns for the well-being of the *bourgeoisie* were, in this, irrelevant.

So, almost immediately after the Craig Lowries left, he had turned to his host Robinson and excused himself with his usual *sang froid.* 'I want to make sure the windows of the glasshouse are closed. You can't be too careful with the temperatures in the Highlands,' he said. 'Even now a sudden chill could kill the more delicate of my new flowering plants.'

Robinson suppressed an impulse to make a polite protest and acknowledged the Duke's pressing need to return to his orchids. Smiling affably, he made the best of a ludicrous situation as the Duke bellowed at those of his followers still close to him and marched off.

The ballroom suddenly seemed much emptier but Robinson's evening was not over yet. Finally eschewing the punch, he poured himself a whisky and watched the servants clear up. This he found a soothing occupation that gave him time to consider everything that had happened. There was much to think about. Events spun through his mind and questions arose at every turn.

*Still, when in doubt,* thought the lawyer in him again, *do nought.*

He sipped his whisky, thoughtfully, and then realised 'Ah, that was what it was. Emma did look very fine but she was wearing riding clothes, not a ball gown. I should've paid more attention to my lady's art. Only she could create a riding habit that looked sufficiently like a ball gown to deceive a whole ballroom.'

'Thinking of whom', he said aloud, seizing a passing footman, 'Where is Lady Robinson?' The man shook his head. He didn't know. He had things to do. He couldn't chat. He ran off. However, Robinson understood everything. *I've lost her,* he thought.

But he firmly put this complex issue on one side for later consideration in his journal. There were more immediate matters to attend to. Almost, but not quite overwhelmed, he now turned his attention to the supine Pettigrew and flung punch over his head. He was just forcing his inert colleague into a sitting position – propped against the table leg – when he felt his sleeve tugged urgently. It was the Gatekeeper again.

'Sir William, there's another crowd of them arrived. I can't keep people like this out – not with the gate off its hinges. These people wouldn't have waited anyway.'

Robinson dropped the still hazy Pettigrew and turned in time to see Lord Bamburgh and the Lady Eleanor enter the Ballroom.

'William, you old rogue. What disarray I find you in. Broken gates, campfires abandoned on the lawns and now drunken sots under the tables!'

Had he been fully conscious, Pettigrew's humiliation would have been complete. Even Robinson was at this point close to speechless.

'We thought we'd come on a progress, William. Make use of the long midsummer evening. We've ridden almost all the way from Glasgow in one day. Is that not admirable? Make us welcome now!'

'But why would you do such a thing? Without warning like this?'

'To fetch Emma, of course. But also to see your new bloodstock, don't you know!'

Lady Eleanor tutted. 'I could not care a fig for your bloodstock,

William. I want to see my daughter – and at once. Where is she, William? Is she safe? Your letters, they were so – incomplete! Really!'

Sir William was by now a little recovered. 'You've just missed her,' he said. 'And her husband – if that's what he is. And the Duke of Argyll...'

Edwin, Lord Bamburgh, helped himself to a glass of punch. Then he tossed a sugared almond into the air and caught it between his perfect teeth. 'A small gathering of intimates, then,' he grinned.

# Chapter 31

## Robinson Park, Arduaine
## 22nd June – Midsummer Night – 1793

OVER THE LAST FEW weeks, Adele had never been as sure as Emma that the 'rescue' would work. When Emma came back from meeting Jamie on the fringes of the Park, Emma was delighted at the boldness of it all. *An abduction in plain view – what could be safer?* But Adele knew Robinson had turned the Park into all but a fortress, with sentries and soldiers at every point around its perimeter, and that Emma herself had only by luck avoided them.

'Why did Jamie not come to the door?' Adele had asked. But, as she did so, she recognised Jamie's wild reputation had long threatened to earn him an attractive price on his head. He was also reputed to be dead. Coming to the door had not been one of his choices.

'And this is so romantic,' replied Emma, brimming over with youth and love.

'One man – a young man – against so many soldiers! He could be killed.'

'He won't. He couldn't be. And please, dear, dearest Adele, will you help us?'

So, although unconvinced by the overall plan, Adele had agreed to create for Emma the most cunning of riding habits – one that could double as a ball gown. Throughout her whole life, her talents had been leading up to this moment and so, deftly, her fingers worked to produce a masterpiece.

The abduction had then unfolded like a well-constructed eightsome reel. People had changed partners, people had stood idle, people had moved into the dance and become the principals and all with seamless success. Of course, Jamie's Jacobite Highland gentleman motif was a gratuitous and flamboyant touch – introduced to stun the crowd to silence and immobility. And the chief architect of the plan, Malcolm Craig Lowrie, had apparently indulged his young cousin on this dubious point.

Though his own arrival had been no less spectacular in its way, Craig Lowrie's initial role in the escape had been more low-key than Jamie's. Coming as a guest, to Robinson Park, he had been forced to walk weaponless past Robinson's private army. And he had depended totally on Jamie making it through the kitchens with everything they would need. Adele shuddered. So many aspects of this plan could have gone wrong but, thanks to Jamie's exuberance and Malcolm Craig Lowrie's experience, nothing had. But the Midsummer Ball – the first ever to be held in the painted palace of the Robinson Hall ballroom – was now well and truly over.

The Craig Lowries and Emma had dissolved into the night – their brilliance clouded by darkness – as if before the eyes of the watching company. The more superstitious had crossed themselves. And, after that critical moment, the Duke had bellowed in frustration and marched towards the exit, cuffing his attendants into life. In the turmoil that followed, Adele had moved away from the crowd and into the shadows of Robinson Hall's corridors seeking out her own apartments.

On her way, she met one of Robinson's servants, hurrying to the ballroom.

'Is the Lady Emma gone?' she asked.

'Aye, madam. Taken by the Craig Lowries. I don't know what's happened. But, she seemed willing.'

'Just tell me – are they all three gone?'

'Yes, like magic. They just disappeared.'

'And His Grace? Where is he?'

'Last I heard, My Lady, he was going back to Inveraray. He was calling for his horse. I must go, My Lady. Please.'

'Yes, yes. Off you go. But wait – where is Robinson?'

'Sir William is in the ballroom, My Lady. Now please, I must go.'

She released him. He was not willing to be drawn further. She could in any case picture the recriminations in the ballroom – and the anger. She, on the other hand, wanted to be alone. She wanted to think about the events of the evening and she wanted to think about Malcolm Craig Lowrie.

During her dislocated and lonely life, there had been men who had filled her with loathing. Pettigrew was one – with his sniffs and snorts and splutters and sliding, malign eyes. He made her flesh crawl. But now Malcolm Craig Lowrie was demanding feelings from her she had never felt before. She paused,suddenly unsure. How could a man like Malcolm Craig Lowrie ever love someone like her? After so many solitary years, she was meek and mouse-like, plain and dull. There was also a shadow about Malcolm Craig Lowrie, a powerful mystery she couldn't read. It made her wary. And, worse, she felt close to despair when she thought what Malcolm Craig Lowrie might think of Robinson's hold over her. Even the servants called her by Robinson's title. Did Craig Lowrie think she was already wed? Faced with Robinson's spinning wizardry with words, how could Craig Lowrie be anything but taken in by the old lawyer's tricks – tricks designed to cloud the truth? How could he not be revolted by the thoughts of *'mariage'* between Robinson – as lascivious and foul as any French courtier – and herself? But then, Adele thought again of the admiration Craig Lowrie had given her across the ballroom. And his smile. His frank and brilliant smile. And she hugged herself with delight.

As she walked the corridors, the Robinson family portraits gazed down at her. The whimsical half-smirk – inherited by Sir William – seemed as usual to mock her. But, for once, she did not care. Instead, her head and heart were filled with snatches of music from the ball. In these, she could hear the spirit of mountains and woods and sea. Was the music of the dance a spell? Or had she come to feel this country was her home now?

She started to run, suddenly afraid of a future of which her homeland of France would never be part. For a moment, she longed for the pavements of Paris once more beneath her feet. But then, she paused to press her feverish forehead against the cool glass of the windows giving out on to the wild, intractable land of Scotland and she thought of the dance, the eightsome reel. Malcolm Craig Lowrie's arms had encircled her with such strength, such tenderness. Such boldness in a dance was breathtaking. Whatever went on in the closet areas of the French court – and as a child she had been forced to witness it all – the formal court dances were false and passionless coquetry. She wanted to be free of that. When she thought of France now, she missed only the love of her mother, the kindness of Marie Antoinette and the joy of Gabrielle. The rest meant nothing to her.

At last, she crossed the linkway and smiled at the servant, crouched at her door.

'Goodnight,' she said.

'Goodnight, My Lady. Sleep well!'

The man, she thought, would sit there all night, keeping her safe. When Jamie took Emma's hand in the ballroom, the sea change in Adele's life had taken her breath away. Her strange world was shifting, her bizarre safety exploding. But there was still comfort to be had in this servant's face. She smiled again and thanked the servant for his patience.

'A pleasure, My Lady,' he replied, returning her smile. A French servant would not have done that. Yes, there is real comfort to be had here, she believed, in this Scotland. How could she have thought otherwise? And she thought of Malcolm Craig Lowrie again.

In her rooms, the candles had been lit and the fresh linen sheets turned back. Although it was midsummer night, it was chill and fires had been laid and torched in the huge hearths of her sitting rooms and bedroom. She felt cosseted. Then she found herself wondering whether Castle Craig Lowrie would be as comfortable. She blushed at the thought. Her rooms of a sudden felt stuffy. On impulse, she undid the shutters and opened the doors onto the night. There was a breeze, gentle, sleepy, from the sea to the west, scarcely moving the now darkening air. A trace scent came to her from the rose parterres. She stepped outside into the warm light of the amber moon. She remembered the ordure in the streets of Paris and she was glad to be away from there. She had indeed come to belong here – yes, even to love this strange cold land, for its beauty and for its purity.

For a moment, she stood there on the terraces, absorbing the silence and the layered blues of a Scottish midsummer night. Everything seemed poised and waiting as she looked at the stars. Who else would be looking up like her? Marie Antoinette and Gabrielle – so far away in Paris? Emma – with Jennet Awe to keep her safe – would they be looking at the stars together? And Malcolm Craig Lowrie – would he be looking at these bright stars alone? Adele shivered. That was folly. She turned and moved back into her rooms, her *Petit Trianon,* her sanctuary. For sanity and safety's sake, she should not think such things.

'Even so,' thought Adele with something like sadness, 'with Emma on the run, a friend is lost to me now. And I am alone again.'

After years of solitary living, the last few months spent in friendship with Emma had been almost like being at home with Gabrielle. The contrast was bitter. 'But,' she thought, 'at least Emma will be with Jamie. That is a comfort.'

She went to sit at her dressing table, straightening her combs and hairbrushes. She admired her favourite cutting shears. These shears were her badge of honour. Adelaide of Fontenoy of Burgundy was a talented seamstress. That was what they said. She smiled and began to unpin her hair. Now, from her richly shining curls, one by one, she pulled out the roses. They were still fresh. She placed each in the silver bud vases on her dressing table, her fingertips lingering on the candlelight-warmed rose petals. But, glancing across them, she also noted in the mirrors, how longing had now replaced despair in her eyes.

And then she heard the click of the door behind her.

* * *

It is Pettigrew.

'Where is –?' She is looking past him for the servant.

'Gone, My Lady. To the servants' hall. I told him Sir William requested he helped there. Oh, he wouldn't have left you alone. But I re-assured him. That I would be having a word with you. That you would not be alone.'

He slides the door-lock into place.

'No, My Lady, you will not be alone,' he repeats. He smiles and then, as he walks across the room towards her, she sees his sharp, yellowed teeth chewing his lower lip. Pettigrew – frustrated in his ambitions – is dangerous. But, with frustrated ambition over-laid by humiliation and lust, Pettigrew will be deadly. Fear stabs at her lungs, making it difficult to breathe, and then, before she can speak, his hand is across her mouth. She twists at the stench but his other arm holds her. She is unable to move.

'No, My Lady. No more words. No more quips and jokes and parodies. Oh, yes, I know, you see. You and the Lady Emma. You mocked me – together – you mocked me. But now...'

His breath stinks of too much snuff and too much stale wine and his grip is unforgiving. His free hand begins to explore her body. He clamps his damp fleshy lips on her mouth and she cannot cry out. He snuffles and snorts like a pig feeding on her. He pushes her backwards onto her bed and pins her down, even his scrawny form too much for her to push him away. She searches for a weapon but her hands can find only soft down bedding and she cannot avoid the insistence of that slobbering mouth. It sucks and splutters across her face. And, now hard between his legs, he is beginning to fumble with his breeches. *The weight of him, the odour!* she thinks and she is suddenly more afraid than she has ever been in her life.

But now, she does not hesitate. As he forces his fleshy tongue into her mouth, she bites. He yowls with pain, pulling away, and, spitting blood, he draws back his fist. He seems to pause – for a long, long moment. Then, he snarls and hits her and hits her again, his rings raking her flesh on cheekbone and jaw. The pain to her head and face is so great she thinks she will pass out, as Pettigrew seems to be gathering himself for an even more brutal attack. He is breathing hoarsely and his body – with its previously slight muscles – is growing ox-like with strength and power. Then, suddenly, she sees his face change. Lust and anger go. Terror replaces them and she sees the ice-like shine of a dirk at his throat as he staggers backwards, twisted from behind, his spine almost cracked. In the same moment, she hears a cool voice say, 'I think not, Englishman. I think not.'

* * *

At that moment, John Stewart Macdonald appeared from the terrace through the open windows. And, for the first time ever, Adele heard her chaplain's voice crack with fear. 'Craig Lowrie – no! He's not worth hanging for,' he said.

'Now who's going to hang me for killing a mad dog?'

*Robinson!* thought Adele. *He will hang you.*

'No, let him go,' she begged.

'So that he can come after you again. Some other time, some other place. I don't think so.'

'Please. You know – he has powerful friends.'

Adele was waiting for the dirk to move away from Pettigrew's throat. It did not.

Father Macdonald added. 'She's right, Craig Lowrie. Haven't you enough to contend with, without the charge of throat-cutting an un-armed man.'

'It's true,' said Pettigrew, wall-eyed with fear. 'I am – unarmed.'

At this, Craig Lowrie's grip slowly eased and Pettigrew slumped in front of him, inert with relief. Craig Lowrie sheathed the dirk and booted Pettigrew to the floor. Adele felt his hand take hers and pull her towards the open window and, she knew that this was all she wanted. But then she saw Pettigrew stir and leap to the dressing table. He seized the cutting shears and launched himself at Craig Lowrie. Adele screamed. Craig Lowrie turned, swept Pettigrew's arm aside, the shears slashing at the air impotently. Pettigrew repeated his attack but met Craig Lowrie's fist before a second breath was drawn. Pettigrew staggered but lunged again. Craig Lowrie's dirk, unsheathed once more, flashed across Pettigrew's throat. A rill of blood appeared on the mottled, sickly skin. Pettigrew froze and then sighed and then crumpled. There was no doubt. He fell backwards but, before he reached the bed, the man was dead. Silence hung over the room, swirling like the Corryvreckan. Adele thought she would never breathe again.

John Stewart Macdonald was the first to speak.

'You'd best be gone, now. This is evilly done.'

'But it was in defence,' said Adele.

'D'you think any would believe that? Pettigrew and Black Malcolm Craig Lowrie. That Pettigrew was attacking Craig Lowrie? Do you really think they'll believe he had the courage. It will be seen as murder. Plain and simple. Murder.'

'No worse than I'm already accused of.'

'Then, t'is a pity, Craig Lowrie, that you're so famed for such crimes. And this time, you've killed an Englishman, of the King's Party. There will be no defence.'

Craig Lowrie drew out the dirk from the inert Pettigrew. He wiped it on the brocade of the drapes, re-sheathed it and then shrugged. The old priest made the sign of the cross and then said, 'Come now, you must away. We'll arrange things here.'

'Now why would you do that for me, priest?'

'For her.'

Adele, shocked and silent, felt her chaplain look at her. Malcolm Craig Lowrie followed his gaze and then stepped forward. He extended his hand again and said, 'Will you not come with me, lady?'

*This was why he came back,* thought Adele. Joy surged through her, She wanted to accept the hand before her. But then she found she could not. She shook her head, feeling the air fold over her, like the sea.

'But why not?' For the first time, she thought she heard a shadow of uncertainty mist Craig Lowrie's voice. 'Are you staying for him? Staying for Robinson?'

Adele shook her head again. 'It's my sister. It's for Gabrielle.'

Then she began to shake, as if she would never stop. She felt the old priest put his arm around her shoulders. She couldn't control the shaking and all the words in her head seemed to jumble up together. She didn't know what was English and what was French any more. Speechless and shocked, her bruised and bleeding face and head were beginning to throb, her body ache. She saw Craig Lowrie's face close down. There was a nerve twitching in his cheek and, in those few seconds, she came to know terror. Her world swirled and her hands clawed but could grasp nothing.

John Stewart Macdonald intervened. 'Her sister, Gabrielle. There is such danger for Gabrielle – in France. And we had hoped to bring Gabrielle here. Go, Craig Lowrie. Go now.'

Between them all lay the stiffening hulk of Pettigrew, his lifeblood on Adele's sheets. Craig Lowrie hissed between clenched teeth and then he was gone from *Le Petit Trianon.*

But, as he picked his way across the Park, he saw the heavy moon – the Moon of the Horse, sacred to the old gods – now tipped a hostile light over the land. Anything moving – including Craig Lowrie – was starkly visible. And the Wolf of Dalriada would now be quarry – hunted by Robinson and his pack – to the end of time.

Meanwhile, lost in grief beyond tears, in the silent *Petit Trianon,* Adele watched John Stewart Macdonald ring for a servant.

# Chapter 31

## Robinson Park, Arduaine
## 22nd June – Midsummer Night – 1793

*PETTIGREW*
*You're not going to like what I have to say in this letter. But it is, I am afraid, unavoidable. Your son, sir, is a cad, sir. And later this morning I'll ask him to remove himself from my house and grounds and return to you in Carlisle. The reason? You may ask the reason, sir, and I can tell you, last night, at a ball we were holding here at Robinson Park, your son disgraced himself. And worse, besmirched your good name. I don't know what possessed him but he treated the Lady Emma Bamburgh, as if she were a common whore, sir. I send this letter to apprise you of the facts – no matter what your son may try to tell you. The letter and he will arrive in the same transport, I expect, but you need to know why he has been dispatched with so little ceremony...*
(This letter remained unsent.)

**Robinson Hall, Oban**
**22nd June 1793**
*My dear Pettigrew*
*I have the most dire news for you. I cannot disguise it. I will be direct.*

*Last night, when the household was finally to bed after a ball, armed robbers broke into the chamber of my Lady wife. She was badly shaken but your son who nobly went to her aid, I'm afraid, was cruelly murdered in cold blood. I have taken steps to alert the authorities but hold out little hope that the felons will be appre-*

*hended. The trail will now be too cold for the coroner's men to make any progress. I am so sorry.*

*When the inquest is finished, shall I return your son to you and his mother? It would, I feel, be best if I were to make arrangements to return him to you. It would be more appropriate for him to be buried in Carlisle with full funeral rites, than up here in this outpost of civilisation, where you I know are loath to visit and would be able to attend his grave but rarely.*

*Words cannot express my regret sufficiently regarding this turn of events.*

*Yours ever*

***Wm. Robinson***

## *Robinson's journal – 22nd June 1793*

*So young Pettigrew has had himself killed. Well, I should imagine that was only a matter of time. But, oh, how very inconvenient that it should be here. And now.*

*Even so, there are some grave questions raised by the death.*

*Pettigrew was in Adelaide's rooms and, I am told by the servants, he attacked her. The man had run mad, it seems, but why? And I can guess the identity of the 'intruder' who murdered Pettigrew. I'd wager the King's crown that it was Black Malcolm. It appears he entered from the garden. But why was the door to the grounds left open in the first place? What is the extent of collusion here? And how far is my 'beloved wife' implicated?*

*The bond between MCL and Adelaide is too, too powerful. I saw it clearly last night. If it blossoms – I cannot but fear it has done so already – there will be the Devil to pay. Where will all my grand sacrifice and hope for redemption stand then with the Almighty? No pure and innocent Adelaide – no atonement to offer. No amazing grace! In accordance with my oath. Zounds to that! Weighed in the balance, there will be nothing I can offer Him as recompense for my sins. Nothing. Does that trouble me? Never used to. But now? Well, yes, it assuredly does. Now less of my life on earth remains, and the day will soon and inevitably come when I shall be judged. Perhaps even damned. Forever. And now I can feel the breath of devilry on my neck. Almost smell the sulphur...*

*And I fear I have truly reared a jade in my own home.*

*Yet, so many times I resisted the urge to take her. So many times. And for what? So that – in the end – she could give herself to what appears to have been a total rabble! If she had offered herself to me – just once – I could bear it. But no! Not one word of welcome have I ever had.*

*I've always tried to be kind to Adelaide. For years. Other men in my circumstances would not have been so. I resent it. I do. I've even loved her – in my way. And I've not laid a hand on her – kept her pure and virtuous, or so I thought! But, in spite of all this restraint, and her behaving as though she and her virtue were somehow unimpeachable, has she been indulging in licentiousness with others? And have I been rejected – for this? For liaisons! With brigands like Craig Lowrie. Or worse, with fools and bullies like Pettigrew!*

*I cannot bear to go near her. Never again. Absolutely never again.*

*But what to do? I would return her to France – she has often asked for that. But to do it safely it might involve more expense than she deserves and more than I am now prepared to give. Or I could cast her out and let her take her chances with the brigands she seems so to favour.*

*And that creeping priest! That's another indulgence I've allowed. Induced by that rogue of a seminary bishop. Unbelievable. Here in a protestant, Whig House, we've had a Catholic priest sliding about corners, doing what he wills at all times of the day and the night. Eating at my table, even. I've been had for a fool by the pack of them. But, now at last here an opportunity to remove at least him from the household.*

*Some evidence of what really happened last night will surface at some point, I've no doubt. The coroner's men are on to it. But, in the meantime, arrangements must be made. Pettigrew Senior will no doubt have wishes to be complied with regarding his son's disposal. I'll await his instructions. But, of course, it is not convenient to have young Pettigrew in my ice house, awaiting collection. A good thing Scottish summers are cool.*

*Now, the Lady Emma. Bamburgh or Craig Lowrie – I wonder which she is. I have a strong sense that she is not yet married. I base this on the fact that I have seen her returning from a midnight walk in the Park. No doubt – in view of all that's happened – she was meeting young JCL. And to be honest, why would she bother to come back if she was married?*

*I think Argyll was a fool to make JCL a* cause célèbre *by putting a price on his murderous cousin's head. Messy – with no evidence – no witness statement. Although it did suit me, of course – the fiction of JCL being a clansman loyal to the Campbells and the King and then murdered by MCL.*

*But then was perhaps MCL, the cousin of the allegedly murdered whelp, the real quarry right from the start? There's a depth to Argyll's animosity regarding MCL that goes back years, I'll wager. The cause? I'd like to find it.*

*Argyll will of course now put a price on both their heads. Not sure how this will help. True, more people will be looking out for both of them. But it would be better, I opine, if MCL were considered the sole agent for evil in the region. Otherwise, my case is diluted. This needs more consideration. How can I turn this to my advantage? Or do I need now urgently to seek an interview with his Grace? Now we have met socially, as it were – if you can call that fiasco at the ball a 'meeting' – it may be easier. Pettigrew may have had his uses after all. But so many questions. Such poor intelligence. I can't be doing with this not knowing what's really happened. Good that Edwin's here – he'll distract me. And the lovely Eleanor. I can't write more of that.*

*Time for bed, I think.*

# Chapter 33

## Robinson Park, Arduaine
## 22nd June 1793

FROM THE WINDOWS of her rooms in the guest quarters of the Hall, the Lady Eleanor watched her husband and their host stroll across the lawns towards the paddocks by the sea. The previous evening, one had had his daughter abducted by brigands and the other had had a house-guest murdered yet now they walked and chatted about equine blood-lines as if these terrible events were no more than usual in the normal course of life. *Perhaps it was for men,* she thought and shuddered.

She returned to the fireside where her morning chocolate was waiting for her. She sipped this, savouring the taste, allowing its warmth to ease into her mind. She was considering what to do next. *Because what to do next,* she thought, *seems to be my decision – if I can call it that.*

A moment later she was navigating the corridors of Robinson Hall, searching for Lady Robinson's apartments. And at last she swept along the linkway to Adele's sanctuary.

The servant whom Pettigrew had deceived was now back in post. Penitent, he barred her way, his arms outstretched like a crucifix. 'I'm sorry, My Lady, Lady Robinson will see no-one.'

'Nonsense!' came the reply and the Lady Eleanor was through the door and into Adele's rooms before he could stop her. But what she saw then gave her total pause. Shadows had come out of the corners. They now covered everything – all the furniture, all the furnishings, all the *Objets d'Art,* all chosen with such care and delight – with a pall as colourless as dust. A man had been murdered here.

As the Lady Eleanor moved through rooms that were lit only by sunlight, filtered through thin cracks in the shutters, she noted the body had been manhandled out and the sheets had been stripped. The bed had been re-made but it stood empty. And, on a chair by the dying embers of a fire sat a silent woman, masked by grey darkness. This was the Lady Eleanor's first view of Lady Robinson and, angered, she said, 'Child, you cannot stay here. It's too awful. How could Robinson leave you in this place? Here, let me open the windows.'

Without waiting for permission, she drew back the drapes, flung open the windows and the mirrored shutters and allowed summer sunlight to flood the room. Then she turned and then she gasped. Adele's body above her ball gown was blackening. Her face was blood-smattered and one eye was swollen, useless. She did not raise her gaze from the fire. She shivered – constantly and in silence.

'Oh child, you cannot stay here,' repeated the Lady Eleanor, holding out her hand. Adele hesitated but then reached for it, trying to stand. Weak, she sank back into her chair. And Eleanor repeated, 'How could Robinson leave you here – and like this?'

'Robinson has not seen me.' The words were spat through the bruised lips, like broken teeth. 'He will not see me.'

'But why? Has the man run mad?'

Eleanor pulled a blanket from the bed and wrapped it round the young woman, calling for the servant to help. Then together they supported Adele back along the linkway and up the servants' stairs. At each step, Adele moaned softly but, at last, they reached Eleanor's rooms. The servant then withdrew, with instructions to send a maid immediately and the maid was to bring with her fine soap and warm water from the kitchens. Adele needed to wash.

While waiting, Eleanor stripped away the shredded ball gown. She tutted. Standing there, in the huge room, wearing nothing but a shift, Adele looked to Eleanor like a lost child. In need of protection. But this child, thought Eleanor, has fought with every ounce of her strength to defend herself. How could anyone think otherwise? Think her less than innocent and wronged?

Wrapping Adele in one of her own shawls, she led her to a chair by her bright and vigorous fire. The girl's face remained expressionless. Eleanor bit her lip. *Resignation* – a French word – was a draining, darkening bruise upon the soul and Eleanor knew she must find a way of somehow reaching Adele, before her spirit moved so far away into *resignation* it could not be re-called. The danger was dire and immediate. But, once bathed and dressed in one of Eleanor's own nightgowns, and encouraged to rest in Eleanor's own bed, Adele could at least sleep. And, Eleanor would watch over her till she was sure the shivering was stopped and there was no fever.

To occupy herself in her vigil, Eleanor looked about for something to do. She settled upon repairing Adele's torn ball gown and made herself comfortable by the window. In the sunlight, she was warm and peaceful but, as she stitched, her anxieties about her daughter surfaced again.

She had made enquiries the night before but Robinson remained silent on the matter and, little came of quizzing the maid assigned to her for her stay, Eleanor realised the Master of the House kept the servants either ignorant or cowed. Almost nothing could she glean. However, her 'maid' did let slip that Adele and Emma had become friends. And so, it seemed, of all the people thrown so haphazardly together in this God-forgotten place in northern Britain, the young French woman, Adele, might be the one person able to tell Eleanor what she needed to know about her daughter. Even so, some days passed and, only when Adele's bruises had turned from black to yellow and purple, did Eleanor feel she could seek some answers.

'Is Emma married then?' she at last asked Adele.

No longer entirely obscured by bouts of pain nor by laudanum, stark memories of midsummer night were now returning to Adele but, even so, some memories resolutely would not come. Eleanor could see the struggle. Then Adele suddenly asked, 'Did you agree to Emma's engagement?'

Adele's directness almost shocked Eleanor but she decided to treat it as an invitation to talk about some of her own long-held misgivings. Neither her husband nor Robinson had taken these into account. She laid aside her sewing and said, 'I have to say, I was never happy with Edwin's arrangements with Campbell Craig Lowrie. Campbell Craig Lowrie was merely the chieftain of a sept. This would place Emma, an earl's daughter, with a cadet of a minor Highland clan and that seemed a strange sort of "throwing away" – for Edwin who spends his life calculating profit. I couldn't guess what he was thinking.

'However, I know Edwin and I knew things would never be so

simple. In due course, he confessed to me that money was on offer. Irresistible. As we always seem short, this is always a concern. And, of course, the Craig Lowrie lands – mainland or on the Isles – they resound with wealth. Edwin told me, "Cattle grow fat looking at the grass. Forests cluster over mountains rich in minerals. The rivers are thick with fish." Edwin simply could not have said "No!".'

Conversation, no matter how unsuitable for the sick room, was more satisfactory than Adele's lack-lustre silence. So Eleanor smiled as Adele said, 'But the Craig Lowries, of all people! Their reputation! As brigands! Would Emma's engagement not be rather frowned upon by the English court?'

Eleanor waved a hand and said, 'It would not necessarily be cause for concern at court. Who knows? Men do not fully explain these things to women.

'But, I never liked the old man, Campbell Craig Lowrie. Mairi MacDonald, his wife, was my friend. We spent time together at Holyrood. Different rank – but two young girls together in the strange, political world that men create around themselves. You can imagine how close we grew. But then Mairi died. Suddenly.'

Eleanor now began to tell Adele some of the old stories surrounding the Craig Lowries. These spoke of Glencoe and of how Malcolm Craig Lowrie's great-grandfather, a MacDonald, had been brutally murdered by Campbells after they had received food and shelter from his hands.

'They had taken MacDonald salt,' said Eleanor, 'and to a Scot, this is cause enough for a hundred years of hatred. But the story of the Craig Lowries, of course, has more twists than that. After Glencoe, the family fled to Jura. And then, much later, a bastard son of the Campbells grew to power in the Isles. None could withstand Campbell Craig Lowrie there. Nor did they want to. As their chieftain, he fed them. Well. Sometimes – for the clan, for anyone – that is enough.'

Adele fretted the sheet and Eleanor stood to check her forehead for signs of returning fever. There was none but Adele felt cold and clammy to the touch. Eleanor drew a cashmere shawl – soft and light and pretty – around the young woman's shoulders. She helped her sip some water. Then she returned to her chair by the window, took up her sewing, and carried on with the tale, 'Finally, Campbell Craig Lowrie followed the drover's road from the Isles via Carsaig to Tayvallich. Thereafter, rock by rock, he seized land from the Campbells. This was a neat revenge for Glencoe – and all the other "slights" – real and imagined. But bloody. So bloody.

'Yet Campbell Craig Lowrie carried Campbell blood in him. Blood seems to rage against blood in that family. The clansfolk say the land still runs red where Campbell Craig Lowrie rode. And now, it seems, Malcolm Craig Lowrie follows in his ilk.'

Adele slumped on her pillows as though Eleanor had struck her. Eleanor noticed but did not remark upon this and continued, 'It was an ill day, when Campbell Craig Lowrie took Mairi MacDonald as his wife.'

*Century-old wrongs – as bright as yesterday's – stalked these lonely places,* thought Eleanor. She felt the heart-tug, bred into stone and sky, of the land beyond the Robinson Park gates. And, she wondered, could her daughter ever ask a Craig Lowrie to deny it all? Yet, if he did not walk away from this, would they ever be free of the need for revenge? It was in his blood. Horror made Eleanor edgy.

Adele was restless, too. Eleanor was aware of some conflict within her but – even as tears edged the young woman's lashes – she did not ask its nature. She simply crossed to her and offered her some warm chocolate to drink – bitter-sweet to the tongue.

Although she fussed and chatted on, Eleanor's attention never left the young woman convalescent in the bed. But, for her own sake, it suddenly seemed important to say, 'Marriage can sometimes be a way of healing some of these endless feuds. Mairi MacDonald certainly believed that. But no healing came. Only more feuding, constantly, between the MacDonalds and the Campbells and the Craig Lowries. Only more cause for hatred. It's surprising that any of them are still alive.

'And, Campbell Craig Lowrie believed in cruelty – as others believe in God. He offered it everywhere – to his tenants, to his livestock, to his enemies, even to his kin...If you ever see Malcolm Craig Lowrie's back, you'll see the scars of it. Yes no living thing was safe from him. Even his son. Campbell Craig Lowrie used to beat the child till he bled. That man said: "I beat that boy until he bleeds and still he does not cry." Oh, yes, Campbell Craig Lowrie was very proud of his son – and the boy's silence. In his cups, he used to boast to his kin that Malcolm would be the greatest of all his tacksmen, a worthy member of the Craig Lowrie *daoine uaisle*, of the noble people. A true *sith!* So Campbell Craig Lowrie said. But Mairi would not bear Campbell Craig Lowrie another child. She consorted with witches to avoid it. And, rumour has it, the witches killed her.

Or perhaps, in truth, it was Campbell Craig Lowrie killed her. Either way, she died.'

Eleanor paused for a moment, laying down her needlework with a sigh. Then, she picked up a new thread, adding, 'And we have what we have now.'

Breathing painfully, Adele now asked 'And Jamie?'

'Another branch,' Eleanor said, glad of the switch of conversation. 'Same family. But softer, brought up by another Craig Lowrie tacksman of lower rank. Not by Campbell Craig Lowrie. Jamie seemed gentle enough and his prospects reasonably good. When Edwin proposed him as a match for Emma, I hoped possibly against hope that for once we were to favour something other than political ambition. But, no. The Bamburghs may possess some ancient influence in the world but the Craig Lowries – the Craig Lowries possess the key to unimaginable greatness. They are key to the Auld Alliance – between France and Scotland – and to Europe. And even the Bamburghs – obscure Northumbrians – are infected by this ambition. It was a very attractive part of the marriage brokerage.'

Eleanor snapped the thread and found a fresh part of the gown to work on while Adele remained silent. Eleanor felt ashamed of her own impotence. 'Nothing – not birth, not up-bringing, not native wit – nothing releases women from the snare of men's games,' she said.

But a new thought occurred. She suddenly stood up to study the far hills from the huge window. A moment passed before she declared: 'I absolutely do not believe those Craig Lowrie boys have turned into criminals. I simply do not believe it. There is more to this than appears on the surface.'

Adele shifted painfully in the bed. 'But the stories...'

Eleanor raised her hand. 'Stories? Who tells the stories? Not the Craig Lowries, not one man of the clan, I'm sure of it, would speak ill of his clan chief, Malcolm Craig Lowrie. So where do these stories come from? Ill-wishers? Merely.'

Then she softened, returning to help Adele be comfortable again. She plumped the pillows vigorously. 'The truth is buried deep and I don't suppose that we shall ever know it,' she said, 'Here let me brush your hair for you, my dear.'

With rhythmic, soothing strokes, Eleanor now brushed the rich, curled mane of her patient. She noted its beauty was undimmed. Without the bruises distorting face and body, Eleanor thought, Adele could have looked like a princess of legend, her hair swirling around her like a shining dark cloud. A princess for a *sith,* she wondered and smiled at the playful thought. But, then, weary, Adele sank back onto her pillows and Eleanor put away the brush.

'Would knowing the truth about the Craig Lowries make any difference?' Adele asked.

For a moment, Eleanor said nothing as she poured some tea for Adele. Then she returned to her sewing. Pulling two rough edges of the silk together, she said, 'Knowing the truth about the Craig Lowries probably wouldn't help any of us over much. And, whatever that truth may be, we shall all just have to persevere, shall we not?'

Then she looked at Adele sharply and asked, 'Now – tell me – what really happened on midsummer night?'

# Chapter 34

## Robinson Park, Arduaine, Oban
## Late June 1793

DINNER IN THE DAYS following the ball was indeed a quiet affair. With Adelaide too ill to come down, Emma gone and Pettigrew in the Ice House, Robinson was obliged to instruct the housekeeper to prepare simple meals for himself and the Bamburghs.

'We won't stand on ceremony,' he said. 'The house steward and two footmen will do. No more than ten dishes.'

After one such dinner, seated in the drawing room over tea, Edwin appeared to be reading a newspaper but in fact Robinson was aware his old friend's attention never wavered. 'You have a plan,' Edwin said at last.

Robinson took out his spectacles and polished each lens with a silk kerchief. The fire crackled. He was waiting until the tea had been served by the footman who would then withdraw to a far distant door and he, Edwin and Eleanor would be alone. As he watched the pleasant splash and swirl of the golden liquid in the delicate porcelain cups, Robinson thought, *if only life were like that.*

During the pause, Eleanor was coming to the end of her repairs to Adele's torn ball gown, her tiny stitches pulling together the ragged material. 'There,' she said, cutting the thread. 'Never as lovely as it may have been before. But it could serve. *Diner à deux.* The two of you. Quietly. At home.'

'Those days are over.' Robinson snapped. But then, he smiled at Eleanor and forgot what he was about. Now Adelaide was beyond redemption, he remembered that Eleanor had for so many years been the Queen of his heart. And she was still lovely. Thirty-nine years old – with fine lines etched around her eyes – but still lovely.

Edwin coughed. It reminded Robinson where they all were. 'Your plan?'

Robinson began. 'I think we could rescue Emma from these brigands.'

'Really?' said Eleanor, her face a mask. 'How thrilling!'

'At your suggestion, Edwin, I hired a private army of English mercenaries to protect Robinson Park. Much good did it do, when it came to it. But, with Emma gone, these men are kicking their heels in the grounds and – I gather – finding themselves involved in murder and mayhem in the villages. I've even had a deputation from the Oban townsfolk today! It's apparently only a matter of time before there's an unfortunate incident down on the docks. And, as Oban is where at least some of my livelihood comes from, I am not inclined to permit that.

'So I either dismiss them now or I give them some employment. Your original notion was that they should help me retrieve Emma's inheritance as Jamie Craig Lowrie's widow. I think we could improve on that.'

Edwin – not yet fully engaged – made a show of turning his newspaper page.

Robinson placed his spectacles on his nose and lowered his voice even further. 'With these English mercenaries and the Duke of Argyll's men combined, we could flush out the Craig Lowries.'

'Why should we want to? Emma is clearly not a widow.' Edwin was becoming uneasy.

'But we don't know yet whether she is a wife.'

Eleanor lost patience. 'I knew we should never have allowed Emma to come on her own.'

'The King required us at court.'

'So we had to miss our own daughter's wedding? So now we don't know whether she's married or not? So she is now in the hands of goodness-knows-who and goodness-knows-where? Is this what you call a plan, Edwin? William?'

Robinson intervened. 'Of course not, Eleanor, my dear. My plan is: we simply join forces with the Duke of Argyll. He is, even as we speak, burning village after village near the castles of Craig Lowrie and Dunadd.'

'Dunadd?' Edwin found the geography bemusing.

'Jamie's home stronghold. Really Edwin, you must remember that. Do try to keep up.'

'And has he any news of Emma? Resulting from all this arson?' Eleanor sat forward.

'It is a matter of time.' Edwin turned another page.

'Edwin – for heaven's sake – we are laughing stocks. We have misplaced our daughter. Do something.' And, with that, Eleanor stood and, pausing only for the footman to open the door, swept out of the room.

Edwin stopped smiling. 'She's right. Although I would never admit it to her. Between us, we have mishandled this.'

Robinson was aghast. He spluttered, 'I disagree. I was quietly going about my business in my office in Oban and in walks your daughter. She then spends months silent on the subject of her "wedding" and the next thing I know, Argyll is hunting her across my dance floor. I have been the entirely innocent party is this affair. And – if I may say so – it has so far cost me dear. I feel very strongly about this.'

'Very well. Whoever's mishandled the matter, we have to do something about it now. I'm quite fond of Emma – I'd like to think of her as happily married to a Scottish landowner, with the lands and prospects of a Craig Lowrie. But now she seems to be in the thrall of a Scottish landowner with the prospects of the gallows. We have to do something about this.'

'Join forces with Argyll, then?'

'I'm not sure. I'm not convinced. I don't understand why Argyll is so vigorous in finding Emma. And why all this blood lust? There is more to this than clearances in preparation for the arrival of some Cheviots or than pursuit of my daughter.'

'Well – partly – he wants you.'

'Me?'

'You.'

'By now, he will have heard of our arrival. If you are right, why seek a young girl when her father is here, with you, admiring your racehorses?'

'I couldn't say. But, I know, he is reputed to want to build a connection with Northumberland. Northumberland and Argyll, now that would be an alliance maintaining a balance of indisputable power in the United Kingdom.'

'Well, if that's his game, why bother now with the Craig Lowries? I could be his broker with Northumberland.'

'Personally, I think all this tinkering with local brigands is a nonsense, a smokescreen. But Argyll's never forgotten the bloody nose Campbell Craig Lowrie gave his family when he took the Dalriada lands. Even so, Argyll is canny. I think his motives are grander. I think his interests lie with the rich and fertile Craig Lowrie lands on the mainland. And beyond those, the Isles and, perhaps, even the route to France. The Auld Alliance.'

'Argyll? Interested in my daughter's lands?' The forgotten broadsheet slid to the floor from Bamburgh's grasp. His mouth was squared with curiosity, reflecting a mind spinning with the possibilities.

'Possibly your daughter's lands.' As a lawyer, Robinson was pedantic about these things. He added, 'Formerly, his. Well, his father's and his father's before him.'

'So what is in all this for me? And for you? Which side do we back? Argyll and his interest in power? Or the Craig Lowries and their wealth to which we, possibly, have a claim?'

At this moment, Eleanor walked back in. 'And, another thing,' she began, 'Lady Robinson is innocent...'

'Eleanor, my dear,' said Edwin, bending down to retrieve his newspaper. He waved some of the sheets at her. 'William and I are thinking how to rescue Emma. He really does have a plan.'

'Really?' Eleanor showed surprise at Edwin's warmth.

'Not sure I'd call it a plan, Edwin.' Robinson resorted to polishing his spectacles again.

'You are too modest, William. I think it's excellent. I'll ride to Argyll tomorrow, find out his thinking and be back before you know I've gone, my dear Eleanor.'

'How will that help?' Eleanor's eyes narrowed.

'Indeed,' added Robinson, 'how will that help?'

'We can't make a decision without knowing what in fact is going on. Argyll is prepared to create bad blood. What is he thinking? That's what we need to know.'

'Do you think it will work, William, your plan? Do you think we'll find Emma?'

Eleanor laid a hand in appeal on her old friend's arm and looked into his eyes. She had no intention of telling either of these men what Adele had told her of the Craig Lowrie 'plan' for a wedding. And she would not be telling Edwin or William that she had some notion of where Emma was – well, not for the moment, anyway. She needed first to know which – if either – of these men, she could trust.

* * *

In due course – after the inquest – some Oban undertakers were made responsible for managing Pettigrew's cortège – a solitary lych wagon – on the road south to Carlisle from Robinson Park. They were not best pleased with their commission, nor with their fellow travellers. In the Robinson Hall stable yard, as they prepared for the funeral journey, a nervous dispatch rider bearing Robinson's letters to Pettigrew Senior, mopping his brow, was muttering, 'Safety in numbers'. And several of the ill-famed English mercenaries had also been detailed to escort the cortège. These were sulking. They would only be released from this tedious contract when the coffin reached its southern destination without harm or damage. But, before that, miles lay ahead of them – with Craig Lowrie country up in arms – and timid undertakers as company.

There was then a further change of plan. Robinson, without prior notice, placed the cortège under the protection of Edwin, Earl Bamburgh, and his elite guard. The Oban undertakers did not feel this was an improvement. They could see their new 'protector', Edwin Bamburgh, enjoyed the clatter and excitement of a stable yard as much as anyone – bawling at his men and tweaking the reins of any horse that was not in order. 'But this is hardly suitable for a funeral cortège,' the Oban undertakers thought, 'Where will be "respect for the dead"?'

At last Bamburgh chose directly to address the Pettigrew cortège. He was bellowing above the uproar in the yard. 'The journey to Inveraray will take less than one day's ride. I promise you will have my help as far as the Garron Bridge. You can then follow the military road south towards Carlisle. You'll have less to worry about after Inveraray.'

The Oban undertakers greeted this with an impenetrable silence.

Bamburgh bellowed on, 'The journey from Arduaine to Inveraray will be the most dangerous part of the journey – through malcontent Craig Lowrie lands. You will be glad of me then.'

The dispatch rider and the Oban undertakers remained unconvinced by these assurances. And, to their dismay, it all came about as they feared.

Far from being 'just one day's ride' as Bamburgh promised, the journey south took two days. During these, Bamburgh seemed blind to the difficulties of managing a cortège – with due dignity. The cortège had to travel along forest trails scarcely suited to the purpose and the chivvying Bamburgh gave the undertakers made them fretful. One man even ran back towards Oban – without pay – after only three hours of it.

Meanwhile, the woods of the Craig Lowrie demesne surrounded them and, there, even at the height of day, the light was dimmed to green darkness. When forced to make camp overnight, the undertakers had no choice but to find comfort in huddling close to the coffin. And they even found themselves glad of the cordon of steel that Bamburgh and his troops provided. They had all heard the tales of the Craig Lowrie Witch Mother, angered with all mankind over her early death at the hands of Campbell Craig Lowrie. And through the silence of the night, they could hear the boom of the Corryvreckan whirlpool – where she was said to wash her plaid and drown mortals in the maelstrom.

But, the next day, the party finally reached the Garron Bridge, east of Inveraray Castle. They waved farewell to the Bamburgh troop and pushed the lych cart – with Pettigrew – into the stable-block of the nearby coaching inn. Away from the Craig Lowrie lands, the undertakers were allowing themselves to feel more cheerful. And, on the morrow – though still in company with four surly English mercenaries – the funeral party could journey on to Carlisle on better roads and tracks and with considerably less menace. Who knew – even the English mercenaries might cheer up?

# Chapter 35

## Robinson Park, Arduaine, Oban
## 1st July 1793

WHEN BAMBURGH and Pettigrew's cortège clattered out of the yard of Robinson Hall and Robinson returned indoors, Eleanor was waiting. 'William, when are you sending to Oban for a doctor?' she said.

'A doctor? For whom? Are you sick?'

'Not me. Adele.'

'Adelaide? Really? Now why should I do that?'

'Because she needs one, William. She could lose an eye...I'm sure of it.'

'And why should that concern me?'

'William, you must stop this. What are you thinking? This is a young girl who is under your protection.'

'And has made a fool of me.'

'William, you are making a fool of yourself if you persist in this.'

'Perhaps. Perhaps not. But I am determined. She is leaving this household.'

At this point, they moved into the Library. They were both anticipating a heated exchange.

'William,' began Eleanor. 'Whatever you are thinking, that young woman is innocent. And she is hurt, and her heart is broken.'

'Not my doing. None of it. It's the price she must pay for cavorting with brigands and fools in her rooms.'

'William – she needs a doctor.'

'Eleanor – I'm not sending for one. It's a ruse. Just a ruse – to delay her departure. I'll not stand for it. She, and that priest, as soon as she can ride, they are leaving.'

'Where would they go?'

'Not my concern.'

'I'll send for a doctor myself.'

'I forbid it.'

'She will be better more quickly if you do.'

Robinson paused. He sat and then stood up again and walked to the window. 'All right. Send for your doctor. There's one in Oban.'

'Will you not come to see her for yourself.'

'No. No. That would not do at all.'

'You're an intractable man, William. And I'm glad I didn't marry you.'

'That you would not marry me is – it's true, and has always been – a source of grief to me. But I will not see her.'

'I suppose this quality of firmness is what has helped you amass such a fortune.'

'I suppose it has.'

'But it has kept you single.' Eleanor stood to leave.

'And she may not take the thoroughbred with her.'

'Sirene?'

'If that what she calls her. Well then yes, Sirene. She may not take her with her.'

'But what can she ride? You will not be allowing her to take the carriage, I assume, either.'

'You are correct.'

'But Lady Robinson...?'

'Does not exist.'

'William...'

'I am sorry to grieve you, Eleanor. But no, Lady Robinson does not exist. Adelaide de Fontenoy is to make her own way in the world. Finally.'

# Chapter 36

## Inveraray Castle, Argyll
## 3rd July 1793

MEANWHILE, BAMBURGH and his troops moved noisily into the castle courtyard of Inveraray. Bamburgh was ready to demand an audience with Argyll, believing he had the whip hand.

'Not the baronial hall, then,' Edwin thought. Now swordless, he was walking along corridors away from the staterooms where he expected to be received. There seemed little daylight to be had – unlike William's newish fresh architecture – but Edwin had always taken comfort in ancestors' portraits and mounted stags' heads. The community of the dead, human and animal, endorsed what he was and, when he reached the glasshouse, where he was to meet Argyll, he was smiling.

There the orchids made a pretty show. Edwin was unused to the delicate skin of the petals combined with the brilliance of the colours. Northumberland had neither the weather nor the hothouses to shelter such and so people thought little of them. But Argyll clearly did. Edwin tucked away the information in his brain, as potentially useful. A taste for the exotic, perhaps even the continental, he thought. With an absent mind, he was drawn to touch the silken flowers before him.

'I shouldn't,' said a voice apparently from nowhere. 'The dirt and sweat on your hands will damage them.'

'Your Grace?' Edwin had located the source of the voice. A shabbily-dressed man turned from his work re-potting some of the more mature flowers.

'Indeed,' said Argyll. 'Good Evening, Bamburgh.'

'Good of you to see me without warning.'

'Isn't it?'

Argyll passed his hands through a water bowl and then wiped them on a damp cloth. His eyes never left his visitor. Then he gave Edwin his ringed hand and Edwin bowed over it. *A fulsome bow for a northerner,* thought the Duke. *What does he want?*

Argyll waved towards two chairs, his own on a slightly higher dais. Recognising the message, Edwin bit his lower lip – a small movement not missed by the Duke – and then took his seat.

'You've ridden hard to visit me.' Argyll's voice was quiet.

'Indeed.'

'Your purpose?'

'Justice, Your Grace.'

'Ah. Justice. That is one of my strengths. The dispensing of justice. Sometimes rough. But, on the whole, just, in my view. What can I do for you?'

The last question was abrupt and sharp. Edwin was surprised but decided to meet like with like.

'My daughter, Emma. She has been abducted by the Craig Lowries.'

'Really? I thought she had married into that pack.'

'There is some doubt...'

'And what would you have me do?

'Find her.'

'And why would I do that?'

Edwin was finding this all more difficult than he had imagined it would be. But he persevered.

'There is the question of the marriage settlement.'

'How much remains to be paid?'

'Some Craig Lowrie lands on the mainland.' Edwin's eyes did not blink nor move from the Duke's face. And some of the lands on the Isles,' he added.

He was rewarded with what he saw next. It was almost imperceptible but it was there – the slightest hardening in the Duke's eyes, covered at once by that eerie quietness of manner. *That's it,* thought Edwin, *the Lordship of the Isles. That's what he wants with the Craig Lowries.* He smiled. And was then unnerved to find the Duke smiling too. Both had realised that each liked the other.

Half a bottle of claret later, the Duke was saying: 'I have a new idea every morning of course. Rather the way I think of a new source of plants. I'm a plantsman, you know.'

'I saw, Your Grace.'

'But my political ideas require almost as much work. At the moment, Edwin, the route to Northumberland is taking up my time. An alliance with Northumberland – given the geography of the kingdom – is almost inevitable but it still needs careful planning. Which is why I need you on my side.

'What would be in that for me? My duty is to His Grace, Northumberland.'

'Of course, of course, my dear fellow. But, as we dine, let me explain...'

With Bamburgh's influence, Argyll explained, the alliance would become reality and the alliance would hold the balance of power in the kingdom poised between the courts of Edinburgh and London.

'Your daughter was to be my house guest, you know. Until you and I could – talk.'

Really?' Edwin was entertained by the way the Duke expressed it.

'Yes, I need you to persuade Northumberland of the sound sense of this plan. He and I, we are two of the great Northern lords. Where we go, others – such as Cumberland – will follow.'

'So why are you burning Emma's villages?'

'Ah, the clachans, as we call them here. You know, if you are to have fiefdom over some of this land, you really must learn the correct terms.'

'But why are you? Burning the clachans?'

'Because I'm a Campbell. Because they are not loyal. Because I want the land. And – because I can.'

Edwin could not but admire such brutal honesty. 'So what have you in mind?'

'The best plans are always the simplest. What I have in mind is a power share. With you, over the Craig Lowrie lands on the Mainland. The Isles will be mine. But, even so, the mainland territory is rich, you would be well pleased with the revenues.'

'And what do the Craig Lowries think of this?'

'I haven't asked. And anyway, I don't believe they know how wealthy they are and the true value of what they possess. I do. It was mine, before it was theirs. No, I haven't asked what they think of my burning the villages. Or any of my other activities.'

Here the Duke broke off, leaning across to cut more meat from the bone with his dirk – Highland style. Edwin noted the vigour with which the Duke performed the operation.

'Why not?' asked Edwin. Candour seemed to be the mood of the moment.

'It's not important.' The Duke sat back. He seemed to be chewing the flesh with distaste. Edwin felt the mood of the moment change. 'What is important is how we are going to control these lands. You could help me again in this matter.'

'Really? How?' Edwin felt that to the Duke at the moment these manoeuvres and plans were of more interest even than power-broking between England and Scotland. That was the plaything of a great man testing his power. This Craig Lowrie business was more visceral.

'I suggest we place young James Craig Lowrie and the Lady Emma at Dunadd. That castle has a significance for the peasants. The Ancient Kings of Dalriada were invested there. Yes, we could place "the loving couple" there and rule through them.'

'But you've outlawed Jamie Craig Lowrie.'

'Hmm, yes, that was an oversight. He irritated me. Teenage boys do. All that flamboyance and posturing. Like the other night. At that fiasco in the north. Turning up like a Highland Laird at Culloden – that could have been expected of James Craig Lowrie. Had we known he was alive.'

Edwin affected ignorance and said nothing.

Argyll recovered himself. 'Yes, putting a price on his head, that was, I suppose, going too far. I rescind it. Anyway, your daughter will rule him. From what I've seen of her, she's a remarkable young woman.'

'Very like her mother,' said Edwin. 'And good with horses.'

The two men smiled comfortably at each other. This was going well.

'And you, of course, will rule James Craig Lowrie through her.'

'And – in this alone – I am to take my orders from you?' This would be a dangerous step. Edwin needed to be clear of his role so that, if necessary, he could explain it to his liege lord, Northumberland. Argyll inclined his head.

'But the Lordship of the Isles?' Edwin asked.

'Is mine.' The mood had changed again. Argyll closed down.

Edwin changed direction. 'And Malcolm Craig Lowrie?'

'That is the price they must all pay. He must be dispossessed. He must bow his head over my ring. He must take my name and swear an oath of allegiance – to me. He must eat with me and ride with me and if necessary fight and die with me. Or – he must go.'

'Why?' asked Edwin, knowing the cause of all this hatred must be buried deep. He was unsurprised when he received no answer. Argyll rose. He paced up and down in front of the fireless hearth. Edwin remained seated – to show his independence. He remained silent, waiting. The Duke went to a low window and opened it onto the night, still light from the solstice. He looked out and said as if by way of explanation, 'I know he's out there.'

'How? How do you know?'

'For a few days, we burned the clachans and nothing was found – not a trace of him. Then suddenly it all changed. My men started to come home with more than bloodied noses. And the burnings – well, shall we say they became less effective. The fires were out more quickly. I know he's there, somewhere in the thick of it. And my men can't find him.'

Dinner, thought Edwin, was clearly at an end. He prepared himself for the ride back, unfed, to Robinson Park.

Then Argyll smiled. 'Come, Edwin. Smoke a pipe with me. Tell me about the St Leger. I have a fancy to enter some of my horses, you know. Come, let us talk horses.'

'Your Grace.' Edwin dipped his head and then followed the Duke from the room. He smiled. This was all going very well indeed.

# Chapter 37

## Robinson Hall, Arduaine, Oban
## 15th July 1793

'YOUR WIFE, sir –'
'She is not my wife.'

'Well, Mademoiselle de Fontenoy' continued the physician, 'has severe bruising, a cracked rib and a black eye. She was lucky.'

'Lucky?' said Eleanor, her eyes widening.

'Whoever did this to her intended her extreme harm. His – I assume, it was a "he" – attempt did not succeed. She was lucky. The intervention, from whatever source, was timely.'

'How soon can she move? Travel, even?'

'William.' Eleanor was close to exasperation.

'Not for some weeks still. By then the bruising will have gone down. And if she rests, the cracked rib will heal.' The doctor began to assemble his equipment and pack his bag.

'And her eye?' This was Eleanor's main concern.

'Will heal. I have seen this injury often before – though not, it must be said, in a lady of the quality. Sometimes it can go either way. But, if she stays in a dark room, rests it from the light...'

'And the gash to her face?'

'A permanent scar, I'm afraid. And there is some evidence of sepsis. Some leeches will clear that up.'

Eleanor moaned softly.

'But, I want to know, when will she be able to travel?' pressed Robinson with impatience.

'Not for some weeks, I'm afraid. But six weeks at most.'

'Oh, really,' said Robinson. Then he handed the doctor his fee and left the room. The doctor took his leave. And Eleanor smoothed the bedclothes across Adele. Both women were weeping.

* * *

'I have made a decision,' said the Lady Eleanor one evening, some days later. 'I must attend my daughter's wedding.'

Adele said nothing.

'Edwin's gone – for goodness knows how long. William is sulking – I thought better of him than that – but no, he's sulking and for goodness knows how long as well. And I have been given a second chance. I will see my daughter wed!'

Eleanor let fall the information piece by piece. 'As soon as the priest is ready, I know, he will ride south to offer the sacrament. I believe, he is making arrangements to do so as we speak. I will tell him when I meet him that I will ride south with him – whenever that shall be. It may of course be weeks yet.'

Adele shivered. She gazed at the older woman and wanted to beg her not to leave her but her lips could not easily say the words. Of course Eleanor would need to be with Emma.

Eleanor sat on the bed and took Adele's undamaged hand in hers and continued, 'Whenever it is, I will see Emma wed and then I will ride straight back here. And we'll see what happens then...I can't believe William will continue with this. I really can't. As for you,' Eleanor explained, 'you will be allowed to stay at Robinson Park until you can travel.'

The irony of the situation had not escaped Adele. For the briefest of moments, it seemed, she had allowed herself to hope Craig Lowrie would rescue her from the living death that Robinson meted out. Now, by a turn of fate, Robinson himself was setting her free. This was what she had longed for, for years, but, she thought, 'What will I do with freedom? Where will I go? How will I live?'

And had she gone with Malcolm Craig Lowrie – as she had so wished to do – what would he have offered her instead of the psychological and physical isolation of Robinson Park? The imprisonment of a different kind of life? How would she have borne that?

But, remembering the dance on midsummer night, she calmed. She felt again the strength of him around her, saw again the flash of his azure eyes, and knew that, no matter what, she would love Malcolm Craig Lowrie to the end of time.

Then, she had to remind herself, had she not refused him? If he had been her only hope of love, by refusing him, she had destroyed her own future. And, her vision of a life with Malcolm Craig Lowrie now appeared an impossibly small dream, mewling in the night, only to die in the sun.

Adele had also seen the bleeding child of Eleanor's Craig Lowrie tales in the man. When Adele had refused to go with Malcolm Craig Lowrie, she had seen his face lose life, turn as cold as stone. And that was breaking her heart. But, she knew full well, she would now have to learn to put away that grief. She shrugged.

At present everyone knew riding was out of the question. She could not even have thought of riding south to Emma's wedding, much as she longed to be there. So, however much she must dislike it, she was still, under Robinson's protection. She was still safe for the present. She must take some comfort in that.

But, at some time, when she was stronger, she would have to retrieve the letters from Gabrielle, hidden in the secret wall compartment of *Le Petit Trianon.* And then, whenever she was asked to leave, Adelaide de Fontenoy would be prepared. She would leave with almost as little as she had brought but she – and her pride – would be intact.

Even so, in spite of all her plans, day in, day out, her head ached relentlessly and she felt she was on the edge of an abyss. She longed for Gabrielle and the safety of a world now out of reach. As children, she and Gabrielle had enjoyed the rare and miraculous sunshine of a Queen's smiles and they had thought the Queen's world would last forever. But it had not and a new order had come in its place. And Adele knew, as Gabrielle would no doubt say to her, she must now resign herself to her fate, no matter what that would be.

Then, one day, the realisation came to her. As she woke with the sunlight flooding Eleanor's room, she found herself gasping for breath. Gabrielle in France! At any moment, Gabrielle might find herself denounced. She might find herself tried, sentenced, murdered...And for what? For looking after an old father and managing to make a living. Having to make that living. Because she had no rights of property! Adele fought back tears. That would all be so unfair, so ironic.

Of course, she would have to try to help Gabrielle. Somehow, she would pay for the passage to France to find Gabrielle. Though her quarters on any ship would be as she could afford, would not be grand, would not be comfortable, she would go. And, as she would have nothing to steal, perhaps she would even be left in peace. Peace was the best she could hope for now. And the prize? The prize would be to be re-united after so many years with Gabrielle.

Adele stood up. It was, without doubt, time she made her way back to *Le Petit Trianon.* The servants she passed offered her help without comment but she gently refused and continued step by painful step through the corridors.

Walking into *Le Petit Trianon* again, she almost lost her courage. The rooms – once so beautiful and cared-for – were dark and dank. Had she been away so long? But she lit two candles and held the candlesticks aloft. With the flickering light, she could see her way to the secret compartment in the walls and once there she pulled out Gabrielle's letters. These were something of 'home' and full of love and she needed that. Quickly, she slid them into two letter holders, bright with the flowers, which she and Gabrielle had stitched as children. She was now ready to go back to Eleanor's quarters.

Then, for a moment, she paused by the dressing table. She arranged the candlesticks upon it and sat down. The roses she had worn in her hair for the ball were still standing in the bud vases, where she had placed them but they had dried through the neglect of weeks. Still enchanted by the memory of the ball, she took out the best-preserved rose and held it against her hair once more. But, then, she caught sight of her face in the mirror. That was what had been missing before. Eleanor had had all mirrors removed from her quarters so Adele should not see her ruined face – with its swelling and its bruises and its cuts – but now she saw them all. Her fingers touched the dressing covering the place where a deep and permanent scar would be and she hissed softly. It could also be that this scar would protect her from the attentions of those who would wish her harm – in the new life which waited for her outside *Le Petit Trianon.*

Her sewing shears were lying on the dressing table where she had left them. Constant companions since she left France up until Pettigrew's attack, five weeks before, she could not leave them behind. There were objects and trinkets she would have to take with her. These were among them.

On impulse and though in severe pain, she pulled out from a cupboard the shabby leather travelling bag which had come with her on board that dreadful ship in 1783. Calmly, she placed inside the bag everything she valued. She put in the letter envelopes with Gabrielle's letters, her sewing shears, her glittering silver thimble and *chatelaine* needle case and pin-cushion, the milky and smooth mother of pearl thread winders – all the tools of a seamstress, all so dear to her. She rolled up her riding clothes, a cotton batiste night-gown and the tiny court dress she had travelled in a decade before. She put them inside the bag. She also put in the jewellery that, over the years, in some gross ritual of possession, Robinson had placed upon her body. Throughout her sojourn at Robinson Park, she had rarely if ever chosen to wear any jewellery other than a tiny silver cross at her throat. But, now, too desperate for pride, she knew she could not leave behind all these heavy pieces – vulgar, mostly in gold. She was sure these were the pieces that would most persuasively pay for her passage to France. To the sides of the hold-all, she strapped her new leather riding boots. Then, for good measure, she blew out the candles and put in the silver candlesticks. *What I have packed is enough,* she thought. Then she hesitated.

Helped by evening sunlight straying through the shutters, she picked out a desiccated rose. She could smell the trace of summer in its fragrance. Then she wrapped it in a silk kerchief, placing it carefully among the folds of her riding habit in the bag. Now the bag – not too heavy for her returning strength – would have to wait for her in an *armoire* until the moment came for her to leave.

*And one final task.* Adele went to the centre of the room where the *mannequine,* given to her by Marie Antoinette, stood in the twilight of *Le Petit Trianon.* Trembling, she touched its face and murmured, *'A Dieu!'*

Now she was ready.

# Chapter 38

## The Three Fishes Inn, Oban, Argyll 15th August 1793

MALCOLM CRAIG LOWRIE was shivering as he opened the door. He had slept on the ground for almost two months. *And Scottish summers were not French,* he was thinking. *Freak winds that in an hour could cut across the land from Kintyre to Culloden...Rain settling on your skin and in your bones...The only comfort of the bad weather is the relief from the midges...*

But here in his rooms at *The Three Fishes* on the Oban North Quay he knew he would find a fire and cooked food – venison stew, perhaps, to be washed down with fine claret. There would be a decanter, left ready for him on the wine table, its crystal facets gleaming in the firelight. This was all as he hoped. But what he also found was Father John Stewart Macdonald.

'I've been waiting for you. They said you would come today.'

'So you have. And they – whoever *they* may be – were right.'

He was irritated to be kept from his comfort but Craig Lowrie did not show it. He tossed his riding cloak to Rabbie MacDonald waiting by the door, and moved to the fire. Taking a moment, as the warmth eased its way through the cold in his limbs, he said nothing – waiting for the other man to explain his presence. He had recognised long ago that John Stewart Macdonald was not a man to be rushed. But when John Stewart Macdonald remained silent, longer even than his custom, Craig Lowrie grew curious. There was something about the man this night, something different.

'Will you take a glass of Madeira with me?' Craig Lowrie touched the decanter.

The older man nodded. Then, at Craig Lowrie's signal, he took a seat, drawing a letter from the folds of his cloak. Its pages moved slightly in the draught from the hearth but neither man commented on the unseasonable need for a fire. Without a word, the old priest handed the parchment to Craig Lowrie – in return for the glass of Madeira. And then, he sat back and watched. Recognising the broken seal, Craig Lowrie neglected to pour his own restorative. The letter was from Gabrielle.

'You opened this?'

'It was already open. When the new contact – he came in on the *Espoir* a week ago – gave it to me.'

'He had read it?'

'He couldn't.'

Craig Lowrie indicated to the old man that he should drink, while he placed himself where the candlelight fell across the torn and stained pages. The writing was wild with distress.

*A, Chérie!*
*Terrible, terrible news. Marie Antoinette, she is to be tried. In October – or whatever they're calling it now. They are certain to call her guilty – they will say she is guilty of the most unspeakable crimes. She is innocent of course. But they will say 'Guilty'. I cannot bear it.*

*But, even worse, even closer to home. An instruction has gone out. We women are to go into the streets and berate men as cowards who do not join the Army – so France can fight these foreign wars everyone keeps talking about. We are to go out like common whores, parading up and down, shouting and swearing...*

*And, yet worse and even more dangerous, the old men are bid to come with us and tell the young men what an honour it is to fight and die for our country. Everyone, everyone must be out on the streets – or denounced.*

*But, you know, you know, Ma Chère A, our father has only two themes. One is you and what he did to you! And the other – well, it is how well we knew Marie Antoinette. You can imagine how dangerous that is – now, out there on the streets, in public. That we will die for such a lie, such a fantasy, such a small thing of gauze and ribbon, that tiny, tiny chapeau – that that should bring our ruin and our deaths. Oh, it is so unfair.*

*I am trying to sell the family silver. If we can just get away, in secret, before the edict becomes law, we may yet be saved. But the pawnbrokers are glutted with family silver. They chew their broken teeth and insult us with their small change.*

*My only, only comfort is that you are safe. That you are away from all this. You may even have to live for us all. This may be my last letter, but, my beloved sister, I want you to know you still have all my love. Have my children for me, have my life for me.*

*Yours – for as long as I may live – Your sister, Gabrielle.*

Craig Lowrie stood up. 'If someone has already read this, she is already dead.'

The old man whispered, 'And do you know what this will do to her? To Adele? May I ask if you still care?'

To give himself some time, Craig Lowrie re-filled the older man's empty glass. Had she not refused to come with him because of Gabrielle? And he had been so sure she would come. As they danced, not a word had been spoken. But he felt sure – that she would come to him was the contract. As he had ridden back for her, he had been so sure she would come. And now, there was perhaps no Gabrielle...He shuddered at the harshness of his own reasoning.

John Stewart Macdonald continued, 'And there's worse to tell you.'

*Could there be?* thought Craig Lowrie. He asked, 'Adele? She is ill?'

'Aye, she is ill. Pettigrew – Pettigrew beat her very badly – you know that. He didn't rein in his blows. And she, a lassie.'

'Aye.'

'And now, there is worse. When she mends, Robinson expects her to leave. To fend for herself. To live on the streets. He feels she has somehow cheated him, made a mock of him. He is implacable in this.'

Anger broke through Craig Lowrie, like a river in spate, carrying all before it. Adele's proposed expulsion by Robinson and the Highland Clearances had similarities that did not escape him. Men of power could play with the lives of the vulnerable as he hoped he never would. Even so, when he spoke, he was again in cold control. 'How long do you think we have – before this "eviction" takes place?' he asked.

'Some weeks more. Not fewer. She'll not ride for several weeks...If Robinson will allow her a mount, that is.'

'Allow her a mount? Would he not?'

Craig Lowrie understood vengeance. He had felt the long-simmering pain it could cause. The hillside massacre at Ardnackaig was never far from him. The faces of the murdered boys rose, whenever he closed his eyes to sleep. He heard the cries of his kin dashed on the rocks. He knew that he was waiting for the moment when he could take revenge and he could recognise revenge waiting in others.

He could also understand Robinson's obsession with Adele. Did he not feel so obsessed himself? But he would never understand Robinson's coldness. Coldness like this seemed a perverse cruelty, spinning, causeless.

And, although Craig Lowrie knew how to wait and would wait long into the Celtic night of vengeance – as long as any man alive – Craig Lowrie favoured straight dealing. But Robinson did not. Robinson's way of dealing was covert, twisted, unnatural to Craig Lowrie. Robinson would not help the woman he professed to have loved. *And he has no code,* thought Craig Lowrie.

Craig Lowrie would never like the man.

Adele, on the other hand, would try to find Gabrielle. And Craig Lowrie must now try to dissuade her from that. For her own sake. But also for his. He sipped his Madeira and said, 'she mustn't see this letter. She will go to her death. And for what? Gabrielle is, I think, already dead. Or will be soon.'

'So I thought, when I read it. So I thought when I looked at the face of the messenger. So I thought, when I looked at the whole crew of that French brig, running scared for their lives, down on the Quay. Too scared to go back. Too scared to go home.'

The fire crackled between them and then the old priest took a deep breath. 'What do we do now?' he asked.

He was not best pleased when he found out. Though old and tired, at Craig Lowrie's bidding, he was to go to France to attempt to fetch Gabrielle. The Craig Lowrie's trust was heart-warming but the priest's old bones ached at the thought of it. 'Still,' he said, 'I will do it. For Adele. One last trip.'

'We'll wait till you return. There can be no wedding without you. You, you'll bring Gabrielle with you south, and, if he can travel, the father. To the Cave.'

'I shall. Well, I'll try. And you? Where will you be?'

'Ah, well – knowing that is the real trick. Argyll is hard upon my trail. I don't know how long I can stay ahead. But, I have to keep his men off my people somehow. And there is the unresolved matter of Ardnackaig.'

The priest's face was a blank. Craig Lowrie wondered at it. How could the old man not know about Ardnackaig? But he clearly did not, so Craig Lowrie continued, 'Word will come to me wherever I am and I will be there at Jamie and Emma's wedding. Perhaps, even with Adele.'

'I'll do my very best. My very best to bring them.'

'Either way,' said Craig Lowrie, 'stay safe, Father. There can be no wedding without you.'

With that, Craig Lowrie reached into the leather pouch on his belt and once more drew out the signatory ring. The cabuchon emerald, its rounded sides gleaming in the firelight, held the contract between the two men in its depths. Craig Lowrie reached for the priest's hand and slid on the ring. Gently, he eased it over the joint, deformed by the pain that now plagued the old man. And, in accepting it, John Stewart Macdonald became a Craig Lowrie man.

# Chapter 39

## Robinson Park, Arduaine
## 15th August 1793

THE WALK TO THE stables seemed endless. Adele could scarcely manage a step. But she did – and without a stick. This gave her hope and when she arrived in the yard, her heart leapt. Grooms were busy, horses impatient. She smelled the smell of the stables – hot and sweet – and heard the sounds – metal, stone, equine, human. Here everything seemed normal and she felt huge gratitude, not for the first time, that Emma had taught her to ride.

'Glad to see you are well, My Lady.'

The Chief Groom did not know, then, that she was to be banished without title or shilling. She smiled at him. But when she looked him closely in the face, she suddenly realised he did know. Of course, he did. Nothing escapes servants – ever. Of course he knew. He was showing her kindness.

She found she was leaning against a stable wall. 'Sirene?' she asked.

'This way, My Lady.'

'I don't think you should call me that. We are equals. Always have been.'

'Sirene is this way, My Lady. And you always will be – "My Lady", that is.'

'Thank you.'

She took his arm. Surprised at her trust and her touch, he led her across the yard towards the old stable block where the large stalls were. As they walked, every step on the cobbles jolted her cracked rib but Adele could see Sirene watching her. Even after seven weeks' absence from the stable yard, she was still welcome to Sirene. The mare had an intelligent, inquisitive expression. *She knows,* thought Adele, *she knows not all is well.*

Adele stepped into the loose box and reached out her hand to stroke the animal. Sirene moved quietly towards her, lowered her fine head and gently snuffled the young woman's skirts, trembling with pleasure at Adele's touch. She raised her head and Adele breathed softly into the horse's nostrils, letting the horse nuzzle her hands. Adele looked round. The groom appeared not to be listening any more. He was looking into the middle distance. *A man of tact,* Adele thought.

'Sirene, Sirene, will you come with me?' she whispered in French, 'I have to go – will you come with me?'

But before she could say more, she was interrupted by commotion in the yard. The farrier had arrived, Robinson was greeting him and they came towards the stable.

'She's in here,' Adele heard Robinson say. He was jovial to his equals – as ever. But the two men stopped in their tracks when they found Adele in the stable. There was nowhere to hide so, standing by Sirene, Adele raised her head and stared Robinson in the eye.

'My Lady!' said the farrier.

'You – here?' said Robinson. 'Are you able to ride now?'

Scarcely able to stand, Adele almost fainted as the cruelty in his voice washed over her. But – quite distinctly – she heard Robinson say, 'Well, as you see, Sirene will no longer be your mount. She is in foal.'

# Chapter 40

## Oban, Argyll
## 15th September 1793

MOLLY BALLACHULISH was overjoyed. Heaven had blest her twice that morning. Firstly, she had been taken up by the Lady Eleanor Bamburgh herself! She, Molly Ballachulish, had received an invitation to wait upon the Countess immediately at Robinson Park. And secondly, new pattern books (fifth hand) had reached her from Edinburgh. Cups seemed to be running over in every direction.

A plan had immediately presented itself. She would hasten to see the Lady Eleanor. They would take tea and discuss whatever it was that had prompted the invitation. All the ladies – *well, not by all accounts, the Lady Emma* – would be in the drawing room at the same time. And, then, perhaps she, Mrs Molly Ballachulish, could invite Adelaide, Lady Robinson, to wait on her at Ballachulish House in the town. She was not deluded enough to think she could ever presume an acquaintance with the Countess. But the possibility of friendship with Lady Robinson was more reasonable. It shone with the promise of a new dawn. And Lady Robinson could explain to Fiona exactly how she could adapt the styles in the pattern books so that she could best enhance her own face and figure.

*At seventeen, Fiona is the right age to be seen at her best,* thought Molly Ballachulish, whirling through her dressing room to select her afternoon tea attire. 'Fiona needs a husband.'

In truth, on the extraordinary occasion of the Midsummer Ball, Mrs Ballachulish had seen a look in Fiona's eye that she did not like. After all, she reasoned, tempting as wealthy brigands such as Malcolm Craig Lowrie might be, Oban was now full of young professionals, doctors and lawyers and architects, and any one of these would fit Mrs Ballachulish's bill for Fiona very nicely.

Mrs Ballachulish sighed. Though it pained her to think it, she knew her daughter Fiona was a frump. *But Lady Robinson – with her French elegance and natural charm – is just the sort of woman Fiona needs to bring her on.* And she, Molly Ballachulish, would manage the rest.

A phaeton was assiduously prepared and – after a comparable degree of attention to her own appearance – Mrs Ballachulish left her dressing room strewn with all the contents of her emptied drawers and set off for Robinson Park.

All the way, she rehearsed over and over again what she would say to encourage Lady Robinson to come to visit her. But, when she thought of it, even more intriguing was the puzzling question of why the Lady Eleanor – a Countess, whom she could not remember meeting – would send for her particularly. Perhaps she had met her – but, no, she would certainly have remembered that. No, it was all a mystery. *And a delightful one!*

Shown into a drawing room of Robinson Hall, the wonders continued. Mrs Ballachulish noted the soft velvets and rich brocades and their melting, breath-taking colours. She saw nothing she would have chosen in a thousand years. (In fact, at home, for her furnishings, she had selected Mr Ballachulish's family plaid – and very daring it was of her to do so). But her eyes were now opened to other, more subtle possibilities. What she was seeing here in the elegant receiving rooms of Robinson Hall was an education. The hallways, it was true, still retained a masculine austerity about them. But, no, the receiving rooms, she felt, were divine. And she made herself a promise. *Much will be changing at Ballachulish House when I return home.*

Settled comfortably on a delicate mahogany Chippendale two-seater, and stroking the striped ivory jacquard upholstery, she again rehearsed the interview that lay ahead. She envisaged the moment when the Lady Eleanor would appear and what she would say and how she, Mrs Ballachulish, would reply. But when the moment came, Molly Ballachulish was totally unprepared for what happened.

Eleanor whirled through the door in a state of high distress. Without polite form or courtesy, she seized Mrs Ballachulish by the arm.

'Did you see her? Did you see her on the road?' she asked.

'See who?'

'Mademoiselle de Fontenoy!'

Molly Ballachulish could not speak.

The Lady Eleanor asked again, 'Did you not see her on the road?'

Molly Ballachulish gulped. Finally, she understood. Without note or warning, Adelaide had left.

# Robinson's Journal

## Robinson Hall, Arduaine
## 15th September 1793

*WELL, NEVER TRUST a Frenchwoman. I had thought she was too ill to move. But no, the minx was clearly biding her time – until the moment was right. Until my back was turned. And now, night's coming and we still haven't found them. I sent that silly woman Ballachulish back to town to alert the constabulary and the Port. I've had the servants combing the gardens. I've had the groundsmen combing the Park. I've had the English mercenaries combing the hills. Nothing. Absolutely – bloody – nothing. And that horse – that foal – worth thousands of guineas. It couldn't be worse. Gone, too. The mare's breeding was all towards speed. Well that's certainly come back to bite me now. They must have moved like lightning. But that girl, Adelaide, can't leave the Port with the horse – no. No ship will take it on board now – not with the soldiers on the Quay. She won't even get close. Even if she had money to bribe some French sailors. And that's the one thing I've – wisely, it seems – made sure she never had. Perhaps we should concentrate on the road south. Yes, that's it. Away south. That's the route she'll take. To join her friends, her 'brigand' – that whole pack of the Craig Lowries. This joke at my expense gets worse by the minute. I'll have her killed for this. And him. Well, I was going to do that anyway. But she, she is dead.*

# Chapter 41

## The road to Oban
## 15th September 1793

ADELE CLUNG TO Sirene's saddle bow and trod carefully. The rocks beneath her feet shook and rolled and Sirene's hooves caused sparks on the uneven ground. Concealed in sightline by hummocks and woodland, woman and horse were moving north parallel to the Oban road but not on it.

Adele's hair had become unpinned, her dark curls blowing freely in the wind. Her day gown was now torn and two shawls – both rich and expensive Paisley – soiled. Concealing the leather travelling bag with its saleable valuables, now slung across Sirene's saddle, one shawl was stained with horse sweat and dusty from the road. The other shawl was pulled tight about Adele's bruised body in an attempt to stop pain but also keep out the early autumn chill. But she had at least thought to exchange her lavender slippers for her leather riding boots, which, although not ideal for walking, at least surpassed silk.

If anyone saw her from the road, she would cause comment. But at least, Adele thought, none would be able to accuse her of theft. Except of Sirene. Sirene had never been hers but how could she have left Sirene behind? But the twenty-mile journey would now take woman and horse six painful hours. It would demand all of Adele's strength of will and all of Sirene's love. And it would be hard for both of them. They heaved and scrambled over boulders and slid on the grassy slopes and, above all her troubles, Adele could hear the call of the whirlpool of Corryvreckan. The sound made her shiver. The whirlpool pulled together so many threads of her life and had drummed its way constantly through her lost years. It reminded her how frail she was and it mocked her. It told her she was incapable of resisting forces beyond her control. *Best to turn back,* it seemed to say. *Better not to have done this – for both of you.*

*But,* Adele thought, *now we have skirted the loch and crested the hills behind it, the north-facing slope to the south of Oban will lead downhill almost all the way towards the Port. We are in sight of where we need to be.*

The going was tough now. Especially in descent, the strain on the whole body was the same for woman and horse. Sirene had slowed her pace to help Adele and Adele, realising the slower movement put a greater burden on the pregnant animal, tried to forget the stabbing pain of the cracked rib in her side and move more quickly. Sirene was scratched, bleeding and mud-spattered and Adele was weeping for it.

But, eventually Adele and Sirene broke from the woodland under the cliff into the lane at the side of the Oban Distillery. Then, without a word to the distillery watchmen, who stood aghast and in silence at the gate, woman and horse passed by, following the smell of fish to the North Quay.

Within minutes, Adele had located the gangplank of the French brig, *Espoir,* tied up alongside the granite quay. The setting sun was now capturing the glints of quartz in the stones but she had no time to admire it. She had to find the brig's captain before the evening tide took his vessel out from Oban into the Firth of Lorne. She caught up with him just as he was about to go up the gangplank after some business in town.

*'Bonsoir, M'sieur le Capitaine!'* He turned and she could see plain shock on his face to hear French courtesy on a northern Scottish dockside.

'I can help you, *mademoiselle?*'

'I have need of passage to France – with my horse.'

He glanced at her appearance and she found herself blushing at the frankness of that glance.

'That will not be possible, *mademoiselle.* My sailors, they are superstitious. They do not like women on board ship. And your horse, we have nowhere to stable it.'

He was about to turn away.

'I have money, monsieur. I can pay.'

'I regret, *mademoiselle.*'

'I pray you.'

*'Mademoiselle,* I will be honest. I am not going anywhere. Not until I hear more news from France. There is Revolution there, you know. And I am certainly not going home. Until I know.'

Adele bit her lip at the word 'home'. He saw that and softened – but only slightly.

'I regret, *mademoiselle,'* he repeated. Before stepping onto the gangplank, his eyes swept over her again. The quality of her Paisley shawl, pulled tight around her, seemed to interest him but, she realised, her pretty lavender silk petticoat and skirts were in shreds and, above her riding boots, her stockings were holed.

'And you, *mademoiselle,'* he said, though not unkindly, 'look like trouble.'

With that he left her and for a moment she stood on the quayside, at a loss.

Then a familiar voice made her turn. 'This was not well done, My Lady.'

Now behind her stood Robinson's Chief Groom. He was stroking Sirene, as she stood behind Adele, and Sirene was nuzzling the man. She would find the apple treat he'd brought for especially for her. He said gently to Adele, 'I'll take her back home now – she'll be better cared for there when her time comes.'

Adele was about to protest but her eyes filled with tears. She had almost subjected the lovely Sirene to a sea voyage and a birthing in a strange land. Impulse, Adele now recognised, could have killed them both. 'Yes, yes. Of course,' she said but she clung to Sirene's neck. Her world was falling away from her now. *How could she have been so thoughtless?* She sobbed – a deep, despairing dry sob – with her face buried in the soft mane. For a wild moment, she wished she could be nine-years-old again. That she could start again. That none of this had ever happened.

Then the Chief Groom tried to ease the reins from Adele's reluctant grasp. When she had relinquished them, he said, 'My Lady, forgive me, but the Lady Eleanor...she bade me find you and take you for safety to Mrs Ballachulish. You can stay there until the Lady Eleanor returns. She will have to go south any day. She has no choice. But she told me to tell you she will come for you – as soon as she can.'

'Ah yes – south – for the wedding.' Adele could see the groom was uncomfortable. He clearly did not feel it was his place to pass on personal messages. But perhaps he recognised how important the

Lady Eleanor felt this message would be. He is so *sensible,* she thought, using the word in the French way.

Abruptly the Chief Groom turned away to remove Adele's travelling bag from Sirene's saddle and signalled to a stable lad standing not far away. The boy now took Sirene's reins from the Chief Groom's hands and led the horse away. Adele watched him for a moment. The patient boy would wait by the cross-roads on the road south until the Chief Groom, remounted, joined him. Then they would begin the two-hour journey back to Robinson Park. Sirene would be exhausted and, unless they were very careful, she might lose the foal. Adele could hardly speak for guilt. But, as she waved *'A Dieu!'* to Sirene, she knew herself that the mare would be safer with these kind and loving Highlanders than foaling on board the brig or alone in some field near St Malo in Brittany.

Close to collapse herself, she then took the Chief Groom's arm. He hefted the bag and they walked slowly along the Quay – heading away from the bustle of the Port in the direction of the increasingly genteel end of town and the newly-constructed Crescent, near the North Shore. Here they found the Ballachulish town-house.

As Adele climbed the steps up to the huge and freshly-painted door, she was aware the groom behind her did not move. *He is a good man,* she thought, suddenly sorry to leave those who had been kind to her, in so many ways, at Robinson Park. Then she braced herself and rapped the imposing brass door-knocker. And she was surprised to find Molly Ballachulish open the door herself.

'Oh, my dear, my dear, I have the Lady Eleanor's confidence. I saw you coming up the Crescent. You need explain nothing. Come in. Come in, Mademoiselle de Fontenoy.'

Adele could not help but raise an eyebrow. However, standing in the polished and furbelowed hallway of the Ballachulish town residence, she felt aware of how shabby she must look and shame made her humble. She stood still and waited as, delighting in her newfound intimacy with the aristocracy, Molly Ballachulish swept on, 'What a fright you gave us all! Come, you will want to change. I shall send my maid to help you. She is French, you know.'

'No need for a maid.' Adele had managed without her own maid for years – with the exception of the occasional request for help from the housekeeper. Now, in her changed circumstances, 'managing without' seemed a matter of pride.

'Oh, but I insist.' Mrs Ballachulish was joyous, almost fainting with stress and stays. 'You are my honoured guest. I shall send her to you directly. And then we shall take tea in the drawing room. You will have dined, of course.'

Adele did not demur and, finally, out of politeness, she submitted to the suggestion of the French maid. A few moments later, in the Ballachulish House guest room – which, clean, neat but not grand, was to be hers for the duration of her stay – she met her fellow countrywoman. But, although Adele greeted the maid in French, hostility underscored every movement the woman made. The weary Adele was silenced. For some moments, the slamming shut of drawers was the only sound in the room.

Then the child's court dress was given its own hanger within the *armoire*. Sensing satire, Adele tried again. 'I beg you,' she said. 'Have I done you harm? How can that be? We have not met, I think.'

The maid peered at Adele with unnerving frankness. 'I am *La Veuve,* Madame Marie Le Pecque. I was married to Monsieur Jean le Pecque,' she said. No further explanation was given.

But, as the strangeness of Breton French washed over Adele like cold sea, she gasped at the chill of it and at what she had just heard. Why was the Widow Le Pecque here in Scotland? Acting as a maid? And why would she not answer Adele's enquiries and remarks, made so warmly and in French?

But, without saying more, the maid continued her work. In tight silence, she slid the cotton nightdress under the pillow and then lastly untied the Paisley shawl knotted around the leather travelling bag. She examined the shawl and cast the now ragged cloth to one side, as if for cleaning. From the bag, she drew out Adele's jewels, the letter envelopes, and the candlesticks, inspecting each item before laying it on the bed. She then stood back to look at the paltry and eccentric display, with a glacial sigh.

Adele, however, looked at these 'treasures' and was glad she had managed to retain some vestige of her French common sense. The trove of jewels and silver would pay for much, she thought. Then, losing patience with the sulky maid, she waved her to one side and took out her sewing kit herself. Seated on the bed, she fingered each tiny tool, enjoying its quality and feel. This would feed her, somehow, somewhere, she was sure.

But, suddenly, she felt uncomfortable. Marie Le Pecque had drawn close, staring at the soiled dressing still clinging to the wound on Adele's cheek. However much Adele wished she could hide it, the wound inflicted by Pettigrew was still prominent. No-one who looked at her could miss it. The maid tutted her disgust and then withdrew, unsmiling and still without a word, leaving Adele shivering in the semi-darkness of her new surroundings.

But Marie Le Pecque returned a moment later with towels. Two bemused footmen followed, carrying a copper bath, and some giggling maids came in, bearing ewers of steaming hot water. The whole household was clearly unused to waiting on ragged visitors, Adele could see. Their dignity had been affronted.

But, with Mrs Ballachulish waiting in the salon, there was no more time at present to explore this. *Perhaps the hostile French widow will mellow,* thought Adele. *These things happen. Even Sirene grew to love me in time.*

Again, taking with her the junior maids, Marie Le Pecque left the room. And, Adele was just wondering what to do next when, to her surprise, the French maid re-appeared. She was clutching the means of changing the dressing on Adele's face and, although still unsmiling and wordless, she did this with unexpected care.

Mrs Ballachulish had herself laid out some clean clothes. These would hang loose on her frail form but – from their cut and fabric – Adele knew they must have been expensive. She was grateful. And when she was at last bathed and ready, she glided down the stairs and appeared in the drawing room transformed from a ragged vagabond. She was now dressed in a black high-necked silk gown; her shoulders were covered with the finest white linen; and, resting on her soft hair, she wore a modest but exquisite Quaker cap. She wore no ornament other than her usual tiny silver crucifix. She embodied the respectability of a *bourgeoise.*

Even so, a chill moment of silence greeted her re-appearance in the salon. And, while it lasted, Adele could hear the sounds of Oban as its denizens roosted for the night. Like the gurgle and boom of the Corryvreckan whirlpool, muffled calls and the thunder of carriages penetrated the new glass windows. Nothing would pause for the private grief of a young French woman savagely attacked, friendless and far from home.

Adele also noted that the eagerness with which Mrs Ballachulish would have sought for a single word from 'Lady Robinson' on the night of the Midsummer Ball had disappeared like mist in the wind. And, in its place, there had come a clattering formality. But, the customary exchange of compliments and courtesies between the mistress of Ballachulish House and her humbled guest could not be avoided for ever.

There remained an undertow. Adele knew Molly Ballachulish would want to gauge how entertaining the disgraced Lady Robinson would affect her burgeoning social standing. This was a powerful conundrum for her. However much they would both have wished things otherwise, the events of the past few months had happened and, because of them, Adele wondered, would she ever be permitted to be part of the Ballachulish household – as the Lady Eleanor had seemed to hope? She was disgraced and, in spite of the Distillery Manager's wife's warm heart, this might cause difficulties for her social aspirations.

Adele accepted this and, waiting for some sign from Mrs Ballachulish, she stood patiently, just inside the door to the sumptuous salon of the new town-house. But she did not have to wait long to see what would happen next.

Presiding over the teacups, Mrs Ballachulish began proceedings. Continuing to address the standing Adele, she said, 'I promised her, the Lady Eleanor, that, if I found you, I would look after you...secretly. She will any moment have to ride south for her daughter's wedding. And she will be gone, distraught with worry about you, you know. But the wedding is pressing. Of paramount importance. Lady Emma and Jamie Craig Lowrie must be married soon. The Lady Eleanor told me, the situation is intolerable. If it doesn't happen now, there is every chance Emma will die an old maid...'

Adele felt there was some enhancement of the truth here but said nothing. She bit her lip and concentrated on the hectic Ballachulish plaid that newly graced the windows, the cushions and the chairs of the freshly-decorated salon. Mrs Ballachulish – with a gesture that finally invited the standing Adele to take a chair – said, 'But I am very happy to help you, my dear.'

She poured the tea and then offered milk or lemon. Adele took neither. But she then listened in surprise as Mrs Ballachulish declared, 'I never liked that man, Sir William. Too greedy, by far. And ostentatious.'

There was a pause. Adele said nothing and, to cover the moment, looked around the room again, about to remark on the originality of the furnishings. But, before she could, her eye was caught by her hostess's daughter, Fiona Ballachulish, seated by the fire. A screen, designed to protect complexions from the heat of the fire, partly obscured the young girl's face – to sinister effect. Adele smiled at Fiona. No smile was returned but in the eyes of Miss Fiona Ballachulish was puzzlingly but unmistakeably an expression of triumph.

*Do these Ballachulish women know everything?* Adele was uncomfortable at the thought.

Mrs Ballachulish swept on, 'And in return, while you are here, Mademoiselle de Fontenoy, you can do something for me...'

At this point, Adele realised the brooding presence of Fiona Ballachulish was significant. Molly Ballachulish smiled, breathless with delight and, here, Adele knew, was coming the truth of it.

Mrs Ballachulish announced, 'I want you to help Fiona acquire some of the grace and charm that you French ladies, Mademoiselle de Fontenoy, have in such abundance.'

Aghast at the boldness of the request, Adele gazed at her hostess. *How could Mrs Ballachulish be so insensitive?*

Then, somewhere a bell rang in the silent house and a maid came in to call Mrs Ballachulish away to below stairs. With a grimace, the Lady of the House bustled from the room. 'Really can no-one else deal with traders?' she tutted, over her shoulder.

But now, left alone, Adele and Fiona looked at each other.

Fiona spoke first. 'So...you are much changed, Mademoiselle de Fontenoy.'

Adele bowed her head.

'They won't queue to offer you their sword arms now.'

Adele was startled. Insensitivity seemed to be a Ballachulish family trait.

'He won't offer you his sword arm – not now. Not a man like that. Not Malcolm Craig Lowrie.'

Adele gasped. She felt as if slapped by her salon adversary. But then she rallied. She had been brought up in the court of Marie Antoinette and would not be faced down by heavy country manners and an ill will. She replied, 'If you wish to be charming, Mademoiselle Ballachulish, you must first study to be pleasant.'

'Making friends, are we?' Molly Ballachulish bustled in again to take her place at the teapot. 'That's wonderful.'

Adele took up her cup. The tea was perfect, the colour of a bright copper. She was taking Fiona Ballachulish's salt. She was taking her coin. She must resign herself to a life of domestic service. She drank her tea.

# Chapter 42

## The Knapdale Forest
## 30th September 1793

ALL SUMMER, the evictions had served Knapdale ill. On the tops and emerging from the shattered slopes and broken woodland of Argyll's forests, a sense of loss had filled a waiting landscape. And now, as the air browned with autumn, the glens once thronging with families lay deserted. And clachans were no more than heaped and broken stones, covered in grass. But, for the fugitive hoping to move down to the ferries and on to the Isles, these ruins gave unexpected shelter as the wind bit and chattered round the unprotected head.

And today of all days, as she lay in the truckle bed within the rough-hewn bothy in the sheiling, Emma thought also to be sheltered – by something that she could not yet identify. Something close. It was her wedding day. Nothing would harm her, she was sure of it. Her wedding day would hold its own magic. She and all she held dear would be safe today.

She was waiting for morning. There was no light but the moon and stars yet she was aware of the silent hulk of Jennet Awe between her and the night sky. *This,* she thought, *is the last time I'll sleep in a bed with a maidservant keeping me from the terrors of the night. Whatever those may be.*

And tonight the 'hulk' beside her would be Jamie. She ran her hands over her body and imagined what it would be like, to lie – finally – in the arms of the boy she had loved since she was seven. *Almost half my life,* she thought. It would be so different, to sleep with a man, not a maidservant. She would have to wait to know for sure but she could imagine. In the dark months, while she had thought Jamie dead, she had thrust thoughts like these away into the lightless places of her heart. But now they came back – strong – and she hugged herself. The Harvest Moon was right above her and she felt blessed.

Then she remembered her mother. Eleanor had spent time with her child. They had played and talked and learned together. *If only she could be with me today,* Emma thought. Suddenly, she felt a loneliness she had not recognised before. Throughout the long months, since the eventful night at Castle Craig Lowrie when Jamie had been torn from her grasp and her dreams shattered, this loneliness had clung to her life, like cobwebs in a cave. *But I can't cry,* she thought, *not on my wedding day.* She stuffed the sheet hard in her mouth to stop any sound escaping from her into the perfect night and gripped her fists so the pain of her nails pressing into her palms stopped up her sadness.

But then, Jennet Awe stirred. The older woman rose from the truckle bed, moved towards the door and, once outside, she gazed at the Harvest Moon – or as she called it, in the old way, the Moon of Songs. Silent and intent, she stood with her head cocked to one side. From the clearing, surrounding the bothy, the wooded hills sloped down to the Sound of Jura and the boom of the Corryvreckan rose with the mist. The woodland night creatures snuffled and squealed as owls swooped by on silent wings. But Jennet Awe did not seem to hear these. She was speaking to someone Emma could neither see nor hear. In the night wind, Emma clutched the words, 'My Lady!' but no more. Then Emma remembered the half-forgotten tales she had heard of the Craig Lowrie Witch Mother, the woman who had spawned not Jamie but his cousin, Malcolm. She crossed herself but she could not resist the lure. Enchanted, she drew closer. But heaving sobs of fear wracked the stalwart frame of Jennet Awe.

'Protect us all, My Lady' she pleaded with the Scottish night and Emma backed away without a word. She hoped she was leaving Jennet Awe to the comfort of the Celtic Moon's songs and...Emma did not know what.

But the morning star brought a brisk and efficient Jennet Awe and the scent of rose petals to Emma's side – as the woman poured water from a pitcher into a copper bath.

'For you, My Lady!' was all she said but she helped Emma undress, folding away the girl's cotton nightgown with immense care.

Emma studied this kind woman with the flour in her hair.

'Jennet Awe,' she said. 'Were you ever married?'

'Aye, once. He was killed – by Campbells. Before our child was born. And then the bairn – he died too. Too little food. Too much fear. Fear's the very Devil for the milk in your teats. But, after his death, my milk came again and I nursed Malcolm for the Lady Mairi. I had milk for him, when she had none. Fear, again. Fear because she was wed to Campbell Craig Lowrie.'

Emma remembered the strange events of the night.

'Tell me about the Craig Lowrie Witch Mother,' she said. 'Was the Lady Mairi the witch of the Corryvreckan? Will she drown Malcolm Craig Lowrie's enemies?'

Jennet Awe looked startled. 'Now why d'ye ask about those old stories?'

'The Craig Lowrie fascinates me. And I am soon to become his kin.'

'On your wedding day? To be thinking of someone other than your husband to be – why, bairn, you're in danger.'

'No', laughed Emma, 'Not a bit of it. Jamie is the Craig Lowrie for me. But his cousin – you must admit – he is a puzzle.'

'You won't be the first and you won't be the last to say it,' said Jennet Awe, swirling the petals in the water with her muscular hands – an unexpectedly tender gesture. Then she stood up, stretched her back and fetched some linen wraps.

'But Jamie, he's so different...' Emma nestled into the bed. 'Jamie is so kind. And funny. And...'

'He was never raised to be Laird.'

The words broke from the woman moving heavily around the bothy in the dying light of the Moon of Songs. But she seemed to regret her harshness and said quickly, 'The water's cooling, My Lady. Time for your Wedding Day bath.'

This was all she would say. She would not be drawn again and so Emma said nothing more about the Craig Lowrie cousins. Instead, sliding under the steaming water, she said, 'Today will be the best day of my whole life. Nothing, nothing will go wrong this time.'

Then she sat up, adding, 'It would be a dream too far, Jennet Awe, but I would so have liked my mother to be here...'

A new voice emerged from the night. 'And so she is, child.'

The Lady Eleanor walked in.

'Mother, how came you here?'

'I rode. Of course. Two days on the trail. The footmen held me up. They were so slow. And of course we came over Craig Lowrie land.'

Emma was full of admiration. For a Lady such as her mother to ride without armed escort through such wild country was courageous. But then 'My Lady Mother' could never be said to lack courage.

Eleanor nodded to Jennet Awe as the woman moved back into the shadows. Then, picking up the warmed linen, Eleanor swept it round her naked daughter. Emma, in Eleanor's eyes, was a child who had suffered much, unwarranted – and without her mother's comfort. And, in Eleanor's mind, there was no doubt where most blame should lie. Edwin Bamburgh had behaved with extraordinary callousness towards his only child and she, Eleanor, had been forced to comply. Resentment was festering in her like a plague boil but, she reminded herself, this was not the day for it.

One hour later, clean and warm and sipping tea, mother and daughter were examining the wedding dress that Adele had prepared for her friend. The soft gauze was caught at the waist with a silk ribbon sash the colour of rose madder. The contrast with Emma's autumn-coloured hair was rich. And, here and there, along the lines of the gauze, Adele had embroidered a touch of rose and a trace of *muguet*. It was a masterpiece.

A straw bonnet, trimmed with fresh flowers sat neatly on Emma's cropped curls. *The effect is charming,* thought Eleanor. But Emma removed it.

'No, this would be better for Adele,' her daughter said, her voice rippling with delight. 'It would frame her beautiful face. Mother, Adele has looked after me so well through all this unhappiness. I am so grateful.'

'And I am, too,' said Eleanor, her fingers tracing the embroidered flowers on the shimmering veil of the dress. Then she sighed.

'Is she safe? Is Adele safe?' Emma had caught a grace note of regret from that sigh.

And, more brusquely than she intended, Eleanor replied, 'She is – now.'

'Where is she? Did she not want to come?'

'She couldn't. I will go back to her, soon. I think she will need me. But I wanted to see you wed.'

'Oh, yes!' Emma could have been distracted by happiness. Jamie was alive. Her mother was here. She was about to be properly married.

And what had happened in the past seemed a bad dream. But from that dream, the ghost of Adele seemed to call, seemed to persist.

Emma's anxieties over her friend threatened to rattle the air. So Eleanor now told her daughter what she knew of Adele's journey to Oban and her current sojourn at Ballachulish House. But there was too much, too sad, she judged, to be repeated on her daughter's Wedding Day. She did not tell Emma all of it.

'Well, I'm glad she's among friends,' said Emma, playing with her sash. 'But what possessed her to leave? She may not have liked Robinson but she was safe there. Is she trying to return to France?'

'Well, I'm not too sure of the "whys" of this. So here let us now think of you and your day.'

'I'm still sad she won't be here. Did she not want to come?'

'Oh yes. I think you may be sure of that. And look at this lovely gown. Do you not think she would have liked to see it worn?'

Of the three women in the room, only Eleanor knew how much Adele had wanted to see Emma wear this gown. Before the Midsummer Ball, Adele had worked late into the night to create the wedding dress. And the plan was that she would bring it to Emma on her wedding day, wherever and whenever that may be. But, after Pettigrew's attack, as Eleanor watched over her, Adele had struggled with bruised and swollen hands to complete the remaining touches to the dress. She had ensured it was ready for Eleanor's saddlebags, when needed. *Oh, yes,* thought Eleanor, *I know how much it cost Adele to make this dress. And how much she longed to see you wear it.*

But now, to replace the bonnet, Eleanor took up some flowers, wove them into a coronet and graced her daughter's curling chestnut crop with it. Then she said, 'You are ready.'

Outside the bothy, Berry stood waiting in the clearing. A Craig Lowrie clansman, at Jennet Awe's request, had brushed his coat till it shone, removing all the mud the Scottish autumn had thrown at him. Then Jennet Awe had plaited his luxuriant mane with silken ribbons and bells. The huge Friesian stood quiet and gentle, as Emma mounted and her mother arranged her gown over the stirrups, And, then, followed by an armed guard of clansmen, and flanked by the Lady Eleanor and Jennet Awe, Emma rode down the woodland track towards Loch Caolisport. She knew, this time, her bridegroom would be waiting without fail by the ancient cave of St Columba. And, as she rode, Emma felt even the forest was waiting in reverence for the Holy Sacrament of Marriage.

* * *

Once at the cave, Jennet Awe helped Emma dismount and Eleanor stepped forward to check that the wedding could proceed. She moved aside the fronds of fern – heavy with Autumn rain – and the darkness of the cave lifted.

In the ninth century, half way back towards the lifetime of the Christ, St Columba had sailed from Ireland to bring Christianity to this wild peninsula and he had sheltered here in this place. Eleanor was silent for a moment but then, she was afraid. She thought, *In spite of all its power, this cave is no church.*

'Is this holy?' she asked. 'Is it holy enough?'

'This,' said a deep, strong voice behind her, 'is the holiest of places.'

Elsewhere, John Stewart Macdonald was usually marked out as a priest only by his black clothes and hat. But now he wore the full wedding regalia of the Catholic Church. These declared he had all the authority necessary to perform the marriage between the Jacobite, James Craig Lowrie, and the Lady Emma Bamburgh and Eleanor took comfort at the sight of him. And she knew *What had been half-done at Castle Craig Lowrie all those months ago, this holy Father would finish.*

'We meet at last, Father,' she said. 'How truly delighted I am to find you here.'

She was also gratified to find the bridegroom at the mouth of the cave, ready to meet her daughter. 'I am the bride's mother,' she said, 'And here she is! Isn't she lovely?'

James Craig Lowrie was gazing in frank admiration at his bride-to-be, his features awash with love and hope. Looking at him, Eleanor could have hugged herself with delight. *My daughter will be safe with this husband,* she thought.

But his groomsman, his cousin, was another matter. She studied Malcolm Craig Lowrie covertly. Also at the mouth of the cave, he stood kilted and bedraggled. His white shirt was stained with grass; and, though wrapped closely and pinned with the finest silver, his plaid, similarly so. He bristled with weaponry – a broadsword, a flintlock, and a dirk – and a musket was propped up against the cave wall at his side. *This man is dressed for war, not weddings,* Eleanor thought.

'Are you expecting trouble, Malcolm Craig Lowrie?' she asked. A challenge.

‘Always,’ he said. His teeth were white and shining through the grime on his face. She noted his mouth smiled but his eyes did not. *And those eyes, turquoise as the sea of the Isles.* She shivered. *This man is dangerous.*

Her quick ears also heard a puzzling exchange between Father Macdonald and the Laird.

‘You are alone,’ the younger man said to the priest, quietly looking around.

And the muttered reply did not escape Eleanor. Father Macdonald whispered, ‘Aye, as we thought, the old man could not travel. She would not let him out of the house. She will come when she can – which I fear will not be soon. And things are bad. I – even I – met with discourtesy.’

As he spoke, for a moment, he seemed to crumple. Shuddering, he began to search the folds of his robes. At last he found what he was looking for – a signatory ring – and offered it to Craig Lowrie. ‘Here,’ he said, ‘I shall not be needing this again. I can do no more in France. It is no longer a Christian country.’

Eleanor saw the young man nod, touch the old priest’s arm, take the signatory ring and slide it into the leather pouch hanging from his belt. Then, without a word more, Laird and Priest separated. Father Macdonald assumed authority again and the Lady Eleanor leaned forward to take the bouquet from her daughter’s hand. Then bride, groom and witnesses turned towards the stone altar. The crucifix carved into the rock above shone out of the shadows and the rough chapel was bright with white heather and candlelight. *Yes, this is perfect,* thought Eleanor. ‘Begin. There is no holier place than here,’ she said.

The ceremony reprised and, in less than the time it took for the sun to move across the mouth of the cave, James Craig Lowrie and Emma Bamburgh became man and wife.

Then, Edwin Bamburgh arrived. The flank of hill lying before the cave was suddenly a mass of leather and steel and Craig Lowrie clansmen – carrying only targe and dirk and concealed in the woodland that fringed the clearing – suddenly found they could not reach their Laird.

Malcolm Craig Lowrie was trapped.

Edwin Bamburgh smiled.

‘Well, Emma, my dear, I came to your second wedding anyway!’

‘What are you doing, father? Did you know about this, mother?’

'Of course, not. And, yes, Edwin, what are you doing here – with all these soldiers? It's your daughter's wedding!'

'It's quite simple, my dear. I have been dispatched by His Grace, the Duke of Argyll, to bring in the outlaw, Malcolm Craig Lowrie.'

'But he is no outlaw! He is the Laird!' Jamie was aghast.

Eleanor managed, 'And you chose this moment to do this?'

'And on what charge?' John Stewart Macdonald stepped forward. Passions were close to spilling over. Bloodshed would soon follow. But Bamburgh did not answer and signalled to the four soldiers closest to the Craig Lowrie. They laid hold of him before he could move.

But he did not move. He stood still and spoke in a loud clear voice. He said, 'My Lord Bamburgh. I am a Scottish laird in Scotland. By what right does an Englishman try to hold me?'

Bamburgh smiled. 'I repeat, I am the agent of the Duke of Argyll, and I arrest you on the word of an English magistrate.'

'Edwin!'

'Of course, my dear, I'll show you.' Something of meekness laced Bamburgh's voice as he drew from his cloak a letter from Sir William Robinson. It was addressed to himself and at Inveraray. He handed it to his wife, ignoring his soldiers smirking behind their chainmail.

In silence, Eleanor read the first part which ran, *'My dear Edwin, tell the Duke of Argyll if he wants to capture Craig Lowrie there's every chance he'll be at your daughter's wedding. This won't be at Craig Lowrie Castle – the Duke has his troops all over that part of the region. My agents – whom I have paid well for the information (of which more later, along with the cost of the army you bade me hire), they say the most likely venue for this wedding of yours is the Cave on Kintyre. The Cave known as Columba's. And there you'll find the whole nest of them – perhaps even my former wife, Adelaide.'*

'So,' Eleanor tutted, 'here's the reason for all this hunting and tracking and riding all over the countryside. Adele. That's what William wants. But, Edwin, really! Why did you involve yourself in this?'

Eleanor read it again and said, 'You can't believe this, Edwin. You can't.'

'What? Not believe our old friend Robinson over the word of this, this ruffian? Are you so taken with the fellow? My wife and daughter, both taken in by such a – such a ruffian.'

'A ruffian, perhaps, but of your rank,' said Malcolm Craig Lowrie, his voice cold as the morning. The shieling now rippled with menace.

'What is the charge?' Father Macdonald attempted again to contain the situation. His attempt was doomed to fail.

Bamburgh was smug. 'The charge is what gives me my authority here, father. Murder. The murder of an Englishman. The murder of Silas Pettigrew.'

No-one could deny that the Laird had killed Silas Pettigrew. But Jennet Awe suddenly gave a soft mewl and then fell to the ground. Her wailing began low, like an animal in pain, but then it swelled till the woods and the rocks and even the sea seemed to shatter.

'She is possessed,' said Emma. 'I've seen it before. It's the witch mother. It's the Craig Lowrie Witch Mother!'

'Nonsense,' said Bamburgh, kneeing his horse, which had scented something on the wind and was twisting to be free. But even Bamburgh was alert with superstition. And amid the waves of sound, his soldiers, crossing themselves, were backing away from the keening woman and Craig Lowrie's guards loosed their hold. After all, they believed, they were in the presence of the Craig Lowrie Witch Mother, speaking through the yowls of Jennet Awe and they had no wish to take on a Devil's Spawn. They released Craig Lowrie as if he burned their hands.

The Witch Mother's son did not wait longer. With speed – later reported as superhuman – Craig Lowrie sprang across the rocks at the cave side. He leapt straight onto Barbary's back and Barbary set off down the woodland rides, scattering Emma's wedding flowers as he went.

Now, though they had been penned by Bamburgh's soldiery, the Craig Lowrie clansmen threw their bonnets in the air – applauding their Laird. And, then, to a man, they began to shout. Realising they were still unable to break through the lines, they howled in rage. The war cry that drew the blood to their hearts rang out as one word across the hills. They shouted it as though their hearts would break. They shouted 'Ardnackaig!'

On his plunging horse, Bamburgh cursed his men for letting Craig Lowrie go. But then in the same breath, he told them not to fire their hastily-mustered flintlocks. 'You'll kill the horse, you fools! I'll not have him hurt.'

And, clinging low on Barbary's back – to offer no target for a lucky shot – Craig Lowrie rode him hard towards Loch Sween. Barbary responded and soon man and horse were swallowed by oak woods, no longer green with summer but red with autumn fire. None would catch them, neither there nor out on the bare hills between Ellary and the West.

The hag-ridden rabble of Bamburgh's escort – its weaponry at sixes and sevens – now turned back to its business of disciplined soldiering. But they found the Craig Lowrie clansmen were no more than memories and the warcry of 'Ardnackaig' no more than an echo. The wooded hillside was empty. And James Craig Lowrie was smiling as he kissed his bride's hand and said, 'We do seem to have eventful wedding days but let's make this our last.'

In disbelief, Edwin Bamburgh stared at the empty woodland ride. He clicked his tongue against his teeth and then cloaked his fury with a courtly smoothness. 'Well said, Jamie!' he agreed. 'And now we're to take you to your new home, Emma. Jamie, this is the gift of Argyll.'

'And what would that be?' Jamie could not help but be intrigued.

'Castle Craig Lowrie,' replied his new father-in-law with a sudden grin. 'The bounty on your head has been retracted. You and your wife – you are now in possession of all the Craig Lowrie lands, of Dalriada itself. And your Laird is no longer Laird,' concluded Bamburgh, wheeling his horse to the north.

The remnants of the wedding party mounted in shocked silence.

'I'll keep it only until my cousin comes to claim it,' Jamie managed to say.

'Nonsense, boy,' said Bamburgh. 'Malcolm Craig Lowrie is an outlaw and, because of that, none can give him shelter. Now don't give me cause to imprison you on your wedding day.'

Jamie was about to say more when Emma rested a hand on his arm. His face softened as he pulled Emma up beside him on his mount and held his bride in his arms for the first time. The time would come to challenge her father. But not yet.

The whole cavalcade set off towards the north, towards Castle Craig Lowrie. And only Eleanor marked John Stewart Macdonald peel off down the woodland ride towards Loch Sween but, she decided to say nothing. Driving her horse forward, she beguiled her husband with tales of the wonders she had seen on her ride south. Bamburgh was now enjoying the ride and basking in what he thought was Eleanor's forgiveness. But as she examined his face, Eleanor considered the man she had married. She did not like what she saw.

# Chapter 43

## Inveraray Castle Stables
## 16th October 1793
### Under a Hunter's Moon

ARGYLL HEARD THE CLICK behind him but continued to feel the forelegs of the black brood mare. 'Come in, Craig Lowrie. I've been expecting you,' he said at last.

Sirene twisted her head between the two men and Argyll smiled like a conspirator across her broadening back.

'Unthinkable amounts of money have changed hands for this horse,' he said companionably. 'Unthinkable to anyone else, any-way, but Sirene was cheaper than could ever have been hoped for.'

Argyll enjoyed hard bargaining and felt cheated that Robinson had had a vulnerable spot that made him easier to handle. The story whispered in village tap rooms – no doubt circulated by Robinson's agents – was that 'Lady Robinson' had taken against riding and wanted the horse removed from the stock while she visited friends in the Borders. So, the Duke had surmised, nowadays, the lawyer could not even bear to have Sirene in the stable yard and this had entertained Argyll immensely. Even so, he thought, the Argyll agents had done well in the negotiations, shaving yet more off a reasonable price. He could not help but congratulate them.

But, Sirene was unhappy, unsettled. The loose box, certainly large enough for a duke's darling, now seemed too small for her highly pregnant form and she did not like the present company. She was taut with the tension between the two men – stamping, trying to pace, as her tail lashed Craig Lowrie's bare legs. Argyll noted, the Highlander did not flinch.

Craig Lowrie was waiting in silence, his face unreadable – seemingly unmoved by tales of horse-trading in taprooms. The Duke decided not to offer him his ring to kiss. In the present situation, he did not deem it a political advantage to have fealty denied and none of his people were there to persuade the Craig Lowrie to comply. Instead, he said, 'I think we could find a more congenial place to discuss the matters between us.'

Craig Lowrie slid his dirk from the sheath lying across his chest. With the honed tip, he started to clean his fingernails, while resting his shoulders comfortably against the stable door – blocking ingress and egress. 'I think this suits me fine,' he replied.

The Duke had to agree. As a place to trap a man, the stable was perfect. It was dark and closed and the castle grooms were no doubt rounded up and penned in somewhere by Craig Lowrie clansmen. There would be no-one to hear him call. He swept up some hay to rub Sirene's flanks and calm her. The gesture was nonchalant. 'So,' he continued, 'What do you want?'

'Information.'

'Information?' The Duke stopped his grooming. 'This is not my usual currency. Not at all.'

But, after a pause, he added, 'I suppose – quite naturally – you'd like to know why you've been outlawed. And dispossessed. Not just killed. Yes, I suppose that must be something of a puzzle.'

Argyll spoke quietly so as not to alarm the pregnant mare further and, in the imperfect mix of light and shadows, he observed Craig Lowrie's almost imperceptible nod. The Duke turned to gentle Sirene again, with long rhythmic strokes to her neck. She began to gleam in the torchlight.

'She's a fine animal, is she not? She has no hot spots and undoubted strength. Yes, and the foal will do very well, too. Very well indeed. Due in Spring sometime, I believe. Yes, give it a few years and then, the St Leger, I think. When the foal's of age, I'd like to pit it against that horse you stole. The Earl Bamburgh's very proud of that horse, y' know. You did yourself no favours there – racing off with his St Leger. Oh yes, I hear everything, y' know. But, I assume, the horse's still in good condition. Berry was his name, wasn't it?'

Both men knew Argyll was pretending ignorance. Craig Lowrie replied, 'Barbary. "Berry" is what the Lady Emma calls him. Yes, he's tied to a tree outside Castle Craig Lowrie now. No harm done. Good service rendered.'

'Happy to hear of it. A strong mount, that one. I'm glad he's unharmed. In spite of his size, Bamburgh'll run him again and again in the St Leger, you know. And when the horse is close to losing...why then, I'll run the foal – perhaps three, four years old by then. But strong enough to take on Barbary, certainly...And he'll have been raised in secret. So I'll make some money. I'm glad I don't have to add horse-stealing to your list of crimes.'

'And what about yours?'

'My crimes are not the issue here. Now yours...that's another matter...I could have you hanged for the things you've done.'

'So why do you not?'

'Ah, now, have you not guessed?' The Duke let the question hang in the air between them. It was a feint, designed to stir a response. But, though Argyll was listening like a checked hound, Craig Lowrie's voice in reply gave him nothing. Argyll could not fathom the young man's thinking – yet.

'Setting that aside,' Craig Lowrie said, 'you know why I'm here.'

There were several possibilities, as the Duke acknowledged, but he was unprepared for what Craig Lowrie said next.

'Ardnackaig.'

'Ardnackaig?' While busy with the mare – a ploy to buy time – Argyll appeared to search his memory. Then he said, 'Ah, the new Craig Lowrie war cry, I gather. Well, yes, yes, I admit Ardnackaig was unfortunate.'

'Unfortunate?' For the first time, emotion flashed into the Highlander's voice.

Argyll's foil had found a mark. *Perhaps now they would at last make some progress,* he thought.

Angry, Craig Lowrie continued, 'The murder – in cold blood – of two boys not old enough to bear the dirk? Their disemboweling – unshriven? Their deaths – away from their mothers' arms?'

'Put like that, I can see why you are so upset.'

'Upset?' Hefting the dirk, as he spoke, Craig Lowrie was now standing between Argyll and the light. Argyll resisted the temptation to blink, sharply aware that his situation had suddenly become dire. 'You could say that, Uncle,' continued Craig Lowrie, 'And what would you care to do about it?'

'Well, well, yes.' Argyll's chosen defence was to appear at his most affable. 'You can have the men who did it. They were over-keen. It was a mistake to let them loose without direction.'

He peered through the half-light, checking the impact of what he was saying, 'You can pick them tomorrow. They'll be on the ride to Oban. Unhorsed. Maybe a bit confused...' he continued.

'You'll hand them over? Just like that?'

'Just like that. They deserve it. They were – uncivilised.' Impatient, Argyll did not want further to discuss the hillside at Ardnackaig. *A few rogue clansmen, drifting about the hills,* he thought. *Was he supposed to control everything on his vast tracts of land? All of the time?*

After that day in February when Craig Lowrie had first come to him about the massacre, Argyll had as a matter of course made enquiries of his stewards. But he doubted he had learned much. He knew that, the stewards would certainly have recognised his anger at being so embarrassed. As a result, what they knew they would certainly have hidden from him and, what they did not know, they might even have made up. Argyll also knew, he might even be made to feel some personal regret for the two boys – particularly if pressed by Craig Lowrie.

But, he had no intention of being brought to book by some wild hill men from the untamed corners of a region he was about to claim as his own. *No, he would not be held accountable by such.*

Craig Lowrie was speaking again. As he did so, Argyll heard the freezing over of streams in a Scottish winter. 'On the road, you say. I'll be telling the boys' kin where to find them. And they'll be given to the women.'

There was a pause and then Craig Lowrie said, 'I dislike the ease with which you've just handed over your clansmen to their deaths.'

Sirene laid back her ears and flung up her head. But, Craig Lowrie moved to where she could see him in the torch-lit and shadowed stable. And – soft as summer wind in woodland trees – he breathed into her flared nostrils. He ran strong hands down her neck. He stroked her face – from forelock to nose and gentle mouth. He murmured in the Gaelic. She lowered her head.

With the sound of Gaelic rippling through his mind, Argyll thought suddenly of Craig Lowrie's mother. His heart clutched in his chest. He gasped with delight, admiring the young man as, still murmuring, Craig Lowrie slowly untied Sirene's tether, retrieving an apple core from his plaid for her. He let the treat fall into the straw and, snuffling in her bedding to find it, Sirene bowed in pleasure at Craig Lowrie's touch.

To his surprise, like the mare, Argyll found his guard was down. This was a state dangerous for a politician, he felt, and forced himself to recover, asking brusquely 'Was there anything else?'

Craig Lowrie answered softly, as if still gentling the horse. 'Well, there is the somewhat pressing matter of your giving the lairdship of Craig Lowrie to my little cousin, Jamie.'

'Ah, James Craig Lowrie. Young, passionate – and a blusterer.'

'But he'll not know what to do with the lands and people of Dalriada. As you know. He was not bred to it, as I was.'

'I thought that might come into it. But,' Argyll found himself unexpectedly drawn to explain his strategy, 'giving James Craig Lowrie the Craig Lowrie lands is a way of controlling him. Keeping his mind off flamboyant, empty gestures. And a boy's rebelliousness. No, now he'll be controlled by his responsibilities – and the Lady Emma, of course. I had the pleasure of her acquaintance, as you know, last summer. A spirited girl. With a strong right arm, as I recall. Poor Pettigrew, what a night he had of it. His last, too. And who will control the Lady Emma? She will be controlled by her father, I trust. And her father...'

'Is liegeman to the Duke of Northumberland.'

'You are well-informed. But there will be no conflict between the small services I shall ask of Bamburgh and his bonds to Northumberland. In fact, it may be a useful way of endorsing a pact...'

'Northumberland knows of this pact?'

'Not yet, but he will. Dinna fash yerself.'

'And where does my dispossession fit in with all this?'

'You – ah yes, you. You are many things. You are difficult. Always have been. Disruptive. A gentleman – living in the heather. Irritating. No bar bills at a London Club for you! But, as I have asked before, I now ask you again, will you ride with me, Malcolm Craig Lowrie? Will you fight alongside me? And will you and your kin and your kin's kin carry the name of Campbell? I have the right to ask. You know that. Will you?'

'I cannot.'

'Others have before you!'

'I know. You have sucked in small clans and septs the length and breadth of Argyll and Bute. But I cannot. I will not.'

'Then, you must leave Dalriada.'

'Better that than live as liegeman to a Campbell. I'm no man's tacksman. Certainly never yours.'

Argyll was quiet, suddenly saddened.

'But why would you let me go? Why would you not have me hanged – as you say you could?' Craig Lowrie continued.

'I've my reasons.'

'They must be strong.'

'They are.'

'So you offer me safe passage.'

'I do.'

'And my kinsmen? If they choose to stay, will they stay safe? These are their heartlands. Not all will want to go with me.'

'You underestimate yourself. But, no. I'll not treat them worse than my own.'

'As poorly as that? No, it is not enough. The burnings, the killings, the clearances – these must stop. The Craig Lowrie kin must be safe. And free.'

'They will be. If you go.'

Craig Lowrie appeared for a moment to be considering accepting the idea.

*Perhaps,* thought Argyll, *freedom from a Laird's obligations has its appeal for the Craig Lowrie. After all. It's duty drives Craig Lowrie. He'll save his clan. And he'll dispossess himself, if he must, to do it. But his passions lie elsewhere. Perhaps, at last, I have found the way to manage Craig Lowrie. Craig Lowrie wants freedom. But to do what?*

Argyll was surprised but he did not press the matter. Instead, he said, 'Some things for you to weigh in the balance when you consider the options.'

'If I go – and it is by no means certain I will – you will keep your word? My people will be safe?'

*Ah,* thought Argyll, *not entirely malleable, then.* 'Certainly.'

'If they are not, I will hear of it. And I will bring that once more to your door.'

'Are you threatening your Laird?'

'Not mine.'

'Your Laird!'

Craig Lowrie shrugged. Argyll tutted. He disliked that French habit the young man had picked up so long ago, long before he came back to Dalriada. But Argyll had further business to settle. Pleased with the general progress he had made, with new vigour in his voice, the Duke said, 'You are also the last Lord of the Isles.'

'Long since gone, that aristocracy.'

'Even so,' the Duke pressed on, 'you carry that title among your others. And you carry it in your blood. Not your father's blood. Your mother's blood. I believe you are the last in the line. And I want that title – I want it for Argyll.'

Argyll felt rather than saw Craig Lowrie's eyes narrow. 'Now why would you be wanting to take on that title? What right of blood or lineage would give it to you? What advantage would there be for you to hold a title long lost?'

'I want the title. For power, influence, land...impute what you will.'

'Is that why you want the pact with Northumberland, too?'

'If it pleases you to think so...'

'But I still don't see how a defunct title will help...'

'Somerled – the First Lord of the Isles – his name has an old magic. And I need that title. I choose not to explain why.'

'And why should I give it you...?'

Argyll was becoming irritated by the word games, twisting and spinning and whirling around him. Craig Lowrie could have been a lawyer with a mind like that. He decided to cut through to the heart of the matter.

'One thing is truth – your father was a Campbell.'

'Aye, Campbell Craig Lowrie was his name.'

Argyll had warmed to his theme, forgetting Sirene would be startled by the ramping tension. He faced Craig Lowrie, saying 'That is precisely the point in dispute.'

It was now Craig Lowrie's turn to be startled. Argyll had fed him an entirely new thought. Was the man who had beaten him, all through his childhood, not then his true father? And if not, then who was?

Argyll watched as Craig Lowrie calmed and re-tethered Sirene, giving her another treat from the folds of his plaid. He is looking for time and space, thought Argyll. Craig Lowrie seems – for the first time – wrong-footed.

The Craig Lowrie dirk glittered again. Cut down from the claymore of Campbell Craig Lowrie by the skilled cutlers of the Isles, it was a fine piece of weaponry. Then the dark leather sheathed it against Craig Lowrie's chest. And Argyll knew he was back in control.

# Chapter 44

## Tayvallich Quay, Argyll
## 16th November 1793
### Under a Moon of Mourning

IN THE DARKNESS of a wintry evening, again on the quay at Tayvallich, Father John Stewart Macdonald clutched at his saddle and slid painfully to the ground. For a moment he paused, resting his forehead on his horse's shoulder and then he breathed deeply and shook himself free.

'Are you well, Father?' The kind concern in the voice almost made an honest man of him. He was close to weeping, but he pulled himself up and said briskly, 'Fine, thank you, my son. Fine.'

The fisherman was about to return to his work when he hesitated and said, 'There'll be no more sailings this night, Father. Tomorrow, perhaps – if the storms calm.'

*He won't already have gone, will he?* wondered the priest. Turning to the fisherman, he asked, 'Did you see passengers on earlier ferries this night?'

'No, none.'

The man's reply was spare. He had nets to mend.

*But there's something else, something he isn't telling me,* thought Father MacDonald. 'Are you sure? Did you not see anyone?'

The man clammed hard. 'Anyone? No – I saw no-one. No-one on board the boats, Father.'

*He is finding it hard to dissemble to the cloth,* thought the priest. He pressed him further. 'Did you no see a Craig Lowrie down here? At the quayside?'

'Now why would you be wanting to know? No I'll no take your

money, Father. That's not what I'm after having.'

'And what is it – you're after having?'

A sign, a sign of friendship to the Craig Lowrie, as if the weary priest did not recognise this. It had been a mistake to return the signatory ring to the Craig Lowrie at the wedding. But, when the priest had last returned from France, he could not have imagined that he would need the signatory ring again. Relieved to be back here, in Scotland he had felt safe but now all his certainties were tossed about the sky. He almost envied those Highlanders travelling to the New World. There perhaps they would have control of their lives. He hoped with all his heart this would be the truth of it for them.

'I have nothing,' John Stewart Macdonald sighed, gesturing helplessly to the fisherman. 'Nothing but my word.'

'Even your word may not be enough, Father. These are dangerous times.'

'Then I shall not hear your words.'

'No, you'll not hear my words.'

*So Craig Lowrie may already be away to the Isles. But I cannot be sure,* thought the old man and, trailing his mount behind him, he turned towards the quayside inn. He could see the inn was almost identical to *The Three Fishes*, or any other inn, in any seaport up and down the West Coast. Craig Lowrie could be in Oban or Campbelltown or further north or further south. He knew he would have to search them all. All the inns in all the ports until he found the Craig Lowrie, the only man – fugitive though he was – who could help. John Stewart Macdonald felt tired to his bones. He wanted peace and certainty. *But I also need to help My Lady. One more time, I need to help My Lady.* Through his fatigue, the thought persisted. His love for the child – holy as it was – this had been his guiding principle since he had first been summoned to Robinson Park all of a decade before. But the child? Where was the child now? She was a young vulnerable woman – and she was all but lost.

* * *

From Tayvallich, earlier that day, boat after boat had left for the Isles, the Craig Lowrie heartland, where neither man nor woman would betray or surrender their Laird. But the rough old trawlers had left without Malcolm Craig Lowrie and now the wind from the west carried storm with it, driving boats, large and small, into port.

Standing on the quayside watching the shipping, Craig Lowrie could feel the rain, hard with ice, bouncing off his plaid and, when it touched his face it felt like knife points. *Not the night for travelling further,* he thought. And it was then, across the waters of the dock, that he saw John Stewart Macdonald.

Craig Lowrie watched as, limping, the stooped old man was following the light of the inn. Craig Lowrie could have called out to him but first he waited a long moment to see who else was watching. No-one else broke cover. Cautiously, Craig Lowrie circled the dock and, on his way, he met the fisherman who had first spoken to the old man. Craig Lowrie paused alongside him.

'No, Laird, he did not say what he wanted. But it was you he was seeking. And he seemed gey sorrowful not to find you easily. I think he is ill, Laird. But I think what he has to say is a great matter.'

Craig Lowrie thought about this and then moved on. The man touched his greasy cap and then watched him go before picking up his torn nets again.

'I thank you', said Craig Lowrie from the darkness.

Now obscured in the inn doorway, Craig Lowrie viewed the scene inside. The old priest was speaking to the landlord – *taking a room, perhaps?* – but then he winced with pain into a far corner of the tap-room, by the fire. A serving woman bustled across and without a word pushed in front of him a bowl filled to the brim with rich and steaming mutton broth. He began with little enthusiasm to dip rough bread into the liquid and spoon up the barley from the edge. Agreeing with the fisherman, Craig Lowrie thought, *He's playing with his food. He should be hungrier for that broth. The man is ill.*

The brigand was about to seek out the priest, when his attention was caught by a French brig – Oban-bound – putting in. This was not part of her voyage plan but the weather was making the Gulf of Corryvreckan impassable and the wind had pushed the boat off course eastwards and up the more sheltered Loch Sween and into Tayvallich Haven. However, after the brig was made fast in the deep channels and the skiff had begun its ferrying, sailors tumbled ashore – some noisy, buoyant, in a gang, others walking as singletons. Craig Lowrie could smell the fear on these.

Intrigued, he changed his target. *What was the news here?* He chose to follow one sailor who walked alone. The man was dressed as the others, but he did not walk in quite the same way. He was not bow-legged with a long-serving sailor's gait. And, when he paused for a moment, uncertain which way to go, Craig Lowrie saw it. The sailor was standing with one heel to the arch of the other foot. The man had a court stance. That was enough for Craig Lowrie. This was no mariner ashore for comfort.

The Frenchman gasped as he was slammed against the dock wall, with Craig Lowrie's hand to his throat and the Craig Lowrie dirk to his ribs. Then Craig Lowrie addressed him politely in court language, asking what the news was from France.

'Please, please, *m'sieur.* Keep your voice low. I must speak Breton. Do you know Breton?'

'Do you know Scots?'

'No – I'm afraid I don't.'

'Then we must make do with Parisian French', said Craig Lowrie, without releasing his grip.

'Please, *m'sieur.* My compatriots, they must not hear us.'

'Really? Now why would that be?'

'I think you know, *m'sieur.* I think you play the games with me.'

'Perhaps I do. Perhaps, it is not kind, as a gentleman to treat so unmannerly another gentleman visiting my country.'

'And you, *m'sieur.* May I have your name?'

'No – but I will have your story.'

The dirk drew blood – not much, just enough – and the man gabbled his news. 'I was there. That day. When everything ended. When Marie Antoinette was killed.'

'Truly? The Queen? Dead?' Craig Lowrie felt the cold – suddenly. *Someone perhaps walking over his grave,* he thought. 'Continue, *m'sieur.*'

'*M'sieur,* I saw it all. Her beautiful, beautiful hair – she had shorn like a boy's. And the colour, it was drained. It was white. White with sorrow. And she, so pale, so thin, blushing when some lout called out the names of her children. But she was still so beautiful. And so queenly. All the way from the gaol – until the tumbrel reached the *Place de la Révolution.* Shaken so roughly about as the wheels hit the cobbles! But she remained queenly. Even there, where a scaffold was waiting for her. She stepped up, so grave and so dignified. She was wearing a pure white gown. Clean. Not a mark on it. Though she had been in prison all those months. All around, people shouted and laughed, peered at her shamelessly. Jeered. Dreadful, dreadful.'

The man faltered at the memory, shifting slightly in Craig Lowrie's grip. The grip tightened. 'And you? What role did you have in all this?'

'Merely a bystander, *m'sieur.* There was nothing, nothing I could do.'

Craig Lowrie considered the truth of this and then asked, 'What happened then?'

'She knelt and she prayed. Then she stood up and turned her head towards the towers of the Temple. Where she thought her children were being held.'

The man gulped. Craig Lowrie released his grip slightly – but not by much. For a moment, neither man spoke but the Frenchman at last broke the silence, 'The poor lady. I cannot believe she is dead. But I saw it. With my own eyes.'

'This was hard for you.'

'And even worse was to come. Later, I heard, the gravediggers – they were tired with their work – so many corpses to bury, they could not finish the task that day. And so she lay – body and head – above ground all night. Like a pauper. No respect. That was truly the end. The end of it all, for us.'

There was a pause. Then, the Frenchman said, 'And now, *m'sieur,* will you help me? I have told you all you asked. All I know. Will you now help me?'

Craig Lowrie looked down at the squirming courtier. He could cut the man's throat and push him into the sea. That would certainly be tidy – and quiet. It had its attractions. But he baulked and, instead, he pushed the wretch into the dock. At once, the man began to bawl. He could not swim. *'Au secours! Au secours!'* he screamed. Fishermen ran from all quarters to pull him out and, in the confusion, Craig Lowrie slipped inside the inn. He picked up John Stewart Macdonald's bowl of broth and, without a word, he took the old man by the elbow and was up the stairs to the old man's lodgings before anyone noticed.

'Malcolm Craig Lowrie!' said the bewildered priest.

'Indeed!'

'I was looking for you.'

'Well I am here. Now sit by the fire and eat, Father.'

'Did you cause that hubbub down there?'

'That? Dinna fash. Here, eat.'

The old man now ate rapidly, taking pause only after a final smear of bannock across the bowl. But before he could bring himself to tell his own news, politely he asked 'Well? You wanted to speak to me, Laird.'

Seated on the settle across the fire, Craig Lowrie now leant forward, hands on knees, and said: 'I have such a tale for you!'

Listening to the story of Marie Antoinette's death, the old man rubbed his eyes and said, 'But what do we do now, Laird?'

Craig Lowrie took out Gabrielle's most recent letter from the leather wallet slung across his chest. He had carried it there in safety in its crested cylinder ever since the priest had brought it to him in summer but, now he re-read it. He rolled up the letter and stowed it once more in cylinder and wallet. He had made a decision. He said, 'Now, in all honour, we have to show My Lady this letter.'

He stood and paced the room before he added, 'But we have also to dissuade My Lady from going to France.'

'You think she will, Laird?'

'This, this news of the Queen, this is powerful.'

Craig Lowrie stopped moving and returned to sit by the priest. What came next was painful for him to remember. 'Her sister – Gabrielle. She was the reason My Lady would not come with me, the night of the ball. I'm certain, Gabrielle was the reason. God forgive me if I am presuming too much but otherwise, I believe, she would have come. I am sure of that.'

On the night of the ball, Craig Lowrie had felt such fire crackling between himself and Adele – like summer lightning. That fire seemed all-consuming. She loved him, he thought, and, sure as earth, he loved her. But she had been chained by a silken dream of family, no more substantial than the friable leaves of parchment he carried next to his bitter heart. 'Yes,' he said, 'this is all very powerful. And, with this news, My Lady will now want to go to Gabrielle.'

The old man nodded. With the death of the Queen, French life, as Adele knew it, was gone. As he had recently travelled across Brittany and Normandy to Paris, he had himself witnessed the changes happening in France. Some changes, it was true, were fine and noble but some were despicable, craven and bad. Yet, he knew, Adele would try to go back. She would try to find Gabrielle. And he knew why. She would want to rekindle the impossible dream of a family life for them in France. This chimaera had sustained her throughout years of incarceration at Robinson Park. It had become her life-blood. Why would she not go? Even if it meant death, she would go. Especially now...

Silence prevailed for a moment and then Craig Lowrie stood up and crossed to the window again. He looked out onto the tiny Scottish port with its shouting sailors waving torches and, yes, the silent agents in the shadows. 'This will be an argument for her leaving

Scotland, returning to France. She will slip the old man's leash now. I am sure of it. And we must be there, when she does.'

'It is too late,' said John Stewart Macdonald. It was now time for him to tell Craig Lowrie of Adele's abrupt leaving of Robinson Park. He concluded, 'After I returned from France and, before the wedding, I went to Robinson Park but there was no sign of My Lady. I knew she must already be trying to get to France. To Oban first, but then, to France. But I could find no trace. The trail was cold. And then I was obliged to ride to Kintyre.'

Worse news was to follow. 'Robinson is now intent on hounding her out of Scotland. He feels fooled. He is proud, and angry and vengeful. He is as ready to commit mortal sin – murder, even – in cold blood as Pettigrew was in passion. As you were.'

Craig Lowrie shrugged. He had never cared about Pettigrew or his murder. But, thinking of Adele, he said, 'Concealment of her whereabouts from Robinson, I suspect, will not be possible much longer. The Englishman's agents are everywhere and they are ruthless.'

The priest sighed. 'There is one possible reason for hope. I have had no confirmation of this and I have been too ill to travel alone to find out. I had to conserve my failing strength to find you...'

'Yes, yes, but what is this "reason for hope"?' Craig Lowrie was at the old man's side again now.

'I did not see the Lady Eleanor. She could wait for me no longer. When I returned from France, she had already started the ride south – she and her riding servants and some on foot – hastening to the Lady Emma.'

The old man paused, rubbed his eyes again and then added, 'Yes, hastening to see her daughter wed. But also, I am sure she would have been scouring the clachans for news of My Lady. But there was no news. No word left for me. There was nothing for it. When I returned, it was time to ride south.'

John Stewart Macdonald sighed. A trick may have been missed, he thought but said, 'because I was away – the Lady Eleanor turned to the Distillery Manager's wife, Mrs Ballachulish, for help. And, if My Lady is not yet gone to France – in Oban, with Mrs Ballachulish, that is where, I believe, she will be now. The woman Ballachulish will have been eager, very eager, to please the Lady Eleanor. She will have her, I'm sure of it.'

'Then,' said Craig Lowrie, with a smile, 'when you are rested, we will pay a call.'

# Chapter 45

## Ballachulish House, Oban
## 16th December 1793

ADELAIDE DE FONTENOY was almost enjoying herself. It was the tenth time that she had made Fiona Ballachulish 'glide' down the stairs to the Salon on the first floor of Ballachulish House. She stood at the bottom of the flight, calling out, 'Head up! Don't look down! Use your ankles. Rely on the house architect – the man who has built this house – he has not made the steps uneven...!'

'Oh, really. Do I have to?'

'You do want to make an entrance don't you? You cannot do that if you treat the stairs like a rocky hillside – moving from one hoof to the other, heavily, like a cow. Again. If you please!'

Fiona tried again.

'And now, this time, the smile! Not the frown. The smile. Not the grimace.'

'How do you know so much?'

'I was a child in the French court. Everyone there knew how to be charming. I watched them. It is what your dear Mama wants for you.'

'It feels strange.'

'With practice, it will not. Again! Smaller steps. And the smile!'

**Molly Ballachulish's Journal 16th December 1793**

*What an impossible day it's been! And where is Mr Ballachulish when I need him? Birmingham, that's where. Really!!!*

*Oh it all started well enough. I was standing on the landing, watching my 'girls'. It was a delight. This is precisely the sort of lesson in refinement I had in mind for Fiona when I decided to involve myself in Adelaide de Fontenoy's 'adventures'. There is no-one, no-one else who could teach Fiona to be 'charming' in the French manner. What luck we have had.*

*I'm helping the Lady Eleanor Bamburgh too, of course – someone far superior in rank to Sir William Robinson. Although he is a local dignitary and going against him like this is not ideal. Certainly, as far as I'm concerned, regarding Adelaide's sojourn here, secrecy is vital. I don't know how long the Lady Eleanor will be here in the north and I may need to be friendly to Sir William again some time. So I've instructed all the servants to be silent.*

*But, if Sir William were to find out – seeing how things are between them – not that dear Adelaide ever speaks of it, frustrating though that is. If Sir William were to know, I'm sure we'd be off his list. And that would be dreadful! Simply dreadful!*

*On the bright side, I certainly hope, when Fiona – in her newly refined form – bursts upon Oban's social scene this Christmas, the impact will be sure to enable her to ensnare some well-off, respectable and law-abiding local gentleman. It can't fail. Surely. I expect an offer for her by the New Year.*

*At least that's what I had thought until now!!! Oh, how events do fool us!*

*I was just thinking to myself that the only problem with teaching Fiona flirtation – or as Adelaide would put it, 'engagement' – was that, before the Terrible Event, Adelaide de Fontenoy could never have descended a flight of stairs without admirers. But poor Fiona, well, poor Fiona is quite the opposite. She will probably have to do precisely that – descend without admirers – until she can trap someone...*

*Anyway, that is what I was thinking when suddenly the doorbell rang.*

*I was obliged to repair instantly to my Salon to receive my callers – having bundled Adelaide and Fiona into the snug to prepare themselves. I always say you can never be too careful at Fiona's age! The very next corner of the street may conceal the very man you will wed. You have to be constantly at your finest. You cannot falter for a moment! Exhausting as that is for poor Fiona.*

*Anyway, how things do run away so. Then, a maid showed the visitors in. The silly girl had no success whatsoever at removing the visitors' outer clothing, rain-sodden and smelling of horse as it was.*

*I was glad – at that point – the Ballachulish plaid was still covering the furniture...But I had absolutely no idea who these visitors could be, until the older visitor revealed his face.*

*'Father Macdonald!' I said – I was so surprised, I must have squeaked. I hadn't seen him for weeks, not even at the ball. Though I suppose, on mature reflection, a ball would not have been appropriate for his calling. But I, foolish as I was, said, 'How lovely to see you! And...?'*

*At this point, everything fell apart. Malcolm Craig Lowrie removed his hooded cloak and smiled. 'The neighbours' I shrieked and collapsed onto the day bed. I was truly without the power of speech. And, all lessons in sophistication forgotten, Fiona was shouting for the maid. But I did register that Adelaide had remained in the snug. 'Where is Adelaide?' was all I could think of to say before I swooned properly. And even when the smelling salts worked their magic, all I could say was 'Fetch Adelaide.' She is so practical and comforting in a crisis. But where was she?*

*Complete disaster. Complete disaster on every front!*

When she heard the old priest's name bawled by Molly Ballachulish in the Salon, Adele thought to run to his side. But then she heard a shriek. There would be some social embarassment disturbing Mrs Ballachulish's equilibrium. *But what?*

She paused and listened and then she knew. Having not seen him since midsummer night, here, almost at Christmas, was the man she longed to see most in all the world. But she wanted – so desperately – to cling to the memory of that midsummer night. How Craig Lowrie had looked at her. The unspoiled memory of midsummer night – before Pettigrew's attack – was her only comfort now.

But the moment he saw her, she knew that memory of dancing on midsummer night – so perfect – would die for both of them. There remained the concomitant slaughter of Pettigrew. The dancing and the killing – how could she remember the one and forget the other? She touched her cheek. To forget was impossible.

And, while she remained at the Ballachulish town-house, jealousy would ensure Fiona Ballachulish used every opportunity to remind Adele of what she had lost and engineer every opportunity to humiliate her. Sure enough, now at the door of the sitting room where Adele was concealed, now calm with cruelty, Fiona's voice scythed the air, saying, 'Mama needs you. You must come.'

When Adele arrived in the Salon, Molly Ballachulish was lying inert but conscious on the day-bed. Adele attempted to make her comfortable, pressing a cool kerchief to the woman's forehead. Then, as she recovered, Mrs Ballachulish waved her away weakly. At this point, Fiona signalled to Adele that she should take the seat at the left hand side of the hearth.

'There' she whispered, sibilant with triumph. 'A fire screen – to protect your poor face.'

Malcolm Craig Lowrie was watching Adele cross the room. Her profile was as lovely as he remembered it from the midsummer ball and he felt heady with its beauty. But, he also noted Miss Ballachulish's insistence that the young French woman seat herself to the left of the hearth. Adele spoke not a word, keeping her head lowered. Then, suddenly, she turned and raised her beautiful eyes to his.

And now he saw the scar. Poorly-stitched, it ran close to snagging her eye, while gouging a jagged trail down across her perfect cheekbone towards her soft mouth. Silas Pettigrew's signet ring had marked Adelaide de Fontenoy for life – as much as if he had taken a branding iron to her.

Craig Lowrie said nothing.

And, in the silence that followed, a smiling Fiona Ballachulish was heard to ask, 'Will you take some tea, Mr Craig Lowrie?'

**Molly Ballachulish's Journal 16th December 1793 (cont'd)**

*He really is a handsome man. And he was dressed in a gentleman's clothing – none of this Highland dress people make so much of, all stained and covered in bits of straw. When I saw how well-cut his jacket was – French, perhaps? – I thought there is a chance, just a chance, that no-one from the Crescent will have recognised him, no-one will know that I have entertained an outlaw here in my Salon. Oh, the thought of it – and the new furnishings have not arrived. I so wanted them in place before visitors. And, oh, I do so hope no-one in the Crescent's noticed.*

*And as for Fiona, simpering and smiling in that way! Does she want to encourage people like this – brigands and Catholics – to visit us? The sooner that girl's married the better! And why, oh why, is Mr Ballachulish not here to protect us all?*

There were only a limited number of comments anyone could make about Scottish weather and Mrs Ballachulish had made them all by the time Adele rose and addressed her 'employer'.

'Would you excuse me, Madame Ballachulish? This is not an opportunity to be missed. May I have a few words with my Chaplain in private? You must understand, Madame. It is some time since my last confession.'

'What on earth could you have to confess?' Fiona Ballachulish was relentless in her unpleasantness.

'Much,' persisted Adele. *'Madame?'*

'Yes, of course, my dear. Use the sitting room next door – if that would serve? I don't know what your requirements might be, Father Macdonald? But you are welcome to anything I can offer you. But, I do agree with Fiona, Adele dear, I can't imagine that you have done anything needing confession.'

This was kindly said and Mrs Ballachulish concluded by pointing to the door to the snug. Adele left the room followed by the priest carrying his riding satchel but, as she went, she felt Craig Lowrie's eyes upon her and she trembled. *Yes,* she thought, *Yes, it is over now.* But there was still grief to come. Within the half hour, she had read her sister's letter and John Stewart Macdonald had told her what he knew from Malcolm Craig Lowrie of Marie Antoinette's death – and the death of the France Adele thought of as home. Her misery was now complete.

**Molly Ballachulish's Journal 16th December 1793 (cont'd)**

*The whole house is in uproar. Adelaide de Fontenoy is determined to go to France. Fiona says she will have no man other than Malcolm Craig Lowrie as her husband. And Marie Antoinette is dead – BEFORE I CAN FIT OUT BALLACHULISH HOUSE IN THE STYLE OF VERSAILLES. OH – IT'S TOO, TOO BAD. MY FURNISHINGS ARE OUT OF DATE BEFORE THEY'VE ARRIVED!!!*

*When will Mr Ballachulish ever come home?*

# Chapter 46

## Robinson Park, Arduaine
## 25th December 1793
### Robinson's Journal (no longer under lock and key)

*WELL, THAT WAS AN appalling evening.*

*Of course, none of this is helped by Edwin snuffling around after His Grace. His new master by all accounts. And Eleanor – where's she when I need her? Too busy settling that girl of hers into married life and Castle Craig Lowrie to look after an old friend! I haven't seen her since September. Still, as I gather from the servants, that may not last too long. Jamie Craig Lowrie continues to protest he holds Castle Craig Lowrie only until MCL comes back.*

*But that's another nonsense. From whence is that man to come back, I ask? I believe Argyll's intent on keeping MCL from Dalriada. All my agents say so. The question is: Are his clansmen still loyal? If they're not, he won't be back. How could he be? Who would hide him, if he did come?*

*And MCL! That man has reason to hate and to bless me! Is he my friend or am I in danger? At one point, when I had Adelaide 'under my roof' – shall we say – I could have been in danger. As that fool Pettigrew turned out to be. But now I've driven the lady out, Craig Lowrie should be thanking me. Still, I'm not convinced he would. Perhaps he doesn't want her now she's scarred and damaged by the ghastly Pettigrew.*

*But I don't understand MCL's thinking at all. And I won't be the first lawyer who's crossed him and felt the worst of it. Having Emma Bamburgh here was, as I thought, a huge mistake. Cut right across his plans. And MCL's violent – demonstrably – and clever – also demonstrably. And I'm at risk. I'm sure of that.*

*What complicated lives we lead! A trace of mist in the sea wind – that's what these Scottish peasants say MCL is. They're full of admiration, of course. And no small tinge of pride. But no help whatsoever to me! No-one, even if they know, is prepared to say where and when he'll next appear. So the questions for me are: will he come again – as he did on midsummer night – with murderous intent? And this time would I be the target? But, also, if so, why?*

*Whatever his motive, I'll clearly have to double the guard again. So I can't dismiss all those mercenaries yet. Zounds, the cost of all this! I'll be forced to live in poverty soon. When will it end?*

*And another thing – this is still my house and I'm eating like a Highlander. That Christmas meal – cullen skink. Peasant food. Really. In the six years, since she had the management of it, Adelaide has never allowed cullen skink at my table. And I haven't had a decent dinner since she left.*

*And the fires were not lit! There was I, standing around like a loon, while footmen scurried about with logs...*

But Robinson was deriving no satisfaction from his journal that night. He rang the bell and a sleepy servant appeared in the Library doorway.

'My coat,' said Robinson and, when booted and ready, he whistled up the dogs. The servant made as if to accompany him but Robinson waved him away. Then, heavy-hearted, he followed the gravel path alongside Adelaide's rose parterre. The emptiness of the rooms behind it made him grimace with cold.

'Of course, if Eleanor had married me when I asked her, I should never have been in this situation. I should never have known Adelaide de Fontenoy. Zounds!' he said to himself, broken in heart and pride.

As soon as he could, having crossed the sweeping lawns that led to the seashore, he picked his way along an eastern ride that led up the coastal hills and onto the ridgeway. Even after a thirty-minute walk, he knew, he would still be within the Park boundaries. *And still safe,* he thought. The Christmas Moon was high and bright, penetrating even the thick but leafless branches of the Robinson Park woods. And, though there were fewer soldiers than there had been on the Robinson Park boundaries in the last year, his step was sure on his own land. As he walked, he raised his eyes to the Ridge.

From the high ground, he knew, he would be able to see the Firth of Lorne, milky in the Christmas moonlight and he would be able to look towards the west. And he would be able to look towards the Isles. In the west and to the south, he knew, as far as man could see, islands lay, hulking dark against winter waters – Shuna, Luing, Scarba, Jura. Black Malcolm's Isles – they would taunt him with the questions that were fretting his lonely nights. *Is that where Craig Lowrie is? The man who stole Adelaide – and my redemption – from me? Is that where she is?*

The incline was more telling now and he was breathing heavily as he hauled his huge bulk up towards the ridge belvedere. Between gasps, he considered the facts of the situation.

*Some of the mercenaries have gone south with the unfortunate Pettigrew. Most of those left in Robinson employ are away, ranging round the countryside, briefed to find Adelaide – who, it seems, has disappeared. And without trace.*

*Adelaide has not gone south. I am now sure of that. No amount of bribery or threat has produced a word about her. East is also unlikely. Beyond the Ridge and the Robinson Park boundaries, the land is unknown to her. Completely.*

He also on reflection dismissed the Isles – Adelaide was not born to live in a croft, however romantic the company might be. *So,* he concluded, *Adelaide must be in Oban.*

He paused to gain breath and, as one who has covered every contingency, thought with some satisfaction, *And the brief for those mercenaries now lining the Oban dock was to find her and bundle her by any means – fair or foul – out of my life! Even so far as to pay for her passage back to the bloodbath in France.*

He walked on and then halted abruptly. If the tale came to be told about how he had thrown her out, there would be outcry among the *bourgeoisie* of Oban – who were, it had to be said, much more given to tittle tattle than the silent Highlanders surrounding their town. The scandal there would be! Middle-class values attacked, the *petite bourgeoisie* led by the Kirk! He would lose clients by the second. 'And Eleanor. If she heard of any ill treatment and rough handling...'

He spoke out loud and, to see if he needed them, the dogs raised their heads from snuffling the undergrowth. He ignored them, still engrossed in his considerations.

*So,* he thought, *how if Adelaide were arrested instead – then what would I do?*

This seemed a more promising solution. As magistrate, he could commit Adelaide for trial. *But for what? Vagrancy? Theft? Yes, theft. That would be it.* In his mind, he argued a good case for not having intended to 'give' her jewellery. Some of the gold pieces she had taken – and with which he had adorned her young body, it was true – had been his mother's, after all. But then he paused again. He could imagine the public salacity. His private arrangements would be exposed. 'Lady Robinson' would be exposed. The murkiness of her position in Robinson Hall would be exposed. And the boost to his reputation – which had derived since the midsummer ball from having a young French 'wife-to-be' on his arm – would be lost in the stark humiliation of prurient interest.

As had been made clear, she had never loved him. Worse than that, it had become clear that she hated him and did not mind who knew it. If it all came out, he would be seen as a sad old man who had fallen in love with a woman just a third of his age. She would be revealed to have led him by the nose for years. And he would be regarded as a fool deceived by a thief. His devotion, his tolerance, his willingness to comply with her every whim – his 'Atonement' – it would all count for nought. That was intolerable enough. But there was also that business arrangement with her father at the French court all those years ago. Few of the new citizens of Oban would understand that little vignette, either. As he perceived the situation, she – a most beautiful, beguiling child – had been rescued by him, Robinson. But, he could hear the Oban middle-classes outcry, 'From what?' He knew – as they would not – with a father like de Fontenoy, corruption would not be far away. If 'the pledge for gambling debts' had not been given to him, Robinson, then the offer would have been made to some other dupe.

*Perhaps de Fontenoy blood was bad blood,* he thought. *His own blood was not particularly 'good' so her bad blood was not the particular issue. But the Oban bourgeoisie might not see it like this.*

And, yet, Robinson – *foolish, foolish man* – had hoped for years that one day Adelaide de Fontenoy would love him. And she had not.

'Bah, bad blood will out', he found himself saying aloud. The dogs again checked at the sound of his voice but he said no more. They continued their hunting. He continued his climb. From the next twist in the path, he looked down and saw Robinson Hall. It lay lightless in the moonlight, on the sea bank below. He remembered the night of the ball. The blaze of candlelight when the midsummer sun had dipped below the hulk of The Isles – so precisely orchestrated by Adelaide. Perfect. How proud he'd been of Adelaide's arrangements! How bathed in the light of her his life had seemed at that moment!

*Until Pettigrew ruined everything – with his greed and his overweaning ambition and his uncontrollable lust. Yes, Pettigrew's lust! Ridiculous at the time. But sickening. Sickening. The way Pettigrew went after the Lady Emma...so crass, so vulgar...And almost drooling like a spaniel over Adelaide...*

The dogs at his side whined as a sudden and dread possibility loomed and scampered around his mind. *What if everyone had been right? What if Adelaide had been innocent?*

Robinson stabbed the hard earth with his thumb stick and achieved the final heave into the belvedere. Now he stood up straight and said, petulantly, 'But why then would she say nothing in her own defence?'

'Because you did not give her the chance.' He heard Eleanor's voice on the wind – as clearly as if she was standing along side him.

*But Malcolm Craig Lowrie?*

'A coincidence.' Eleanor's voice cut him like frost.

But Robinson had seen how they looked at each other. *That was love.*

'Can you blame either of them for that?' Eleanor's voice rippled through his head again. 'William, you have been the fool of fools. The night of the midsummer ball was the first time Malcolm Craig Lowrie and Adelaide de Fontenoy met. There was no collusion. How could there have been? She was sealed up by you, a prisoner, in Robinson Park. And the night of the ball was the first time Malcolm Craig Lowrie had stepped foot inside the Hall!'

And Robinson saw the truth at last. None of the ills of that night – except the murder! – could be laid at Craig Lowrie's door. He gasped. Chewing his knuckle, he thought deeply. Adelaide had not welcomed his own advances nor submitted to him in any way – unlike many a servant girl before her. And, perhaps in spite of herself, she had come to treat him as a man of power and of influence. She had, after all, even asked *him* to go to rescue Gabrielle. She had appealed to *him* in trust. He had refused her, of course. But, he recalled, the request at the time had seemed almost a sign that she was softening. The time of her asking now seemed idyllic, a time of warmth. And perhaps she was innocent.

Then Robinson's mind raced on.

*The advantages of reinstating Adelaide were many,* he thought. *No public humiliation. She could again run his household with flair and style. There would still be the hope that she would love him. In spite of that scar, she was still a beautiful and elegant woman whom it would be a pleasure to watch moving round his rooms and his life. And surely she would be grateful. A little at first. But, enough perhaps.*

He leant on his stick and scanned the view. It was the same as that from the great window of the Hall. He remembered Adelaide as she had been framed there against the setting sun on the night of the ball. That was the last time he had been happy. And he knew now that his discomfort had all been caused by Pettigrew. *It had all come about because of Pettigrew!*

'That was it,' he said. His dogs stood up at his side. He would send word to the captain of the guard with changed orders. *No, better than that, he would ride to Oban himself and bring home his bride.*

Eleanor's voice rang again in his head. 'William, let the girl be. Wherever she is, she is not for you. You know that. She was never yours. And she never will be for you. What you intend – keeping her locked up as your "wife" or "mistress" – certainly as your housekeeper – is cruel and unjust. She was a child when she was sold to you. And now you want to treat her again as if she were some thoroughbred horse...to be held against her choice...kindly or unkindly...as it pleases you. And bred from perhaps? William, this is not worthy of you...William, do not do this...'

But, whistling to the dogs and startling the night creatures, Robinson started off straight down the slope. *And no more cullen skink for me,* he thought.

# Chapter 47

## Oban, Argyll
## 26th December 1793

AN UNWASHED HUMAN smell pervaded the lawyer's office and, gagging, Robinson scrabbled in a desk drawer to find a pastille. There were two pastilles to choose from – lavender- or cedar-scented. Without hesitation, he chose cedar – the stronger of the two fragrances – and using a sliver of wood as a spill, he lit the pastille in the castle-shaped burner on his desk – the handsome gift from a grateful client intended for precisely such occasions as these. Then he sat and waited for the clouds of spicy perfume to fill the room.

Meanwhile, across the desk, Robinson's agent was also waiting. He was a scrawny man who, it seemed, chose not to care much about his appearance. In Robinson's view, the agent seemed rather to glory in grime than otherwise and, when in the past Robinson had challenged him about this, he had been told, 'I need to blend.'

Robinson could only agree. Mixing with the likes of fishwives and potmen in the professional pursuit of information meant there was little point in the agent paying too nice an attention to his personal aroma. However, when the agent attended interviews with people of Robinson's rank, Robinson believed the man should make an exception and wash. The agent did not wash. He also preferred to be paid in the coin of the realm – no paper notes unfortunately – and to remain anonymous.

'Why do I have to deal with such people?' Robinson often wondered, resentful of those such as Edwin Bamburgh who did not. On this occasion, Robinson also feared information worth having would be unlikely. Up at Robinson Park, he had been waiting for weeks now for news of Adelaide and nothing had emerged. There had been no hint among the servant girls whom he regularly interrogated for gossip. No rider had come hotfoot from the Port. There had been no whisper on the wind. So, it was with a discouraged heart that, from the desk drawer, he now withdrew a shilling and placed it on the desktop.

Both men studied it for a moment and then, moving his hand towards the coin, the agent spoke. 'I may have something for you.' Robinson slapped his hand down on the coin. 'What?' he said from behind the clouds of cedar scent.

'She was seen.'

Robinson moved his hand slightly so the silver gleamed through the smoke in the candlelight. He could also see its reflection in the other man's eyes.

'Where?'

'The quayside.'

Still as a stalking cat, Robinson watched the agent. The man shifted in his shabby shoes and continued, 'Talking to the Breton Brig's captain.'

'That was weeks ago. I know all that.' Robinson's hand closed over the coin.

'There's more. Your Head Groom's lad brought the horse home.'

Robinson picked up the coin in silence. As he thought, nothing he did not already know.

The man's eyes flared in panic. 'There's more.'

'There'd better be.' Now impatient, Robinson pocketed the coin.

'Yes, the laddie brought the horse home but the Head Groom took Her Ladyship away. On foot. I followed them. She was a poorly lady then, had to rest on his arm. Looked like an auld couple, they did.'

Robinson ignored the smirk, snapping, 'Yes, yes – where did they go then?'

'Ballachulish House, The Crescent, Newtown.' The man had drawn out his tattered and greasy notebook to lend authority to the announcement. But the drama of the moment was leaving Robinson cold. His in-born suspicions sieved the information.

'Why did you not come to me with this before?' he said.

However, in fairness, he knew he had not been down in the town for some time and, as a matter of policy, he never revealed to people like the agent where he lived. So it was possible – just possible – that this man was honest.

The agent seemed to have finished. It was not much information to go on. Adelaide could be long gone. He would have to go to check it out himself. Wearily, Robinson retrieved the coin from his silk waistcoat and tossed it. The man's eye was quick and his hand quicker. The coin was taken on the wing.

Testing it with his broken teeth, the agent added, 'There's more.'

'Why didn't you say so?' Robinson was irritated. He'd missed the trick. He now had to find another coin and go through the whole game again. Even so, on producing another coin, he learned that Adelaide was still with Molly, that she was largely recovered from her injuries except for the scar and that the French Brig was sitting on the harbour bar waiting for the flood tide. It would not leave for a few days – not until laden, and not until certain of its voyage plan, and not until stocked with passengers for France. 'Fewer of late. France being in the state she's in. Passengers wanting to go there will stand out.'

The man was – however unwisely – playing the old lawyer like a river fish. But, in the course of the sport, most worryingly of all, Robinson also learned, Malcolm Craig Lowrie had been seen on the Crescent. 'Dressed as a gentleman. Dressed for travel.'

Then Robinson dismissed the agent. 'Watch the docks!' he said. 'Let me know if you see any one, anyone at all, from Ballachulish House down there – at any time – at once.'

Smiling as he pocketed the second shilling, the agent slithered out of the office door. Robinson ignored him. Opening the window to clear his head, the lawyer considered his next move.

On entering the drawing room of Ballachulish House, The Crescent, Newtown, Robinson caught his breath. Furnishings – selected and ordered directly from London – had converted the room of this modest townhouse into a mirror-image of his own drawing room at Robinson Park. Even worse, the curtains were identical to those in Adelaide's former sitting room, in the so-called *Petit Trianon.* And, if Molly Ballachulish was hoping for a rapturous reaction to all this refurbishment, he thought with irritation, she would be disappointed. Even though his heart had stopped and his breath had become laboured at the sight of them, he said nothing of the furnishings. His plan of campaign had another goal – endorsed by his first sighting of Adelaide since she had disappeared.

As he walked in, Adelaide was putting the finishing touches to the curtains, late winter roses placed in tiny crystal vases delicately stitched into silk damask. And, as the maid announced Robinson, she had her back to him. The effect of her – a jewel among rich fabric – was perfection. He sighed and she turned and he could see the scar, tracing its angry way down from tail of eye to curve of lip. Its ugliness threatened to unman him but even so his tongue, he found, was quivering in his mouth at the sight of her. Lust almost rendered him silent.

But he recovered and said, 'Good Day, ladies. What a charming tableau! The three of you here, all together. Three such beauties – all together like this...'

Fiona Ballachulish, ringing for tea, simpered. Molly Ballachulish eyed Robinson with suspicion. Adelaide turned back to focus on her appointed task. But, as she did so – placing the final rose in the final vase of the curtains draping the huge light-filled windows of the Ballachulish drawing room – she started visibly. Robinson knew she had seen the three English mercenaries who went everywhere with him now. Eyes afire, she turned back towards him in silent enquiry. He felt he would not disappoint her – in time.

'Yes,' he continued, smiling, playing the fond husband. 'Three such charming friends together. I really am most distressed to have to break up such cosiness. Such domestic peace. But I fear my own cosiness and peace has been compromised. Mrs Ballachulish, you have had My Lady as your house guest quite long enough. I'm afraid I must insist on taking my lovely wife-to-be home. You are wicked. You have kept her away from me so long. I cannot bear another day without my beautiful Adelaide. I regret. I must insist. She must come home!'

Mrs Ballachulish was now racked between wanting to please Sir William and wanting to continue with her programme of refinement for Fiona. This was a conflict of interest to which she did not feel equal.

'It has been certainly very kind of you to spare her for so long,' Molly Ballachulish began with caution. 'And I'm sure you can see how her advice has benefited my humble home, how elegant a style we can now adopt. Even here – even in the North End of Oban.'

Robinson shifted position. He was closing in. 'Madame, I will speak plainly. I gather that my lady wife-to-be's presence has – for some reason known only to himself – attracted the attentions of a well-known local felon. This must have been most distressing for you all. Indeed it must...'

'Felon? Oh, Sir William, you mean...'

'I do indeed, Madame. Malcolm Craig Lowrie has been seen in the Crescent.'

'Oh,' said Fiona, 'Mr Craig Lowrie has taken tea with us on several occasions. You know he has, mama!'

Irritated by her daughter's lack of tact, Molly Ballachulish rallied. 'Of course, he has, Sir William. And very awkward it has been – with Mr Ballachulish so often away in Birmingham.'

'Difficult, Madame, dreadful for you! Indeed. So, I believe if I remove Lady Robinson – whom he has, as you probably know, relentlessly pursued – yes, if I remove her, you will be relieved from the necessity of entertaining this murderer and any of the motley crew of brigands he chooses to bring with him. Rest assured, Madame, as magistrate, I have alerted my men to the dangers of this felon. You will not be troubled further. He will be caught.'

'Oh, do you think so?' Molly Ballachulish was floundering.

'I do, Madame. I consider it my duty.'

'But, mama, so far he has brought only the priest, Father Macdonald, with him. For Adele to make confession! Which she seems to need. Rather often.'

'Really. The confession of sins. A quaint custom. But, quite unnecessary for you, my dear, I'm sure. Your sins – they could hardly trouble the Almighty. Could they?'

Although he had no intention of leaving without Adelaide, Robinson could not resist the opportunity to turn the knife and remind her of her 'damaged' state. A ruined woman – with the mark of violence upon her. She lowered her eyes and he could not see how her mind was casting about for escape – like a trapped animal. But he could imagine.

Mrs Ballachulish, meanwhile, was looking at her daughter. 'There have been those who have pressed invitations upon Mr Craig Lowrie shamelessly,' she said.

'Really, Madame?' interrupted Robinson – much to Fiona's relief, squirming as she was under her mother's eye. 'I hope, I'm sure my wife-to-be was not among them!'

'Oh, mama! I merely asked Mr Craig Lowrie what was his preferred tea and said I would order some for his next visit.'

'A pressing invitation, indeed,' laughed Sir William pleasantly. 'How could the former Laird of Craig Lowrie resist the offer of taking Assam with such a bevy of beauties? But, perhaps you would go and pack, my dear. We need not trouble these good folk longer than necessary, don't you know!'

'And perhaps while Lady Robinson does so, you will take your tea with us, Sir William. Is your carriage without? The Crescent is so narrow the neighbours will find it difficult to pass.'

Molly Ballachulish's concern that her neighbours should see the crest on the Robinson carriage seemed to the lawyer greater than her concern for their inconvenience. The Lady of the House was completely won over to his side, it seemed, as she flew to the window in the hope of observing with her own eyes the Robinson carriage outside her own front door.

There it was, together with the three mounted mercenaries. The neighbours would indeed find an entourage of that size difficult to pass without being aware of its titled provenance. The well-upholstered bosom of Mrs Ballachulish swelled with pride.

And Robinson smiled, pleasantly, again.

Soon after this, under urgent orders from Adele and alert to the need for discretion, Marie Le Pecque was gliding along the Oban quayside. She checked and feinted, whenever she thought she would be recognised or accosted. But, as she moved along, she could not help but remember the last time she had walked these cobbles. Then she had been hurrying to greet the French brig's return and the person who had crossed the cobbles to the quay, then, seemed so young to her now. It was almost a year ago, when she ran across this very road, and found not her young husband, Jean, but a bloodied corpse, with its head crushed to pulp. He had been recognisable to her only by his sweet, sweet hand that was wearing one of the rings they shared. Now she was no longer a young girl full of hope. A life-time had passed.

Of course, before she had come to Scotland, she had known fear. Back home in Revolutionary France, before she had left St Malo, she had known fear. Denunciation ran through that town like cholera. No-one knew where it would strike next. But she and her husband, Jean, at that time, they had such hope that Scotland would be safer. So it came about that Jean signed up to serve before the mast of the brig *Espoir.* Superstitious, he unwisely took the name as a good omen. And, when the brig had first tied up at Oban quayside, she and Jean slipped away and found a dwelling. And they loved each other so much in the following weeks.

But, then, Jean made two mistakes. He signed on again for another voyage with the *Espoir,* to St Malo and back. It sounded simple. But his second mistake, for even more money, was fatal. On meeting Father John Stewart Macdonald – at a private mass for Catholics in the town – Jean had agreed to take secret letters from a French woman living in the hills behind Oban back to St Malo from where a secret postal chain stretched across France to the heart of the country, to Paris itself. Dangerous arrangements. But there would be no danger for him, he said. His task would end in St Malo.

'What then?' she asked him – unsure how this commission would help them.

'I come home. When I have collected any letters addressed to Adelaide de Fontenoy!'

*Adelaide de Fontenoy.* Small wonder Marie had hated the name throughout this past year and, when Madame Ballachulish first offered Marie's services to Adelaide de Fontenoy some months before, she was horrified, detesting the young woman who bore the name. *With good reason,* she felt. Such bitterness had licked at her face when Adelaide de Fontenoy – the woman responsible for Jean's death and for her year-long servitude – was introduced to the household. Marie had immediately known the de Fontenoy woman for who and what she was. Even though, subsequently, Madame Ballachulish had insisted the title, 'Lady Robinson', be used. *Putain,* thought Marie.

But then Marie had seen the scar tracing its way down that once beautiful face. From her maid's bedchamber, she had heard the tears in the night and seen the red eyes in the morning. She recognized them. They reminded her of her own. And she had felt herself, reluctantly, soften. She was now – heart and soul – Adelaide de Fontenoy's French maid.

But as she walked along the quay, Marie became aware of something new in the Oban air. She could hear the snorting and pushing of the English mercenaries' horses, lining the dock. Something was happening. She didn't know what. The fisher folk were scurrying feverishly along the quays, into the alleys, into the cottages and the net halls. Neither they nor the serried ranks of soldiery were speaking. This was serious, Marie could feel it. With a servant's invisibility, she pressed her body against the dock wall. But in spite of her watching, no clues told her what was unfolding. Even so, her fear told her whatever it was had to do with Adelaide de Fontenoy.

Then, Marie became aware of a smell – worse by far than the old fish market, imbued with its venerable savours. Close to her in the crowd, the smell of a man's body made her gag. She tried to wriggle away but, before she could, his hand whipped across her face and over her mouth. She felt rather than saw the knife at her throat.

'Now pretty lady, what are you doing out on your own? Mrs Ballachulish will be missing you. And "Lady Robinson" too, I'd guess. Ah now, "Lady Robinson" – two young French women – you must talk a great deal. And what about, I ask myself, what about?'

The blackened teeth in the purple stubbled face repulsed her as the image of Jean's clear young face rose before her again. Spurred by grief, she forced the man's grip away from her mouth. But the silver candlesticks in her tapestry bag scraped together. Even amid the hubbub of the docks, Robinson's agent suddenly looked sharp. Marie wondered whether he could smell silver but she could recognize greed when she saw it. She took hope. Her chance of escape would come if greed distracted him, if he busied himself with the silver. But, as if he'd heard her silent thought, the man sniffed. He was confident enough to ease his hold on her throat – if only slightly. 'Now "Lady Robinson",' he sneered, 'What are her plans?'

'Why should I tell you?'

'Because I *need* to know. And my master *wants* to know.'

'Your master –?'

'Doesn't concern you. I'm here at present. And you have more than enough to concern you because of it – believe me.'

Just down the Fish Quay, the net halls provided a darkened alley and, without further talk, Robinson's agent dragged Marie sideways and down it. On his mind, she knew, were torture, theft and rape. And, judging by his glazed eyes, rape seemed the most pressing. Theft would come a close second – the silver was still clanging temptingly in Marie's travel bag. Then, lastly, torture would furnish the agent with information, which he would be happy enough to sell to anyone who would pay good money for it.

Even so, for now, Marie's screams excited Robinson's agent beyond caution and he forgot to watch his back. Before he could rip clear his breeches, he crumpled under a sledgehammer blow to his kidneys and, as he fell forward, his rotten teeth shattered on the stones. Unmanned, yelping unintelligible obscenities, and swearing vengeance, with a mouth full of blood, he staggered away into the shadows. And Malcolm Craig Lowrie helped Marie to her feet.

# Chapter 48

## Oban – the North End of town 31st December 1793

AFTER HIS ENCOUNTER with Marie Le Pecque at the docks, Craig Lowrie returned to the Crescent to find it blocked by Robinson's equipage. Marie had told him her lady would already be looking for a way to slide out from under the lawyer's nose – 'no easy task' – so ringing the doorbell could scarcely be the plan.

For several reasons, Craig Lowrie thought, this was not the moment for an afternoon call. Firstly, he was not dressed for such. He had been riding hard for four hours to reach Oban from his lands in the south – harried by Argyll's men. And his plaid was weather-blasted – fit to soil the elegant arrangements in Molly Ballachulish's Salon. Nor was he in the right temper. What Marie had told him about Robinson's intentions had banked up his smouldering anxiety. Adele must not be persuaded to return to Robinson Hall, whatever the inducements, and he believed Robinson could offer her everything but a life worth living.

But Craig Lowrie's mind was working well as he circled down the rear alleyways under the cliff that broke Oban's back. He was unsure what he was looking for but knew he would know it when he found it. And, there, quite by chance, he found Adele.

The young Frenchwoman was sliding out through the kitchen garden gate of Ballachulish House. Although hatless, she was wearing a thick, full-skirted wool redingote, designed for keeping warm riding out in the British winter but also useful for general travel. She was also carrying or rather dragging a leather hold-all. This appeared to be heavier than he would have expected for a young girl's hand luggage.

'Well met, lady,' Craig Lowrie said. 'May I carry your bag?'

Adele was startled and, for a moment – a fragment of second – he thought she would again refuse his help. But she seemed to pause and consider what he had said. Then she glanced up at him with a sudden smile that made him laugh. He was charmed. The efforts of manoeuvring the bag down the garden had dishevelled her hair. Fine wisps and curls had escaped and now floated around her sleek head in the sea air. But when she looked up at him, her dark eyes suddenly sparkled in the winter light. There was no help for it. He seized her bag and her hand.

'Now,' he said, 'run!' And he began to tow her down the back lane behind Ballachulish House, leaping over detritus from the new houses of the Crescent. They dodged dead cats and decaying vegetables and headed south for the docks. As they both knew, Robinson's mercenaries would be in pursuit as soon as the old lawyer realised what was happening.

Craig Lowrie ran at the loping pace that served him well on the hills and, if needed, he would have been able to keep this up for some hours. It was no challenge to him. But Adele had not lived that life. Drawing-room bred and only just recovering from the injuries inflicted by Pettigrew, she managed to keep pace for a little while. But then she began to tire and, quite soon, she stopped.

'Forgive me', she said, gulping for air. 'My heart – it threatens to burst.'

Craig Lowrie pulled her into a gateway so she could catch her breath. No mercenaries had appeared but it would not be long. 'Of course,' he said, 'I should have thought. You are not bred to hill-running.'

'No,' gasped Adele, trying to smile. 'Madame Ballachulish – her house is not well-placed for exercise.'

Craig Lowrie checked the back lanes again for mercenaries saying, 'No sign. We could walk from here, but we will have to walk quickly.'

Her redingote was weighty. Running – even walking quickly – in a riding habit was nigh impossible. He had to do something, he thought, and drew his broadsword. Her eyes opened wide with alarm. The sword was sharp – sharp enough to take off a man's arm, through mail, muscle and bone. But long practice meant he used a sword like a butcher his knife, with precision. By pulling out the skirts and slashing down neatly, he was able to remove some of the fullness from the woven wool. The sorry remnants now lay inert on the ground between them. Then, with a smile, she picked them up and pushed them into her bag. 'No trails,' she said. 'We should leave no trails.'

Craig Lowrie was amused. 'This is not travelling lightly, I think.'

But, he noted, as they began to run again, Adele now ran more freely – no longer having to carry the full weight of the redingote skirts. And, though her skirts were still long, she could hitch them and run, like the young animal she was. Like the young animal he was.

At their next halt, Adele explained why her bag, which he was carrying, was so heavy. She had packed all the crass gold jewellery – Robinson's tokens, claiming her as his own. She would sell them when necessary. Craig Lowrie was relieved. There was no sentimental attachment.

'But, also, I brought my sewing tools,' she added, 'I could not travel without them. They may help me pay my way, respectably, somewhere, at some point. And a change of clothes. This was as well, don't you think?' She smiled and swished her jaunty but now ragged redingote skirts.

Craig Lowrie nodded but, still wary, he sidled to a corner to check their way was clear. It was. *What could Robinson be doing?* Although he was grateful for the delay, it seemed suspicious.

'Where are we going?' asked Adele – suddenly aware she had followed this man without question. It had seemed, she realised, the most natural thing to do.

'My rooms,' he said.

'Not quite what I had planned,' she said.

'Of course not – but this is no time for coyness, lady. And have you a better idea?'

'No, none!'

'We must move on again!' Then he smiled and, taking her by the elbow, walked around the back of the market halls. 'Don't be afraid,' he whispered. 'Of me. Or of what Robinson might do next.'

'I'm not,' she whispered back. 'Merely curious.'

Her courage pleased him beyond his expectations. He stopped walking for a moment and unpinned her hair, as he had wanted to do since the night of the ball. It was fine but full and soft as cloud.

And, as he removed the pins, one by one the shining curls swung down. Fingering the softness framing her face, he almost forgot his hurry. Then he recovered himself, adding, 'Yes, indeed, you are not afraid. Now, walk calmly. And hold your head up. No one will question us.'

Nor did they. Working Oban was used to observing the passage of travellers through its heart. Travellers of all ranks came in from the Isles or off the hills – they came of their own free will or in the sorry gaggles, clustering bewildered on the docks, sold by their Lairds to make way for sheep. These people, Oban observed, left for Ireland or the Isle of Man, even for Liverpool and the Americas or the Continent and preferred on the whole to keep their tales to themselves. Oban folk working on the quay respected that. Only the new middle-classes gossiped. The fishermen, herring women and stevedores also would not comment to anyone beyond their friends if they saw a Highland Laird and a lady. *Runaways,* they would assume. They would say nothing to anyone they did not trust. It was not their business. It would be safer not to speak and they would keep their eyes down, as the Craig Lowrie passed.

# Chapter 49

## The Three Fishes Inn
## 31st December 1793

*THE THREE FISHES INN* reared up over the dockside walkway and its shadow fell across the people working there. Rough as it was, it was to be a refuge for Adele until the *Espoir* was ready to sail and she would have to leave. But, as they circled round the town towards it, from force of habit, Craig Lowrie scanned the quaysides for what might later be useful. He noted where the fishermen had discarded dried-out lobster creels. He saw the herring gutters' rags and the broken crates. He saw the barrels of pitch for the ropes. He saw the pools of birch tar oil. He led Adele past it all and he said nothing of a plan half-forming in his mind. It might alarm her. She was alarmed enough.

The pair glided from the quay, into the inn and up the creaking stairs to his rooms. Rab MacDonald was waiting. He had prepared as ever for the comfort of his Laird but did not remark on the lady on his Laird's arm.

Craig Lowrie, however, offered the young woman a chair by the fire and then went to the casement. He noted on the far side of the quay, some English mercenaries were lounging, armed but slack. At present, they were without orders.

'So what do we do?' asked Adele, smiling. She was glad at last to be seated.

'We wait,' Craig Lowrie said. Outside, ostlers, fishermen, even the mercenaries were going about their business. This was as good as it could be for now. He turned from the window and removed his weapons – sword, pistol, even his dirk – placing each item carefully down on a dresser near the door, primed for immediate use. 'We have three hours before the tide turns,' he said. 'We cannot risk being seen. And Marie is to meet us here.'

*'Vraiment?* But I didn't know you were acquainted.'

'Acquainted? That would be too strong a word for it. A business arrangement, perhaps.'

Adele was not old enough nor wise enough not to ask, 'But what?'

Craig Lowrie quickened. 'Among other things, the letters, your letters, of a year ago...'

'The letters? It was you who had them?'

'It was.'

'I have been slow!'

'A little, aye.'

'Forgive me, *m'sieur.* It is important. I must ask. Marie somehow found them? And sold them to you?'

'In a manner of speaking. But, in a manner of speaking, they were hers to sell. Jean Le Pecque, your emissary, the sailor who fell from the rigging of the *Espoir,* was her husband, after all. And he left her with comparatively little.'

'And Father Macdonald then took them to France for me. He didn't say where he found them. I have been a fool, have I not? She blamed me – for everything...? How she must have hated me! And then to be made my servant!'

'She hated you, yes. But, mostly, for her widowhood.' Craig Lowrie's responses became clipped. So much death. So many widows and keening women. He remembered his mother – the mystery, the sadness of her life. Loss, he did not want to think about it. *Ardnackaig!*

Adele said again, 'How she must have hated me!'

'Aye, so.'

Somewhere inside this short exchange was a reproach. How much thought had Adele ever given the widow of her emissary before? But, at this, Craig Lowrie checked. How much, he wondered, had he ever enquired of any of his people? Rab MacDonald, his tacksman, sitting like a dog, outside his rooms, even as they spoke? Now landless, Craig Lowrie was thinking of going to London, losing himself there, but he would expect Rab MacDonald to come too. He had never thought to ask whether that was what Rab wanted. But should he? And should he also ask who would Rab MacDonald leave behind, who would weep for him? Was there a woman who – like Marie Le Pecque – would find her life destroyed for the loss of Rab MacDonald?

Then Adele shifted uncomfortably on the hard chair. Its creak brought Craig Lowrie back to the reality of *The Three Fishes*. Adele's presence was shimmering through the air in the musty, shabby inn-room. Craig Lowrie smiled. And Adele smiled back at him. Something like summer lightning was passing between them again. He felt as he had felt on midsummer night. But, for the first time since he had helped her escape from the Ballachulish kitchen garden, there was a look almost of fear in her eyes. Distrust?

She was a gleam in his darkness but could *she* trust him now? A brigand endowed with an unsurpassed reputation for murder and mayhem. Could she really trust him? Her dark eyes, deep as the sea, held a promise for him but, at the same time, Craig Lowrie knew, on midsummer night, he had failed to keep her safe.

'You had better eat – I don't know when you will be able to eat from now on,' he said and, before she could reply, he had spoken to Rab MacDonald at the door. Oatcakes, mackerel, cheese and apples appeared.

'One of the first rules,' Craig Lowrie said, 'is to eat when you can, sleep when you can. These are a fugitive's rules.' He sat opposite her and waited while she considered the food placed on his desk at her side.

'I must go to France,' she said suddenly. Her voice sounded small in the dingy upper quarters of an Oban inn. And the task that lay ahead, he now realised, was immense. Here was a girl who had spent almost all her life under protection – the 'protection' of a man as powerful as Sir William Robinson whose money would buy everything she needed. She had been richly comfortable, beyond the wildest dreams even of Molly Ballachulish. But hers had been a life, distorted by wealth and comfort. She had also lived under constant, undermining threat. Craig Lowrie now saw quite clearly that, throughout, Robinson had been hunting her and, at some point, if he had not already, he would close. And then there was Pettigrew...

He leant forward, listening to all that she intended. But, her inner terrors mewed through her words like seabirds. And, shame was seeking absolution from a brigand.

She explained her history. It was an explanation of the inexplicable. 'I – I seemed to just lose hold of my life. Somehow, it fell away from me – as the light goes from the roses at the end of summer – suddenly, without warning. My real life went, never to come back.'

*Has Robinson already claimed her?* wondered Craig Lowrie. *Was the woman here in his rooms – in his heart – really another man's wife?*

Plucking at the fabric of her gown with her long fingers, she would not look him in the eye, as she continued her story. 'I was only a child when I came. I did not know what to do. How to help myself. How to change things. At first, weeks went by. And Father Macdonald was my only friend. But then, at last, I found some pleasures, to be sure. I found I enjoyed planning the rose garden. And I enjoyed managing a household. (I had learned to do this in France). And, arranging *Le Petit Trianon,* it was like a game. Like playing with the Queen's Dolls House. And, that game never stopped – throughout all those years! And now, when I have the game no more, I do not know who I am.'

So, thought Craig Lowrie now, Robinson would be able to suck Adele back into his world. Because it was all she had known, she would be prepared to manage his house again. And, if she had not already, Adele would find herself obliged – finally – to warm Robinson's bed.

*What then?* Loathing Robinson as she did, this lovely woman would have no choice. She would kill herself. Craig Lowrie snatched at his breath. He stood and threw another log onto the fire. *Damnation waits for the suicide.*

He noticed her shuddering, as she looked up. 'So, yes, I must go to France. In spite of all its terrors. The good father, John Stewart Macdonald, he was afraid Gabrielle might already be dead. But she may still be alive. She may need help. 'And,' Adele said, with a sudden shine to her voice, 'this way, there is life beckoning. Without Robinson. I may yet be safe.'

*Would a mistress believe that?* Craig Lowrie thought. *Or is she hoping for some new protector?* He was confused. He remembered the letters he had read in this room a year before. She had detested Robinson then. *Had anything changed?* He could not yet tell. But hunting this quarry – the truth of whether she was Robinson's mistress or not – was exhausting. And he faltered at the direct question. *So did he really want to know? Did he really care? Or would he love her anyway?*

She had turned to the food beside her, taking up the silver fork and cutting through the salted fish carefully, creating small mouthfuls of the unfamiliar food. Then she nibbled an oatcake and she then returned to the fish. And then she found Malcolm Craig Lowrie watching her. With a smile, he teased her, 'You eat mackerel with passion!'

And Adele laughed. 'I'm sorry. Yes, I suddenly found I was hungry after all. Yours is a good rule.'

'Long practice,' replied the Laird, shrugging. 'I've lived off the land since I was a boy. It's what I'm used to. Your wonderfully ordered life – as if you were straight from court – that isn't a farmer's way.'

'Nor a brigand's way?'

'Nor a brigand's way.'

Craig Lowrie took some cheese and went to the window again to eat it. *No change out there yet.* And he wanted time to think – away from the gloss of her dark hair and her shining eyes. The mystery of this woman was almost too powerful to be safe close to her.

'What are you expecting?' she asked.

'Robinson,' he said. The sound of the name broke any illusion of enchantment in the fire-lit room. She pushed the plate from her.

'What do I do now?' she asked, suddenly close to tears.

'When Marie Le Pecque comes, she will have bought passage for you both to France. St Malo, I believe. Then it should be possible for you to make your way to Paris. And, when you reach Paris, you should find Gabrielle, or news of her, at least.

'Here,' he said, drawing the cabuchon signatory ring again from his belt pouch. 'Father Macdonald has no further need of this now. Take it – it will find friends of the Craig Lowrie who will help you.'

She examined the ring – gazing into the depths of the polished emerald – and then she slid it onto her forefinger. It was too loose and, instead, she dropped it into one of the deep pockets concealed in her redingote skirts. Then she nodded. 'It is a good plan. I thank you. Yes, I will do it.'

'But, it will be dangerous, lady. You must take care.'

'Then I had better not stand out too much from the crowd,' she said, standing to pull out her sewing kit from her travel bag. She removed her redingote and studied the slashes.

Craig Lowrie could re-call coquettes from his days at the French court, the extravagance of their movements, the grossness of the language of their bodies, extended in tawdriness to a fourteen-year-old boy. By contrast, this young girl possessed all the beauty of a pure-bred animal, She was unconscious of her immense power – although, standing there in the firelight, her soft muslin chemise dress made her look vulnerable.

At last she began to roll and hem – quickly, neatly, rhythmically – around the edge of the redingote skirt. Because of the way the material fell, when she finished, the slashes would be invisible yet the bulk of the skirts, reduced. It was a simple adjustment and Craig Lowrie could observe her frank delight as the redingote grew whole again. To watch her work gave him huge pleasure.

Adele glanced at him across the fire and said 'It's strange that Robinson – who couldn't bear to look at me at one time – now wants me back.'

She paused from her sewing to touch the scar disfiguring her face – as if from habit now.

'Oh, I can understand his wanting you back,' Craig Lowrie said.

The dark curls nestling to the pale skin of Adele's neck were making it difficult for him to concentrate on Robinson. She smiled and he remembered midsummer night again. Then, she bit through a thread and tossed her glossy hair to one side, the better to see her work. Craig Lowrie sighed. But then he remembered the moment when he had invited her to leave Robinson and she had refused. And, in the face of this bitter truth, Craig Lowrie's head began to swirl.

At last, the young woman rose and began to pull on the repaired redingote, asking, 'Will you help me? Will you make sure it is now respectable for travel once more? I surely shall not need to run like that again. But even if I do, the coat is much lighter now, is it not?'

Smiling at the hopefulness in her young face, he moved across to help her. Adele half-turned her head this way and that as he slowly checked the fit of the redingote, pulling it tighter around her body. He approved. Its thinned down skirts would not now impede speed. 'Yes,' he said, 'it fits. And it clears the ground.'

When she looked up, she found his eyes sparkling with amusement. 'I think, My Lady,' he said, 'it is a useful length.'

But his hands stayed resting on her waist and he did not release her. Instead he turned her gently round to face him. And then, he stopped laughing. He said the words he had wanted to say – ever since she had kissed him in the Versailles Hall of Mirrors all those years before. All of their lives, it seemed. He said, 'Adelaide de

Fontenoy,will you no come with me? I do not know where I am bound but come with me, lady.'

Adele felt his breath gently lift the wisps of hair framing her face, glance her cheek. Her world began to melt away. But then, she thought, *It is happening again.* Craig Lowrie was reaching out to her but she would have to turn him down. She knew she must stay true to Gabrielle. She must. But she loved him so much. *No. I will not lose him, not again,* she thought and, she found herself saying aloud, 'Come with me, Craig Lowrie! Come with me to France!'

For long seconds, only a rough mantel clock, ticking its way forward on the tide, broke the silence between them. She had only minutes left in Oban. And, if he said 'No!' now, she knew eternity would be too short to scope her loneliness without him. She held her breath, trembling.

When Craig Lowrie spoke, it was strangely formal – as though she had hired a riding servant. 'I am at your service, My Lady,' he said.

She gasped.

'But I must dress for travel, first.' He laughed again. 'I can journey to France with less comment if I am not in Highland dress.'

He was pulling off his soiled shirt when hoof-falls and the clatter of tackety boots on cobbles, accompanied by shouts, rived the air. He plunged to the window and that was when Adele saw the scars on his back, the scars made by his father, Campbell Craig Lowrie. Their cruelty trumpeted through the room. She moved close to him and, slowly, her hand reached out to touch the long-broken skin – a net of cuts and the silence of a child. Craig Lowrie turned and, with a gentle hand, he touched her scarred cheek. As she trembled at his touch, Craig Lowrie felt he had come home at last. Their kiss when it came was hard and long and hungry.

# Chapter 50

## Oban, Argyll
## 31st December 1793

THE CLOCK ON THE mantelpiece above Fiona Ballachulish's head continued to tick away some long, slow minutes. The conversation stilled to a trickle. Heads turned to the door. But no Adelaide appeared.

Ever desirous of pleasing a member of the titled classes, Molly Ballachulish said to her daughter, 'Fiona, fetch Lady Robinson. Tell her Sir William waits below.'

But, when Fiona Ballachulish returned, the girl was shrieking, 'Adelaide has gone and the French maid has gone too! And all Adelaide's jewellery has gone missing. Empty drawers everywhere!'

At this point, Robinson made his excuses and left. The chase was now on.

But, ever fastidious, he had to search every street for signs of the fugitive. He trusted she could not have managed to go far. No woman could. *The ridiculous skirts they wear would prevent it,* he thought, and, casting about for news, he knocked at the doors of several of his acquaintance to check whether they had seen her. To maintain appearances, he had made his enquiries in the calm and measured manner habitual to him and endured several delays and unwanted cups of tea in the process. He knew he would have to tell them some soothing tale about confused messages when next he met them but for now, they would have to speculate unaided about the whereabouts of his 'wife-to-be'.

Then, at last, Robinson – on foot and flanked by his mercenaries

– arrived on the far side of the docks from *The Three Fishes*. Standing outside his offices and beyond the North and South Quays, he hushed his men and paused to listen. Alert above and beyond his usual capacity, he could hear the distinctive tones of Craig Lowrie come out of the darkness of the inn's upper room casement. The man was giving instructions.

Then the fugitives appeared at the inn doorway, Craig Lowrie no longer dressed as a Highlander but wearing the great coat of a gentleman over the stock, shirt, breeches and boots of the Continental traveller. He was black and glossy as a raven. Only the weaponry marked him out as anything but a sophisticate and courtier. The weaponry was savage.

But, pausing there, in the shadows broken by torchlight, the runaways were now looking across at Robinson and Adelaide's mouth was a square of dismay. *She really does loathe me,* Robinson thought, suddenly sad. He could see Craig Lowrie was trying to push Adelaide in the direction of the Ballachulish maid. But, Adelaide was clinging to Craig Lowrie in a way that she would never ever have clung to him. Their bodies had fallen against each other as if they would dissolve. Robinson's mind calculated events. *So,* he thought, *so, that is the state of things.*

But then Craig Lowrie pulled apart from Adelaide, his gaze sweeping the docks. And, the lawyer stood still as a stock until Craig Lowrie's eyes settled on him. A look passed between the two men. And Robinson felt a grudging admiration for the Highlander. *To still have his wits about him – so close to Adelaide.* But then he hardened. *Yes, he loves Adelaide and yes, he wants to take her from me. But I want the Wolf's head. I still want his head!*

Robinson's mercenaries clustered to him. Still waiting for orders, they were ready to charge around the quaysides in pursuit of the fugitives. They needed his word only. He looked at their faces – ready to kill on his instruction – and he knew this was precisely what he wanted from them. *Murder!* This is what he had kept them fed and watered for, this whole year, and, now, at last, the pack was sighting the quarry. They clattered off in pursuit. 'Murder!' they yelled. 'Murder! Murder!'

Craig Lowrie felt rather than saw Robinson's eyes boring across the docks, flint-hard and angry. The lawyer was bellowing orders but his voice had a strange, lonely quality and Craig Lowrie knew, as far as Robinson was concerned, Craig Lowrie was already a dead man. He would also never let Adele go. He would kill her first. Even across the waters, Craig Lowrie could read the depth of Robinson's enmity as it exploded into life.

'Come, *madame!* Come!'

Marie Le Pecque was pulling the protesting Adele towards the *Espoir's* skiff moored at the end of the North Quay. Despite her resistance to leave his side, he knew they could not wait much longer. The *Espoir* rode the waves at the bar in the Sound of Kerrera and the sailors were climbing the rigging, setting the sails, excited to be almost off. And, from the town end beyond the South Quay, the clamour of the mercenaries drew closer.

Craig Lowrie had to delay them. He looked around. Ten yards from him, towards the distillery, the quay narrowed. Now it was time to test out his embryonic plan. He flung greatcoat and jacket to Rab and ran towards the net halls. At a bottleneck, he began to drag fish crates and creels together. Then, in an abandoned birch tar barrel, he dunked all the rags, with any rope and remnants of net he could scrape together out of the rubbish. And he drew flint and tinder from his pocket to set the fire that he hoped would save them. The fire caught quickly rattling through the debris and the old timber net hall went up too. Passage along the quay for Robinson's pack of mercenaries was now impossible. And, amid the chorus of shouts from his pursuers, Craig Lowrie heard a single animal scream from Robinson. He almost felt sorry for the man.

He now walked off towards the *Espoir's* skiff. *These are the last few steps I will take on Scottish soil for some time,* he thought. The price he was paying was immense but, he knew, he could no more fail Adele now than walk back through that fire to pass pleasantries with Robinson.

At the spot where, almost a year ago, he had met John Campbell, he paused. This, he was sure, had been the old man's last view of Scotland. But Craig Lowrie suddenly knew it would certainly not be his. He would be back.

He shivered afraid that the reason for his return could very well be that Argyll would renege on the deal struck in the Inveraray stable. The Craig Lowrie swore, if Argyll, burned just one Craig Lowrie clachan, made even one Craig Lowrie child an orphan, there would be no mercy. And, when the *Espoir* sailed, he now decided, Rab MacDonald would be staying behind. In the months ahead, Rab MacDonald would be his eyes and his ears. And if Argyll reneged in even the smallest particular, the Craig Lowrie would know.

Then there was an explosion of the tar barrels in the net halls behind him. And he moved on.

As he drew near to the mooring at the quay's end, he saw that Rab MacDonald and Marie Le Pecque were already in the *Espoir's* skiff, leaning on the oars. But still on the dock, Adele was saying she would not board.

All that could be seen of Oban at present was fire reaching up to the stars, and hot debris from the old buildings was pattering around the fugitives at the end of the quay. Even the shouts of townspeople trying to put out the fire were lost in the hiss of embers raining on the sea nearby.

Rab was arguing 'Come, come, *madame*. We'll miss the tide. The brig will sail.'

But Adele was calling out, 'No, no, I must know whether he is alive! Look at the flames! Is he caught in that?'

Shifting his oars in readiness, Rab chuckled. 'Oh I expect the Laird will find a way. Do not worry yourself, My Lady! He always does. Come, My Lady!'

'No, I'll wait for him here. But you, you go on. And you, Marie. You want to be home! Go! I release you from my service.'

'How could I go – without you? How could I? Please, *madame*, please! I can hear the officers calling on the ship. We'll be left behind.'

Then – out of the darkness – Malcolm Craig Lowrie arrived at speed. Running, he leapt from the edge of the quay, and landed, with a sure foot squarely in the centre of the boat. When he had steadied the rocking skiff, he turned to Adele. She was now terrified that the mercenaries would break through the dying firewall, and was calling out to him, 'Go on, go on without me! I'll distract Robinson. Go on!'

But, at that moment, the moon came out from behind the cloud, trailing its mystery on the air. *It is a wolf's moon, a quiet moon,* thought Craig Lowrie. He watched as the huge moon, the largest of the year, spilled moonlight down through clouds and bathed the scar on Adele's lovely face. And a sudden stillness lay between the Laird and his love. 'Will you no come with me, lady?' he asked.

Malcolm Craig Lowrie's voice crossed the night like a soft charm. Through the darkness, it wound and spiralled and swept on, calling to Adele with unarguable power. It calmed her so that, looking down, Adele saw the only man she would love till she died. And, at last, she took his waiting hand.

THE END

## About the Author

Between reading English Language and Literature at Bedford College, University of London and acquiring an MA in Linguistics at the University of Essex, Elizabeth Gates explored Europe as a teacher of English and Creative Writing. Then she worked as a freelance journalist for 25 years – published in national, regional and local magazines and newspapers and specialising in Public Health issues.

Now Elizabeth Gates has at last turned to her own fiction. *The Wolf of Dalriada* is an enjoyable foray into writing historical adventure and more historical novels are in the pipeline. *The Wolf of Dalriada* will form part of a series entitled *The Craig Lowrie Chronicles* and Elizabeth is currently writing a sequel set in Revolutionary France. A prequel exploring mysticism and legend in the Highlands is also planned.

When not writing, she enjoys her family, friends and travel. She misses her Labradors a lot.


## Acknowledgments

Very many thanks to family, friends and peers – who have supplied endless affection, support and tolerance during the writing of *The Wolf of Dalriada* in all its incarnations.

Deserving of special mention are my peer group, the Sofa Novelists – you know who you are! – who for years have patiently read the story and unfailingly encouraged the author!

But thanks in particular go to Lonely Furrow Company Publishing. Production Editor Michael Bangs has prepared the written manuscript meticulously for publication – ably assisted by proofreader Mia Gates – all the while sustaining the author with some wine and much tea.

Thank you all!